THE IMPOSSIBLE CONTRACT

THE
IMPOSSIBLE
CONTRACT

BOOKS BY K. A. DOORE

The Perfect Assassin

The Impossible Contract

THE IMPOSSIBLE CONTRACT

K. A. DOORE

TOR A TOM DOHERTY ASSOCIATES BOOK
NEW YORK

THE IMPOSSIBLE CONTRACT

A Tor Book
Published by Tom Doherty Associates
120 Broadway
New York, NY 10271

www.tor-forge.com

Tor® is a registered trademark of Macmillan Publishing Group, LLC.

The Library of Congress Cataloging-in-Publication Data is available upon request.

ISBN 978-0-7653-9857-4 (trade paperback)
ISBN 978-0-7653-9858-1 (ebook)

Our books may be purchased in bulk for promotional, educational, or business use. Please contact your local bookseller or the Macmillan Corporate and Premium Sales Department at 1-800-221-7945, extension 5442, or by email at MacmillanSpecialMarkets@macmillan.com.

First Edition: November 2019

Printed in the United States of America

0 9 8 7 6 5 4 3 2 1

This one is for my parents
And for all my queer fam'

1

Drum Chief Eken's end of season party was unflinchingly raucous. The unfettered flow of date wine and the thunder's erratic interruptions only encouraged the partygoers to an ever-greater volume. The wind puffed the sound and smell of rain through open windows and doors. A storm was coming; it was season's end. All of Ghadid was celebrating tonight, safely indoors and away from the strong winds and violent rains. A mixture of excitement and relief pulsed beneath the too-loud conversation.

But Thana felt neither. Instead, she ground her teeth against the crowd's onslaught, thrumming with a nervous anticipation that had nothing to do with the storm or the party. Balancing a tray of wine-filled glasses on one hand and holding a pitcher in the other, she threaded her way through the bodies, attuned only to the tone, not the content, of the words blowing past.

For this event, she'd borrowed a dull purple wrap that sucked away the warm undertones in her brown skin. It served its purpose in transforming her into just another background blur, as unexceptional as the other slaves. She'd even done her hair up in a common slave style, all tight black knots in uniform rows across her scalp.

Her gaze tracked the crowd and snagged on a figure in green conversing with one of the drum chief's wives, his wrap cinched tight with a silver belt: her cousin Amastan. He wore his tagel higher than usual tonight, covering even his nose, but Thana would know her cousin's build and stance anywhere.

She let out a breath of relief. He'd made it.

Not that she'd ever doubted he would. But there was always a chance, however small, that he could've been delayed, or worse, barred from entering the party. Then they would've had to scrap their plan, wasting the months of preparation and planning it'd taken to get them this close to Eken.

After all, this conveniently public spectacle afforded them their best—and only—chance to kill the drum chief.

It wasn't personal. Not for Thana, anyway. The contract had sealed Eken's fate. But it *was* personal for their employer, whose daughter the drum chief had dishonored—one among many, if the rumors were true. If Eken had been anyone but a drum chief, their employer would've approached the Circle for justice. But, although a drum chief wasn't technically above the law, going the traditional route would've allowed Eken to turn the trial into a public spectacle and bring shame upon the girl's whole family, while incurring little more than a small fine himself. The girl had suffered enough already.

Instead, a network of sympathetic ears had brought their employer to Kaseem, the broker of so many bloody deals, who in turn selected Amastan out of all the cousins. Only Amastan had previously demonstrated the precision and subtlety necessary to kill a drum chief. While the family's contracts were now sanctioned—if unofficially—by the Circle, they'd still be exiled or even executed if they were caught killing one of the Circle's own. Drum chiefs were fickle like that. Hence: months spent carefully assembling the pieces of their plan until each was exactly where it needed to be and nothing could go wrong.

Thana averted her gaze as she served the guests, only occasionally sneaking a glance to check Amastan's progress. As she circled the room, she picked out other drum chiefs, their wraps rich and vibrant, their fingers glittering with rings. Ghadid had twelve drum chiefs for its twelve neighborhoods. Half of them were here tonight.

But one was still missing. The night was no longer new and Drum Chief Eken had yet to make an appearance at his own party. Where was he?

A sudden quiet settled on one corner of the room and oozed outward like spilled oil. Heads tracked its spread. A moment later, the crowd near Thana parted and two men passed by, one wearing a wine-red wrap and the other, bone white. The first was broad-shouldered but stout. His extravagant wrap hid most of his peculiar shape, its embroidery and hem of tiny bells pulling the gaze away from a bulging paunch. His equally lush tagel concealed his entire face but for a thin swath of dark brown skin around a pair of even darker eyes.

Thana had worked in his household for three weeks already. She would've known Drum Chief Eken's wide-legged stride and shape anywhere. The other man, though, was a mystery. White was inappropriate for a celebration and Thana doubted he was in mourning. Everything about him yelled *foreigner*, from his loosely wrapped tagel, to his lighter, almost golden eyes and sand-pale skin. He ignored the greetings flung his way as the drum chief led him through the room, all the while trying to engage Eken himself.

Mutters nipped their heels but sputtered out when Drum Chief Eken signaled for the party to continue. The conversations started and stopped and started again, like a tired mule failing to pull its load. Thana caught snatches of worry and confusion as she resumed circling the room.

"—audacity to be seen in public with—"

"—was always saying Eken's a shards-cursed imperialist—"

"—of the Empire doing here?"

Thana kept her expression blank even as worry tightened her chest. Rumors had circulated in the few days about the Empress's man who had arrived along with the year's first caravan. Who was he? And why had he come all this way from Na Tay Khet to their city on the edge of the Wastes?

Now he was here, at Eken's party, in the company of the drum chief himself. The implications were unsettling, but they had nothing to do with her contract. Thana wouldn't let his presence distract her.

"It's true, then."

The voice came from beside her. Thana smoothed over her jerk of surprise with a smile and offered the speaker a glass from her tray. A tall man stood at her elbow, thin but strong like a palm, his dark red tagel almost as loose as the foreigner's. His eyes, though, were as dark as midnight. As he studied Thana, she realized he'd spoken to her. He raised his hand, refusing the wine.

"Sa?" prompted Thana.

The man turned his gaze back to Eken and folded his arms. "The fool has finally arrived."

As much as she might want to, Thana couldn't respond. Legally, the fool was her master and agreeing with the man could see her whipped. So she kept silent and moved away to fill an empty glass. When she glanced back, the tall man was gone.

Meanwhile, Eken had shed the man in white and joined his wife. Amastan greeted the drum chief and pressed his closed fist to his chest. Eken mirrored the gesture, then laughed at something Amastan said, his whole body heaving with the motion.

Keeping one eye on their exchange, Thana weaved through the crowd. She handed out glasses of wine and topped off empty ones as she went, smiling blandly at each passing thanks. Soon, her tray was half-empty. She paused long enough to rearrange the glasses.

Amastan was explaining the history of glasswork to Eken as Thana approached. She twisted the top of one of her rings beneath the tray, then offered her tray to the drum chief. Fully engrossed in Amastan's words, Eken reached for a glass. Thana turned the fuller side toward him and, as she brought her hand back, tipped her ring over the glass that'd soon be nearest him. Fine white powder fluttered into the date wine, dissolving instantly.

With the smallest metallic *clink*, barely audible even to Thana, the ring's cap settled back into place. Thana gave the drum chief her blandest smile, but he took the poisoned glass without even a glance her way. Then she continued on, offering wine to the next guest. She didn't dare linger to see if the mark drank the poison. That was Amastan's job.

Thana glided across the room, her thin smile belying none of the thrumming nerves beneath. This may have been her third contract with Amastan, but it was by far her most important. No one was beyond the family's reach, but killing a drum chief wouldn't come without consequences if they screwed up. Over two decades ago, her mother had killed a drum chief and almost ended the family. But her mother hadn't been under contract and they were. As long as she and Amastan stayed within the confines of the contract, everything would be fine. They'd be fine.

Thana welcomed the nerves. They were a part of the work. *That's what keeps you alive,* her mother had said time and time again. Nerves and anxiety were encouraged. It was the calm you had to be afraid of. Complacency got you killed.

The nerves were well-earned: in the next few moments, all their work would come to fruition. Thana had spent months living among the slaves, while Amastan had spent that time gathering facts and rumors. In the next few moments, they'd either become legends in her family's history or cautionary tales of failure.

Despite the tension of the moment, she couldn't help but feel a spark of jealousy. If they succeeded—and they would, they had to—all the credit would go to Amastan. This was his contract, after all, even if she'd put in half the work. More, if she was being honest with herself, since she'd been the one playing a slave. Amastan would be the one remembered for killing a drum chief, not her. And he didn't even want the prestige.

Thana took a breath and pushed away her jealousy. In its absence, the nerves came roaring back. It was out of her hands now. She had to trust they'd chosen the right kind of poison, that Amastan had calculated the correct dose, that she'd ground it fine enough, that the mark had drank all of it, that the timing had been right, that no one had seen, that Amastan kept their mark engaged, that—

The storm broke, rain pounding against the roof and drowning out the crowd, the air suddenly laden with it. For a moment, Thana couldn't hear anything but the rush of rain. That moment soon passed, but the din worsened as people shouted to be heard above the roar. Slaves rushed from window to window, closing the shutters before the spray could dampen the drum chief's guests. As each window was closed, the storm was further muffled, until its rage was only a distant scream.

Then the shouting started.

Thana turned, her face a mask of surprise as she fought a surge of panic. *We've been found out, someone noticed the ring, the chief can taste poison, it was the wrong poison, Amastan slipped up—*

Drum Chief Eken clutched at his own throat, his eyes so wide that the whites showed all the way across the room. His tagel had been yanked down and his lips were moving, but Thana couldn't hear him over the crowd. Amastan waved one of the drum chief's wives over. No one else was responding to the crisis; the other slaves stood frozen in place, confusion and terror on their uncovered faces. Past the growing chaos, the man in white leaned against a wall, eyebrows furrowed as if this were a mere annoyance.

Froth spilled from the mark's lips. Thana's panic spiked, became paralysis. It wasn't supposed to happen this fast. The mark was supposed to survive the evening, only to complain about stomach pains and die later that night. Even to the healers, it would've seemed as if he'd eaten spoiled meat. The contract required a quiet, inconspicuous death. But this—*what was this?*

Whatever it was, she wouldn't let it ruin their contract. Thana shoved her tray into the hands of another slave and all but dropped the pitcher on a table as she rushed to Amastan's side. Now was not the time to disappear. No one would notice the slaves who rushed to help, but they'd notice any who ran away. She couldn't risk breaking her cover, not when the contract wasn't done.

The mark's wife helped Amastan guide him out of the room. Thana ducked under Eken's other arm, spreading out his bulky weight and using her body to shield his features from the wall of staring guests. Even if the mark was dying, it was still disrespectful to let so many see his bare face, most of whom belonged to a lower class.

Once they were out of sight and in the hallway, the wife pulled over a chair and they guided the drum chief into it. He slumped, his shoulders heaving with each pained breath. He wheezed and hacked as he fought for air and he kept shaking his head like a stunned dog.

His wife turned on Amastan. "What in G-d's name happened?"

"I don't know, ma." Amastan echoed her worry. "One minute he was fine, the next—" He waved at Eken.

A second woman joined them, the gold chain at her waist marking her as Eken's senior wife. She went straight to her husband, her fingers finding first his wrist, then his neck. She tilted his head back and peered into his eyes before prying open his mouth and staring down his throat. She did all of this in the same perfunctory manner as an Azali examining his camel.

She stepped back, shaking her head. "He's having an acute reaction to something he ate. Girl"—she snapped her fingers at Thana, who stiffened—"did you see him take any nuts of any kind?"

Thana kept her gaze averted but shook her head. "No, ma. Just the date wine that was served to every guest."

"Then there must have been some pit in the wine." The senior wife pinched the bridge of her nose, irritated. "The fool should've known better. The cores of some fruits make him very ill. Quick, girl—fetch a healer. We have little time."

"Yes, ma."

As Thana left the room, she made a circle with her thumb and forefinger on her hand nearest Amastan. He grunted and said something, but the noise from the crowd was too loud. She could only hope he'd seen her signal and knew to look for her coded note outside the slaves' quarters later. They hadn't been exposed yet, but the situation was getting away from them.

Thana grappled with what had happened as she slipped outside and down a side street, running through the pouring rain for the nearest healer. The possibility of dragging her feet crossed her mind, but it was just as quickly dismissed: if Eken died because she was too slow, all the blame would fall on her. No, their original plan was shattered. But Thana was still a slave in the drum chief's household for a few more days. There was still a chance they could salvage this contract. Still a chance *she* could fix things.

When Thana returned with a healer, three of Eken's wives waited outside his room. They let the healer through, but one of the wives blocked Thana from following. Thana caught only a glimpse of the senior wife and Eken inside, still alive. She retreated to the slaves' quarters and wrote Amastan the promised note. Then she scrubbed the floor—and planned.

Only one course of action remained. They'd never get those months of preparation back, but Thana was still here, a part of the drum chief's household. Just because the poison would be cleaned from his body didn't mean he couldn't still die quietly tonight. If anything, it'd be less suspicious than before. Eken was old and the reaction had weakened him. It wouldn't be surprising if his heart gave out. Thana just had to make sure that it did.

It'd be risky, acting on her own. For generations, assassins in her family had traditionally worked in pairs. When a murderer had caught several of her cousins alone and unawares, that tradition had become a rule. Of course, her mother had been known to work on her own, but Tamella was a legend. Even forced into retirement, her name was still a whispered warning. Someday, Thana would reach the same level of notoriety.

But aspiration was one thing; action was another. Thana couldn't wait for Amastan. She had to act tonight. If her mother could get away with working a contract alone, than so could she.

While the decision set part of her at ease, it set the rest of her on edge. She was on her own. If she failed, all of Ghadid would learn her name and she'd be hunted. Her family and cousins were tolerated as a necessary evil, a vanguard against corruption and injustice, but only if Ghadid could pretend they didn't exist.

G-d did not condone murder, even when it was for the greater good.

With only a few hours left to act, Thana got to work.

The storm lingered well after it was mere dregs, spitting at empty streets with little enthusiasm, its breath fogging windows. Thana hunkered under the eave of a neighboring building, gaze fixed on one window in particular, as dark as an eye. She'd shed the purple wrap in favor of a dark green one that blended with the shadows. Its lightweight fabric clung wet to her skin and rain ran through her knotted hair and down her face, but she didn't move.

The evening had been trying, full of nerves and waiting. Although Amastan had instilled an appreciation for patience in her, she still hated sitting idle. Slipping away from the other slaves had been a trial in itself. Now she drew in calm with each breath, stilling her shaking hands. She could do this without Amastan. She *had* to do this without Amastan.

The lights in the other windows went out one by one. The wind picked up, whispering unintelligible promises to any who'd listen. A different kind of fear spread bumps along Thana's arms. Guul were said to ride on the tails of large storms, feasting on the disaster and death left behind. Thana touched the cord at her neck, tracing her finger along the glass charms lying cold against her collarbone. But guul were creatures of the Wastes. They never came near Ghadid. Here, she only had to fear wild jaan.

Thana checked her rings and counted her knives. When the rain picked up in one last, petulant burst, she detached from the wall and slipped across the alley as little more than a shadow. Eken was expected to survive the night. A wife was keeping guard outside his room. But no one should be inside, no one by his side. At least, not while the healer was resting.

The rainfall masked the squeak of metal as Thana used her knife to unscrew the bolts of the window hinge. She caught the glass before it could fall and shatter, then climbed over the sill and into the room and its stifling darkness. She pulled the freed window back into place after her to keep the wind out.

She paused and took in the room, her sight already adjusted to the gloom. Damp footprints glistened behind her as she approached the long, low bed. The dry air would take care of those, storm or not. A man stirred in the bed, lips moving soundlessly, but his eyes didn't open.

Thana's fingers found and twisted the cap on one of her rings. She stopped next to the man's head, comparing the face before her with the one she'd seen tagel-less at the party only a few hours before. It was the mark, all right. Drum Chief Eken.

She leaned over the mark and watched his nostrils flare and flutter, his lips part. Holding her own breath, she tilted her hand over those lips until white powder spilled and coated them. The mark grunted. Licked his lips. Resettled.

When the mark started to choke, Thana picked up the pillow beside his head and laid it across his face. At this, the mark started, hands reaching at and pushing away the pillow. Thana leaned in, imagining herself as unmovable as metal. She closed her eyes, feeling instead of seeing the mark's progression from waking to confusion, followed by awareness and struggling. Thana fought back, willing the poison to work quickly. Although she was fast, she wasn't strong like Amastan, and the mark could easily overpower her if given a chance.

For a heartbeat, she knew he would. The mark had hold of the pillow's edges and was gasping for breath as he pushed her back and away. Thana gritted her teeth and shoved back with all her strength, but she wouldn't last much longer. The mark thrashed, feet kicking air, body twisting away from her.

Thunder crashed, long and low and distant. Lightning illuminated the room, outlining the mark's weathered and scarred hands as they clawed at the pillow obstructing his mouth and nose, the assassin's pylon-straight back and tense shoulders, her mouth set in a thin, firm line.

The light was gone just as suddenly, and with it went the mark's strength. He weakened by degrees as the poison worked, numbing his muscles, breaking his will, and slowing his heart beat by beat . . . by beat. He stopped resisting all at once, arms falling heavy back to the bed. But Thana didn't relax, not until the breath she'd been holding burned like acid in her chest. Only then did she let go of the air in her lungs and the pillow in her hands. She stepped back, wary and weary and ready to be done. She freed a knife and waited.

But she didn't need the knife. The pillow slipped to the side bit by bit, then all at once, revealing parted lips and open, sightless eyes. Thana shivered despite the room's warmth. Three contracts, and she'd never gotten used to that sight. She hoped she never did.

Thana touched the charms at her neck as she muttered a prayer for the drum chief's jaani. She returned to the window, settling its glass back in place. But while there was still a small gap, she threw a pebble at the water cup near the bed. It teetered and fell and shattered. Someone gasped in the hallway. In another moment, they'd enter, see the mark dead, and send for a healer. But they'd also send for a marabi to quiet his jaani. No one, not even Eken, deserved to have their jaani go wild.

Thana vanished into the lingering storm before anyone opened the door.

2

Thunk.

A knife protruded from the leather target, several inches from its center. Thana examined the girl at the opposite end of the room. Illi already had another knife in hand, but she waited to throw it as Thana approached. Thana moved Illi's fingers along the knife's hilt, then nudged the girl's rear foot over by an inch. She stepped back, gave Illi another once over, then nodded.

"Again."

Illi threw the knife, her motions as quick and smooth as a whip. *Thunk.* This time, the knife quivered at the target's center.

Thana fought back a smile. "Not bad for a first lesson."

Illi puffed her cheeks. "When am I ever going to need to throw a *knife*? It's wasteful."

Thana's mood curdled. "Do you ask Tamella when you'll need to fight hand-to-hand? Or sprint for several platforms?"

Illi looked away, braids obscuring her sour expression. "But those skills are *practical*." She crossed the room and yanked her knives from the target.

"No," said Thana. "They're not. If you ever have to *sprint* for a contract, then you've already failed, and the watchmen will find you anyway. Tamella isn't teaching you how to run or fight, she's teaching you endurance and confidence. Same here. You'll probably never have to throw a knife as part of a contract, just as you'll never have to punch a mark, but the other skills you're learning—precision, controlled breathing, form—will help you. Now, try again."

"Besides," said a voice from the doorway. "You never know when a contract might specify the mark die by a thrown knife. You should be prepared for any eventuality."

Illi spun, the dagger at her hip already in hand. But Thana took her time. She recognized that voice, jarring as it was to hear it at home. Even more jarring was the sight of the man in her bedroom doorway. He wore a crisp green tagel up to the bridge of his nose. Around his eyes, his skin was as brown as warm tea, wrinkles etched deep by sun and age. His wrap was tight around a wiry torso and rough, callused hands were folded atop an amber-tipped cane.

"Kaseem." Thana tried to hide the tremble in her fist as she placed it over her heart and bowed her head. "How may I be of service, sa?"

Kaseem lifted his cane and gestured at Illi. "I don't wish to impose upon you and your pupil, ma. Please, finish your lesson."

"We're done for the day," said Thana quickly. At least this time, Illi knew better than to contradict her. "What brought you all the way here, sa?"

Thana held her breath, mouth dry. It was an idiotic question. There was only one reason Kaseem would cross the city to show up at her door.

"Your recent work was impressive," said Kaseem, rolling the amber beneath his palm. "The qualities you demonstrated are exactly what another client is looking for."

Illi let out a tiny sound, halfway between a gasp and a squeak. Thana shot her a warning glance, but the younger girl had already smoothed her features into a blank mask, her fingers laced together before her, the dagger back in its sheath. Despite being almost ten years Thana's junior, Illi was far enough along in her training to grasp what Kaseem meant. After all, if she kept training and passed her test, she too might be approached by Kaseem one day.

One day. Thana resisted the urge to bounce. She'd dreamed of this day her entire life. Not every cousin made it through training and even fewer were ever approached by Kaseem himself for a contract. This was it. Maybe, finally, her mother could be proud of her.

"Illi," said Thana, "that's enough for today. I'll let Tamella know how you did."

Illi started to protest, but then her gaze caught Kaseem's and she pressed her lips tight instead. Illi flicked one of her long braids over her shoulder, pressed her fist to her chest, and went to the window. If she stayed, the girl would have a full lesson in how a contract was presented and negotiated, but the details of the contract were privy only to those bound by it. Thana wasn't about to take an untested cousin on as her partner for her first contract.

When Illi had disappeared over the windowsill, Thana gestured to Kaseem and led him down the stairs to the living area. The ground floor was deserted. Her mother was on a rooftop somewhere training the other young cousins, and her father had wormed his way into a drum chief's private library where he now spent most of his days. His own collection filled half the room, shelves of densely packed scrolls that contained too many details about things that had happened in Ghadid. Amastan was in love with all that history, but Thana couldn't be bothered. *Now* was more interesting—and relevant—than *then*.

Kaseem took his time on the steps. He wasn't especially old, but he was as frail as a grandfather. Not for the first time, Thana wondered how old he really was. He claimed he'd shattered his thigh in a fight once and now relied on a cane to get around. But he leaned too readily on it, turning his weakness into a display—like a feint. If he'd been part of their family, he would've made a great cousin.

When Kaseem was on level ground, Thana went to the hearth and swung the waiting kettle over the fire. Only once the water had boiled, the tea steeped and been poured, and the two were seated across from each other did Thana dare speak.

"The mark's funeral isn't until tomorrow, sa."

"I know." Kaseem ladled a third spoonful of sugar into his tea. "The execution of that contract was impressive."

Thana snorted. "We nearly botched it. Should've known the mark'd have a problem with date pits, of all things."

"Yes. You almost did. That was foolish of you not to inquire into any potential cross reactions. But the key here is that you didn't 'botch' it. The mark is dead and his household doesn't suspect murder. At least, not any more than usual."

Every death was suspect in Ghadid, where healers could cure you of almost any ailment if you could afford the water—and drum chiefs could always afford the water. The family was responsible for relatively few of those deaths—or had been. Entire years used to pass between contracts, but they were still working through the glut after a twelve-year ban. Long-suffered injustices had to be righted, and it wasn't as if the marab or the Circle was going to do anything about them.

Thana tasted her tea and wrinkled her nose; she'd let it oversteep. She sipped it anyway, using the bitterness to center herself as she waited for Kaseem to get to the real reason he'd come.

"Your quick thinking and success despite the kind of failure that would've rattled any of your other cousins was notable." Kaseem placed a glass bottle in the middle of the table. "Which is why I'd welcome your expertise on a new contract."

Thana stared at the bottle, pulse thudding in her ears. This was it. She'd been expecting this, *wanting* this. She'd worked three contracts with Amastan already, passed the test five years ago, and trained her entire life—longer than most of her cousins by a decade. Amastan had received his first contract barely a year after earning his tagel. But then, that was Amastan, the only cousin who'd ever tried to fight Tamella. He was . . . unique.

But she was the Serpent of Ghadid's only daughter. She needed to be more than unique, she had to be exceptional. Thana straightened. Whatever contract Kaseem had brought her, she'd prove her worth by completing it.

She examined the bottle. Its throat was sealed with wax, but the glass itself was clear. The bottle was filled with baats, the metal coins glittering in the hearth's firelight. Even without counting, Thana knew there were more than she'd ever seen in her life. It was easily a merchant's fortune or a drum chief's allowance. A year's worth of water, at least.

On top of the baats was a folded note. The contract. She'd have to break the seal to read it. Her hands stayed in her lap.

Kaseem was watching her closely. "Go on, take it."

Thana met Kaseem's gaze and tried to read those eyes. "What are the obligations?"

The edges of Kaseem's eyes crinkled with a smile. "The removal of a mark. This time, however, the client prefers that the cause of death is quite obvious. The word they used was 'messy,' but you may use your discretion. You'll be paid the second half upon confirmation of the mark's death. You may share this contract with another. You have as long as you need to complete the contract, but once you read the details, you may want to act quickly. Of course, I wouldn't presume to tell you how to do your job."

"And if I fail?" The question was a formality; Thana knew the answer. Failure meant the end of her career, maybe her life.

"The usual. Return the baats you were paid upfront, plus a fine. Judgment by the drum chiefs, if you're caught." Kaseem paused, took a sip of tea. "But this client has one additional stipulation: if you don't complete the contract, your body will be forfeit."

Thana frowned. What could the client possibly want with her body? If she survived, perhaps they meant to own her as a slave. If she died, though, her body would be worthless. Unless all they wanted was to ensure her jaani was not quieted. She grimaced. That would be a step further than mere humiliation; that would be blasphemy.

Did her potential employer mean to intimidate her with that obligation? If so, then it was insulting. Thana was a cousin, a professional. If she took the contract, she'd complete it. Threats were immaterial.

"Who's the mark?"

"Do you accept the contract?"

Thana eyed the bottle. Of course she would, but she still had to ask one last question. For it to be a legitimate contract, the mark's guilt must be beyond the law. "What's their crime?"

Kaseem's eyes all but disappeared in a wide smile. He let out a low rumble of a laugh, at complete odds to his thin, bony frame.

"It would be simpler if you asked what crime they *haven't* committed. Your potential mark is guilty of the most egregious acts against both their fellow man and G-d. The world will be a much safer place without him."

Him. Thana drew the bottle close, marveling at its weight. She was struck again by the gratuitous amount of baats inside.

"The note includes your exact instructions." Kaseem spoke quickly, belying his own eagerness. "But I can tell you this much: a foreign friend visits our city and your employer would like to see that he's given a *proper* welcome."

"A merchant?" guessed Thana, appreciating the musical clink of metal on metal as she turned the bottle. She set it down and pried off the wax seal with a knife.

"An ambassador, of sorts. From the Empress herself."

Thana froze, the bottle half turned and the paper still caught inside. The ridiculous number of baats made sickening sense. This contract was going to be Political, with a capital *p*. A drum chief was one thing—Ghadid prided itself on dealing with its own problems. But the Empress?

The Mehewret Empire claimed Ghadid, although the city had never acknowledged foreign rule. There had been no war, no surrender, no fanfare. Over a century ago, the Emperor had simply redrawn his maps and declared that Ghadid and the other cities on the edge of the Wastes were now on *this* side of the Empire's border. At the time, no one had bothered to correct him. Ghadid had its own problems, including a seven-year drought and a spike in banditry. A messenger had arrived to announce the change. He'd been ignored.

Years passed and the declaration was forgotten. Then the Empress came to power. It wasn't enough that the map of her Empire included Ghadid. No—she wanted tribute. She wanted control.

The first tax collectors the Empress sent never returned to Na Tay Khet. Soldiers accompanied the second group and camped below Ghadid, among its pylons, as the drum chiefs deliberated what to do. The decision had nearly torn Ghadid apart, but in the end they sent the soldiers away. That time, the army had come unprepared for a siege against the City in the Sky. Perched above the ever-shifting sands upon metal pylons that burrowed deep into the earth, Ghadid was unconquerable.

But the third—

Thana remembered them. The Empress had sent a smaller

force, one that arrived with a caravan and rode the carriages up into the city, hidden in plain sight among the other foreigners. Thana had been too young to understand what was happening, but she remembered the proclamations that had appeared overnight, pasted on buildings and bridges. She could still feel the jostle of bodies as her family joined the others in the long, twisting lines for the census. She could still hear the cold, quiet anger in her mother's voice and the intermittent bursts of outrage in the streets.

Thana would never understand how those collectors returned to their Empress alive. Many in Ghadid regretted the act of clemency. The Empress's proclamations had rolled in a few years after that: long, curling lengths of vellum read by tarted-up citizens of the Empire, their skin pale as milky tea and their clothing little more than a skirt around the waist, their faces and chests indecently bare. The proclamations were frivolous, but their intent was plain: the Empress owned Ghadid.

The family's business had picked up. A few years back, the Empress had retaliated by sending a small army. But Ghadid had drawn up its carriages and gleefully rained down rocks and burning pitch and broken glass until the soldiers gave up and left. Another group had tried the infiltration trick, but it didn't work a second time. Their bodies were never found.

And now the Empress had sent an ambassador, with a list of crimes to his name that impressed even Kaseem. What was she planning?

Thana slid the note out and opened it, smoothing it against the table with her palm. She read. Instead of bringing clarity, though, her confusion and concern only deepened.

The mark had arrived a week ago with the most recent Azal caravan. The note described him as average height, pale featured, and having a predilection for wearing white. A cold realization filled Thana: the foreigner at the party. Was this contract related to Eken's? Then she read the last line:

Heru Sametket is the second advisory marabi to the Empress.

"He's a *marabi*?" Thana stared at Kaseem. "You want me to kill a *marabi*?"

"The Empress's marab are no holy men," said Kaseem. "They don't bother themselves with funerals or quieting jaan like ours do. They are a different breed altogether, preferring their studies over action. There is very little of G-d about them."

Still, Thana's heart hammered. Holy man or not, a marabi was a man of G-d and they could protect themselves in ways that went beyond mere knives and poisons. It was rare for a contract to be written on a marabi, but when they were, the crimes were significant.

"Why is the Empress's marabi here?" Thana sipped her tea as she considered a different question: did Kaseem know that Heru was already hard at work among the drum chiefs? If he'd spoken to Eken, then he'd spoken to others. Was he trying to start an uprising?

"I don't know." Kaseem's gaze unfocused in thought. "But there're guesses, conjectures. I suspect the Empress is testing us. She might be searching out weaknesses for another siege. Or she may be sowing dissension. It wouldn't be the first time."

Thana ran her thumb along the note's edge. "But killing the marabi, an ambassador . . . that would guarantee a war."

Kaseem steepled his fingers and met her gaze. "Yes."

Thana considered. Her mother had taught her to question the motives of any potential employer, but Amastan had taught her to consider the bigger impact. A contract might be justified against a particular mark, but if it didn't serve Ghadid, it didn't serve the family. In its own way, the family protected Ghadid. Starting a war didn't sound like protecting the city.

Then again, war had been brewing between Ghadid and the Empire ever since the late Emperor had added them to his map. If the Empress didn't send an army now, then she would in the months or years to come. Wasn't it better to have that war on their own terms, rather than at the Empress's whim? If Ghadid reacted strongly enough, perhaps the Empress would strike the city from her map and be done with them.

In a way, it was already too late. If the Empress had sent her own marabi to Ghadid, even as an ambassador, then she'd already shot the first metaphorical volley. If they didn't respond strongly, they'd look weak, perhaps even accepting. The tone would be set for future discourse. Ghadid couldn't risk it. Thana couldn't risk it.

She folded the note and slipped it into a pocket. "What else can you tell me, sa?"

"I have only rumors."

"Then give me rumors."

Kaseem poured himself another cup and took his time stirring in sugar. He set the spoon down and took a sip before answering. "The Empress's marab are a breed apart from our own. They attend the dead and their jaan, but she has encouraged them to pursue nontraditional studies and research. There's even rumor that she has removed restrictions on some previously banned lines of study. This has seeded her court with marab who are not wholly devoted to G-d. This ambassador in particular is one of the worst offenders, intent on twisting the word of G-d into blasphemies. He's a keen but cruel man, whom few but the Empress can abide. And, most importantly"—Kaseem held up a finger—"he's traveling alone."

Thana frowned. A loner would be tougher to lure out. A loner would notice if someone went through their things. A loner wouldn't leave their drink unattended or their back unprotected. A loner would be on their guard.

Then her frown curled into a smile. It was a difficult contract, yes—but Kaseem had come to *her*. She wouldn't disappoint him. And with Amastan as her partner, nothing could stop her.

"I accept. Let's talk payment."

3

"But a two-pronged approach won't work," insisted Thana. "Not this time. There's no way to drag the mark out. We have to go to him."

She sat in the window of her room, legs tucked to her chest and hand dangling. Beyond, the sky was a cloudless blue, any mugginess lingering from the storms too thin to be felt, the air quickly returning to its usual stink of hot stones and sand. The gnats had all but disappeared with the rain, but a few still insisted on buzzing by her ear. She swatted at them in vain.

Amastan paced her room, hands clasped behind his back. On the small table by her bed was the note that detailed her—*their*—contract, alongside an empty teapot. Thana had found Amastan as soon as Kaseem had left and invited him into the contract. He'd accepted, of course. Then he'd begun to fret.

His tendency to overanalyze every angle of a contract had ensured their success in the past, but *shards and dust*, was it annoying. It'd already been several days since the eventful party and they'd made no progress. Their mark had kept his head down and was holed up in an inn. Whatever had driven him to seek out the drum chiefs was gone and now he kept to himself, leaving the inn at odd hours and avoiding routine. For an ambassador, he was surprisingly private and skittish.

No, the two-prong approach that'd brought them so close to Eken wouldn't work here.

Amastan's nose wrinkled as he chewed his lip. He'd tied his tagel low for this meeting. "We need to draw him out—"

"How? He's not talking to anyone."

"A disturbance. You go in as a servant at the inn and—"

"If we'd known ahead of time, we could've slipped in before he arrived. But he's spooked—he won't trust any new servants."

"It doesn't need to be a servant. The inn is full of iluk and other foreigners this time of year."

"What then? I try to talk to him? He's an ambassador, the only people he wants to see are drum chiefs, and I don't have to explain why impersonating one of *them* would be a bad idea."

Amastan stopped pacing and turned to her. "Then what do *you* propose?"

"Kaseem said we need to be quick. So: a poisoned arrow. We can hit him through a window—"

"The further away we strike at him, the higher the chance he'll survive."

"So you're not gonna like my idea of slipping into the kitchen and poisoning his food."

"Unless we can guarantee he'll eat it. And I doubt either of us wants to risk another reaction like Eken's."

Thana winced. That oversight belonged to both of them, but she couldn't shake her own guilt. They'd come within inches of disaster. Poisoned drinks and food were out, then.

Quick and messy, that's what Kaseem had implied and what the contract demanded. She knew, then, what they needed to do. She also knew Amastan wouldn't like it. Well, he'd just have to handle it, because this was her contract, not his. *Her* shot at making a name for herself. And if they messed up, it'd be on her. So they wouldn't mess up.

"We'll track his routine for a few nights, then slip in while he's asleep and slit his throat." Thana wiped her hands together as if brushing off dust. "Simple."

Amastan's frown was slow, considering. "He'll have wards, charms, and who knows what else. We might not be able to just sneak in."

"We'll visit Salid and he'll sell us stronger charms. We'll ask Menna and she can tell us how to break his wards. And if we run into something else, there's two of us and one of him. He won't have a chance."

Amastan's gaze slipped past her and out the window as he thought. Thana waited as patiently as she could. She was right. He'd see it too, he had to see it—

"Yes," he said. "You're right. I understand now why Kaseem chose you for this particular contract. He saw some of Tamella in you."

Thana bristled but bit her tongue. If this contract went right, then maybe Amastan and Kaseem and all the rest of her cousins would stop seeing her as just the Serpent of Ghadid's daughter.

"But we still need to be careful," continued Amastan.

"Of course," said Thana. "We'll watch him for a few nights— he has to have *some* kind of routine. The building next door has a glasshouse, but it doesn't take up the whole roof. We can set up there. When we feel good and comfortable, then we go in and do whatever it takes to finish the contract."

"We can't assume we'll have more than a few days," warned Amastan. "We don't know how long he plans on staying."

"We won't need more than that."

Slowly, Amastan nodded. "I see no obvious flaw in this plan."

Thana prickled with pride. From him, that was high praise. She smiled and slid off the windowsill. "Then we'd better prep. We're going to have some long nights ahead."

Heru Sametket sat alone at a table on the edge of the inn's over-crowded common area, oblivious to everything and everyone around him. His attention was fixed on the paper unrolled across his table and the pen in his hand. He wrote in furious bouts only to pause for long stretches and chew on the end of his pen.

He wore a dark blue tagel up to his eyes, but he itched at the fabric like a young man unused to the cloth. Despite his class, he wore neither charms nor any jewelry. He had on the same white wrap he'd worn at the party, which glared bright and conspicuous in the gloom.

The color choice was perplexing. Only the grieving wore white, the shade of sun-bleached bones and death. Thana had found a little about the Empire and its marab in her father's library, but only learned that they preferred red or even black and certainly nothing to confirm Kaseem's salacious rumors. Ghadid's own marab wore gray. Only mere whimsy could explain his choice, which irritated her more than she liked.

Across the room from the mark, Thana prodded a half-eaten bowl of porridge and traded verbal jabs with a handful of her cousins. She'd talked them into joining her tonight, but they didn't know she was actively working a contract—and they wouldn't suspect. Only those of her family who'd been chosen for the profession would've had the training to notice Thana's disengagement. She'd chosen cousins in other lines of work, so no one commented when she picked at her food and stole glances at the mark.

Outside, Amastan was nestled on a neighboring rooftop. He'd

pick up surveillance when Heru went upstairs, which he always did after dinner. If he wandered away on an errand instead, then Amastan would follow. Amastan was less skilled at tracking than Thana, but he had already spent two evenings inside the inn. They couldn't risk his presence becoming familiar. Besides, he could use the practice.

The server plopped a mug next to Heru and moved on. Heru took it, lifted his tagel, brought the mug halfway to his lips, and paused. His eyebrows formed a hard line and then he was on his feet. He grabbed the server's elbow and yanked him back to the table. Thana dabbed at her porridge with a piece of crust and tried not to stare.

Heru stabbed his finger at the mug. "What is this?"

The server tried to shake free, but Heru held fast. "It's your drink, sa."

"No, you imbecile. There's a crust around the edge and a stain on the lip. This mug is filthy. How dare you serve me in a dirty mug?"

The server blinked. "It's as clean as it gets, sa."

Heru shoved the mug at him, spilling half its contents across the floor and the server. "Then clean it again!"

The inn's owner, a man by the name of Idir who was solid if slow, approached from the kitchens, drying his hands on a towel. "What's the problem, sa?"

The server fled and Heru turned his anger on Idir, brandishing the mug like a weapon. "I don't know what kind of clientele you normally serve at your establishment, but even the lowest slave wouldn't drink from such a disgusting mug."

Idir took the mug, glanced at the offending rim, then gave it a quick rub with his towel. He handed it back. "There. Clean as new."

A lone chuckle burbled up from the back of the room. A man

wearing a tagel as red as blood had paused his card game to watch. Something about him tickled Thana's memory, but she shoved it aside. Heru took the mug back reflexively but didn't bother to inspect it. He opened his hand and let the mug fall. It hit the floor and split in two with a jaw-shuddering crack, spraying dark wine across the stones. The room went silent.

Idir looked down at the mess. "I'll add that to your bill, sa."

Heru grabbed Idir by the shoulders and stepped close. He hissed into the other man's ear. Idir's expression shifted from annoyance to amusement, then concern, and finally wide-eyed terror. When Heru let him go, Idir was trembling. Shoulders slumped, he bowed to the marabi, picked up the remnants of the mug, and hurried from the room.

The whole inn was staring now, but Heru ignored them and returned to his seat. Within moments, he was reabsorbed in his work and the scratch of his pen was the only sound in the room. Slowly, the other patrons picked up their conversations and smothered the eerie *scritch scritch scritch* with murmurs and strained laughter. Thana's companions exchanged nervous glances.

"Who does he think he is?" muttered one cousin.

"He better not be staying long," said another. "He'll get himself marked if he keeps that up."

Thana hid her smile by taking a drink.

Heru paused, then put his pen down and reached under the table to a small sack. He pulled out a blue glass bottle and poured some liquid onto a cloth. He used this to wipe both the table and his hands. He'd performed this same ritual twice just this evening. Thana could only guess at its significance.

A woman slid into the seat next to Heru, her unnaturally straight hair tumbling across bare shoulders. Her wrap dipped dangerously low, and she leaned forward a little as she turned toward him. Thana's cheeks warmed and she twisted her gaze back to the marabi's face for his reaction. But he ignored the woman and began writing again.

A cousin jostled Thana's elbow and she peeled her attention away. She nodded once or twice, too distracted to parse her cousins' conversation, and snuck another glance when she took a drink. The woman—she had to be a whore—pouted. Her eyes were lined with thick kohl and her lips had been painted a bright, painful red. She'd leaned in close to Heru and was fluttering her lashes. Then her gaze dipped to what the marabi was writing. Her pout deepened into a frown, but she didn't draw away.

Heru finally looked at her, his pen still hovering over the paper. His gaze was cool and analytical, as if the whore were merely an insect. His tagel fluttered as he spoke. The whore replied, a sly smile pulling back her lips to reveal yellowed teeth. She wiggled her chest, but Heru's gaze never strayed from her face.

The woman, unperturbed by his lack of enthusiasm, slipped an arm around his shoulder. Heru abruptly stood, rolling up his papers and recapping his pen. The woman offered him another pout, but Heru was already stalking toward the stairs that led up to the private rooms. The woman frowned, then glanced toward the back of the room. The man in the blood-red tagel made shooing motions at her. Rolling her eyes, the whore followed Heru.

Thana finally recognized the man in red. He'd been at Eken's party, had made that strange remark. His presence among Eken's guests meant several things, most interestingly that the late drum chief had been in the habit of inviting whoremongers to his public events. What was he doing here in the same inn as the mark? Perhaps he meant to take advantage of a foreigner's ignorance and rob him.

Well, he could have the mark's baats when the contract was complete. Thana wouldn't need them.

"Did you hear that, Thana?"

Thana bit her cheek and smiled. She was being too conspicuous; might as well run with it. "No—I was hoping that whore would give up and come over here."

Her cousins all laughed. Guraya slapped Thana on the shoulder, her hand heavy with wine. "She's too much for you."

"Oh come on, a girl can dream." Thana elbowed Zdan and wiggled her shoulders in a parody of the whore which was only exaggerated by Thana's small chest and modestly tied wrap. "Don't tell me *you* weren't watching."

Zdan rolled his eyes at her but didn't deny it.

Guraya giggled. "You better act quick. Another caravan just arrived, so they're going to be pretty busy. I can't wait for the market next week, there's going to be—"

Thana zoned out again. A week felt so distant when she had a mark to kill in the coming days. She pretended to listen, but kept checking the stairs, waiting for the whore to return. Guraya was right, the inn was overflowing with iluk who'd be easy pickings for such attention. The whore wouldn't waste her evening on one mark. Any minute now . . .

But the whore didn't reappear. Gradually, the other patrons paid up and either took their leave or retired upstairs, some with whores at their side and some alone. A handful were locals, but most belonged to the caravans. The extra cloth around their shoulders and heads, their longer tagels, the dust that lightened every inch of uncovered skin marked them as iluk, probably Azal.

Eventually only Thana, her cousins, and two people in the far corner remained, one of which was the man in the blood-red tagel. Thana had watched the whores return one by one, but the woman who'd followed Heru still hadn't appeared. Unease had slowly filled her along with a need to *act*. She'd been sitting in this stuffy, crowded room for long enough. It was time to find Amastan and see if he'd learned anything new.

Idir began to sweep the floor, his only warning that whoever didn't leave soon would find themselves tossed out. Thana left the baat for her drinks on the table but hesitated as her cousins headed for the door. She needed to know what Heru had said to Idir that had shaken him so. Anything could give them an edge.

Idir didn't look up from his broom when she neared. "How may I help you, ma?"

Thana kept her voice low. "I was only wondering what that man said to you, sa. It isn't too late to call the watchmen. If he was intimidating you—"

Idir stopped sweeping and looked up. "You're Tamella's daughter, aren't you?"

Thana started. "How did you know?"

Idir's eyes crinkled with a friendly smile. "You have her cheekbones, ma. I'll never forgive her for marrying Barag. Such a strong woman shouldn't be held down by a soft-skinned poet. But that's not your fault." Idir glanced down at his broom for a heartbeat, then rolled his shoulders back and met Thana's gaze. "If you were anyone else—aside from Tami—I wouldn't answer your question, but . . . you seem cut from the same cloth. You won't think I've been touched."

Idir gestured with his broom toward the stairs. "I know they say he's a marabi, but whatever he worships, it's not G-d. He spoke of things that should be forgotten." His fingers tightened around the broom. "I've seen a lot over the years, there's been mad men and wild jaan beneath this roof, but neither have chilled me as much as him. He threatened to bind my jaani. And, ma—I fear he can."

Idir's words stirred Thana's memories. She'd begged stories of monsters and jaan from her father when she was younger.

Scary stories she'd giggled over and that had later kept her awake in the dark of her room, jumping at every creak of the cooling stones. Stories about jaan that stole into your mind and whirled your thoughts into madness. Stories about guul that stole bodies and picked apart corpses for parts. Stories about sajaam that had once commanded storms and ruled the world.

And stories about en-marab that had once been marab until they turned against G-d. No longer content to quiet jaan, they'd learned how to control them. *Bind* them. Where the marab maintained the balance between the living and jaan, the en-marab subverted that balance to enslave both. If you misbehaved, the en-marab would steal your jaani while you were still alive.

But while jaan and guul could be found in the Wastes, sajaam and en-marab were long vanished from the world, if they'd ever existed at all.

"Some advice?" said Idir, voice low and close. "Don't cross that man, ma. Stay out of his way. Our city will be much safer when he's gone."

Thana glanced at the stairs and touched the glass beads at her neck. She'd bought them only yesterday from Salid. Her fingers counted five: one against jaan, two against magic, three against deception, four against bad luck, and five against G-d. Through her wrap, she almost thought she felt the charms' reassuring warmth.

"Yes. We all will be."

4

"He entered his room," said Amastan. "Then he closed the shutters. The light went out a few minutes later and since then it's been quiet."

Thana lay on the roof next to Amastan, the stone under her elbows and upper arms still exuding the day's heat, watching the dark window that he'd assured her was the mark's. True to his word, nothing stirred beyond. She scratched her head, fingers hesitating as they encountered little resistance. Gone were the slave knots, replaced by a close shave and several days worth of soft fuzz.

She'd taken leave of her cousins at home, feigning exhaustion as they'd tried to pull her along for a round of midnight tea, then backtracked to the inn and climbed to where Amastan had been watching, waiting. She'd told him everything that had happened inside, from the mark's fit of anger to the whore's ignored attentions to the threats against Idir. His evening had been dull in comparison, broken up only by a handful of drunken fights below.

"You didn't see the whore?" pressed Thana.

"No. But she could have stayed out of sight until the mark closed the windows."

Thana considered what they should do if the whore was still inside as she stared out across Ghadid's nightscape. The moon was only just rising while stars flickered and stared, occasionally obscured by a lost cloud. The city glowed with torchlight, hued glass transforming the light from orange to blue or purple or red. Glasshouses glittered across the roofscape, their budding contents only dark shadows within.

The vents of the glasshouse behind them were still open, taking advantage of the water-thick air. The churning smell of dirt and cut leaves and crushed dates seeped out, overwhelming any other scents. In another week, the vents would be closed and the glasshouse sealed to retain as much precious moisture as possible. But for now, Thana drank in the smells of life.

A group of singing iluk crossed the bridge to the next platform, their camels in a line behind. Thana idly traced the path that would lead them all the way to the city's edge. There, carriages waited to take them down to their caravan. She wondered what those iluk men thought about her city. She'd overheard foreigners talk about Ghadid as if it were a strange and impossible place, but it was stranger that others would build their cities so close to the ground and risk being overrun by dunes.

Ghadid soared above the sands on pylons built before written history, pylons which burrowed down and down through sand and dirt and clay to the sprawling aquifer below. Each pylon supported a metal platform, which in turn held a dozen and more buildings. Bridges linked the platforms to each other and cables linked the city to the sands. Ghadid crouched like a hesitant cat on the edge of the Wastes, curving around one corner of the unmapped and uninhabitable desert like a crescent moon. Other cities joined Ghadid, some on pylons, some on stilts, some braving the interminably shifting sands, and some had long ago succumbed to dunes.

Only iluk traveled the sands by foot. Some daring types left the platforms to venture onto the sands alone or in groups, searching for enlightenment, adventure, or G-d. Amastan had been down there twice. Thana herself had only once set foot on the sands, egged on by her cousins. The way the sand had shifted under her sandals had been unnerving. Then, too, there were the wild jaan that haunted the sands, stealing into the minds of the unwary.

"I think we should move tonight," said Amastan, breaking through the silence and her thoughts.

"What?" Thana sat up. "Are you sure? Do we know enough about the mark?"

Amastan's smile was subtle, barely touching his eyes. "What do you think?"

"Now you sound like my mother."

"It's your contract."

Yes—it *was* her contract. Thana straightened. Amastan was never hasty; if he wanted to move tonight, then he had a good reason.

"The whore," she said slowly.

Amastan didn't meet her gaze, but he nodded. "She'll have distracted him, maybe even kept him from putting up wards. And if she, uh, did her job, he should be dead asleep."

"I didn't see her go back down. She could still be in the room."

"Is it worth the risk?"

Thana eyed the window, but Amastan's conviction was enough for her. "Yes. We just won't wake her. You're right—this is the best chance we've got."

"We'll knock her out first," said Amastan. "I'll take care of that, I've had more practice and we don't want to risk killing her."

Thana sucked in the warm night air, then nodded. "All right. You'll go first, get the lay of things. We're assuming that the mark and the woman are both in the room and asleep. If that's true, signal me and I'll follow. You neutralize the woman, I'll take the mark." She slipped a knife from the strap on her arm and showed it to Amastan. "Heart first, throat second."

"And if he wakes?"

"Throat first."

"Before you can reach him?"

"You take him," said Thana. "You're stronger."

"And when do we run?" pressed Amastan.

A smile came unbidden to Thana's lips. The familiarity of this back-and-forth was reassuring. Nerves still flickered and spat like lightning beneath her skin, but she was in control.

"We don't," said Thana. "We have one chance and we can be as messy as we need. If we leave the mark alive, he'll know there's a contract on him. We can't risk that."

Amastan nodded, the motion both agreement and confirmation that she'd answered his questions well. She rolled her eyes at him; ever the teacher.

They got to work. With smooth and practiced efficiency, they divvied up the tools of their trade from the pack they'd stashed earlier on the roof. Amastan retied his wrap and tagel, snug and tight, and Thana counted her rings as she'd counted her charms. Two held powdered poison, but the rest were studded with worn stones that would maim flesh if she needed to use her fists. The contract better not come to that; she'd never been good at close combat.

Thana tied a tagel around her face, then looped a garrote and rope through her belt. She checked the knots of her wrap before finally nodding to Amastan. He returned her nod, then swung over the edge of the roof.

He reappeared a few moments later, climbing the wall to the mark's window as silent and quick as a spider. He crouched on the window ledge, head tilted, listening. But it was quiet, or at least as quiet as it ever got with the wind whistling between buildings, flies whining in their ears, and the occasional clatter or shout across platforms.

Seconds stretched into minutes as Amastan waited, testing even Thana's patience. When he finally moved, it was as if he'd never stopped. His fingers spidered around the window frame, feeling for weakness. The frame creaked, moved. Amastan froze. Then, with one finger, he pushed at it. It swung inward.

Amastan glanced at her and Thana understood his hesitation. Why was the window unlocked? Either the mark was naïve or . . . or he didn't have to bother with locks. Kaseem's warning about the Empress's marab echoed through her thoughts. Thana touched the glass beads at her throat as Amastan again glanced from the window to her, the movement a question. Abort? Or continue?

Thana made a circle with her fingers. Amastan made the same sign back, confirming. Continue.

Amastan looked inside. Then his hand danced through a series of signs. Two fingers: two people. A circle, then a closed hand: sleeping soundly. He paused, then signed that the mark was in bed. A longer pause. It took Thana a moment to understand his next sign, but when he repeated it, it was unmistakable, even across the distance: the second person was on the floor.

That was . . . odd. Amastan's next sign indicated that the person on the floor wasn't a threat. It must be the whore, then. Thana hadn't seen anyone else go up with the mark. She repeated Amastan's signs back to him to confirm. He nodded and gestured for her to join him.

He went in first. Thana followed, her bare feet hitting the stone floor with only a whisper. She closed the window, its tinted glass subtly shading the room blue. The air was unexpectedly sharp with peppermint and a large, rough bed took up most of the room's space. In it, a man slept beneath an unreasonable pile of blankets.

Amastan touched Thana's arm, then motioned to the floor. Her gaze swept across a dresser, a side table, a trunk, a pair of traveling bags, and—Thana squinted. What was that? Hidden in shadow at the end of the bed was a large, unmoving lump.

Two fingers. When Thana peered closer at the lump, she could trace the shape of a wrap and the outline of hair splayed across the rug. But the woman wasn't dead. Her chest slowly rose and fell with shallow breaths. At least they didn't have to worry about silencing her.

Footsteps thudded in the hallway, growing louder as they approached. Thana's pulse quickened, loud as drums in her ears. Light accompanied the steps, shining through the crack beneath the door. The light flashed across the floor, the dark rug, the bright red lips, and caught the whites of half-open eyes. Then the light was gone and the footsteps with it.

Thana let out a startled breath. Amastan shot her a warning glance, but the mark didn't stir. Neither did the woman on the floor. Anger as hot as the midday sun blew through her in a rush of realization. The woman was out cold, either by drugs or force. No wonder she hadn't returned downstairs. She hadn't been able to.

At least she wasn't dead. Thana looked closer, searching for any wounds, any blood. But the woman appeared fine—aside from those half-open eyes and shallow, intermittent breaths. A hand touched her arm and Thana started; she hadn't heard Amastan draw near. He signed: was she okay? Thana took a deep breath, then nodded.

Amastan made a circle with his fingers. Thana mirrored the sign and freed a small knife. They'd proceed as planned.

Amastan would keep an eye on the woman, senseless as she was, and Thana would take the mark. Nothing had changed. If anything, things had gotten easier.

Thana approached the bed, her footfalls quieter than wind-blown sand. The mark's chest rose and fell and rose again with each breath. Even in the dark, without his tagel, his pale features were familiar. It was the same man from Eken's party all right. In her head, she pictured what was about to happen, mentally practicing the motions before slipping into a calm, focused state as easily as she put on a belt.

Gently—but swiftly—Thana clamped a hand over the mark's mouth. He started awake, his body stiffening with surprise, but already she was on the bed, straddling him, her hand pushed hard against his mouth, against his jaw, as she slid the knife up beneath the ribcage and into the heart. She twisted the blade, then leaned into it, putting all of her weight on the knife and smothering his screams with her fist as the mark thrashed. Weakened. Stilled.

At least, that was how Thana had visualized it. She'd only brought her hand halfway to his mouth when something grabbed her shin. Fingers. It took all of her training not to jerk away or yelp. Instead, she froze. Something scuffed across the floor behind her, hitting the wooden dresser. A tinny, jangling sound zinged through the room. One of her charm's beads shattered, glass drizzling down her chest. The fingers holding her twitched but didn't let go.

Thana made the mistake of looking down as she twisted away. She choked on a cry. Fingers were indeed wrapped around her ankle, fingers attached to a hand on an arm that belonged to a body. The woman's body.

She'd twisted on the ground until her head was tilted up at an unnatural angle, open eyes staring at Thana. No—*through*

Thana. Those eyes were unfocused and unseeing. The woman scrabbled at Thana with her other hand.

Thana recoiled, stumbling and flailing for balance when the woman didn't let go. She glanced to Amastan for direction or help or *anything*, but he was just standing there, as if he'd been fired to glass. What in all of G-d's holy names was wrong with him?

Then she realized he wasn't looking at her, but just behind. He shouted a wordless warning, his hand finally going for one of his knives, but Thana was already turning. Too late. Darkness burst, filled her vision. On its heels came pain, sharp as a whip in her skull. A second glass bead shrieked and shattered. While the darkness and pain quickly faded to echoes, her neck burned from the heat of her remaining charms. Thana completed her turn, knowing what she'd find. But she hoped—dreaded—all the same.

The mark sat up in bed, awake and naked but for the sheets piled at his waist. He was blinking away sleep, one finger hovered mere inches from her skin. Thana jerked back, out of reach. The woman weighed her down, kept her from getting far.

The mark shook his head as if he could clear it, his gaze sharpening on Thana.

"Who in all the fifteen hells are *you*?"

Thana never had a chance to reply. At that moment, both the door and window burst open and men poured into the room.

5

Shards and fucking dust—

Two men crawled in through the window and three more blocked the doorway. Thugs, by the look of it. Had the mark hired them for protection? They wore differing cuts and colors of wrap, as if they'd just walked in off the street. Perhaps they had. They certainly weren't professionals; they moved with all the grace of drunken mules. That didn't mean they still couldn't get in her way.

Thana briefly entertained the idea of taking them out, but just as quickly dismissed it. One or two they could've handled easily. But five upped the chances that she or Amastan would have to kill, and they'd only been paid for the one life.

Two more glass beads sang and shattered as something brushed her arm. Thana jerked and turned. In her momentary distraction, the mark had lurched forward and touched her again. Now she only had one bead left. Considering the strength of that last attack, it might not be enough.

She needed to grab Amastan and get out of here. *Now.*

But as the men advanced, steps stumbling and slow from drink, Thana caught a flicker of confusion in the mark's eyes, his gaze flicking from her to Amastan to the men and back again. He didn't know who these men were, either. All the better—

maybe they'd kill him instead. Thana wasn't going to wait around and see.

First, she had to get free. Thana pried at the woman's fingers with her dagger. But before she'd freed two, the woman's other hand grabbed her wrist and yanked Thana to the floor. As Thana fell, the men rushed forward, hands raised but otherwise weaponless. What were they *doing*—?

Darkness surged again across her vision, but this time there was no pain. Bodies thumped the ground like drumbeats, the vibrations pulsing through the stone floor and up her cheek. Before Thana could extract herself from the woman's viselike grip, another hand grabbed the cloth at her neck and hauled her back. The woman finally let go as Thana's new attacker tossed her to the ground in the center of the room.

Thana's head hit the stones with a sharp *crack*. Black spots burst before her eyes and she hastily blinked them away. Pain spread down her neck and shoulders, but it was sharp and shallow, only a distraction and nothing to worry about. Her real problem met her gaze with too-pale eyes.

Heru Sametket stood over her, expression calculating and cold.

Thana felt a thrill of the same fear she imagined Idir must've felt back in the inn. She still had one charm left, but the others hadn't been very effective against the marabi. Whatever wards he was using were beyond Salid's protections.

Calm slipped across her, cool as old leather. Thana was going to die. Her mother had taught her how to recognize the moment when failure was imminent. *You'll know you've lost when you can stare death in the eyes and know only calm.*

But that didn't mean Thana had to accept it.

Thana kicked, caught Heru across the back of his knee, and

twisted her body away to avoid whatever he might throw at her next. She freed two small knives and flicked them at the mark. This close, her aim wasn't perfect. One knife struck and bounced off his sternum and the other slid through ribs to lung, but not heart.

Heru grunted, staggered back. Thana was already on her feet, running for the door. She grabbed Amastan and pulled him along and out of whatever fugue he'd fallen into. In another moment they'd be free of the room and flying down the stairs, putting as much distance between them and the marabi as possible, the contract shattered, but she and Amastan still *alive*.

Then the men got up.

Heru let out a strangled, wet curse. One of the men was between Thana and the door. She skidded to a stop, just shy of running into him. Amastan slipped her grasp and attacked the man with his dagger. Thana shook her garrote free and stepped behind the man while Amastan had him distracted, waiting for her opportunity. Amastan scored hits on the man's arms, shoulders, cheeks.

The man's counterattacks were awkward and slow and he didn't bother blocking Amastan's blows. When Amastan came in for a jab to the temple, instead of blocking or moving out of the way, the man stepped close and struck her cousin hard across the jaw. Amastan's head snapped back and he stumbled, eyes crossing.

That shouldn't have happened, couldn't have happened. Before Thana could process it, the man had wrapped his fingers around Amastan's throat. He yanked her cousin into the air, feet kicking. Thana didn't hesitate—she jumped onto the man's back, wound the garrote around his neck, leaned back, and pulled.

"That's not going to work."

One of the men crumpled to the ground, revealing Heru.

Within moments, the man started gathering himself up again. Heru looked from the man to his fingers, streaked red with blood. Then he pressed the sheets against the seeping wound in his chest and backhanded another of his attackers.

But two more men converged on the mark, ignoring his attacks as if they were nothing. Hands outstretched, they grabbed at Heru. Although he ducked out of their grasp, they seized his makeshift wrap. It came half off and Thana returned her attention to the man she clung to.

Heru, unfortunately, proved correct. The man ignored her even as she twisted the garrote so tight that the wire cut into his neck, releasing thick, oozing blood. He lifted Amastan higher, then tossed her cousin across the room as effortlessly as one might a sack of grain. Amastan hit the edge of the dresser with a sickening crack.

"No!"

Thana twisted the garrote's wooden dowels. The wire disappeared into the man's flesh, sliding through his skin like cheese. Although the sight turned Thana's stomach and sent a fresh pulse of blood down his neck, the man still didn't fall. He gurgled and spat blood, then slammed his back—and Thana—into the wall.

Thana dropped, leaving her garrote behind, still stuck in the man's neck. Her breath was gone and her chest throbbed with pain from the impact, but she glanced across the room to Amastan. All she could make out was his crumpled form on the floor, dangerously still. Then the man before her shifted his stance, and the light from the hallway caught and glinted off milky, staring eyes.

No wonder a wire through the neck hadn't stopped him; he was already dead.

Shards and dust and shattered glass. But Thana didn't have time to panic. The man lurched forward. Thana scrambled back. She tried not to think about Amastan, his crumpled body like a discarded doll's in the corner. She couldn't do anything for him until she brought this man down. At least she didn't have to worry about accidentally killing anymore.

But before Thana could attack, the woman barreled into the dead man and tossed him aside. She hurtled through the open door, Heru following at a halfhearted jog. He'd managed to hold on to the blood-stained bedsheet around his waist but wore nothing else save for a leather bag thrown over one shoulder. He'd removed the knife from his chest, the fool. Fresh blood pulsed from the wound, smearing his front.

Heru paused in the doorway, lips thinned in concentration. Then his gaze met Thana's and the concentration tightened into a smirk. He shook his head, then winced, his free hand grabbing at his chest. He stepped into the hallway and slammed the door shut. A key turned with a loud *click* in the lock.

Thana lunged for the door, but it was too late. Even if she'd had her picks, she didn't have time to open the door. She let loose a string of curses as she turned and surveyed the room. Five dead men were between her and the window, their attention fixed on her even as they staggered upright. Amastan lay in the corner, unmoving but—*probably*—still alive. Her garrote was stuck in the neck of one man, but she had a dagger at her hip, several smaller blades at hand, the rings on her fingers, and the throwing knives in the middle of the floor. All of her calm had evaporated, replaced by a buzzing, vindictive energy. By G-d, she was going to live and so was Amastan.

She feinted to the left and tumbled to the right. The men ignored her feint and lurched toward her. One grabbed her arm, another her shoulder, their grip viselike. Thana kept moving, dragging them with her for a half dozen steps before her strength failed.

Pain seared in her right arm. One of the men bent over her, his teeth against her flesh. *In* her flesh. The shards-cursed son of a mule had bit her! The anger that flashed through Thana gave her enough strength to yank her arm away. Her blood was reassuringly bright and red, in stark contrast to the dank stuff still oozing from the one man's neck. She drew back her uninjured arm and punched him. Even though her rings opened trailing red gashes in his cheek, he was unfazed.

She freed her dagger and drove its blade through his eye and into his brain. His fingers spasmed and his grip weakened. She tried to shake him off, but another man still held her shoulder. Thana twisted and stumbled and fell, bringing the man with her, his face within inches of hers, breath foul and burnt, eyes empty. Thana tried to shove him away, but his fingers dug into her shoulders, fingernails cutting skin, digging into muscle—

A blade burst through the man's neck, its tip stopping a hairsbreadth from Thana's nose before twisting and receding. He emitted a wet, guttural moan and blood trickled from the gaping wound to spatter across Thana's face. Then somebody was dragging him back and off her. Not far, but just enough for her to slide away.

She yanked her dagger from the other man's eye, his body twitching but not yet dead—well, no *more* dead—and accepted Amastan's proffered hand. His grip was weak, but he helped her up, then braced himself against her as he dragged in shallow breaths. Two more men lunged for them, but Thana resisted the urge to attack in turn. She was never going to win this fight. Already the man with a dusting *knife* in his skull was getting to his hands and knees.

Instead, she pulled Amastan toward the window. She should've been in agony from the wounds in her shoulders and arm, but sheer nerves kept her going. If Amastan could move even though he'd been unconscious moments ago, then she sure as the sun could.

She pulled herself onto the window ledge, then turned to help Amastan. He ignored her hand and scrambled up on his own. It took two attempts. His left arm wasn't working like it should, and he avoided placing any weight on the left foot. Even in the darkness, Thana saw the bruises spreading across his neck and the pain that flashed in his eyes with each ragged breath. Hopefully those ribs were only bruised, not broken. Didn't matter. He'd live. He had to.

Thana glanced at the ground so far below and swallowed the panic that filled her throat. She yanked the rope from her belt and gave one end to Amastan. He didn't hesitate or object. He looped it twice around his waist, then tied a knot and nodded. Thana looped the other end around her own waist, then gathered the rope and braced herself against the window. She nodded to Amastan.

He stepped backward off and over the ledge. Thana was ready for the jolt, but she wasn't ready for the hand that grabbed her leg. She started, slid forward, but didn't give. Ignoring the fingers digging into her calf, she played out the rope, hand over hand, as Amastan rappelled safely to the ground. As soon as the rope went slack, she let go and turned and slashed at the fingers holding her. Her dagger took three before she could slip free.

Then she was sliding over the window ledge, toes scrabbling blindly for holds. She found them, and then she was climbing back down. Her arm and shoulders screamed with pain every time they took her weight. Her own blood trickled down her chest, almost as distracting. It was all she could do not to fall, let alone keep going.

And then she couldn't hold on anymore. Her fingers slipped. She knew the fall was coming before it happened, so as her stomach dropped, she pushed away from the wall and hoped she'd climbed far enough.

The ground rushed up to greet her, only a half story away but still far enough to daze and jolt. Her bones were still singing from the impact as she straightened out of the crouch she'd landed in. A hand touched her shoulder and Thana staggered, her dagger cutting the air as she turned but it was only Amastan. He was gray as stone and equally bloodless and *pointing*.

The ringing in her ears faded as Thana looked. White blurred the end of the alley. Thana blinked her eyes clear. The mark. He blocked their way, one bloody fist raised in their direction, malevolence smeared across his eyes. Something whispered through the air like a blown kiss. Her fifth and final glass bead pinged with heat before shattering.

He snarled and tightened his fist, spattering fresh blood onto the stones. Thana didn't think; she moved her body between the marabi and Amastan. Pain stabbed in her chest and—

A grunt echoed through the alley. The pain loosened as Heru looked up. One of the men had climbed onto the window ledge. He stared down at them with those awful milky eyes. Then he stepped forward. And out onto nothing.

The man landed with a fleshy, sickening thud, but within a heartbeat was already clambering to his feet. Heru stepped back, his bleeding fist shaking at the man instead of her. Thana seized the opportunity and Amastan's hand and ran.

They'd reached the other end of the alley when the second man fell from the window with a fleshy plop. Thana didn't bother glancing back. She prayed the dead men would finish their job.

Thana slowed once they'd put a bridge and a platform between them and the inn. Only then did she finally stop and breathe and examine their situation. There were dead men loose in Ghadid, unkillable and unstoppable. But that wasn't her problem. No, her problem was that she hadn't killed the mark. Her problem was that the marabi now knew of them and their intent. She and Amastan were going to have hell to pay if she didn't fix that, and soon.

Bur first—

Amastan had collapsed to his hands and knees and was shaking so hard Thana thought she heard teeth rattling. Shock. Thana checked him over for wounds, careful and quick. Both his ankle and elbow were twisted unnaturally, and when her fingers brushed across the former, Amastan jerked back. Broken. But more concerning were his wet, rasping gasps. Nothing she could handle on her own. He needed a healer and now.

Fear filled her chest, tight as a cable, but she pushed it down as she pushed her shoulder under Amastan's good arm, leveraged him upright, and began their slow, agonizing retreat.

6

"Dogs."

The healer deadpanned the single word, her disbelief almost palpable. She stood behind Thana and out of sight as she washed out the wounds the dead man had dug into her shoulders.

"Yes, ma."

Thana was too tired to give a better excuse. She shrugged instead. A mistake. Pain spiked down her back and she sucked in a sharp breath. She glared at the bowl of water glowing faintly blue on the table in front of her, focusing on that instead of the pain. The healer tutted under her breath, finished bandaging Thana's shoulder, then moved in front to start on her arm.

"Next time, ma, maybe you should bring the dogs a treat."

Thana snorted. Then she said, "Did you see anyone else last night? I'm looking for a friend. He'd've had chest wounds, but nothing major."

A full eight hours had passed since their ill-fated assassination attempt. Thana had ended up half carrying Amastan to the nearest healer, but she'd cleaned the blood off herself and waited until dawn to seek care for her own injuries. Her wounds weren't dire and it was better to avoid undue attention.

Amastan would be okay. Thana had been right about his broken bones, but she'd missed his crushed windpipe. Nothing that couldn't be fixed given enough time—and water. The healers didn't charge for their basic services, but those who could afford to pay for the water were strongly encouraged to, and to pay beyond that if they were able. Thana had asked for more than a little life saving and it'd been expensive. But with the baats Kaseem had already given her, she could pay. Baats she'd owe if they didn't complete this contract.

They *would* complete this contract.

The healer raised one eyebrow at Thana's description of the mark, but her face remained impassive. "Chest wounds? Was he attacked by dogs, too?"

"They were pretty mean dogs, ma."

"I'll remember to keep my distance." The healer fished out a needle from a pocket and began sewing up the rougher portions of Thana's arm. "Unfortunately, your dogs had dirty mouths and dull teeth. I want you back here in a few days so we can repack the wounds and make sure they're not festering. The worst is yet to come, I fear. As for your question"—the healer tugged at the thread and tied a knot—"I haven't seen anyone like your friend. But Mo was here all night—you should ask her."

"Thanks, ma."

Thana gritted her teeth as the healer finished wrapping her arm. Both wounds throbbed, the kind of persistent pain you couldn't fully ignore. Thana preferred the kind of pain that came on bright and took your breath away but faded quickly. Throbbing pain was a distraction. But both were better than none at all. She could be dead. She'd come very close to it.

The water in the bowl was gone when the healer slumped forward. She slid a hand across her sweat-slicked forehead as she checked her work. Then she wiped her hands off on a towel.

"Get plenty of rest and drink this twice a day, ma. Come back if you develop a fever. Otherwise, I'll see you in three days." The healer pushed an herb-stuffed pouch into Thana's hand, then motioned toward the curtain on the other side of the room. "Mo is through there. And ma—stay away from dogs."

Thana smiled and placed a baat next to the empty water bowl. She had enough baats from the contract to heal her wounds completely, but that would've been conspicuous, not to mention immoral. If they had unlimited water, the healers could cure almost anything. But Ghadid struggled to conserve enough just for daily needs. So the healers used the minimum amount of water necessary to stabilize their patients and allow the body to heal itself.

The curtain led to a second room. Another healer tended to a child with a scraped knee. Her back was to Thana, but she was smaller and younger than the first—this must be Mo. Her braids were shorter and only a third of them had salas, the fabric healers received for every life they saved. Each grateful person gave what they could, so among the finer, colorful cottons and silks were dull strings and threads. Mo's salas consisted almost entirely of the latter, the thin lines of dull color braided into her black hair.

The curtain rustled as it fell back into place, but Mo didn't turn. The boy locked gazes with Thana, his stare bold and daring, trying—and failing—to hide his fear. Mo finished cleaning the blood off and applied a bandage. She gave the boy his instructions and shooed him away before finally turning and standing and acknowledging Thana's presence.

"What?"

Thana forgot what she'd been about to say as heat rose unbidden in her cheeks. Mo was almost an entire head shorter, but she stared up at Thana with bright eyes and a straight back. Her wrap was loose, obscuring her figure, but her skin was smooth and dark as midnight, her face heart shaped, her chin small but pointed, her lips wide and full. She was *beautiful*.

You always had a problem with pretty faces, chided Amastan's voice.

Thana pulled herself together. "The other healer said you might be able to help me, ma." Her words tumbled out too quick. "I'm looking for a friend—did you treat a man with a punctured lung last night?"

Mo pursed her lips. "A friend, huh? And what were you two doing that your friend sustained a lung wound?"

"It was dogs, ma."

"I don't take that kind of nonsense from children, so what makes you think I'd take it from *you?*"

Thana stepped back as if she'd been slapped. "I—uh—"

"You people." Mo's words were sharp and clipped. "You think you can get away with anything and we'll fix you up. I don't get it—it's *your* body. Don't you want to take care of it? And the *waste*—while you're out having fun with your friends and puncturing lungs and breaking legs, there're people dying of thirst right outside our doors. Those baats could've given them water to live instead of healing your sorry hide what shouldn't've needed healing in the first place. Maybe if you pulled your dust-stuffed heads out of the sand for once, you'd learn some responsibility and empathy. The sands don't just cover *you.*"

Thana bristled, any infatuation gone like smoke before a storm. "Look, I was just asking a question—"

"'Just' a question," interrupted Mo. "*Just* a little tumble from a roof. *Just* a knife fight with your girl's lover, *just* a run across the sands on a dare. Oh don't mind me while I *just* go waste a few skins of water for fun."

"I didn't come here for a lecture."

"Then maybe you shouldn't've been playing with dogs!"

Thana answered Mo's furious glare with her own. She didn't

have time to get into a shouting match with a rigid-as-iron healer. Her cousin had almost died, a dangerous man was loose in their city, dead men were walking, and this woman was treating her like a street kid. "Look—ma. I just want to know if my friend's all right. Did you see him or not?"

Mo held her glare for another moment, then sniffed, satisfied with her small victory. "The foreign marabi in the white wrap? I treated him myself. He left a few hours ago." She eyed Thana. "He didn't ask about friends."

"He wouldn't," muttered Thana. "Did he have anyone else with him? A woman?"

"No. He was alone." Mo narrowed her eyes. "But I can tell you which direction he took when he left."

Thana didn't rise to the bait. Sands take it, the mark was still alive. She shouldn't have hoped, but—

The bell over the entrance jangled with a new arrival. The healer called from the other room.

"*Mo.*" It wasn't just a summoning, but a warning. Mo stiffened, glanced at Thana, then hurried out. Thana followed at a slower pace. She needed to go home. She needed to rest. And then she needed to plan.

But the scene unfolding in the other room caught her and kept her from leaving just yet. What was at first a flurry of motion and cloth and limbs soon slowed and condensed and became several men, some moving tables, others carrying burdens. The tables screeched as they were dragged together and then groaned as heavy burdens were laid out on them. Four unmoving lumps of flesh. Four bodies. The color of their wraps was unforgettable. And now, too, the smell.

Thana crept closer despite the overwhelming stench of rotten flesh. She needed to know for certain. One man was missing several fingers, another his head, and a pair of wooden rods dangled from the neck of a third, the wire cut deep into his skin. Even as bile rose in her throat, Thana was relieved.

It was them, all right. And they were now very much dead.

But there had been five.

Mo scanned the line of corpses. "What in G-d's holy names—?"

Thana lingered near a watchman, a golden sash and tagel marking his position. He didn't answer Mo; his attention was fixed on the corpses. The other healer walked the line of bodies, checking pulses and pulling back wraps to reveal cool, graying flesh beneath.

"They're all dead," she announced.

"We know, ma," said the watchman. "They'd been dumped in an alley in Aeser, left like a pile of trash."

The healer rounded on the watchman, who took a startled step back. "Why did you bring them to me, sa? I can't return life to the dead."

Mo picked at the garrote wire in the neck. "Enass—they've been mutilated."

The watchman frowned. "Well, that's how he was killed, wasn't it? And that's why I'm here, ma," he added, addressing the other healer—Enass. "Something is off about this. If you can tell me how they died, ma, that could help us find their killer."

Mo tugged the garrote free and held it up, congealed chunks of gore dropping to the floor. "This was done posthumously."

"Why do you say that?" The watchman stepped closer to examine the wire. Even his tagel couldn't hide his disgust.

The other men shifted uneasily. One raised a hand. "We free to go, sa?"

"Oh, yes." The watchman waved them away. "But report to our scribe before you head home. I need your accounts of the evening in writing. The Circle will want to know every detail. Thank you for your assistance, sai. And your discretion."

The men murmured their assent and filed out, leaving Thana exposed. She stood at the end of one table while the watchman peered at the neck wound. Mo frowned at her, but turned back to the body instead of calling her out.

"There's not enough blood," explained Mo. "If this wire had killed him, then he'd have bled out and his wrap should be drenched with blood. Look how deep the wound is. Not to mention a garrote is used to choke, not to cut. This was done after his heart had stopped, by someone strong or desperate."

Mo ran her hands along the man's body with expert ease, unknotting and folding back his wrap to expose dark flesh beneath. She brushed her palms across his chest, arms, and thighs. Then she filled a nearby bowl with water and settled her hands on the man's chest. She breathed in and closed her eyes. The room grew still with her.

The moment stretched into a minute. The water level in the bowl gradually lowered, but this was no ordinary healing. Blue light scattered across the water's surface and Mo's skin, tendrils snaking across her body. Then the light snapped and Mo fell back as if she'd been pushed. She turned wide-eyed to the watchman.

"What magic is this, sa?"

Enass had just finished the same examination on another of the dead. Now she flipped the body, pulled the wrap past its waist, and motioned them over. Mo and the watchman hurried, but Thana moved more slowly. When they joined Enass at the table, the marks were clear to all. Dark lines had been cut into the man's skin as if by a hot scalpel, their edges curled and burnt. A dozen and more slashes formed symbols that seemed to be letters from a language Thana didn't recognize.

Mo turned the next man over and ripped his wrap down. More lines covered his back, the symbols similar if not exactly the same. The other men proved no different. In a matter of moments, the living were surrounded by bodies crisscrossed with bizarre burnt cuts. They exchanged uneasy glances.

The watchman was first to break the silence. "We'll look into it, mai. I don't know if this is the work of a cult or a madman, but I've got the feeling these won't be the last bodies we see like this."

Mo clutched at her arms. "No, sa."

Enass wrapped an arm around Mo and drew her in close. The watchman gave the nearest body another once-over, then stepped back with a shake of his head.

"We'll find him, mai. Someone who can do this—he won't be able to hide long in our city." He glanced at Thana and frowned. "You're not a healer."

"I—was just leaving, sa." Thana moved toward the door.

Mo waved her off. "She's a patient, sa. Got attacked by dogs."

"Dogs again?" The watchman's frown deepened. "There've been a handful of dog attacks lately since the caravans started arriving. Until those iluk learn to control their beasts, we should all be more careful."

Thana barely suppressed a laugh at Mo's incredulity. Instead, she said, "Definitely, sa. No more dogs for me."

"Get going, then. And don't talk about this to anyone. We don't need to cause panic over a handful of unexplained deaths." The watchman considered the corpses again. "Not yet, anyway."

7

Amastan lay in the same bed she'd left him on, eyes closed and completely unresponsive. The wide room was quiet, emptied of its lingering patients in the aftermath of the storms. Thana had stolen a few hours of sleep at home, slipping in through her own window to avoid any questions from her mother. She pressed his hand between hers and watched his chest rise and fall, rise and fall. Not for the first time, she thought about speeding his recovery. But no matter how much she needed him, the stigma against wasteful healing held her back. His healer had already assured her he would live. That had to be enough.

Besides, wasn't it a little selfish to heal Amastan only to drag him back into danger? Mo's words, however ill-informed they'd been, had left their mark. Whatever Thana did next, she needed to avoid healers, which meant avoiding any unnecessary risk. But that begged the question: what *should* she do next?

Amastan would know. He'd have answers. He'd sit her down and they'd discuss their plan over tea and she'd stop being so *afraid*—of the mark, of the dead men, of breaking their contract, of disappointing her mother, of failing.

Of losing him.

"What do I do?"

But Amastan didn't answer. Thana sighed and pressed the heels of her hands against her eyes. What would Amastan do?

He'd lay out the situation, piece by piece, like a master player preparing for a siddat tournament. Piece one: the mark knew. Piece two: Thana was on her own. Piece three: the dead men were now thoroughly dead. Four of them, anyway. What had happened to the fifth?

Thana touched the empty cord at her neck, all of the charms shattered and gone. They hadn't done her much good, had they? But then, they were supposed to protect her from jaan and basic wards, not from dead men and whatever the mark had done. And what *had* he done? He'd stopped the dead men, if only for a moment. He'd commanded the whore. He'd used magic Thana had never heard of, let alone understood.

Her fingers tightened around the cord and she knew, then, what Amastan would do. You couldn't fight what you didn't understand, which went double for the charms. Salid had as great an understanding of jaan as the marab—if not better. He was no longer the best charm maker in Ghadid, but he was discreet, never asked questions, and was very good at what he did.

To make his charms, he had to know everything about curses, bad luck, and jaan. He might even know what in G-d's names the mark had done, or even how dead flesh could walk. He could give her an edge against the mark.

If nothing else, she needed new charms.

Thana left her cousin with a kiss on the forehead, then headed for the Telem neighborhood. She adjusted her wrap as she walked, knotting it at a respectful height just below her neck. As she dodged merchants' carts and felt the sun's hot breath on her skin again, last night's monsters were seasons away. She even paused for a minute to watch two street performers dancing with blades and silk, occasionally trading rehearsed blows to the appreciative gasps of their small audience. Thana couldn't share that awe; the performers' moves might be pretty, but they'd be useless in a real fight.

A tinny bell announced Thana's arrival in the shop. An old man hunched at his worktable, a pair of spectacles strapped across his eyes, his brown tagel barely covering his mouth. He held tweezers in one bony hand and a small glass orb in the other. As she waited and watched, breathing in tea-bittered air, he furrowed his bushy eyebrows and inserted a scrap of paper into the glass. Then he set both down, pulled back the spectacles, and peered at her.

"Ah. Tamella's daughter. What now?"

Thana undid the leather cord around her neck and dropped it in front of Salid. He started to pull it to himself, saw it was empty, and shoved it back to her with no small amount of annoyance.

"Is that a joke, ma?"

"No, sa. That's the same charm you sold me three nights ago."

Salid had so little of his face covered that Thana could watch the frown creep up his features before reaching his eyes. "I don't see any charms."

"Because they broke, sa. All of them."

"What?" Salid leaned back, looking from the cord to Thana. "My charms don't fail." He held up a finger before she could refute him. "They don't fail against jaan and curses. Only something powerful could have done this. What did you meet?"

Thana took a seat across from the charm maker at his low table. "We were attacked by five dead men, sa."

Salid's brow furrowed. "Dead men? Do you mean they were possessed? Even in a body, a jaani couldn't break those charms. I've worked with Menna on that design and we've tested them—"

"The marabi broke them," admitted Thana. "But he was associated with the dead men. And no—they weren't possessed, at least not as far as I could tell. Trust me—they were very much dead."

"A *marabi* broke my charms?" Salid sounded insulted. "That's not possible. Marab don't use that kind of magic, at least none that I've met. . . ." He trailed off, gaze sliding past Thana. When he focused on her again, his gaze was hard and cold. "You're not speaking of the man from Na Tay Khet."

It was more plea than question. Thana swallowed, knowing she was on thin glass. She wasn't supposed to talk about the contract with anyone except Amastan. In dire circumstances, exceptions could be made for other cousins. But Salid was an old friend of the family, and if Salid knew anything that could help . . .

Thana picked her words with care. "The dead men attacked him. I stabbed one, but he didn't even flinch. Didn't bleed, either, not properly. And the healers found marks on their backs, cuts in their skin that looked like symbols or words. Do you have any idea what it means?"

"Marks on the skin?" Salid drummed the tabletop with his fingers. "Are you certain they were dead? If so, that sounds like . . . well, I don't want to think about the possibility that Ghadid could harbor something so foul."

Thana huffed her exasperation. "They were *dead*, sa. They didn't breathe. They didn't bleed. They jumped from a second-story window and got up like it was nothing. I shoved a knife through one's eye and into his skull and he kept going. I know a corpse when I see one."

"That's enough. What you're describing isn't the work of a marabi. It's a form of magic that hasn't been practiced for many generations. I've never seen it myself, though—only read about it. But the practice died out centuries ago along with the last of the sajaam. But . . . how well do you remember the markings? Could you draw them for me? I don't want to jump to conclusions that will probably prove unfounded."

"No, sa. They were too complex." It'd be easier if she could bring Salid to the bodies, but she should avoid being seen with the charm maker. She needed to contain this mess, as much as that was still possible. "But I could bring you a rubbing. Do you have any paper and kohl?"

"Yes, yes—that'd do. I have some right here." Salid pulled a metal crate out from under the table, full of odds and ends. He rubbed his temples, then shuffled through the jumble. "I really hope you're wrong," he muttered under his breath.

"What do you think it is?" pressed Thana.

Salid only rustled through the box louder. He produced a roll of parchment followed shortly by a small box of kohl, both of which he shoved across the table at her. "You'd laugh if I told you. To you, they're nothing but stories."

"The Serpent is nothing but a story to most of Ghadid, but we know better. Tell me."

Salid considered her for a moment before sighing. "En-marab."

Thana did laugh, but it was a tired, dry sound. "If the dead can walk, why not the madmen used to scare children?"

"I'm not joking."

"Neither am I."

"It fits the pattern," said Salid. "What you described is a binding—a jaani bound to a corpse."

"So, a guuli."

"Not a guuli." Salid held up an admonishing finger. "I said a *jaani.*"

"But guul live in corpses—"

Salid rolled his eyes. "Listen first, ma. And don't interrupt again. If a jaani enters a living body, the mind will break under the strain of two jaan—its own and the wild one. If a guuli enters a living body, the body will break. They aren't interchangeable creatures, even if they're of the same substance. A guuli in a corpse is what you find in the Wastes, wild and vicious and predatory. A jaani bound to a corpse is controllable, a slave. It is *created*." He held up a finger. "But not by a marabi. Such a creation is blasphemy of the highest kind. But look—*that's* why I don't want to jump to conclusions. The implications are disturbing. Now go. I want to see these marks while there's yet light."

Thana took the parchment and the kohl and stood, leaving the empty cord behind on the table. "I'll need more charms, sa."

"Here." Salid grabbed a leather pouch off the wall. "I don't know what good they'll do you against this kind of magic. I'll look for something stronger while you're gone."

He dropped the pouch into Thana's waiting hand. She rubbed the leather between her fingers, counting the beads inside. Five charms.

"As long as you stay away from that foreign marabi and those bound, those charms will see you safely there and back."

Thana tucked the pouch inside the neck of her wrap, thanked Salid, and left. Even knowing the charms wouldn't do anything against the dead men, she still felt safer.

At the healer's, Mo stood next to the same corpse, as if Thana had never left. The other bodies had disappeared and the tables were back where they'd been, the air a bit less rank than before. Thana hoped someone'd had the sense to burn them instead of putting them in the crypts. Beside Mo stood a man wearing a white wrap, his posture rigid. Thana was halfway across the room before Mo noticed her. The healer puffed her cheeks.

"You're back," said Mo. "Your friend's here, too."

"Friend?" echoed Thana.

The man in white turned. Heru Sametket met her gaze, a clean blue tagel covering his face from the eyes down. The floor tilted beneath Thana. She froze and watched the same recognition flit across Heru's eyes, then harden into something cold and deadly. The tension filled the room so thick that even Mo noticed and glanced between them.

"Friend." Heru's voice carried no warmth.

"This *was* the guy you were looking for last night, wasn't it?" asked Mo.

"How kind of you to check in on me," said Heru. "I'm so sorry we didn't run into each other sooner."

"Yes, that was unfortunate," said Thana, recovering her wits even as her pulse thudded loud in her ears.

She forced herself to approach them and the corpses. If the mark tried anything, at least Mo was right there to help. But likewise, she couldn't just stab him and be done. They were at an impasse—she could only hope the mark realized it, too.

Heru eyed her with no small amount of distrust as Thana joined them. Then he abruptly returned to the examination she'd interrupted. The wrap had been removed, leaving only a naked body facedown on the table. Its head was twisted unnaturally, arms askew, and half its scalp had been sheared off in a bloodless chunk. Like the others, marks had been cut into its skin. But, unlike the others, two large gashes ran long down its back.

"This one's new," said Thana before she could stop herself.

"Yes, my *friend*." Heru all but hissed the word through his teeth. "He attacked me not even an hour ago. I'm starting to get the feeling that someone wants me dead." He looked pointedly at Thana.

"He's the same as the others, though," said Mo. "Posthumous wounds with minimal bleeding. Someone broke his neck after he was dead. See—no bruising. You need flowing blood for bruises."

Heru grunted, tracing the marks on the man's back with his finger. "I don't recognize this writing, although it's familiar. I *should* know it. This is my—" He cut himself off and turned to Mo. "What scholars do you have in your town?"

Thana swung her bag down. Heru stepped back, hands raised, but when Thana pulled out the kohl and parchment, he relaxed.

"Jumpy, aren't we?" said Thana.

"Considering the circumstances . . ."

Thana held up the parchment. "I need to make a rubbing."

Heru narrowed his eyes. "You're no scholar. What could you want with those marks?"

Thana chewed on her answer. She didn't want the mark to know any more than was necessary. She should've turned around and left as soon as she saw that white wrap, her lie to the healer be damned. She could still leave. But then she caught Mo's gaze and saw her curiosity and Thana's hesitation solidified into resolve.

Thana shrugged. "I have a friend who might know something."

Heru gestured toward the corpse. "Then by all means."

Keeping Heru in her line of sight, Thana spread the parchment across the dead man's back, careful to keep its rough paper between her and the skin. She held the paper down and scraped kohl back and forth across its surface. The marks took form in the negative space between the thickening black kohl. When she'd captured all of them, Thana wiped the kohl from her fingers off on her wrap and rolled the parchment back up.

"Thanks," she said needlessly, and turned to leave.

A hand touched her wrist. Thana stopped and Mo stepped back, her hands clutched before her.

"Let me come with you," said Mo. "I need to know what's causing this. I want to help stop it. Whatever this is, it came here, to me. I can't let it go any further."

Thana swallowed. It was selfish to do anything but dissuade Mo, but a part of her wanted to be selfish. Amastan was right: she really couldn't resist a pretty face. Besides, Mo didn't seem to be the type to idly stay behind. And once Thana found out who or what was creating these monsters, she'd need someone to take the problem off her hands. She still had a contract to complete.

"That's fine. But doesn't someone need to stay here?"

"Enass will be back. I'll leave a note."

Mo stared at her expectantly until Thana realized what Mo wanted, sighed, and ripped off a clean piece of the parchment. Mo took the scrap with a nod of thanks, then swept away to a table. Heru sidled over as Thana re-shouldered her bag. She stepped back and crept a hand toward her belt and the dagger there, hoping he couldn't see the fear clawing at her throat.

"I fear we have not yet been properly introduced, *friend*," said Heru, voice low but even. He extended a hand. "I am Heru Sametket, second advisory marabi to the Empress Zara ha Khatet, long will she live. But, I understand you know that already."

Thana didn't take his hand. The charms at her collarbone had grown warm.

"Thana," she muttered when Heru didn't move. She wasn't sure why she gave him even that. A mark had never known her name before. Then again, this contract was already being smothered by firsts.

"How's our other friend faring?" asked Heru. "I assume from the lack of appropriate grieving garb for your culture that he is still unfortunately alive."

Thana bristled. "He's fine."

"Ah." Heru poured a great deal of disappointment into that single sound. He ran a hand down his chest. "What prompted the knives? I would like to know so I might avoid such an inconvenience in the future. Your healers may perform small miracles, but they are quite stingy with their water."

Thana took another step back. Mo needed to hurry up with her note. "You threatened me."

Heru raised an eyebrow. "Oh? Really? I recall *you* slipped through *my* window."

"You're not exactly innocent. What about the whore you brought up and—"

Thana stopped herself, the implications clear as everything finally clicked into place. She just hadn't thought it all the way through yet. She'd been stupid, so stupid. In all the excitement between the corpses and the marks, the broken charms and Amastan's condition, she hadn't had a chance to *think*.

The woman had been unconscious, hurt even—that was indisputable. Then she'd attacked Thana, risen and run across the room. She'd been alive, but her body had moved as if it were not her own. As if her jaani were gone, or . . .

A jaani bound to a body is controllable, a slave, Salid had said. The stories of en-marab varied in many ways, but they had one thing in common: where marab invoked G-d to quiet jaan and drive wild ones from the possessed, en-marab bound jaan to their will. Whatever blasphemous magic had created the dead men was the same magic that had commanded the woman. The same magic Heru had used.

If that magic were so rare and dangerous that Salid couldn't be certain of even its existence, then what was the chance that *two* en-marab were in Ghadid at the same time?

"—And?" said Heru.

"What kind of marabi *are* you?"

Of course he'd created those men. She saw it now. Amastan must've tripped an alarm and Heru had lost control. Maybe he didn't know what he was doing. It didn't matter. What mattered was that the mark, sent to their city by the Empress herself, was an en-marabi who had no qualms using jaan to bind both the living and the dead to his will.

A true monster. And Thana was supposed to somehow *kill* him?

If Thana took another step, she'd be through the door. She didn't have to wait for Mo. She could be gone, far from this awful man. But she was also wary to let him out of her sight and she couldn't leave Mo alone with him. Mo didn't know what he was, what he'd done.

"The kind you wouldn't want to meet at night," said Heru softly. "Do you have any intentions of trying to kill me again? Because I would advise against it. You were fortunate last time, but—" He grabbed the front of her wrap so suddenly that Thana didn't have time to back away. He dug his fingers through the fabric and around the charm pouch beneath. "These pretty baubles won't save you again."

The glass charms glowed bright even through the layers of cloth, then shattered all at once. Heru released Thana and stepped back, hands at his sides as if he'd done nothing.

"You'll take me to this scholar," he continued. "There are few things worse than death, but I am capable of most of them."

"You don't scare me," lied Thana.

Mo had finally finished her note and now hurried back to them. She'd tied her braids away from her face with a wide blue ribbon and Thana couldn't help but look. Heru followed her gaze.

"I'm not threatening *you*."

His words were a punch. How dare he threaten someone who couldn't fight back, who didn't have a half dozen knives close to hand. "Don't you dare touch her."

Heru tilted his head. "Who hired you?"

Then Mo was between them, thumbing through the keys on her belt. "Come on, let's see this friend of yours. . . ." She trailed off, looked at Thana. "What did you say your name was?"

"Her name is Thana," supplied Heru.

Thana glared at him. Behind Mo's back, Heru kept his gaze fixed on Thana while he ever so slowly reached out as if he were going to brush his fingers through Mo's braids. Thana's first impulse was to dig another blade into his chest. But Heru had already broken her charms with a touch and Thana had no idea how much damage he could do in the second it took her to draw a knife.

What harm was there in bringing him along? This situation couldn't possibly get any worse, and if she kept the mark near, she could at least keep an eye on him. It'd give her more opportunities to study him—and find a way to complete her contract. When she nodded, Heru dropped his hand.

"Right," said Thana. "Let's learn about monsters."

8

Salid didn't bat an eye at the small entourage Thana brought with her. Instead of asking about her new acquaintances, he brewed a pot of tea, grabbed extra cushions, and found a bowl of sugar. Once everyone had settled around his worktable, the tea had been poured, and the sugar stirred in, Thana dropped the kohl-blackened parchment on the table. Salid pushed the teapot to one side and spread out the parchment. He weighed down the corners with pieces of unpolished glass and examined the rubbing.

When a few minutes had passed and Salid had only made a handful of throaty grunts, Heru snapped, "What do you make of it, old man?"

Thana narrowed her eyes at him, but Salid shrugged. "It's . . . puzzling, sa. And worrying. I—hmm."

Salid began rummaging in a large trunk beside the table. Mo sipped at her tea, gaze wandering the small workspace. Thana looked, too, following Mo's touring gaze as if she were seeing the shop for the first time. The room was congested, stuffed full of cords and pliers and feathers and hides and all manner of glass beads—in jars, in bowls, even clustered on the workbench. A panel of glass windowpanes hung along the back wall, in various hues of blue and green.

Thana's gaze came full circle to Heru, who'd pulled up the

bottom of his tagel and was checking his teeth in a knife's reflection. He picked at something and Thana turned away in disgust. Finally, Salid set a large, leather-bound book on the table with a heavy thump. He stood back long enough for them to appreciate the size, then leaned in and began flipping through its pages, each one filled to the edges with tight, spidery script. At last he paused on one page and scanned its contents with a trembling finger. Then he sat back as if he'd been pushed, all his air coming out in a gust that fluttered his tagel.

"I—well . . . that's unfortunate."

Heru stowed his knife and wiped his fingers clean on the table's edge. "Who is he?"

Salid stared at the marabi with confusion that soon narrowed to suspicion. He gestured to the page, its vellum yellowed with age. "This is a very old magic, a kind that hasn't been seen in centuries. It's a type of binding that goes well beyond what's necessary. A marabi may bind a jaani to its body, but only to keep it from going wild and only until the seven years have passed. The jaani cannot harm anyone in that state. Even though it's inside its body, the jaani does not *possess* it. Those men you found, though—that could be called possession, but unlike anything even wild jaan do. This is intentional and directed. The men who once used this magic were branded *en*-marab because they were everything the marab stood against."

Mo shuddered. "Why would anyone make such creatures *intentionally?*"

"Control." Salid spread his hands. "Power. The same things men have lusted after ever since G-d told us not to. The en-marab were once as numerous as marab, until G-d struck them down. Well—G-d and the old kings. It turned out no one likes power-hungry men who can bind anyone they want to their will. The last notable en-marabi lived centuries ago, and he was a remarkable scholar as well as a monster. He pushed the boundaries of binding beyond anything en-marab had done before." Salid tapped the vellum. "These symbols bind and control jaan effectively and efficiently—and he was the one who invented them. What I don't understand, though, is how those symbols came to be in our city, today. This knowledge should've died with their creator."

"But the knowledge is in your book," said Mo, confused. "And that survived him."

Heru snorted. "It takes more than knowing a few symbols to bind jaan, girl." Then, to Salid, "Who is this man?"

"Djet Khentawpet. But he's been dead for some time."

"I doubt death would stop him."

Salid and Heru shared a glance. Thana leaned across the table to read the book, but the script was illegible and interspersed by the symbols she'd seen seared into the men's flesh. Old books and history—Amastan should be here, not her.

"So how do we kill these bound jaan?" she asked.

Salid scanned the page. "I'd imagine disrupting or removing the symbols should be enough—ah. Yes, it says so here."

Heru nodded. But then, he'd already known that. The gashes across the dead man's back had been just that: disruptions. They'd torn straight through the lines of symbols. But what had happened to the first group, the men who'd attacked her and Amastan? When the watchman had brought those corpses in, their marks had been unaltered.

Thana eyed Heru. If he'd created all of them, why had he unbound only the last man? It was as if he hadn't figured out how to undo the binding until after he'd been attacked a second time. Which meant he was either still learning this horrible magic, or . . .

Thana didn't want to complete that thought. She closed her

eyes, trying to refocus. She was getting caught up in the wrong things. This wasn't her problem. She only needed to understand Heru's magic well enough to finish the contract. Stopping the bound jaan he'd made wasn't up to her.

"We need to find who's doing this," said Mo. "If someone is misusing jaan, we need to stop them. This is blasphemy."

Salid nodded without looking up as he reread the page, then flipped to the next. "Whoever created these bound must be obsessed with studying Djet's magic. The art of jaan binding is complex enough, let alone with the complications that would arise from using a corpse." Salid ran a hand across his forehead, smearing sweat and dust; with four people in the small room, what was already stifling heat was quickly becoming unbearable. "Tell me everything you already know about this en-marabi."

"His creatures targeted me," said Heru.

"They did?" But Salid's tone held no surprise; he'd already guessed who Heru was. Hopefully, he'd keep his mouth shut. "Who else have they attacked?"

Thana raised a hand. "Just me, as far as we know."

"And your friend," added Heru.

Thana swallowed a groan. She'd hoped Heru had forgotten about Amastan in all the excitement.

"Which friend is this?" asked Salid.

It'd be less suspicious to come clean. "A cousin who was also attacked. He's been stabilized, but it'll take some time for him to recover. I'd rather not bring him into this."

"Cousin," mused Heru.

"Heru was attacked again, later," continued Thana, hoping to steer the conversation away from Amastan. "Were you alone then?"

"I was."

"So the common thread here is you, sa," said Salid. "Assum-

ing these were the only attacks. Do you have any idea why someone would target you?"

Thana bit the inside of her cheek. Heru could out her in a
heartbeat, not just to Salid, who could up until he did at least
protest his ignorance about her true vocation, but to the healer.
Yet Heru didn't even look at Thana. Why not? Was it because his
own secrets, the ones she knew and the ones she suspected and
the ones *he* thought *she* knew, were far worse?

"I don't know," said Heru after a moment's consideration. "Or
would you like me to select from one out of a hundred possible
reasons? I'm not free of enemies. One could say I'm a popular
man."

"Yes, well, perhaps you should've stayed close to your Empress," said Thana.

Heru replied with a cold stare.

Salid picked up his teacup, but didn't take a sip. "I take it that
means you're the ambassador sent by the Empress Zara, sa?"

Heru turned his cold stare on Salid. "That has no bearing on
our current situation. Let us focus on the task at hand. Or do I
need to remind you that these creatures have made an attempt
on my life twice now? I do not wish for a third." He held his
hands out to Salid. "May I borrow your book?"

"Certainly, sa." Salid hefted the book and placed it in Heru's
waiting palms. As Heru scanned the page before him, Salid
added, "Just be careful with the binding. It's been passed down
through many generations of my family, so it's very old and—"

Heru ripped out several pages and dropped the book on the
table.

"*Sa!*"

Heru tossed a handful of foreign coins onto the table and
headed for the door. Salid picked up the ravaged book and
clutched it to his chest. He gently set the book back within its

trunk, then, clenched fists shaking, shouted at Heru's departing back.

"I'll call the watchmen on you!"

Heru waved a hand dismissively, then the bell jangled and he was gone. Thana and Mo exchanged a glance. Mo was the first to run after him, a dozen muttered apologies in her dust. Thana grimaced but met Salid's accusatory gaze.

"*You* brought him here," snapped Salid. "I don't know what you've gotten yourself into, but if you or anyone in your family ever wants charms again, you'd better return those pages. Otherwise, I'll curse the Basbowen family myself."

"Peace, sa." Thana bowed her head. "I'll return them. On my mother's name."

"I'll look into these monsters of yours, if only because they're a threat to the city." Salid glowered, then his eyebrows unfurrowed and he drew a circle in the air around his chest: a ward against evil. "But girl—I fear you're in over your head. May G-d protect you."

"I know," said Thana. "And thank you."

She paused just outside Salid's door. The sky was a washed-out blue, not a single cloud to mar its vast breadth. When Thana was much younger, she used to lounge on the roofs with her cousins and pretend that the sky was the ground and if they let go, they'd fall and fall and fall forever. She wasn't sure if the dizziness that swelled in her now was only a memory or a symptom of her exhaustion. But she couldn't rest yet and she couldn't let go.

Heru and Mo had already disappeared. Back to the healers was Thana's best guess, so she started off in that direction. She couldn't leave Mo alone with Heru, not when Mo was the only one who hadn't yet realized just how dangerous he was.

And whose fault was that? Thana had pretended Heru was her *friend*. The first rule of being an assassin, the rule that didn't even have to be said because it should've been so extraordinarily obvious, was: don't fraternize with the mark. A rule she'd broken as soon as she'd seen Heru at the healers and hadn't turned right around and left.

Thana hurried through the streets, busier now than two weeks ago but still thinned out by the midday heat. She scanned for her quarry—one in healer blue, one in mourning white—among the city's lifeblood. She pushed through clumps of people and passed children playing with a ball in an alley.

There—just over the bridge and on the next platform. Heru's white wrap stood out among a group of merchants approaching the bridge. He was shoving his way through, Mo only a few paces behind. The merchants around them formed a living wall, so Mo and Heru couldn't see what was coming.

But Thana could. A man stumbled out from a side street, movements clumsy and awkward, tagel askew. There was no doubt that the man was another of those creatures—what had Salid called them?—a *bound*. She started to run, but the merchants reached the bridge before she could, filling it and blocking her path. Mo and Heru continued on just a gap away, heedless of the danger ahead.

The bound spilled onto the road and grabbed at Mo, catching her wrap. Startled, Mo jerked away. But the bound held fast and lunged for Mo's arm. Thana didn't think. She stepped to the side of the bridge so she had a clear shot, then drew a knife and—in the same movement—threw across the gap between platforms, hitting the bound in one shoulder, spinning it off balance. Mo yanked her wrap free, stumbling back.

Heru followed the knife's trajectory across the platform and the gap to Thana. He considered her, then turned and yanked her knife from the bound's shoulder. He sidestepped the creature's retaliating swipe and rolled up one sleeve. Even at this distance,

Thana could see the thin white scars crisscrossing his skin. He drew the blade across his inner arm and pressed a piece of fabric to the welling blood.

The merchants cleared the bridge. Thana ran onto it as the bound leaped at Heru. He stumbled back, but not far enough. The creature slammed into Heru's shoulder, then fell past when Heru turned with the blow. He slapped the blood-stained cloth against the bound's forehead, but the creature grabbed his other arm and they tumbled to the stones together.

"No!" Mo rushed forward while Thana slowed, hopeful, still several feet from the end of the bridge.

Unfortunately, Heru was already rolling out from beneath the creature. He stood up, brushing his hands off on his wrap and smearing blood and dirt across its pristine white. He nudged the prone body with his foot and, receiving no response, gave it a solid kick. The creature didn't move.

Mo pulled up short. "What—? What did you do?"

Heru ignored her and crouched next to the body. Thana reached the platform just as he yanked off the figure's tagel, revealing a scraggly beard and a slack jaw, skin ashen and sagging. Then Heru rolled the body over and pulled the wrap down to reveal a disconcertingly familiar set of seared symbols in its flesh.

Mo gasped. Thana winced. Heru used her knife to slash through the marks. The skin opened under the blade like the peel of an overripe orange. Thick, dark blood oozed from the fresh wound. A darkness gathered in the broken flesh, then burst forth in a hissing stream like a swarm of locusts.

Heru and Mo both stepped back, attention fixed on the swarm. Thana saw her opportunity in that brief moment, while Heru was distracted and her only witness was the healer. The platform was otherwise deserted. Thana was still over a dozen feet away and Mo hadn't noticed her yet. In the blowgun on Thana's belt was a poison that mimicked a heart attack. Mo would assume the bound was responsible for Heru's death. Could it be that easy?

Heru held the knife in front of him, as if to shield himself from the swarm. At the same time, he slid something small from his pocket. Thana held the blowgun to her lips. The swarm began to taper off. Thana filled her cheeks with air. Heru held out the object in his open palm; it was a small, glass bauble. It started to glow and the swarm bent back and down, aiming for Heru's hand.

Thana blew. The dart cut through the air like a diving hawk, aimed perfectly at Heru's neck. She couldn't miss.

Then Heru took one step forward, reaching higher with the glass bauble, and the dart sliced past his neck to *thunk* into the chest of the corpse. Heru glanced at the dart. Thana made the blowgun disappear just as he turned to lock gazes with her. Mo followed that gaze, started when she saw Thana, and waved. Thana swallowed her disappointment and forced a weary smile.

When Thana reached them, the swarm had disappeared and the glass bauble was glowing a sickly orange. Heru slid the bauble back into his pocket.

"I'd appreciate it if you didn't destroy the prized possessions of everyone I introduce you to," said Thana.

"Or what? You'll try to kill me?" asked Heru coolly. He turned his back on her to examine the body. "This one is older than the others, if only by a few days. See how the skin is flaky and dry?"

Thana crossed her arms as she ran her gaze over the body, searching for the dart so she could retrieve it before Mo noticed. But it was gone. *Shards.*

"What did you do?" asked Mo. She hovered by the head, fingers reaching for but not touching the scrap of bloody cloth still stuck to its forehead.

"I quieted its jaani," said Heru. "I used my blood to form a sympathetic connection and then I disrupted the binding network. I'd explain the mechanisms behind such an approach, but I suspect the intricacies would be lost upon such as you."

Mo bristled but let his insult go. "This is getting out of hand. We need to tell the marab what's going on. If quieting works, then they'll be able to help. I can't believe one of these things was out under the sun. Someone has to have noticed—right?"

She looked at Thana, but Heru answered. "No. If they haven't attacked anyone else, who would notice them?"

Thana nodded reluctantly. "You can only tell there's something wrong if you get close. Otherwise they just look drunk. People probably assume they're iluk."

"The eyes, though." Mo hugged herself. "But these bodies, they must have come from somewhere. They have families, people mourning them. We need to let them know what happened."

Heru pinched the corpse's skin. "Do you carry bases, healer? Some method of burning through flesh?"

Mo dropped her arms and frowned. "No."

Heru tilted his head. "Then what do you do when the flesh necrotizes?"

"Maggots, sa, like any civilized person."

"I wouldn't call that civilized."

"Life begets life," said Mo. "And we don't waste. Which brings me back—"

"Yes, well, you do many strange things on the edge of the Wastes." Heru straightened. "Before I decide on my next course of action, it would be prudent to ensure that those other dead *remain* dead. That little history lesson only confirmed my own conclusion that the marks themselves are dangerous. The slashes may have disrupted the binding and released the jaani, but I must remove the marks completely. They could still be used in a similar form of sympathetic binding, if our opponent happens to be as well-versed in these studies as I suspect."

Mo's frown deepened. "Let's figure that out when we get back. First, I'm going to call a watchman to carry this body back for us. What happened here needs to be reported to the drum chiefs. The station is just up ahead—I'll only be a moment."

Mo left without waiting for them. Thana started to follow, but Heru grabbed her by the wrap. She ripped the cloth from his grasp and they faced off for a second time that day. Except now, there were no healers nearby. No one to intercede.

Heru moved first, flicking out the dart from between his fingers. He held it up. "Do I have to worry about you trying that again?"

"Maybe you shouldn't have destroyed a valuable book."

Heru raised his eyebrows. "Was your friend so upset? I'll pay him more next time. Those pages are necessary to safeguard our great Empire. He should be grateful to contribute. Besides, a sand flea couldn't have possibly known what to do with such precious knowledge. It was wasted on him."

"And *you* do?"

"Of course." Heru straightened. "I'm a marabi trained under Na Tay Khet's foremost scholars. I am the most qualified to deal with this particular threat in your entire sand-swept, backcountry village."

"Then why are you even here?" prodded Thana, relaxing ever so slightly as Heru continued not to try and kill her. While she appreciated the restraint, it was puzzling.

Heru glanced at the body lying haphazardly next to them. A few people had walked past, glances furtive and quick, but no one had bothered them. Drunks were common after season's end, after all.

"I was sent to open civilized negotiations between your little

hovel and the Empire," said Heru. "The Empress is most dis-
pleased at the state of relations around the Wastes, specifically
how a bunch of sand fleas can continue pretending they don't
belong to her. I fear, however, that I'll be forced to cut my visit
short. Your little town doesn't have the resources I need to con-
duct an appropriately thorough investigation into a problem of
this magnitude. The Empress will forgive me for returning early
when there're such terrible things happening within her Empire."

But his tone lacked certainty. It was laughable that anyone,
the Empress especially, believed Heru would be an ideal ambassador. His brusque nature and curt pride made him quite the
opposite. Perhaps that was the point. The Empress must have realized what message dispatching someone as unlikable as Heru
would send to Ghadid. She must have considered that such a
message would be met in kind, either openly or—

"And you?" asked Heru. "Who hired you? What were you
doing in my room last night?"

Thana palmed a knife. "I don't know what you're talking
about."

Heru sighed. "Are we going to play this game? I'm not a fool,
child."

Thana eyed him warily, then asked what she'd been wondering all along. "Then why don't you kill me?"

"You're annoying, but your likelihood of success is very low.
I've calculated that your utility to me as a possible decoy for these
bound jaan is higher than any satisfaction your immediate death
might provide. You can't hurt me and it's in your best interest to
keep me around until this current crisis is resolved. Besides, I
don't have access to the appropriate tools and equipment to make
proper use of your cadaver."

Thana decided to ignore that last comment. "Why're you so
convinced I can't hurt you?"

"If your attempts so far are any indication of your skill, I have nothing to fear." Heru flicked out a knife from between his fingers like a conjuring trick, and pressed its tip to the palm of his hand. Blood welled and Heru caught Thana in his gaze. "But if you are so concerned for my well-being, perhaps it would be in my best interest to bind you."

But before Heru could go any further, Mo rounded the corner with a watchman in tow. The knife disappeared as they approached, but its threat lingered while the watchman examined the corpse, then asked them each pointed questions. Once Heru mentioned the Empress, the watchman was all deference and respect, and promised to help carry the corpse to the healers for further examination.

"There."

Heru held a pinched strip of skin between two fingers an arm's length from himself. He dropped it into a waste basket with the rest of the skin he'd peeled off, then washed his blood-streaked knife and hands in a bowl of water. Mo had led them to a side room this time, where she'd drawn the curtain for privacy so that the sight of Heru removing the skin from the corpse's back wouldn't bother the other patients.

"That's it?" asked Thana. "No more dead walking around?"

"I cannot speak to the possibility of our mysterious friend binding and sending more respiratorialy challenged jaan my way, but I can assure you that, barring any additional mutilations, these particular dead men will, in fact, remain dead." Heru wiped his hands dry on a towel.

"Now what?" Mo gingerly touched the corpse's shoulder, then pulled the shroud over its head. "The watchmen are trying to find out who these men were and notify their families, but we've got to do something to stop Djet from killing more people."

"It may be Djet's work, but we don't know if it's Djet himself," corrected Heru.

"But you said—"

"I said it's a possibility we must entertain that Djet could still be alive today. But it's an equally likely possibility—nay, more likely—that someone else is emulating his life's work."

"Either way," said Mo, "we have to find who's doing this and stop them."

Heru turned his hands over, inspecting them carefully. He rubbed at a dark spot that might have been blood. "That's what I intend to do. Therefore, I will be returning to the capital as soon as possible to continue my research."

He moved toward the door, but Mo blocked his way. "So you're just going to leave us with the problem? You're the only one who can stop these things. You can't just turn tail and flee."

"I'm not *fleeing*. I must seek out more knowledge to elucidate solutions to the problem. I cannot find that knowledge here, girl. Ergo, I must return to Na Tay Khet." He stepped around Mo. "I'd best leave now, if I'm to join the next caravan."

"But—"

"Let him go," said Thana. "I'll bet you three baats the problem goes with him."

"I don't bet when lives are at stake."

"Then don't." Thana shrugged. She didn't have the energy left to argue.

Mo opened and closed her mouth, then she huffed and stalked away to the other room. Heru had paused long enough in the doorway to watch their exchange. Now he slipped out into the afternoon without another word. Thana let him. She was too exhausted to keep chasing him and if she ran into another of those bound jaan, she wasn't sure she'd be able to defend herself.

Besides, now she knew where he'd be, even if she didn't yet know what she'd do with that knowledge. It was time to check on Amastan. He'd better be awake.

9

The healers' room smelled of sweat and sand. Dust danced in the late evening sunlight that poured through the open door. A few more cots were occupied now, the others still bare mattresses and folded linens. Someone hacked and coughed, a healer at their side. Gray streaked the healer's braids, her bright and colored salas twined among them.

Amastan's cot was in a corner, as far from prying eyes as Thana could bribe the healers to put him. He lay flat on his back, a thin blanket pulled up to his chin, his tagel knotted in place. Someone had been kind enough to give him an extra pillow. Although his dark brown skin was still ashen, he no longer looked as if he might blow away.

His eyes opened as she approached and Thana let out the breath she'd been holding too tight in her chest. He was fine. He was all right. She wouldn't have to stumble around on her own any longer. But even as relief blew through her, a heavy realization settled on her shoulders: Amastan was too broken to come with her.

He smiled weakly at her. "What took you so long?" His voice was a rough whisper.

Thana pressed his hand between hers and tried to dampen her broad smile. "Just trying to complete our contract."

Amastan squeezed one of her fingers. "You know you can't finish it without me."

"Shouldn't, maybe," said Thana. "Can't? We'll see. In case you didn't know, you got yourself thrashed last night."

"I only need a few days."

"We don't have a few days."

Amastan's expression tightened into determination. He shifted, trying to sit up. Thana moved to assist him, but he batted her away. She was forced to watch until he'd maneuvered himself upright. The effort left him panting and pale. He scowled down at his own hands.

"I have enough baats—" he began

"Don't. You know how much that angers the healers. And G-d," she added reflexively.

"I've done plenty to anger G-d for my lifetime. What's a little more?"

"Then maybe it's time we both tried to make amends. Do you remember what happened?"

"Last night?" Amastan touched the back of his head. "Hard to forget. Someone threw me into a wall. And there were men . . ." He trailed off with a frown. "They were dead."

"Well, it's worse than that."

"Worse than the dead walking?" Amastan raised an eyebrow. "I don't know. That would top my list."

"I thought you were more afraid of jaan."

Amastan shrugged. "Jaan didn't attack us last night."

"About that . . ."

She told him everything she'd learned since she'd left him with the healers. As she talked, Amastan's eyes reacted to each revelation, widening further and further. For a while after she'd finished, Amastan remained quiet, his gaze unfocused as he thought.

"You'll join the caravan."

It wasn't a question. Thana nodded, reassured that he'd come to the same conclusion. "I have to. I don't have the time or energy to try to strike before he leaves, and I already checked—the next caravan goes out tomorrow."

"Early?"

"Two hours before sunrise."

Amastan closed his eyes. "You can't go alone."

"There you go, using that word again."

"You know what I mean. At least talk to Menna. Her expertise as a marabi would be very advantageous on this contract."

Thana shook her head. "I don't think Kaseem would appreciate me taking Menna on. He was very explicit when he said she'd never work a contract again."

"Kaseem wouldn't need to know," said Amastan.

"Look at you, willing to break rules."

Amastan cracked an eye. "Once a cousin, always a cousin. Kaseem doesn't have a say over that. But you're right—Menna might be more of a hindrance than a help. What about asking Dihya or Ziri?"

"If I had months or even weeks to get used to them and learn their styles—but we don't have *time*. It's better to go alone than to try to work with a cousin I don't know. At least I know what I can do."

"Thana—"

"Amastan," she cut in. "I'll be fine, all right? I'm not like the other cousins. I'm the Serpent's daughter. Besides, the mark's going to be isolated in a caravan for weeks. It'll be easy. Especially if you help me. If you don't, I'm going anyway, and then if I fail we'll both be outed and executed for trying to kill an ambassador. Or worse."

She paused, letting him imagine the "worse." She realized

then that she'd never told him about the contract's peculiar stipulation that her body would be forfeit. Amastan would worry
enough for both of them without knowing *that*.

Amastan let out a long, low sigh. He looked frailer than before, as if their argument had worn him out. "You're just as stub-
born as her, you know."

Thana didn't need to ask who he meant. "Thank you."

"All right." He pushed himself up further with another grunt.
"Tell me what you had in mind."

For the next hour or so, Thana bounced ideas off her cousin.
The familiarity of the back-and-forth helped her relax and loosen
some of the worry tightening her throat. Sitting here with Amastan felt like another training exercise. They were just exploring a
hypothetical situation. Such as: how would she kill a paranoid,
yet gregarious drum chief? How would she enter a windowless
room without breaking the lock? How would she poison a blacksmith who only ate and drank from his personal sources?

How would she kill an en-marabi who could bind her jaani
to his will with only a touch? Who already knew who and what
she was?

Alone?

When Amastan was satisfied that he couldn't poke any holes
in their makeshift plan, he asked, "Do you have charms?"

Thana started to draw the bag of charms from beneath her
wrap before she remembered Heru had shattered them all—
again. She dropped her hands and shook her head.

"They don't do anything to stop the bound or the en-marabi
anyway," she said.

"No, but you'll be out on the sands. You need protection from
wild jaan. Don't underestimate jaan, they're dangerous in their
own way." Amastan grabbed her hand. "Promise me you'll get
more charms before you leave, Thana."

"I promise."

His grip loosened and he fell back into his cot. "I shouldn't let you go alone. I should make Dihya go with you."

"You just made sure I'm not going alone," said Thana. "You'll be with me."

Amastan smiled faintly at that, his eyes already fluttering with exhaustion. "Don't be so sentimental. It doesn't fit you."

Thana snorted. She kissed his forehead as his eyes finally closed and she lingered long enough for him to sink into sleep. On her way out, she passed a handful of baats to the healer and extracted a promise that they'd keep him asleep for the next twelve hours. She couldn't risk him changing his mind.

She felt as if she stood on the edge of a platform, balancing between her familiar city and the unknown sands. She still had time to tell Kaseem that she couldn't complete the contract. An assassin couldn't be expected to drop everything and chase their mark across the desert, nor fight a horde of jaan bound to walking corpses. Sure, she'd end her career and forfeit her body—whatever that meant—but she'd live. Probably.

Once she set foot on the sands, though, all bets were off. The thought of leaving Ghadid and everyone she knew behind scared her more than she'd expected. She'd been on the sands, of course, every child had, but she'd never gone so far that the pylons weren't always there, jutting out of the sand, round platforms dotting a blue sky. She'd heard stories of Na Tay Khet, had even been obsessed by the far-off exotic city in her youth, but she'd long since grown up.

No one would fault her for quitting, at least not to her face. Cousins had worked alone before, but never so early in their careers, never so young, never outside of Ghadid. No cousin had ever assassinated someone within the Empress's own circle. No cousin had ever been forced to deal with such monsters or to kill an en-marabi. Not even her mother had ever had a contract this impossible.

But she wasn't her mother. She was Thana Basbowen and she was more than just the Serpent's daughter. She'd have to be perfect to complete this contract, but then, she'd had to be more than perfect her whole life. And if she did this, if she finished an impossible contract, killed Heru, one of the Empress's personal marabi, stood up to the Empire, and stopped this monster creating monsters—

She'd become a legend.

10

With each step, Thana's sandals sunk deeper into the sand, making even a cursory round to check the straps on her camel a difficult chore. The wind dried her eyes and punched through her wrap, uncomfortably cool in the predawn. The tagel she wore offered some relief from the sand, even if it itched.

It'd been the easiest disguise she'd ever put together. With only a scrap of dark blue cloth across her face and a wrap long enough to cover her sandals, she looked like the others in the caravan. She'd even lined her eyes with kohl, but she knew that as long as she kept her head down and her mouth shut, Heru wouldn't know her from any other iluk, let alone an Azali.

The people who made their lives—and living—on the backs of and beside their camels called themselves the Azal. They were stateless, constantly on the move to find grazing for their many heads of camel. They knew the desert and the sands and the Wastes better than anyone, and it was this knowledge that made them indispensable to caravans. Although their existence was often harsh on the ever-shifting sands, they were left alone. Even during the worst of the old wars, the Azal had been allowed free rein.

Not out of any kindness or benevolence. No, the Azal controlled the salt. Only they could cross the Wastes to the salt seas that lay near its heart, and only they could bring that salt to the cities and people who needed it. Even warlords, it turned out, couldn't survive long without salt.

Thana touched her waist for reassurance. Underneath the thin fabric of her wrap, the hard edges of her new glass belt poked through. She'd returned to Salid before leaving Ghadid. His shop had been shuttered and dark, but he'd opened the door as soon as she'd knocked.

He'd taken his time admonishing her for her earlier foolishness and the trust she'd betrayed by bringing such a dangerous man into his shop. But his anger had been halfhearted, broken by an underlying excitement. The reason for which soon came to light when he'd laid out a belt of glass charms on his worktable.

Making charms powerful enough to thwart even an en-marabi would've taken weeks, if not months, Salid had explained. Even if haste were not of the essence, after yesterday he wouldn't have wasted so much of his time just for Thana. But this belt was an experiment, a type of charmwork he'd been fiddling with in his spare time. He hadn't tested it yet, and there was every chance it might fail against even the weakest jaani, but it was designed with the strength of guul in mind.

"I'd hoped to sell it to the caravans entering the Wastes, but perhaps it will aid you against these monsters," Salid had said. "Perhaps not. It's in G-d's hands now. Just bring me back my pages."

The glass was rectangular and rounded so that it curved with her body. A metal wire ran through the six pieces, cinching them together. Each piece was an airy blue, opaque with a shifting smokiness and a scrap of paper inside. They were, frankly, beautiful, and it was a shame she had to conceal the belt beneath her wrap. When she'd put it on, the glass charms had been pleasantly cool against her skin. Now they were warm, even through the cloth.

Her hand next strayed to her upper arm and the knife concealed there, but she forced her hand down in case someone was watching. Instead, she mentally touched on each of her knives strapped across her body, the blowgun in one hidden pouch at her waist. Her trusty garrote was in another, where it clinked against the glass belt, singing a song only she could hear.

She tightened the straps on her pack and her camel grumbled through its mouthful of hay. Beneath her personal supply of dates, nuts, goat jerky, dried lemon, and tea, she'd hidden her box of poisons, a few more knives, and most of her rings. The Azal showed off their wealth via the dyes in their fabric and the charm bags around their necks, so Thana's fingers were empty and unnaturally light.

Satisfied with her own preparations, Thana approached the nearest V of salt slabs. An Azali man joined her and together they slid the slabs onto the camel's back. The Azali shot her more than one suspicious glance, but didn't ask who she was. Thana had already paid dearly for that.

Helmek, the caravan's leader, had wanted to treat her as a guest, as honored as any other that joined them on their journey. But Thana had insisted that she be allowed to blend in and help. Heru might look twice at a merchant, but he'd overlook individual Azal. Unfortunately, even if she'd had months to prepare, it would've been next to impossible for her to convince the Azal that she was one of their own. The Azal might be spread out across vast and unfathomable sands, but their small number meant they knew each other as if they were family. They'd know Thana for a fraud.

So with only a handful of hours instead of months to learn even the basics, Thana had smoothed her way with an uncomfortable amount of baats. In return, Helmek and his fellow Azal would accept her as one of their own and cover for any obvious blunders she made. In the few hours before sunrise, Helmek had shown her what he could. But now she was on her own.

The wounds in Thana's arm and shoulders pulsed in pain as she finished loading a slab. An Azali came by with a brazier of tea and she gratefully seized the opportunity for a break. By then, dark blue crept across the black sky's far edge. The first travelers had arrived, but the mark was not among them.

As the horizon lightened, the camels seesawed to their feet and the caravan began to move. Thana returned to her own camel, but she was in no hurry. Burdened as it was, the caravan would move slowly. Stragglers would have more than enough time to catch up.

Her camel pulled back its lips, exposing two rows of yellow teeth, and let out a gurgling groan. Thana jerked away. The camel met her gaze with one of its large, round eyes and its groan continued, unbroken and awful. Thana glanced around, not sure what she should do. None of the other camels were making that noise. She tentatively patted its rough neck, whispering assurances to the beast. The camel only groaned louder.

Thana pushed down panic. What was wrong? She'd never had to interact with camels before, only mules and goats. Compared to camels, they were small, docile creatures.

"It's the strap on your bag, ma."

An Azali woman approached. She wore the same dark blue wrap as the others, but she hadn't yet secured her tagel against the wind. Kohl lined her dark eyes, stark against her light skin, and brown hair fell in thick twists to her shoulders. Most of the Azal looked alike to Thana, but she recognized Feti, Helmek's wife.

Feti tugged on the strap and the camel cut off its horrible noise. It puffed its cheeks and blew spit, but was otherwise content. Feti fell into step alongside Thana.

"Thank you, ma," said Thana.

"I've never known a girl afraid of her camel."

Thana bristled. "I'm not afraid—"

"They are harmless creatures," continued Feti. "Just large babies. But they deserve our respect. Don't worry, you and Melwa will be close friends soon." At Thana's blank look, Feti laughed and patted the camel's neck. "That's her name. All of our camels have names. After all, they say a camel is second only to man in G-d's eye. Even G-d cannot cross the sands without a camel."

With that, Feti smiled and took her leave. The sun rose and the caravan marched onward. Thana volunteered to bring the tea brazier to all the Azal and merchants alike. But the mark still wasn't among the dusty travelers. She passed a long line of pack camels, each tied to the other so that only one Azali was needed to lead them. She handed a steaming mug of tea to the leading woman, then turned to go back.

She froze. The caravan kept moving around her. For fear of losing her nerve, Thana hadn't dared look back yet. It would've been futile for the first hour or two anyway while they marched through darkness. Now that the sun had peeked over the horizon, Thana could see more of the sands than she'd ever wanted. The desert stretched endless ahead, only intermittently interrupted by stingy tufts of grass and scraggles of thorny trees.

The view behind, though, was quite different. There were trees and grass and sand, yes, but towering above it all and puncturing the sky was her city and home. Thana felt like a child on the sands for the first time, staring up at her world from a new perspective; loss and wonder tangled together inside her. From this distance, the pylons all but disappeared in their own reflections and the city flew untethered. Thana had heard iluk call Ghadid a hundred different names—the city in the sky, the impossible city, the city of clouds—but only now did she understand. Pride burned hot as an ember in her chest: that was *her* city.

A speck broke off below, growing larger by the moment.

Thana watched until the speck resolved into a person riding a camel. Then that camel split and became two, both laden with packs and people. They'd catch the plodding caravan soon and either join or surpass it. Thana could guess at one of the riders: it had to be the mark. But who was the other?

One of the Azal yelled a challenge as the riders neared. "Hel! Are you sane?"

The mark's clipped voice boomed the expected response. "Yes—I am sane."

But what was unexpected were the same words echoed by a higher, softer voice.

Mo. Dust, why?

Thana listened as they slowed. She chanced a glance just as Mo dismounted and began leading her camel. Heru, however, stayed mounted. He perched on a saddle, its white leather intricately traced with gold threads, splashing out a pattern of stars and constellations that shimmered in the sunlight. His camel was equally exotic, a longer and thinner beast than the pack camels. Its coat was salt white and blazed in the early morning sun.

Heru urged his mount toward the caravan's center, his gaze trailing across the salt-burdened camels with open disdain. Mo stayed back, taking up the rear of the caravan as she matched their plodding rhythm. While Thana was glad to see Mo alive and unharmed, she couldn't for the life of her figure out why she'd come. Heru should have left the healer alone once he was set on returning home.

Thana itched to reveal herself to Mo, ask her what, by G-d, she thought she was *doing*, and then urge her to return while she still could. As much as Thana wished she could pretend Mo was just another Azali, the truth was that she couldn't. Thana knew herself well enough to realize Mo's presence would be distracting.

A caravan was a dangerous enough place without the threat of bound jaan or an errant en-marabi.

But Thana could be patient, *had* to be patient. If she revealed herself to Mo, she risked Mo letting something slip to Heru. They were here together, after all, even if Thana couldn't figure out why. For now, she'd just wait and watch and see.

The hours plodded as slowly as the camels. With nothing but open desert and empty sky all around, Thana had little else to do but turn her gaze inward, worrying over the plan she and Amastan had prepared. The Azal were as quiet as their camels, with only the occasional hummed song or snort of breath breaking free.

By midday, all of the Azal had mounted their camels, but the pace remained languid. When the sun passed its zenith, the Azal stopped and dismounted as if by some silent command and began pitching makeshift tents. Thana gratefully slid off her camel, which had been surprisingly unpleasant to ride. Even with several layers of padding between her and the beast, her rear still throbbed painfully. Thana eyed Heru's saddle with envy, but the Azal eschewed the unnecessary weight and rode bareback— which meant so would she.

Thana unburdened her camel and then helped remove the salt slabs. The camels were let loose to graze on what sparse grass they could find. She knew she should steal what sleep she could while the caravan was stopped, but she was restless and agitated. She'd check on her camel and then she'd lie down.

The sun was impossibly hot. She'd thought she'd known the full blown heat of season, but on the sands the heat was more intense. It radiated off the sand in shimmering, dizzying waves, and the hot breeze did little to soothe her parched skin. No thick-walled buildings stood nearby to slip inside, there was no extra water to sip, and no cool pumphouse for the worst hours.

Her head was pounding when she reached her camel. Unlike the salt-bearing camels, hers hadn't wandered far from the stopped caravan. It—*she*, corrected Thana, remembering what Feti had said—was busy yanking up thin strands of grass, oblivious to the boiling heat. Thana patted Melwa's side.

"Hey. You."

A chill cut through the heat at the familiar voice. Thana confirmed her tagel was still in place before turning to meet Heru's glare. Panic briefly flared in her. Had the mark seen through her disguise? But as Heru stomped toward her, his eyes held no trace of recognition, only a mixture of annoyance and disdain. Her belly warmed as he approached—the glass charms were reacting to his presence.

"Just how long are you going to stay here?" demanded Heru. "I was told this caravan would be in Na Tay Khet within two weeks. I'm not going to make that if you lot spend the whole afternoon dallying. I saw people *sleeping*. I demand you wake them and pack your beasts. Or do you not know who I am? The Empress Zara ha Khatet is awaiting my report—you would do well not to anger her."

Thana blinked, thrown by his absurd requests.

Heru scowled. "Are you thick, sand flea? Can you even understand what I'm saying or should I try pantomiming? Offal and plague—one of you lot has to be able to comprehend basic questions. My last caravan wasn't this incompetent."

"We're a salt caravan, sa," said Thana. "The camels are carrying heavy loads and need a break. It's too hot for travel. Rest while you can. There'll be no time later."

"Tell your leader I don't have time for this."

The mark turned and stomped toward a large, white tent. Thana silently recited Amastan's plan until her anger had calmed and her hands had stopped shaking.

Patience, said Amastan's voice. She'd have her chance soon. Very soon.

11

On the third day, Thana had her chance.

The wind had been gathering strength. It tore at their tents during the midday rest and flung sand into their eyes as they plodded along. Thana was constantly shaking sand out from the folds of her wrap; she'd long since given up trying to get it out of her hair. At least the wind had blown away the flies.

The news that they'd be stopping early for the night rumbled the length of the caravan and was met with a mixture of relief and unease. A sandstorm was building to the north and Helmek hoped they could still avoid walking right into it. Camels were unburdened, but no one bothered with tents. Not with the wind so strong.

Night fell, and to the north lightning arced across the sky. The caravan was even quieter than usual and Thana thought she could hear the hiss of sand between crashes of thunder, accompanied by the occasional hummed snippet of prayer. She settled onto a blanket next to her camel, careful not to knock over the pole she'd stuck in the ground. If the storm veered south, the pole would help rescuers find her beneath all the sand. It wasn't a very reassuring thought, and now, despite her weariness, she wasn't sure if she could sleep. But it couldn't hurt to close her eyes.

The sound of feet slipping through sand snapped her awake.

It was still dark. The wind had calmed, but the air was fresher and sharp with the tang of spent lightning. Thin wisps of cloud smeared across the stars and lightning flickered far to the west. Thana remained still, trying to figure out what had woken her. Then—

A shadow appeared, eerily bright. White fabric: Heru. Thana stiffened, but he didn't even glance at her as he passed. She watched him until he reached the edge of the camp, then she stood on stiff legs and followed.

He stopped a distance away and hunched over something on the ground. Thana slowed, weighing each step to avoid the warning hiss of shifting sand. The glass at her waist warmed as she approached, an unnecessary reminder of the danger. But after three days of endless tedium—and by G-d, how many more ahead?—she itched with the need to act.

Heru brought his hands to his face and water splashed like an achingly familiar song. Anger cut through Thana's concentration; Heru was washing his arms, his hands, his face. He was wasting water. Had he done this every time he'd broken from the group? She'd noticed he took longer breaks than the others, but she'd assumed he wanted the time alone. This waste was unimaginable.

Heru tilted forward, but this time there was no accompanying splash of water. Instead, fabric rustled and the mark pulled a small ebony box from his bag. He messed with the box, but Thana couldn't see what it held from her angle. The wind carried hints of peppermint and soap to her, followed by the *scrape, scrape, scraaape* of blade across skin. By all that was good and holy—was he *shaving*?

It was all she could do not to kill him then and there. But it'd be difficult to explain the en-marabi's sudden absence, let alone a body with a slit throat. The caravan would panic if they thought they had a murderer in their midst. And panic was not conducive to a safe crossing. No, she needed to be subtle. While the mark's death was supposed to have been a spectacle in Ghadid, here on the sands she needed to use discretion.

Thana smiled. She knew exactly what to do.

Heru's camel was unattended, its legs tucked under as it chewed cud. Its head turned and one pale eye watched as Thana approached. The mark's waterskin bulged from under a stack of blankets. When she brushed by, her knife caught the skin and opened a wound as thin as a hair. But it was enough. Water bubbled and oozed from the hole like fresh blood.

Sabotaging the skin was only a start. The Azal would share if the mark asked. But even if he did ask, he'd drink less. It wouldn't kill him, but it'd weaken him.

The desert—and a little poison—would do the rest.

"Hello!"

The word cut like glass through the dawn. Azal paused in their preparations and turned as Helmek hoisted a stake into the air and pointed north. Thana followed his gesture, but it took another moment to make out the figure in the gloom. They were still far away, but they were on foot and alone, a strange and foreboding sight.

Helmek called again. "Hello!"

The figure continued toward their caravan, but did not call back. The figure's gait was off; they appeared to be limping. But it wasn't a limp from a wound, more as if they were unused to walking. Helmek continued calling to the figure, his clear voice belying neither impatience nor alarm.

As dawn spread, the figure resolved into a man. His shoulders were rolled forward in his dull orange wrap, a gray tagel tied loose around his mouth and nose. He carried nothing, not even a small waterskin. His feet were bare and red with dried blood. Thana wanted and yet desperately didn't want to see his eyes. The belt around her waist had grown uncomfortably warm.

Several Azal drew swords. Helmek remained mounted, but he'd dropped his hands and now held tight to his camel's lead. The man stopped a dozen feet away. Finally, the stranger responded in a rasping voice.

"Hello."

The caravan could have been carved from stone. Not a soul moved, not even the camels. Then something white pushed through the caravan toward the newcomer, as sudden and focused as a hawk after its prey.

"Are you sane?" asked Helmek.

The man teetered where he stood, as if he'd lost his balance. Then he tilted his head back and the rising sun glinted red off his eyes. "I am not. Praise be."

He moved suddenly, lunging forward like a striking snake. Helmek had enough time to draw his sword. But Heru stepped between the two and the stranger stumbled short. Heru held up a clenched fist, blood dripping from between his fingers. Thana's belt flared hot as fire and it was all she could do not to remove it.

The man howled. He grabbed at his tagel, tearing at it, then at his hair when the tagel fell away. Heru stepped closer and the man fell to his knees, quaking in the sand. Heru opened his fist, a blood-stained glass orb clutched between his fingers, which he thrust at the stranger. The man babbled incoherently, first holding up his hands as if begging, then lunging for Heru.

Heru stepped back, out of the stranger's reach. The glass burst into light. The man lurched forward and stepped into a patch of bloody sand. His whole body went as rigid as a board. Then he collapsed. A heartbeat later, a redness swarmed from his ears and face, curling up into the shape of an S before being sucked into Heru's glass orb.

Silence filled the space where the stranger's screams had been. Heru closed his fingers around the orb, now glowing a dull red, and slipped it into his pocket. He ignored the staring Azal and examined his bleeding hand with disdain.

"I require the skills of a healer."

The Azal all began talking at once, an incomprehensible cacophony of panic and excitement. Helmek slid from his camel and approached Heru. A flash of blue in the crowd resolved into Mo, her waterskin slung over one shoulder, a roll of bandages in one hand. She stopped next to the prone figure on the ground. Thana had only covered half the distance when Mo reached for the man's neck.

"No!" The word slipped out before she could stop herself. The sound was lost in the ongoing tumult, although Mo paused to glance around.

All Thana could do was quicken her step and pray to G-d that she'd get there before the man woke up and snapped Mo's neck. But by the time Thana reached Mo, she'd rolled the body over and was sprinkling water across the man's face.

"I asked for a healer." Heru gave Thana only the briefest of glances. "Or are you all suddenly deaf?"

"This man is still alive," said Mo.

Thana grabbed the roll of bandages from Mo's side and tossed it at Heru, not bothering to aim. They flew at his face and should have hit, but Heru snapped up a hand and caught them. Now he gave Thana a longer stare, but there was still no hint of recognition.

Her pulse in her throat, Thana slid to the ground beside Mo. She knew she was being stupid and reckless, but she couldn't bear the thought of standing aside and watching when the man woke up and mauled Mo. At least here she could interfere, maybe even direct the bound's attention to a certain someone—

But the man's eyes. They'd fluttered open briefly, pupils too wide for the bright sky, before squeezing shut again. They hadn't been the glazed, unseeing eyes of a dead man. He *was* alive.

"Of course he is," said Heru, sounding more irritated by the second. He ripped off a piece of bandage and blotted at his hand. "He was possessed by a jaani, not *dead*. Now, will you attend me, or do I need to learn how to heal myself? I'm certain I can learn such a simple art, but not before this becomes infected."

Mo ignored him and closed her eyes, her hands hovering over the man's chest. Her breathing slowed. The water on the man's skin suffused blue, the soft color bleeding onto everything around them. The Azal quieted as they watched Mo. For a few long moments, nothing happened.

Then the man hacked violently, startling half the Azal nearby. He sat up, rolled to one side, and vomited a noxious green slime. He wiped his mouth with the back of his hand and this time when he opened his eyes, they stayed open.

Mo rocked back on her heels, out of grabbing distance. "Are you sane?"

"Of course he is," muttered Heru darkly. "*I* took out the jaani."

Thana picked the man's tagel out of the sand, shook it off, and handed it to him. With shaking hands, he wrapped the tagel around his face, obscuring his sunburnt, blistered skin and chapped, bleeding lips. He nodded, then coughed to clear his throat.

"I am sane. Praise be to G-d."

Although the words were rough and low, the collected audience let out a shared sigh. Helmek approached and extended a hand, which the man took. A moment later, the stranger was on his feet, swaying but upright.

He looked around, then passed a hand in front of his eyes. "Where am I?"

Mo turned to Heru, who thrust his hand at her like a petulant child. While Mo bandaged his cut, Thana stepped closer to Helmek and the stranger, not wanting to miss a word.

"You're among friends now." Helmek put a hand around his shoulder, steering him away. "Come. Tell me your name."

Helmek glanced at Thana as she fell in behind, but he didn't shoo her away.

"Amash, sa."

"What was the last thing you remember, Amash?"

"A storm," said the man dully. "I was between camps when it hit. The elder cast the weather before I left. It was supposed to be clear." His voice tightened and he looked down at the ground in shame. "It wasn't."

"What happened to your charm?" asked Helmek.

"I lost it in the storm," said Amash.

Helmek grunted noncommittally, turning as Feti approached. She carried a tea brazier and deftly poured a cup of still-steaming tea, added sugar, and thrust it into Amash's hands without spilling a drop.

"You're welcome to join us," said Helmek. "We're headed to Na Tay Khet. From there, you should be able to find another group to journey home with."

Amash bowed, the tea in his cup swaying dangerously. "Thank you, sa. Bless you, sa. I should be dead, sa. I will never forget this miracle."

"My wife will see that you have a place in our caravan," said Helmek, catching Feti's eye.

Feti nodded and laid a hand on Amash's forearm, guiding him away. When Amash was out of earshot, Helmek spoke, voice low and directed more at the sand than Thana.

"I've never seen such a thing in this life. And I've seen many things on the sands and in the Wastes. A marabi can quiet a wild jaani within a man, even draw the thing out with enough time and water. But this man did it in an instant. With blood." He lifted his gaze and turned it on Thana. "What is he?"

Thana swallowed. "I'm not sure, sa."

Helmek studied her. "I'm responsible for the safety of this caravan and my people. I must be aware of anything that could threaten their safety. For now, he has proven himself an asset. But I wasn't entrusted with leadership because of my ability to observe facts. He's no marabi and it's no coincidence that you and he are in the same caravan, is it?" He paused long enough for Thana to deny any connection. When she didn't, he continued, "If you know something about him, something that could hurt my people, and you don't tell me, there will be a reckoning. By my hand or G-d's." He held her gaze. "So—is there anything else I should know about this man?"

Thana thought about the dead men who'd attacked them in Ghadid, the fear she'd felt when Amash had stumbled out of the desert, the woman Heru had bound to his will. Helmek deserved to know. But . . . would knowing help him at all? What were the chances that any of that would happen out here? There was nothing and nobody for miles around. They were safe.

No—telling Helmek would only endanger Thana's contract. Helmek might let something slip, and Heru would be left wondering how the caravan leader knew more than he should. The less he knew, the safer he'd be.

"No, sa," lied Thana. "Nothing."

Heru held up the deflated waterskin. "Who did this? Where is the thief who stole my water?"

It was two days after Amash had joined them. The caravan had halted for the afternoon. Thana was busy braiding loose ropes beneath a tent with several Azal when the mark stomped up to them.

"Are you well?" asked one of the men.

Heru brandished the skin. "I am most certainly *not*."

The Azal exchanged glances. One stood and opened his hands to Heru, who dropped the skin into them with no small amount of disgust. The Azali turned the skin over and found the gash Thana's knife had made. He poked his finger through and showed it to Heru.

"Your thief was the ground and the air, sa," said the Azali. "The winds from the storm must have thrown a rock. The leak was so small that you didn't notice right away." Unspoken was the accusation that Heru should've noticed sooner, before all his water was gone.

"Fix it, then. And get me more water."

The Azali's fingers played across the gash, but his gaze didn't meet Heru's. "Sa—the nearest well is yet five days out, we've added a mouth, and we're all running low."

Heru didn't move.

"We'll share our water with you, sa," said the Azali reluctantly. "But I want to make clear that there's little available. Your share might not appear to be much, but if you're careful and prudent, it'll see you through until we reach the well."

Heru grunted, but didn't move from the spot. The Azal shifted nervously. They'd been careful to steer clear of him since the incident with Amash, keeping their gratitude at a safe distance. Unfortunately, now that mixture of terror and respect might net him more water than Thana could risk.

She stood and held out her hand for the skin before the Azal could acquiesce further. It was time for the second phase of her plan and she might as well take advantage of their fear. The Azali thrust the skin at her, all too relieved to be rid of the burden.

Thana left the tent with the skin over one shoulder before Heru could make any further demands. Once she had a few tents between her and the mark, she took a sharp turn and headed for her own camel. She had to work quickly, lest Heru lose what little patience he had and tried to find her. She spotted Feti and stopped her.

"Can you fix this?" Thana tilted the skin so that the gash opened like a fresh wound. "It's for the marabi."

Feti took the skin, her gaze briefly searching Thana's. Whatever she was looking for she must have found, for she nodded and walked off. Thana let out a breath and hurried for Melwa. She gave the camel a reassuring pat, then squatted next to her pack and began removing her things one by one. At the bottom of the pack was her quarry: the leather case that contained her poisons.

She held her breath and removed its lid, half expecting the case to be full of broken glass and dried liquids. But despite her camel's jostling gait, all the vials remained intact. She slid one free with a label that read simply MEAT, then closed the case and repacked her bag.

A few drops on her blade and a shallow score across Heru's supply of jerky was all it should take. She sprinkled water on the area to keep the contagion alive, then wiped her blade clean on the sand. Her plan wasn't foolproof, not by a long shot. This poison killed in the same way that spoiled food did, slowly and variably. But out of her collection of poisons, its effects looked the most natural. Thana didn't expect the poison alone to kill Heru, but if she could weaken him, the desert would do the rest.

By the time Thana found Feti, she'd repaired the waterskin and a fellow Azali was helping her refill it. No—not a fellow Azali.

Mo.

Thana stumbled over her own feet. Caught herself. Took a breath. Kept walking. Mo glanced up at her approach, but quickly returned her attention to the skin to avoid wasting any water. Mo tied off the neck and Thana tried to take the skin from her, but Mo held on for a heartbeat. Her gaze met Thana's and her eyes briefly narrowed with suspicion—or was it just the glare?

Then Mo's expression cleared and she released the skin. Thana bowed in silent thanks, suddenly too anxious to risk speaking in front of Mo. She hurried away, finding Heru already mounted on his pale camel while the Azal around folded and packed up their tents. He snatched the full skin from her without a word.

When Thana returned to Melwa, someone was holding her lead. It was probably Feti; several times now she'd dropped by to warn Thana that she'd done something particularly un-Azal. But the tagel was a light blue—healer's blue.

For once, Thana was thankful for the tagel smothering her face. It hid the panic that startled her heart and filled her stomach with fire. Thana pushed the panic down. Mo was probably only here to see how she was doing or request a favor or—

"Who are you?" asked Mo.

That stopped Thana short. "Lemta," she offered. A common enough name.

Mo's eyebrows drew together. "Let me see your face."

Thana stepped back. "The sun is harsh and the wind—"

Mo yanked her own tagel down, revealing a scowl. "You're no man, ma. It won't offend G-d to bare your face. And you're not one of the Azal. I've seen the way the others act around you and how they fix your mistakes. I assumed you were sun-struck, but when I asked about you, no one could give me the same answer. You're not theirs and you're not ours and you're certainly no merchant." Mo poked a finger at Thana. "I wouldn't normally care about your business, ma, but there're other strange things about and I've got enough mysteries. So, I'll ask again: who are you?"

Thana chewed her words, unable to meet Mo's gaze. The choice was simple enough. Tell Mo the truth now, or lie and risk Mo finding out later. What would Amastan do? He'd hold to the story, come storm or drought. If Mo knew who Thana was, she could slip and tell Heru. Mo's goodwill wouldn't help Thana complete the contract. Telling her would only complicate things.

But . . . if Thana told Mo now, when it was still her choice, then maybe Mo would stay quiet. Mo could be an ally, even an asset. Her mother had always told Thana to keep the healers happy. They were so often the slim line between life and death. If Thana made an enemy of Mo, the healer would do everything she could to keep Heru alive. But if Mo were her friend, Thana might be able to stop her from helping him.

Besides, it'd be nice to talk to someone else aside from Melwa on this tedious journey. Sending up a quick prayer that she wouldn't regret this decision, Thana undid the knot of her tagel and let it fall, exposing her features.

Mo's eyes widened with recognition. "It's Thana, right? What are you doing here? I thought you didn't want to help stop Djet."

"I never said that."

"You said as much." Mo crossed her arms. "Why are you hiding? Is this a game for you?"

Thana breathed deep to quell her rising annoyance. "It's no game. I'm as concerned about Djet and his monsters as you."

"Then why hide?" pressed Mo. "Why not join us openly? Isn't Heru your *friend*?"

"He's, uh, more of an acquaintance. We bonded over a card

game." The lie tasted hollow. Mo deserved better than that. Thana glanced around, then stepped in close and lowered her voice. "Look, to be entirely honest, one of the drum chiefs paid me to keep an eye on him. Why send the Empress's marabi as an ambassador? Something else is going on. I was hired to find out what."

Mo tilted her head, some of her animosity fading.

"Unfortunately," continued Thana, "that contract was open-ended. Because of those monsters, I still don't know what he's really doing. And I can't return until I have that information." She spread her hands. "I thought if I could infiltrate the caravan and pose as an Azali, I might find out. I wasn't trying to deceive anyone but Heru."

"You've still got that." Mo glanced in Heru's direction, even though he was out of sight. "For one of the Empress's marab, he's quite . . . unobservant."

"What about you?" asked Thana. "Why did you come with him?"

"He asked."

Thana's mouth fell open, but she immediately snapped it shut. "He *what*?"

Mo folded her arms. "He said he wanted an objective witness to present to his Empress."

"Why not write down what you saw? Asking you to cross the desert seems excessive."

Mo straightened. "Heru might find a way to stop Djet on his own, but I can't trust my city's safety to a foreigner. I'm doing my duty as a healer." Then her expression softened. "Besides, I'll never have a chance like this to leave Ghadid again. Healers are too precious to risk letting them walk on the open sands." Her last words held a bitterness that took Thana by surprise.

"Surely if you'd wanted to leave, no one would've stopped you."

Mo snorted. "Not by force, no. But healing is G-d's greatest gift, and you can't just throw that away. Not when you could save so many people. But now I'm going to save even more people than if I'd stayed put. Enass can't fault me for that."

"No," said Thana slowly. "She can't. Well, you've picked a great place to break your tradition for. I've heard Na Tay Khet has open water."

"And it sits on the sands with a wall all around," added Mo, some of the bitterness easing. "And there's a palace made of gold and markets that span whole neighborhoods."

"Plants everywhere, not just in glasshouses," said Thana. "The sun is so gentle that no one wears clothes. All the women are topless."

Mo's eyes widened. She let out a noise that was half snort, half giggle. "How do you know so much about it?"

"Whenever I was angry with my mother as a kid, I imagined sneaking away at night and joining the Azal," admitted Thana. "Of course that meant I needed to learn everything about the city, since all the caravans end up there."

"Enass healed a drum chief once and used his favor to borrow a scroll about the city for me." Mo's smile tightened. "She thought that would be enough to satisfy my curiosity."

"That only made it worse, didn't it?"

Mo looked away. "She was trying to help. It's not her fault there are so few healers." When she turned back, her smile was loose and bright again. "You're going to tell me everything you know about Na Tay Khet."

Thana couldn't help but smile back. "You're going to see it yourself in another week."

"But that's a *week*. I can't wait that long."

Thana cleared her throat, then caught Mo's gaze. "I'll tell you all the stories I know, whenever I can, but Heru can't see us talking together. He can't know I'm here. Can I trust you not to tell him about me? We'll never know his true reason for visiting Ghadid if he learns I'm spying on him."

"I can respect that," said Mo slowly. A soft smile turned up her lips. "All right, if you can't tell me stories, at least promise to explore Na Tay Khet with me. Don't get your hopes up about Heru, though—all I've seen him do is write in his scrolls. He's a strange man."

Thana's smile widened. "You don't even know the half of it."

12

By sunrise, Heru looked drawn and pale. After they'd broken camp, he'd slowly drifted from the front of the caravan toward the back. Now only a few exhausted merchants were between him and the tail end of the caravan. Thana had matched his pace to keep an eye on him. He'd paused to squat and relieve himself more than a dozen times already: the poison was working.

Now he was trying to mount his camel by swinging up into his saddle while the beast was still walking, like an Azali. He'd managed this before—by the third day, even the least proficient merchant had learned the maneuver. But this time he was having considerable trouble. Finally he gave up, stopped his camel, and couched it. He climbed into the saddle, but by the time his camel rocked upright, his skin shone with sweat. Heru leaned to one side and retched, then used the edge of his wrap to wipe off his mouth under his tagel.

Unfortunately, by the time the caravan stopped for the afternoon, Mo had noticed his illness. Thana was bent over her things, pretending to search for something but listening intently, when Mo approached the mark. Heru crouched shivering beside his camel, sipping from his waterskin. He'd had just enough energy to set up his tent, but it was skewed at an angle and one side looked like the wind was going to rip it free at any moment.

Heru didn't look up. "Took you long enough."

Mo eyed the skin. "You should be careful with how much you drink. The storm set us back almost a full day. With your loss and Amash joining us, we're already too low."

"Heal me," demanded Heru.

"I have some poultices—" began Mo.

"No." Despite his weakness, Heru's voice was sharp. "You will heal me. Then you'll give me your water and I'll leave this wretched pack. I can make the well in easily half the time it'll take these dust-cursed camels and their flea-ridden masters. I'm sick of this protracted pace, and I'll likely die of it. Unless you heal me."

"You can't go alone," said Mo. "There're bandits and jackals, not to mention wild jaan. Besides, you don't know the way. You'd get lost and wander in circles."

"You underestimate me," said Heru.

Then he turned and heaved a yellow froth onto the sand. Thana's own stomach roiled at the splash and she quickly cleared her mind to keep from following his lead. Heru grunted and clutched at his knees as the flies thickened and converged on his vomit.

Mo sighed. "Close your eyes and tilt your head back."

Thana adjusted her tagel and headed for the nearest tent. She couldn't stand to watch Mo undo all of her work. And now she had to plan for the possibility that Heru would up and leave them. But before she was even halfway to the tent, a shout rang out.

"Hold together! Weapons out! Bandits approaching from the north!"

Helmek thundered past, already mounted on his camel. He was circling the caravan, drawing them tighter together as he repeated his warning. Thana ran for Melwa, swinging up for a better view. Around her, the caravan boiled with activity, tents coming down and pack camels brought to its center. To the north, Thana could just see a cluster of dark shapes. A dozen or so, all on foot, and—if the glint of metal was any indication—their weapons drawn.

A dozen bandits against a whole caravan of armed Azal? It was no contest. Yet unease pulsed through Thana. Nearby, Heru stood and turned north. Mo stumbled back, a faint blue glow fading rapidly from her skin. At least Mo hadn't gotten far with her healing.

"Warriors! Form up!" yelled Helmek. He'd stopped at the edge of the caravan. Now he drew his sword and raised it high.

Blades were drawn all around Thana in a collective *shhnk* of metal on metal. Azal surged forward, forming a wall of weapons and beasts between the bandits and the rest of the caravan. Thana let herself be drawn with them, her body singing with eagerness for a fight. She knew she should hang back, stay safe, watch for an opening to further sabotage or hurt Heru, but it'd been weeks since she'd last sparred with one of her cousins, and sticking with her disguise in the caravan had meant no chance for training. Taking out a few bandits would be a welcome exercise.

The wall of Azal hardened as the bandits approached. Thana narrowed her eyes against the glare. Something was off. The bandits' movements were jerky, unnatural. They held their swords at their sides or loose in front of them, as an afterthought. Their gray and brown wraps hadn't been reknotted for a fight, but flapped freely in the wind.

Out of the corner of her eye, Thana caught a figure approaching the Azal's protective wall. Heru. He still looked drawn and pale, but he moved more easily than before. He was on foot, and he stopped just behind the camels. Good. Maybe he'd get trampled in the fight.

The air was hot as flames and stank of camel and sweat and fear. Around her, camels grunted, leather creaked, and Azal cleared their throats. But the bandits approached in absolute silence, the sand sucking up even the sound of their footfalls.

"Hello!" shouted Helmek, his voice cracking across the sands. "Who are you? What do you want?"

The bandits gave no answer.

"Are you sane?" shouted Helmek.

The bandits gave no answer. Still they ran, all but stumbling over their own feet. Silent. Shouldn't they be shouting by now, trying to terrify their prey? The Azal were shifting nervously around Thana. Maybe this was some bizarre new tactic. But Thana's unease only grew.

"There must be a whole camp nearby," muttered one woman next to her. "Look—they carry no water, no supplies. Where are their camels?"

"This is your final warning," called Helmek. "Turn back!"

But the bandits gave no answer. They were close enough now that Thana could see their eyes, open wide despite the sun's glare. All at once, Thana's unease exploded into panic. The bandits' eyes were milky white.

They were dead.

"Charge!"

The camels lunged forward, heads outstretched and riders yelling. Melwa surged with them, although Thana hadn't prodded her. Her ears rang and her mouth was dry, horror cottoning her thoughts. She had to stop them, they couldn't win against the bound, not like this. Why hadn't she noticed sooner?

The two lines crashed into each other. The Azal drove through the bandits with ease, swinging their swords as they thundered past. Their blades struck true, scoring deep wounds and severing limbs. The bandits didn't bother to defend themselves and struck back. A camel bellowed as a blade bit into its side. Another bucked as a bandit scrabbled onto its back.

Thana let Melwa carry her through the chaos, some of her initial shock finally giving way to resolve. She turned her camel and faced the fight. Where had Heru found all these men and why would he attack the caravan? Were they like the men in the inn, bound that had somehow broken from his control? Or maybe this was Heru's way of securing enough water for himself.

The Azal had struck fast and strong, but they were no match for men who felt neither pain nor fear. Two bound had climbed onto camels and now bit and scratched and tore at flesh, catching the Azal off guard. One Azali fell from camel to sand, then another. The bound on the camels turned their savagery on the beasts themselves while those on the ground swarmed the fallen. The fight that should've been over in a heartbeat had turned into a slaughter.

Helmek was among the fallen. He staggered to his feet and swung his sword, trying to hold back the bound. But they weren't so easily dissuaded. Four attacked at once, swarming him like water-hungry wasps. He disappeared beneath them.

Thana shouted and dug her knees into Melwa's neck, steering toward Helmek. She freed two small blades and leaned forward, Melwa's lead pinched precariously between her fingers. She hadn't been able to protect Amastan, but G-d willing, she would protect Helmek.

She swung at the bound on Helmek, then jerked Melwa back around to go at them again. They ignored her and continued tearing at the caravan leader, who had somehow regained his footing and was just barely keeping them back with wild swings from his sword. But his technique, while suitable for the living, didn't work at all against the bound. His sword split open the stomach of one, a slither of intestines falling to the sand. But

Helmek turned too soon to the next, only to be grabbed from behind by the bound he'd just gutted.

Feti strode through the fray like a vengeful angel. She severed one arm and hacked at a leg, then yanked Helmek free from the tumult. She shoved him out of the way and swung at the bound, her more precise attacks knocking them back. Helmek fell, his chest heaving and his wrap spattered with gore. He struggled to his feet, but his leg gave out and he fell again.

Thana jumped from Melwa, trusting her skills better on the sand, and rushed toward Feti. "You can't kill them! Just run!"

Feti ignored her to strike at an incoming bound. As the blade crashed down on the bound's head, a second one grabbed her arm and pulled her over. The first bound ignored the blow to its head and slammed into her. Feti stumbled, lost her footing, fell. The bound tumbled to the sands with her, its hands finding her throat. Feti struggled to stand as the bound strangled her. Thana tried to run faster, but the sand was unforgiving. She was still over a dozen feet away when a second bound rammed its sword clean through the first—and into Feti.

No. Thana slid to a stop as blood spread across the back of Feti's wrap and the older woman stopped struggling. Feti fell. The bound around her lost interest. Their heads turned and sightless eyes fixed on Thana.

Thana slipped backward, turned, ran. Melwa. She needed to find her camel. She wouldn't be able to fight them but she could still outrun them.

Melwa wasn't far, only a few dozen feet away. But bound swarmed over the dead Azal toward the camel. She reared and kicked, her nostrils and eyes wide with panic. She snapped at one bound and tried to run, but another had grabbed her lead and weighed her down, turning her lunge into a stumble.

Thana stopped thinking. She ran. She threw a small knife into the fray of dead attacking her camel, but she might as well have spat at them for all the good it did. One had managed to climb onto the bucking beast's back. With empty hands, the bound grabbed Melwa's neck and wrenched it, hard. Too hard. A crack rent the air.

Thana halted. She could only stand and watch as Melwa collapsed like an old building. She'd spent so much time near that camel, both on her back and walking by her side, attending to her needs and whispering worries into her ear and now—

A keen numbness spread through Thana, heightening her senses as it dulled her emotions. She slashed at the nearest bound, cutting away some of its wrap to reveal desiccated flesh underneath, bloodless and drawn tight across protruding bone. The sight brought her back to the tables at the healers, the corpses on them scored by deep marks. Thana knew exactly what she had to do.

The bound lunged at her. She reflexively brought up her blade and her knife slid into the bound's chest. But it wasn't dissuaded. It hissed, breath like old, rotten meat, and tore at her arm. Thana growled and kicked off from the bound, letting go of her knife. No matter. As the bound spun away, she loosed another dagger and readied herself.

When the bound lunged again—they were so predictable— Thana sidestepped, brought her foot up, and landed a blow in the square of its back. The bound sprawled on the sand and Thana ripped its wrap down, exposing the marks beneath. She ran her knife clean through them, then jerked away before the creature could attack again.

The bound fell limp, as if all the air had been sucked from it. Something thin and dark as smoke rose from the body, but the wind snatched it away. Thana tentatively stepped closer and prodded the body with her foot, but it remained as still as a corpse. She let out the breath she'd been holding, then pulled her blade from the man's chest and wiped it clean on the sand. Finally, she surveyed the carnage, her gaze skipping across the few remaining Azal as she sought out one specific person.

There. A flash of blue amid the turmoil of brown and red. Thana's heart almost stopped. Mo's camel had been torn out from under her, quite literally. Pieces of the beast were strewn across the blood-stained sand. Mo was keeping the bound at bay with only a length of wood—a repurposed tent stake—turning and swiping and turning and swiping. One bound dodged her swipes and, as she turned, grabbed for her.

Thana threw her dagger. It sliced through the bound's arm. Not her target, but it was difficult to aim such a large knife. Still, it worked: the bound was thrown off by the force of the blow and Mo got out of the way. She smacked her makeshift staff across its head as it stumbled past, and then again when it fell face-first into the sand.

Thana ran toward her as Mo yanked the dagger from the bound's arm and glanced around. Her gaze met Thana's for only a moment, then she was sweeping her staff around at knee level, knocking the remaining bound off balance. In that brief moment, though, Thana had seen Mo's terror, yes, but also her determination. She wouldn't go down without a fight.

But a fight might not be enough. Mo was no warrior and even accounting for the bounds' inferior coordination, there were four of them to her one. Thana tried to run faster, but the sand sucked at her momentum. Pinning the bound she'd felled beneath her staff, Mo stooped and tore at its wrap. Then she cut a line down its back with Thana's dagger. The bound stopped moving.

Another was right behind Mo as she straightened. Thana shouted a warning, but too late. Even as Mo started to turn, the bound grabbed a fistful of braids and yanked. Mo yelled and twisted, sweeping the dagger through the air. But her angle was off, the bound too close. It bared its teeth, then bit into Mo's shoulder. Mo screamed.

Thana held another knife, but she couldn't risk throwing it. Mo and the bound were too entwined. If her throw went wide, she risked hitting Mo. Her smaller throwing knives were still sheathed across her chest, under her wrap. But she didn't have time to slow and free them. That left a larger knife at each ankle and the garrote in her pocket.

Thana slung the garrote free as she crossed those last few feet between her and Mo. The bound ignored her, still jawing at Mo's shoulder. Rivulets of blood stained her sky-blue wrap black. Thana slipped the garrote around the bound's neck. Then she leaned back and pulled with all of her strength.

The head popped off like a cork. Thana fell back, surprised. She landed on the sand, the garrote and a desiccated head in her lap. She fumbled the head, then threw it. Mo, meanwhile, had unlatched the clawing arm. Both of her hands were busy with her shoulder, assessing the wound and doing what she could to staunch the flow of blood. All this, while she stumbled away from the corpse, which was still moving in fits and jerks, despite missing its head.

There were still two more bound nearby and both were scrambling for Mo. Thana ripped through the headless bound's wrap and broke the binding with a slice. The body crumpled beneath her, dead for good.

Three down. Thana didn't bother looking around. She listened to the screams from the Azal, the panicked bellows from the remaining camels, the *thwump* and *clack* of staff and sword against dry flesh. Too many to go.

All at once, the bound crashed to the ground, bones rattling like dice in a glass bottle. A stillness settled over the area, screams quieting to muffled groans. Thana stared, her numbness cracking a little, then glanced around. Heru stood more than a dozen yards away, eyes wide, skin ashen and glistening with sweat. His wrap was torn on one side and shredded at the bottom, his tagel pulled down around his neck. Bright red blood smeared his upraised arms, rolled to his elbows, and dripped to the sand. His hair, however, was immaculate.

Then he collapsed.

13

Mo moved first.

She stumbled through the sand, braids falling into her face, one hand clutching at her shoulder, the other her improvised staff. It took Thana another heartbeat to realize Mo was going to *help* Heru. Then the paralysis that had seized her vanished and she ran after Mo.

The Azal had been decimated. Some had been literally torn apart, while others lay stone-still in the sand, necks at an unnatural angle. Thana passed Helmek's corpse, his throat torn out. Bile threatened to choke her. The bound all around were already beginning to twitch. She quickened her step.

In the silence, Thana counted the bodies of the Azal. She came to a number far fewer than had been in the caravan. To the north, though, was a smear of dust and the receding bodies of camels and riders. Even as she stared after them, a handful more joined the fleeing group. First relief, then anger filled her. Those cowards had left her and Mo behind without bothering to help. But even as she thought it, her anger guttered. What could they have done? The bandits they'd fought had refused to die. They'd made the smart choice. She shouldn't blame them.

She did anyway. For now it was easier to stoke that anger into a fire that filled her and kept her going than risk lingering on all the death around her.

Slabs of salt and bags of goods were strewn everywhere, among them broken ropes and saddles and dead camels. The only thing she *didn't* see were intact waterskins. Precious water had been spilled across the sand, the slicks of moisture already vanishing like breath on glass. The Azal who'd fled must've taken the rest with them.

Mo slid to the ground next to Heru. Her hands moved from his neck to his forehead to his wrist. Then she twisted around, looking for something. Her gaze fell on Thana.

"Water!" ordered Mo. "I need water!"

She didn't wait for a response. She ripped off a length of fabric from her wrap and bound the cuts on his arms first. Then she put her shoulder into his side and rolled him onto his back. She brushed away the sand caking his clean-shaven face and put her ear near his mouth.

Thana cast around, not sure if she wanted to find an intact skin if it meant saving Heru. But she found one anyway, stumbling across it partially hidden by the corpse of a camel—hers. She whispered a prayer for Melwa, then stole a moment to rummage in her pack until she found the small bag containing her poisons and rings. She tied this to her belt, then slogged back and dropped the sloshing skin next to Mo.

"We can't stay," said Thana. "Those things are going to wake soon, but we might still survive if we leave him. We need to catch up to the rest of the caravan—they took all the water."

Mo snagged the skin without looking at Thana and undid the knot. She dribbled water into her palm, sniffed it, then carefully funneled the water between Heru's parted lips.

Nearby, a bound spasmed and rolled its head to the side. Thana stepped closer to Mo. Their odds of survival were quickly narrowing. "You're only going to wake him up long enough to die. We can't take him with us and those things will kill him. It would be a mercy to let him sleep through it."

Still ignoring her, Mo ran her palms across Heru's exposed skin and began praying softly. Frustrated, Thana stalked off, only to turn right back around when she reached the hulk of Heru's dead camel. The fleeing Azal had taken all the surviving camels, leaving them just death and dust. She found no more waterskins nor survivors, only bodies. Several bound were clambering to their feet, but they were still uncoordinated and unsure.

Thana tried again. "He's too far gone. We need to—"

"I won't leave anyone behind," snapped Mo. "It's not up to me who lives and who dies. I'm a healer. I swore an oath. I do what I can."

"Yes, I'm aware, but we're all going to be dead soon if we don't *go*."

"Then go, Thana!" Mo sprinkled water across Heru's face. "No one's keeping you here."

You are! Thana wanted to shout. She wanted to grab Mo and drag her away. She'd already failed Amastan and Helmek. She wasn't going to let this stupid healer get herself killed, too. She took a breath and drew a dagger. Fine. If Mo wasn't going to leave, then Thana would just have to protect her. They were going to see Na Tay Khet together, or not at all.

More bound were standing now, some shaking their heads, others taking tentative steps. Stupid again—instead of arguing with Mo, she should've been dispatching the bound. She could've made a dent in them by now. Thana tightened her grip and shifted into a fighting stance. There were nine bound left and only one of her. But she was a cousin and more than enough.

A bound with smashed legs scuttled her way. Thana charged it, slamming the butt of her knife against its skull, then sliced the blade down its back in one savage blow, putting all of her anger and frustration into the action. The bound collapsed again, this time for good.

Eight left. No—Thana blinked, then scrubbed at her eyes. Somehow, there were more now than had originally attacked the caravan. Eighteen, twenty. And still more were clambering up-right. Only a dozen had attacked initially, but more must have joined during the chaos of the fight. Whoever had created these bound didn't want anyone escaping alive.

All at once, they charged.

Thana did the only sensible thing left. She turned and ran.

"Mo! We've got to go! We've got to go *now*!"

Mo glanced up and her eyes widened. Her lips and hands continued moving, though, despite the charging bound. Thana made to grab for her shoulder, but then Heru's body spasmed, his eyes fluttered, and his mouth opened and closed. He sat upright, turned to the side, and threw up a thin, yellow broth. He wiped his mouth with a shaking hand, then wiped that hand on his robe. When he tried to scour the robe with sand, Mo shoved the waterskin at him.

"Drink."

"He's awake! Great! Let's go!" snapped Thana.

Heru paused while chugging water to stare blankly at her. Then dangerous recognition flickered across his eyes. Too late, Thana realized her tagel had come loose, exposing half her face. Heru handed the skin back to Mo and stood. Thana turned with him to face the approaching bound. There was no more time and nowhere left to run. Instead she readied herself for another fight, one they couldn't win.

Heru held up a hand and the sand shuddered beneath their feet, concentric rings like ripples in a water bowl moving out-ward. The bound surging toward them slammed into an invisible wall, some recoiling and falling back, others stumbling and clawing at the air as if they might climb it. Heru's outstretched arm trembled.

"I can't hold them for long," he said. "We need to leave. Where's Anas—my camel?"

Heru walked forward and the bound fell back. Thana and Mo followed a few feet behind. Heru abruptly stopped. He'd spotted his camel's remains only a little further on and a light frown creased his brows. He started again, faster now, and the bound toppled and fell before him as he rushed to his camel's side. He sank next to the corpse almost tenderly and brushed sand from its forehead. The bound scratched and clawed against the invisible barrier, but Heru appeared to have forgotten them.

He withdrew a glowing orb from his wrap—the same orb he'd been holding when he'd cured Amash. He pressed the orb against the camel's side and splayed his free hand on its neck. The scrabbling bound slipped a few feet closer, and Mo grabbed Thana's arm. Thana glanced back at the camel in time to see the orb's light flicker out.

Then the camel's eyes opened.

"Dust," breathed Mo. "I thought it was dead."

"It is," said Thana.

The camel surged up, exhibiting no lasting predilection for death. Heru peered up at it, pride and exhaustion warring across his tagel-less features, his whole body shaking as if caught in a wind. He placed his hands on the camel's neck and hopped, trying to pull himself onto its back, but only made it a few feet before sliding back down again.

The air cracked as if split by unseen lightning and suddenly the dead men were rushing toward them, no barrier to keep them back. Heru slumped against his camel, unaware, while Mo ran for him and Thana let out a string of curses. Heru stirred and tried to couch his beast. But it continued standing placidly, head swaying back and forth, milky eyes fixed on nothing.

They weren't going to make it. Thana briefly considered shoving Heru into the oncoming horde. *That* might give them enough time to escape. But not enough. He was one and they were many and any moment now the bound would be grabbing and clawing at her, dragging her down, not without a fight, *never*—

But the hands didn't grab. Instead, for a second time that day, an unnatural and unnerving silence stretched across the sands. The bound had stopped and now formed a semicircle around Thana and Mo and Heru. They stood as still as stone, jaws slack and eyes empty. Thana glanced at Heru, but he had only just turned away from his camel and noticed the assembled bound.

"Heru Sametket."

The single name was hurled like an insult. The bound spoke in one rasping voice, jaws open but unmoving. The voice was strange: redoubled by the many mouths, but strained as if from a great distance. Because of the distortion, Thana couldn't even tell the pitch of the voice, let alone whether it belonged to any particular gender. It didn't matter, because a horrible understanding was spreading through her.

Heru straightened. "I am he."

"You've taught me well, Heru Sametket," said the voice from too many mouths. "Since you're still somehow alive, I wanted to take the time to thank you."

Heru puffed up with pride. "As you well know, I'm an exceptional teacher. But I don't recall, which student of mine are you?"

"Your skills as a teacher are abysmal," said the voice with disdain. "But I've gleaned much from your bumbling foolishness."

Heru's glowing pride softened to a frown. "I don't know what you're talking about."

"Thrice, I've sent my bound servants to silence you, and

each time you've survived them—and by extension, me. As frustrated as I was with each failure, I've learned more about the weaknesses plaguing my methods and excised those accordingly. You've forced me to perfect and streamline my techniques. So: thank you. You've proven yourself a useful opponent."

Thana closed her eyes. She'd been wrong, so wrong. Heru hadn't been as willfully ignorant and malicious as she'd first assumed. Instead, there *had* been two en-marab. Two, when there should have been none. Heru's confusion was entirely honest, after all.

"Who are you?" asked Heru, annoyance hardening his tone.

"You know me as Djet," answered the voice. "Unfortunately, further collaboration is out of the question. For the purposes of my plan, you're most useful to me dead."

"Djet?" Heru mulled for a moment, then nodded. "As I hypothesized. Before you kill me, tell me—your writing system is ingenious. How did you develop it? Was it based on any particular language or did you integrate aspects from several? I suspect that fusing disparate grammars might've proved most difficult, but potentially rewarding—"

"It was my own creation," interrupted Djet. One of the bound crossed its arms.

"Ah. Then the downward stroke of the intermedial runes wasn't derived from lower Iboljak? I thought that the language's inability to distinguish time present from time past would've been quite useful in—"

"I'm not here to discuss linguistics," snapped Djet.

Heru stepped forward, palms raised. "We could learn so much from each other. Between your knowledge of permanent binding practices and my"—he glanced toward Mo—"long years of research into quieting jaan—"

The bound closed their eyes and a very human sigh of frustration escaped. "The only thing I can learn from *you*, Sametket, is how to avoid dying through sheer luck."

"I'm only saying you should keep your options open. You might be surprised by what I can offer."

"No. I wouldn't. I've watched you long enough to know that your methods are repetitive and tedious, your hypotheses old and trite, and your last breakthrough was largely the consequence of your assistant mixing the wrong proportions of a solution."

"Oh." Heru tilted his head. "Yes. Well. I did firmly reprimand him for that."

"You have nothing left to offer—" began Djet.

"Perhaps not," said Heru quickly. "Your bound servants are already well beyond my own experiments, but have you considered how you might translate your methods to immortality?"

The bound went still and silent long enough that Thana began to wonder if the connection had been severed. But then a high-pitched noise bubbled from their mouths, so sudden and incongruous that it took a moment for Thana to recognize what it was: laughter.

Heru frowned as Thana and Mo exchanged a worried glance. Thana backed toward the camel, blindly reaching for its lead. Then the laughter cut off as abruptly as it'd begun.

"In fact, I have," continued Djet, mirth still tickling his words. "And now that you've touched on the reason I must kill you, it's about time we end our conversation."

Something whispered through the air and the bound resumed their headlong rush as if they'd never stopped, gurgling incoherent cries.

"I think," said Heru, turning to Thana and Mo, "it might be time to take our leave."

Thana pulled on the camel's lead. Its head came down but

it still refused to couch. Mo clucked her tongue. Immediately, the camel folded its long legs under itself and sank down. Heru leaned over the saddle and leveraged himself into the seat. Mo swung herself in front of the saddle, across the camel's shoulders. Heru kneed the camel and it began to unfold and rise.

Thana hissed annoyance, but grabbed the back of the saddle and swung up behind Heru. She'd barely situated herself before the camel started to move, nearly unsettling her. A bound grabbed her foot. Thana kicked, but it only tightened its grip. Heru was trying to goad the camel to go faster than the lurching pace it'd picked. Thana dug her knees into the camel's ribs so hard that she thought she felt something break, then shouted a command she'd heard the Azal use. The camel surged forward and Thana clutched at Heru's blood-stained wrap to keep from falling off.

"It won't be that easy," said the bound still clinging to her leg. Thana snarled and snapped a fist across its face. Finally the bound let go, tumbling into their dust. Thana wrapped her arms around Heru, an unfortunate necessity as the camel galloped across the sands. Each stride felt like she was going to be thrown off. She squeezed her eyes shut, hoping that if she couldn't *see* the ground lurching past, she might stay in place. So she didn't at first notice what lay ahead.

But she felt it.

Beneath the camel's thudding stride was a deeper, dust-shifting shudder, as if the earth itself were shaking. Thana opened her eyes. Something dark and hulking blocked their way.

Mo had also spotted it. "What's that?"

Heru replied, but the wind ripped his words away. Thana didn't need his explanation. The obstruction was low and long and thick. It had stout limbs, a ridged tail, and an elongated, flat snout. When it opened that snout, the creature revealed dozens of daggerlike teeth that serrated the air and tore the breath from Thana's throat.

She'd heard about such creatures, but only in the stories her cousins liked to tell to scare the younger cousins. *Hide like metal,* they'd whispered. *Teeth like shattered glass. Jaws like a smith's clamps. As fast as a sandstorm and twice as deadly. But don't worry,* they'd add conspiratorially, *crocodiles are only found near water.*

This crocodile was very far from any water and much larger than even her young self had dared imagine. Worse, it had milky white eyes and was coming right at them.

Thana freed a throwing knife and waited for that maw to open again. When it did, she leaned out as far as she dared from the lurching camel and threw. The blade pierced its tongue and the monster closed its jaw just as they passed. Thana kneed the camel, urging it to go faster. The camel lowered its head and snorted its annoyance. As the ride became even more precarious, Thana clung desperately to the back of the saddle and Heru, who was sliding sideways himself.

Behind them came a rattling growl. The crocodile had recovered and was running full tilt at them, a sight that was as amusing as it was terrifying. Its stout body swayed side to side on stubby legs, but its long snout was pointed straight at them. It was gaining foot by foot. Thana kicked the camel again and again, panic lodged in her throat, but the beast, weighed down as it was by three riders, couldn't go any faster.

She had other knives, but she'd only be wasting them. She considered jumping onto the crocodile's back, but even if she succeeded in cutting through the marks in its iron-like hide, Heru would leave her far behind. Then she'd be stuck on the sands with neither water nor shelter. But if she did nothing, the crocodile would catch them and tear them apart.

There was another option, though.

Thana tugged Heru's sleeve. He jerked, almost lost his balance, righted himself on the saddle, and glared.

"Can you do your magic and stop that thing from a distance? With, say, cloth?" asked Thana.

Heru pressed his lips together in confusion before twisting them up into a sneer. "There's a technique called *jaani nullification*, and it involves intense concentration, specific reagents, and—"

"There's a bound crocodile about to catch us, save the details for later. Can you do it?"

"While on the back of a lumbering dromedary, in the middle of the desert, trying to hold my failing body upright? Of course." But his words carried no sarcasm. Heru was already rolling back one sleeve, having looped the camel's lead around his opposite wrist. "Give me one of your knives. And not a poisoned one—if I die, you die, too."

Instead of denying the implied accusation, she freed one of her throwing knives and held it out to Heru by its handle. He took the knife and sliced first the fabric of his wrap, then the flesh of his inner arm. He winced and pressed the fabric against the fresh wound, blood only just beginning to ooze up. His lips moved soundlessly.

The crocodile was gaining on them. It'd already made up the distance it had lost earlier. The bound monster put on a burst of speed and clamped jagged teeth around the camel's tail, severing it with one bite. The camel didn't seem to feel it. Of course it wouldn't, being recently dead.

"Are you a good shot?" asked Heru, holding out the bloodied fabric and her knife.

Thana snatched the items from his hand with a dark look. *"Am I a good shot,"* she muttered, piercing the blood-stained cloth with the knife and pushing it against the hilt.

She twisted, careful to keep one hand on the saddle, and took aim. With the camel roiling beneath her and her legs weak from gripping its sides and with exhaustion from so many days and nights of too little sleep fogging her mind, aiming was difficult. But Thana trusted the hours and days and months and years of practice her mother had made her put into honing her skill. She let go of her panic and sighted on the crocodile's head, waiting for the right moment.

"What are you waiting for?" asked Heru with a hint of hysteria.

"Shut up."

Her moment arrived. The crocodile had closed the last few feet between them and now opened its jaws, teeth choked with dried blood and pieces of tail. Thana waited another half heartbeat, until the camel had settled into the bottom of its loping gait, which brought her in line with that mouth. Then she threw.

The knife struck true, right in the center of the crocodile's dark purple tongue. Its mouth snapped shut like a trap closing, but not on them. Its claws stopped scrabbling at the air and its tail stopped swishing back and forth and in another moment, the bound monster had dropped like a stone to the sand. The ground shook with its impact. The camel stumbled, but quickly caught itself and put on a burst of speed. Thana allowed herself a smile; maybe Illi wouldn't complain so much about "useless" throwing lessons after hearing this story if she returned. When.

Thana glanced back to make sure no more bound followed, but the only thing behind them was the camel's long trail of dust. She concentrated on holding tight to Heru, who in turn kept a firm grip on Mo. Blood seeped wet and fresh from Mo's shoulder and her head lolled to one side, jerking upright whenever she startled awake.

Mo wouldn't make it much longer, not without losing consciousness. They'd escaped Djet and his bound, but what now?

Thana didn't trust Heru to know the way to Na Tay Khet, let alone the nearest well. She didn't trust his dead camel not to crumble beneath them.

But she trusted G-d, and that was all she could do right now. She would survive this and make it back to Ghadid. She had to. She was the Serpent's daughter. So Thana ducked her head and closed her eyes against the searing sun and scratching sand. She ignored the pain that ached and occasionally screamed in her muscles, the exhaustion that clamped tight in her chest, the dryness that felt like glass shards in her throat. She settled into the ride's rhythm and didn't think about when it would end— minutes or hours or days from now.

They didn't have water and they didn't know where they were going and now Heru knew who she was. What was the worst that could happen?

14

One moment, the sun sat high in the sky. The next, Thana opened her eyes to swiftly darkening sands and the first few stars of twilight. The direction of the sunset's lingering glow indicated they were still heading north, if a little east. At least Heru hadn't led them off course.

As the day's heat dissipated, a creeping chill stole through Thana. Her limbs shook and her eyelids twitched and her skin prickled, but she didn't sweat. She made the mistake of thinking about water, and then she couldn't push the idea of *just a little drink* from her mind. She clung tighter to Heru, who'd begun slipping, slowly, to one side. No one spoke.

The situation's irony didn't elude her. She'd personally slashed Heru's waterskin and poisoned his meat and now those were the only supplies left to them. She couldn't blame the Azal for taking the rest of the water, but that didn't stop her from silently cursing them anyway.

Time stretched, became painful, then twisted into a particular kind of torture. Every jolt of the camel's stride threatened to break Thana's hold and every time she managed to stay on, her muscles burned hotter. Each second that fell tore more moisture from her breath and threw more sand in her eyes. At least once, Thana found herself wishing Djet had caught them after all, or that she'd revoked her contract and remained in Ghadid, or that Heru had simply died like he was supposed to.

She cursed herself for following Heru, for making that promise to Salid, and then she cursed Mo for joining the caravan. As her tongue swelled from dehydration and every swallow became like gulping broken glass, Thana cursed the sand and the sky, the camel and the Azal. She cursed the grit in her mouth and the pain in her legs and shoulder. She cracked open her eyes and cursed every rock they passed and every new star that dared flicker above. The cursing became a rhythm that soothed and transformed time into something almost bearable.

Cursing was easier than thinking about what came next. Amastan's plan had only extended so far as the caravan's path, and she'd left the bloodied fragments of the caravan far behind. The mark had been *so* close to death and oblivious to the assassin nearby—an ideal that should have ended in a completed contract. Instead, she'd been forced to save the mark and now he knew who she was. Worse, there really were two en-marab, and while the enemy of her enemy should have been her accomplice, Djet certainly didn't seem to think so. His bound were indiscriminate in who they killed.

What a fool she'd been, believing she could take on a contract alone. She'd become a legend all right—the cautionary kind.

When the camel finally slowed and stopped, the sky was rich with stars. A quarter moon had risen, giving them just enough light to see their own hands and imagine the rest. Thana released her tight grip on Heru's wrap and immediately regretted it. She slipped slowly, then all at once, from the camel to the ground.

The next thing she knew, her skin tingled and something cool and sharp pressed against her throat. She tensed but didn't move other than to crack open an eye. The crescent moon backlit

Heru's face, which was so uncomfortably close she could smell the peppermint on his breath. His hand was near her throat. Thana put two and two together and decided to keep staring straight ahead, lest she cut herself by moving. A breeze played across her jaw; her tagel was gone.

"What," said Heru, "do you think is stopping me from opening your throat?"

"Mo would heal me before I bled out?"

"The healer's out of water. She's also preoccupied elsewhere."

"Ah. Then you must be grateful for my help in saving you from the crocodile."

"It was your 'help' that got us into that mess first. If *you* hadn't sabotaged my waterskin and poisoned my food, I wouldn't have *needed* your help."

"How do you know I did that?"

His blade bore down until Thana felt her skin break in a stab of pain. "Who else but the assassin?" Heru leaned in so that his mouth was all but touching her ear, his breath hot. "But I'm not going to kill you because we're still far from any well and we could use your blood to survive in a pinch. For now, you're my walking contingency plan."

Heru rocked back onto his heels, the knife held loosely in front of him. But Thana didn't indulge the temptation to grab it. "You and I both know that I don't need a weapon to kill you. I'd prefer to tie you up so you won't bother me further, but that might bring to light certain . . . details that our healer doesn't need to know. Fortunately, it appears you also have something to hide from her. I suspect she won't take kindly to your attempts to see me dead. So we are, in that respect, on the same page. But"—he shook his knife at her like a chastising finger—"one more rotten meal, one more empty skin, one more of *anything* and I will have *you* dig the well, if you understand my meaning.

And by that, I mean I'll kill you and bind your jaani to my will. I don't think you'd like that."

Thana shook her head, her gaze caught on the knife's point.

"Good." Heru dropped his arm, then looked at the knife as if he'd forgotten it was there.

"What do you want with her?" The question burst from Thana's mouth before she could stop herself.

"I saw an opportunity to expand my current understanding of the peculiar and much-rumored abilities of certain individuals residing near the Wastes and took it," said Heru. "The girl was not coerced into accompanying me, if that's your concern. She understands she has a greater responsibility to humankind in this matter and is willing to learn more about Djet and make certain he's stopped—unlike, apparently, *you*. I'd thought you were at least a *little* intrigued by our shared dilemma, but it's clear that's not, in fact, the case." Hurt briefly turned the edges of his mouth down and Thana wished he'd put his tagel back on already. Even in the dim light, it was off-putting to see his expressions.

"So you just want to study her?" pressed Thana. "Is that why you're so concerned about what she thinks?"

"She could also prove to be an . . . important asset," said Heru. "All available data indicates that your healers are capable of much more than they'll willingly admit, being too blinded by their own sense of moral superiority. You, on the other hand, are little more than a shield made out of meat and bone."

"Where is she?" Thana sat up. A mistake. The world went dark. She blinked furiously, but her sight took its time returning.

"She's searching for water."

"What? You let her go off alone?" Thana stood—another mistake. Her vision darkened again and all of her muscles seized up in protest, tight as cables. She felt as if she'd been run over by a camel. She glanced at Heru; maybe she had.

"The girl insisted."

Thana took a step, winced. "How long has she been gone?"

Heru tilted his head back and observed the moon. "A while."

"Didn't it occur to you that she could be in danger?"

"No. But the point is moot. We have no water; if I didn't let her go, we'd all be dead anyway, contingency plan aside. Besides, she afforded us the opportunity for this lovely little chat." He paused for a heartbeat, then asked, "Who hired you?"

"It doesn't matter."

"It does to me."

"What about Djet? What does he want?" asked Thana, hoping to change the topic.

Heru's expression softened. "The same thing anybody wants, I suppose: to conquer death. I'm very curious about his methods, even more curious about his reasons for trying to have me killed. Unlike with you, where the reason is likely as tired as it is political, it appears my death is a part of his greater plan. But why? I cannot die out here in this G-d-forsaken wasteland before I have a chance to research. It must have something to do with the binding of jaan, in which case . . . but he would need . . ."

He trailed off, his gaze sliding past Thana toward the horizon where the stars abruptly ended and the world began. He pulled a scrap of paper and a pen from one pocket, smoothed the paper over his knee, and began scribbling. When he didn't look up after a few heartbeats, Thana took the opportunity to quietly back away, then walk—jerkily but steadily—to the camel. The beast's head was relaxed toward the ground as if searching for grass, but it wasn't eating. Its eyes were open, staring, and every few moments the camel would huff out a breath, as if remembering that it should.

Those weren't the only signs that something was wrong with the beast. Far more obvious was how the skin had stretched and torn along its neck and back, exposing muscle and sinew and dried blood. Its body had shrunk from water loss and now ribs showed beneath its skin as if the beast were emaciated. In lieu of a tail, the camel had a blood-caked stump. This twitched as Thana slid her hand across its leathery skin.

"Dust, what's he done to you?" she asked.

Footsteps hissed across sand. A dark shape resolved out of the thick night. Thana had drawn one of her knives before she noticed the shape was moving slowly, dragging something behind. A wounded bound? But a wound shouldn't have slowed one of those monsters down—

"Heru?"

It was Mo's voice, thin with exhaustion. Thana glanced around, but the en-marabi was nowhere to be seen. She put away her knife. Mo was limping, pulling a heavy weight through the sand behind her, the wooden stake she'd appropriated as a staff clutched in her other hand. As she approached, Thana heard the distinctly beautiful slosh of liquid.

"Mo!"

Still a few feet away, Mo stopped. "Thana?"

"Are you okay? Let me get that."

Thana grabbed the skin from Mo. Without its weight, the healer sagged. Thana dropped the heavy waterskin next to the camel, then returned for Mo, who gratefully leaned against her.

"Where have you been?" asked Thana.

"Finding water."

Then Mo winced and clutched at her shoulder. She'd folded and knotted her wrap back to make room for a bandage across the wound. The bandage was already dark with blood.

"Mo—your shoulder. You need to sit down and let me look."

"I'm fine," said Mo. But she let Thana guide her a few steps closer to the camel before sliding to the ground.

Mo groaned as she collapsed, as if she'd been holding herself together for far too long. Her fingers stayed wrapped tight around the wooden stake. Why hadn't someone started a fire? The air was growing chill and, though the moonlight illuminated some things, it cast everything else in deep shadow.

Thana left Mo so she could dig through Heru's bag, hoping he would at least carry a—ah, yes. Her fingers brushed across metal and she removed a tea brazier. In its belly was a ball of dried camel dung, which she lit with a spark from the brazier's striker. Warm, golden light poured across the sand and turned the darker blues of Mo's features to soft browns.

Thana stared into Mo's face, at first captivated, then concerned. Mo's braids had lost their tie and now hung every which way, drawing sharp lines across her cheeks and neck. Her eyes were red and puffy with circles like dark bruises, her lips cracked and spotted with dried blood. Every line and wrinkle was crisp, her skin pinched like old leather.

Thana caught herself leaning toward Mo and pulled back, wary of the firelight's sharp intimacy. She looked down at her hands, no longer able to meet Mo's exhausted gaze. Like Mo's face, the skin on the back of her hands was lined and drawn from too little water. She wondered if her pounding heart was another symptom of dehydration.

"Did you just leave me there lying in the sand for half the night?" blurted Thana.

Mo shrugged, but the motion lacked energy. "You looked like you needed rest."

"After I fell off a camel?"

"I made sure you hadn't hurt yourself." Mo hefted her exhausted gaze from the sand to peer at Thana. "He knows who you are. I didn't tell him. He must have figured it out during the fight."

"Yeah. My tagel came loose. It doesn't really matter now. Here"—Thana pulled the waterskin, sloshing, to them—"you need to heal yourself before you lose any more blood."

Mo laid the wooden stake across her lap, then held out her cupped hands for a splash of water. She closed her eyes and the water began to bubble and glow a faint blue. When Mo spoke again, her voice was stronger, more sure.

"Who is he?"

Thana blinked. "I thought you knew—he's the Empress's—"

Mo interrupted her with a sharp shake of her head. The water was disappearing from her cupped palms, its cool glow mingling with the warmth of the firelight. "He's not an ordinary marabi. It's not my place to judge others, but what I've seen him do. . . ." She glanced at the camel standing peacefully nearby, its eyes open and staring. "That creature isn't natural. And when he controlled those monsters, he used blood."

"At least it was his own," said Thana. "But I agree. It's unsettling."

The blue glow flickered, then brightened. Mo shook her head again. "It's not just that. Blood is mostly water, which means his magic is similar to a healer's. But blood is far more dangerous, because there's an inherent connection to the life it came from. He should be able to heal, but I haven't seen him try. He quieted the jaan within those poor men, but the way he did it worries me."

Thana opened her mouth to tell Mo that she had good reason to worry, to tell her about the whore Heru had bound to his will back in Ghadid, the charms he'd shattered, the things he'd threatened her with, and the admission he'd made about controlling jaan and men alike—and then she closed her mouth. Heru's warning beat in her mind like a drum: *details that our healer doesn't need to know.* If she shared what she knew about Heru, then what would stop him from telling Mo about Thana's contract?

For a brief, dangerous moment, Thana contemplated telling Mo everything. Heru was concerned about what Mo thought of him, after all. Why should Thana care if Mo knew she was an assassin? But as soon as the thought solidified in her mind, a wave of fear washed over her. Mo was a healer. She wouldn't even let *Heru* get hurt. What would she do if she knew Thana was here to kill him?

Thana could already see the revulsion on Mo's face, the way she'd draw away. If Mo knew, she'd treat Thana the same way she treated Heru: with cold, clinical indifference. The mere thought of Mo drawing away like that twisted something deep inside Thana. She'd rather liked the way Mo had been warming toward her.

Besides, Mo would try to stop her, and Thana couldn't have that. She still had a contract to complete and she wouldn't let anything get in the way of that. Not Djet, not his bound, and certainly not a pretty healer she hardly knew.

So instead, Thana closed her mouth and shrugged. "I don't know. I leave that kind of thing up to the marab—and the healers, of course."

Mo pursed her lips. The wound glowed a watery blue as threads of light flitted beneath her skin. "Just—be careful. I don't think he has your best intentions at heart. I wouldn't put it past him to pull something when we arrive at Na Tay Khet. He's not a good man."

"Who's not?"

Thana and Mo both started. Mo touched her wound as she turned, the blue fading. It had mostly closed, the violent red gone from her skin, but it could have used another minute or two. Mo didn't take more water.

Thana tried not to glare at Heru. The brazier's firelight had ruined her night vision, but she could make out his hunched shape against the stars. Although she couldn't see his face to judge for sure, by the way he *wasn't* pulling the jaan out of either of them, he must not have overheard the earlier part of their conversation.

"Djet," said Mo stiffly. "We were talking about Djet."

Heru sat next to them and crossed his legs. "Of course he's not." He looked at the brazier. "Is the tea done yet?"

"We were just putting the water on," said Thana. She pulled the skin to her and poured water into the pot. "Where'd you go?"

"I found some footprints and followed them to their inevitable conclusion," said Heru.

"They were probably Mo's," said Thana, annoyed. "Why did you send her off on her own, anyway? There could've been bandits. Or more bound."

Mo laid a hand on Thana's arm. "It was my idea. Don't blame him." *For this,* her gaze seemed to add.

"Why?" asked Thana. "How did you even *find* water?"

Mo and Heru both looked at Thana with surprise. "I'm a healer," said Mo. "Every healer can find water, if there's water to be found."

She leaned over and unhooked a small bowl from the skin, filled the bowl with water, and handed it to Thana. When Thana hesitated, she added, "There's a well, not more than a half hour's walk east. We'll have to fill up again before we continue, so go ahead and drink as much as you need." She ran a hand along the side of the skin, her fingers finding and snagging on a poorly patched rip in its side. "All we have is this skin, and it had a hole in it. I've done what I can, but it's still leaking. Even with a full skin, between three people we'll still be out of water in a day or two."

Guilt flushed Thana's cheeks. She looked down. She could feel Heru's accusing stare on her—*he* knew, even if Mo didn't—as she watched the moisture bubble and ooze from the poorly sutured rip. It must've been ripped further during their flight and there was only so much some string could do. Thana sipped from the bowl. The water was brackish and sour and filled with grit that grated between her teeth. But it was water, and she couldn't stop drinking once she'd started. Mo refilled the bowl twice, then passed it to Heru.

"They weren't hers," said Heru suddenly, between sips. "The footprints. They led north, not east. They brought me to some very terrified sand fleas living nearby. We can use their shelter for the night."

Mo stood up so fast that some of the water in her bowl sloshed over its sides. "There are people here?"

"I assume they maintain the well," said Heru. "They won't bother us. I made it overtly clear that they should make themselves scarce for the duration of our stay."

"What did you do to them?" asked Thana before she could stop herself.

The edges of Heru's mouth twitched upward. "Nothing. We merely had a civil disagreement." He stood, brushing off his wrap with fluttering hands. "Come. I need proper rest and we won't get that out in the open. We'll drink and sleep. Then, when we're well-rested, we can make our own skins and continue our journey."

"Why don't we ask these people how far the nearest city is?" said Thana. "Perhaps we're only a day's ride out, or there's another well on the way."

"In my presence, they were non-verbal. If you believe you can talk to these simple and primitive sand fleas, be my guest." Heru turned to his camel. "But it's my sincere hypothesis that you're only wasting your time."

"Maybe you shouldn't have called them sand fleas," suggested Thana. "At least, not to their faces."

Heru grunted. His bound camel trotted across the sand, easily carrying all three of them, its energy unflagging despite its slowly decomposing body. Mo had talked the "sand fleas"—a couple and their son—into allowing them to spend the rest of the night and the following day sheltered in their home. The woman had pressed clean water into Mo's hands, calling Heru a demon and begging Mo to leave him for someone better. Like her son.

According to the couple, Na Tay Khet was still a three days' journey away. Heru was confident they could make it in one. They'd ridden nonstop since taking their leave the evening before. Thana's fingers grew numb, followed by her hands, as she clutched at Mo's sides and the saddle for long, unchanging hours at a time. The night's chill only deepened, drawing on what little strength Thana had gathered from their rest.

Soon, the eastern horizon lightened, then blossomed with deep blue. Light spread across the sky in waves and suddenly Thana could see the details all around. The endless sand had changed overnight to a landscape punctuated by scrub and short trees. To the north and south stood short hovels. Between them, clusters of date palms stretched like fingers to the sky.

Then the land dipped and the sky paled and to the east, something vast peeked over the horizon. Like a dark stain, the city of Na Tay Khet spread across sand and hills. An occasional tower sliced through the sky and the massive, shining structure at its center hulked like a couched camel. As the sun rose, that structure blazed like a second sun.

The sand resolved into a path, then a road compacted by many travelers over many years. Heru dug his heels into the camel's side, urging it faster even as the road grew crowded. Na Tay Khet's wall was vast, built from many thousands of broad sandstone slabs, each easily as tall and wide as their camel. Farmers and caravans and merchants with their wagons clogged the road as they approached one of a dozen gates along the wall.

Heru careened through the choking mass of dust and foreign grumblings until even his camel was forced to slow and stop. Still, he kicked the beast a few times before giving up. An order to the chaos soon became obvious. They'd joined a shifting, mutating queue that would eventually take them up to and through one of the gates.

Thana tried not to stare at the people and beasts thronging them, but it was all so fascinating—and so much. Most of them appeared desert-worn, their clothing and skin and hair covered in a fine layer of dust. A handful of travelers were almost pristine, clothes and jewelry shining with care, hair uncovered and well-kept, beasts unburdened. These must be the drum chiefs of Na Tay Khet. She tilted her head back to take in the whole wall, now stretching high above them. How many drum chiefs must a city this size have?

As the crowd's jostling worsened, they were forced to dismount. Thana leaned on the camel for support as the sun lurched higher and higher. They'd crossed countless miles over the course of one night, yet the last mile to the gate was taking them most of the morning. Her head swam and the wound on her arm had started throbbing again. Despite their long rest and extra water, she was still weak and exhausted. Now, at least, she knew better than to close her eyes for any length of time. Even with them pried open, the ground swayed dangerously.

While they waited, inching along, she retrieved the small bag she'd salvaged from Melwa. A pang of grief, sudden and unexpected, shot through her at the memory of her camel. She paused a moment to send up a brief prayer for the camel's jaani, then rifled through the bag for her rings. Their gentle weight on her fingers was reassuring. When Mo was preoccupied by a scuffle

between two merchants, Thana slipped the folded cloth containing her poison darts into the pocket of her wrap, safely nestled
next to her garrote.

After that, she kept an eye on Heru as the line inched nearer the
gate, Mo's warning thudding in her head like a drumbeat. What
would Heru do, now that he was home? This was his city; he knew
the layout, the people, the politics. He was the Empress's own
marabi. That had meant little to her while they were in Ghadid
and on the sands, but now worry gnawed ragged bites in her confidence with its sharp teeth. Here, Heru had the advantage.

When the last group ahead of them disappeared through
the gate, Thana found and held Mo's hand. She squeezed and
when Mo squeezed back, Thana felt a little stronger. She could
do this. She had to do this. She would kill Heru and return to
Ghadid and forever be known as the cousin who'd trekked all
the way across the sands to complete her contract, the cousin
who had faced monsters and sandstorms to bring down the Empress's marabi, the cousin who had struck the first and final blow
against the Mehewret Empire.

The *how* still eluded her. But she had time for that yet.

They stepped up to the gate, which was a metal lattice that
hung suspended over their heads, the spikes lining its bottom an
unspoken threat. The guards had positioned themselves on either
side of a metal grate on the ground, already out of the way in case
the gate came shrieking down.

Two guards stood to one side, arms folded across bronze chest
plates, spears propped against the wall. Their gold wraps were
tied at the waist, like a half dress. They wore no tagels, but dark
blue fabric cascaded from the crown of their heads down the
sides, held in place by a circlet of bronze. From a distance, it had
looked like impossibly straight, black hair.

Aside from a ring of kohl around their eyes, the guards' faces were unadorned. Every twitch of the lips or the cheeks was visible and Thana fought the urge to look away. Clearly, it wasn't the custom here for men to safeguard their thoughts and feelings. Thana forced a nonchalance she didn't feel as they stopped under the gate's shadow, just a step from the metal grating and the spikes above.

A third guard blocked their way with his spear. "What's your business here?"

Heru straightened and stared the guard down with familiar disdain. "To see her royal highness and present news of no small import."

The guard grunted. "You got to do better than that, friend."

"It's true, sa, we're here to warn—" started Mo.

But Heru cut her off. "Do you know who I am?"

The guard widened his stance and stiffened, ready for a fight. "You really going to try that on me?"

Thana counted her knives and marked the places on the guard's body that would result in either shock or significant blood loss. The bronze plate that protected the guard's chest cut off at the armpits, displaying a pair of biceps that were each larger than Thana's head. She'd be no match against the guard's strength. She'd only win this fight with speed.

The other guards grabbed their spears, and while they didn't join the first guard just yet, they were no longer relaxed. Heru didn't bother to look at them.

"I am Heru Sametket, second advisory marabi to her Imperial Highness, the Empress Zara ha Khatet of the great and mighty Mehewret Empire—long may she live and reign."

Any annoyance or boredom in the guards was instantly gone, replaced by an electric tension like the prelude to a storm. Two stepped back.

"I beg your pardon, friend," said the first guard, not quite meeting Heru's gaze. "But our captain—you must understand—he will demand some sort of proof."

Heru let out a tight, annoyed sigh, then slipped his hand inside his wrap. The first guard moved his spear in front of him, as if it were a shield.

"Please don't touch me or come any closer, sa," he said.

Heru huffed. "I'm *showing* you your proof." He flicked open a short roll of vellum and held it up for the guards to inspect.

The first guard leaned forward, eyes scanning the skin. Thana craned her neck, trying to read what was on it, but only caught some excessively complicated script before Heru was rolling the vellum up again. He tucked the scroll away and crossed his arms.

"Th-that is sufficient," said the guard. He glanced to his companions for help, but both of them had already backed away. "You may pass, Sametket-sai. Long live her Imperial Highness the Empress."

"She will," said Heru.

Leading his dead camel, Heru passed the guards. Thana followed, her hand still twined around Mo's and her gaze trained on the ground. Heru hadn't explained their presence, but hopefully the guards were cowed enough not to ask.

Then Heru stopped and held up a hand. He turned back to the guards. "Oh, and I almost forgot—this healer is my guest, but this other one has come to assassinate the Empress. I would appreciate it if you arrested her."

15

By the time Heru's words had seeped through Thana's exhaustion and she'd realized he'd betrayed her, the guards had already grabbed her. She jerked away, but tired and desert-worn as she was, she was no match against their strength.

"Thana!" Mo started forward, only to freeze with her hands held before her when a guard pointed his spear at her chest.

"Stay back," warned Thana. Then to Heru, "What do you think you're doing? This isn't funny."

Heru didn't even bother to meet her gaze. "This woman has on more than one occasion voiced in my company her desire to find and kill the Empress. It's my understanding that she was sent by her masters to accompany me here so that she could assassinate our great Empress and declare open war on our Empire. I befriended her so that I could keep her close and turn her in at the most opportune time. To preserve the Empress and the Empire at large, it would behoove you to lock her away. A trial would be nice, but it's not necessary. This is, of course, a direct order from her Imperial Highness's second advisory marabi."

"What?" said Thana. "That's—*dust*! I never said anything like that! Why would we want to kill the Empress? That would be suicide."

Mo chewed her lip, brow creased with worry. She looked from

Heru to Thana and back again, weighing what Thana had told her only a day earlier versus what Heru was saying now.

"We had a deal!" snapped Thana.

Heru finally looked at her, self-satisfaction oozing from every pore. "I haven't broken any deals."

Thana could only stare, amazed at his audacity. But it was true. Heru hadn't divulged her real secret, even if he'd guaranteed her execution. The en-marabi was more clever by far than she'd given him credit for.

"Come." A guard tugged her arm up and behind her back. "Don't make us do anything you'll regret, rat."

"Let her go." Mo raised her makeshift staff, the wooden stake she'd taken to carrying with her. "She's innocent. She's not here to kill the Empress—let her *go*."

Fear pulsed through Thana, sharp as glass. She couldn't let Mo protect her. Mo would only get herself hurt. Besides, Thana *was* here to kill someone, even if it wasn't the Empress.

"Mo—don't. Please."

"But Heru is wrong. You're here to help us find Djet, not kill this Empress."

Thana swallowed hard and prayed she wouldn't regret this later. "It . . . might be part of the reason I'm here."

The shock that cut across Mo's face was almost worse than letting her get hurt. Thana told herself that she could pretend it was all part of a clever plan later, that Mo would understand—and forgive her. But the betrayal that followed Mo's shock hurt more than she'd feared and for a moment, Thana knew how the bound must feel when a knife cut through their skin and severed the jaani animating their flesh. Thana looked away. Heru's appreciative nod only made it worse. She couldn't wait to drive a blade through that awful man's heart.

Thana slumped between the two guards, radiating defeat. Mo made a choked noise, but finally moved out of the way. Thana twisted her head to watch Heru stride imperiously through the gate and into the thickening crowd. Mo followed a few steps behind. She didn't look back. In another moment, the crowd had swallowed her.

The guards marched Thana down a street that hugged the inside of the wall. She tried to memorize every road and building they passed, but she quickly lost her bearings. It was all too new and strange and overwhelming. She was left with only the impression of both immensity and stifling closeness. The buildings stood multiple, treacherous stories tall, leaning over narrow alleys that shouldn't have fit a single camel, let alone the crowds that funneled through them. They passed sprawling glass-less gardens that slashed like oozing green wounds through the city's flesh.

And then there was the noise. While Ghadid could be loud at times, the pylons forced distance between the neighborhoods and the sands drank up the rest. Here, the wall caught the sound and doubled it back, louder again by half. The sheer cacophony of crying voices and rattling carts and clanking wares and bellowing camels made Thana's head throb.

When they'd put more than a dozen streets between them and the gate, Thana forced herself to focus. She didn't know how much further the prison was and she didn't intend to find out. She counted her assets: one good arm, one throwing knife strapped to her chest, a longer knife at her thigh, a half dozen darts in one pouch, the glass charms around her waist, the garrote in her pocket, and her burning anger at Heru's treachery.

Thana stumbled, but the guards caught her and kept going. A second stumble earned her curses from the shortest guard. His grip tightened as he hauled her back up, then loosened again as he adjusted his grip. Just as she'd hoped.

Thana went limp, jerking her arm out of his grasp as she fell. The guard on her other side tightened his hold and pulled up to keep her from hitting the dirt, but now one arm was free. Thana channeled all of her fury and frustration at Heru into a kick aimed at the back of the short guard's knee. His knee gave and he fell forward with an undignified yelp of pain.

"No you don't," spat the third guard, moving in to grab her.

But the taller guard was already lifting her one-handed off the ground, annoyance plain across his bare features. Pain shot through her shoulder and down her arm as he dug his fingers into her skin. Thana sucked in a breath, twisting her body in a way that she was going to regret later, and punched the guard's face, her rings gouging lines across his cheek.

He let go and flung his hands—too late—to his face. Thana hit the ground. The fall knocked the breath from her lungs and scattered dark spots across her vision, but she still spun out of the way of the third guard's lunge. Then she was on her feet and sprinting down the sandy road.

The sound of pursuit was right on her heels. Thana didn't dare glance back. She gauged that the guards were only a few short strides behind, but being lighter and smaller than all three of them, she was faster. But speed wouldn't be enough if she didn't find somewhere to hide, and soon. Already each breath shot pain through her chest and her legs felt like jelly. The excitement of capture and escape had given her a rush of energy, but exhaustion was only heartbeats away.

Thana pivoted from the wall and into the city. The guards cursed behind her as she pushed past merchants and servants and women carrying baskets and men laughing together in doorways.

The sights and sounds were so distractingly unfamiliar that it was difficult to keep her eyes trained on the path to freedom.

Then—*there*! The alley opened up onto a tumultuous marketplace that sprawled across the road. People mingled, pushed, and shoved around colorful merchant stalls. Thana slid into the crowd and slowed to a walk. Not more than a few feet behind her, the guards shouted as they entered the marketplace.

Thana ducked her head and browsed the cages of white geese and striped quail. She observed her immediate neighbors, took in how they talked and walked and gestured. She was struck first by how very pale they were and second by how little clothing they wore. She'd noticed that the guards were not as dark as she and Mo, but seeing so many with sand-toned skin brought her up short. With her full-body wrap and dark skin, she stuck out like a palm on the sands.

Men and women alike browsed the stalls. Most of the men wore little more than a skirt at the waist, their bare chests shining with sweat. The women, too, walked around half-naked, their breasts and navels uncovered. Some wore flashing bands of gold around their wrists and necks, some had equally naked slaves in tow, and some were clearly lower rank, their skirts tattered and coarse. It was one thing to hear about the locals' brazen customs from stories, but another thing entirely to see it. Thana's cheeks warmed as she focused on the birds in front of her.

Thana fought her initial impulse to tug her wrap over her head; no one here covered their hair, let alone wore a tagel. Instead, she sucked in a breath and pulled her wrap from her shoulders and retied it at her waist. She immediately felt naked and exposed. Despite the warm, cloying air, her skin erupted with goose bumps.

The stall owner raised one kohl-thickened eyebrow, but said nothing. Kohl lined every eye here, finger-thick, despite the shade cast by the buildings. She'd have to find some if she wanted to blend in. She leaned over a crate of small white birds as the guards' voices grew louder. She tensed, one hand hovering just above the dagger strapped to her thigh, and whispered a prayer under her breath. If they grabbed her, she wasn't sure she could get away this time without killing one of them.

But no one grabbed her. The guards' voices thinned as they drifted away and soon they were swallowed by the market. Thana flashed the merchant a smile, then slipped into the steady flow of people, letting them draw her along. As she walked, taking her cues from the rhythm of the marketplace, she became more aware of just how much she stood out. How had the guards missed her? Even her simple, unadorned wrap marked her as *other*.

All around her swished skirts of gold and beige and white, a steady background of sand tones that was broken by the vibrant blue of her wrap. What they lacked in color, though, they made up for in detail. Gold and silver thread traced intricate geometric designs that shimmered and flashed when they caught the light. Chained and twisted silver bracelets jangled on wrists, and gold glittered around necks and from ears.

In among all the flash and shimmer were occasional breaks of plain fabric and bare arms. Slaves. They wore their skirts belted at the waist and kept their gazes averted. Their heads were shorn clean, so Thana could clearly see the brands that had been seared into their scalps, right above the ear. They wore neither shoes nor headwear, but they shared something in common with Thana: many of them were just as dark-skinned.

The realization soured her mood further. The Empress merely wanted to expand her Empire and force Ghadid to pay taxes, did she? What other cities on the sands had she seized and plundered?

Thana tightened her wrap, its edge just covering her belt of glass charms. They'd grown cold since leaving Heru and Mo behind, which had led her to realize how warm they'd been for most of her journey. Their chill was a reminder that she had to keep moving, that she had a contract to complete.

But first, she needed to find sanctuary. She was an obvious foreigner in this strange and choking city, and as soon as word spread that the guards were looking for someone like her, it'd become impossible to hide.

And Mo—what about her? The healer was alone with Heru, and while Thana knew he wouldn't try to hurt her, not yet, Djet's bound were indiscriminate. Every moment Mo was near Heru, she was in danger. Thana could only hope she was also safest near him. He'd had every right to betray Thana—she *had* tried to kill him, after all. If he hurt Mo, it'd be through neglect or ignorance. Heru had been clear that he wanted her alive and near. That should mean Mo was safe—for now.

Sanctuary. Rest. The words repeated in her head, as insistent as the beat of a calling. It was just past midday and the air was thick and stifling, but it was nowhere near as relentlessly oppressive as it had been out on the open sands. Here there was a breeze, moist and scented with something irrefutably green.

Thana left the market behind and walked further into the city. The buildings thinned and shortened, but the crowd thickened. She passed open gardens and unguarded pools of standing water. Her stomach gnawed with hunger and her mouth was parched, yet she didn't dare stop. She fumbled the few baats left in her pouch, but she was wary of trying to spend Ghadid's coin. What did they even use here?

She was choking on her own ignorance. She didn't even know where to start. In Ghadid, she'd worn her city like a second skin. She'd known the customs, the different ways to knot a wrap and what each meant, the height and color of a tagel, the shoes of a slave. She'd known which watchmen were bribable, which healers wouldn't ask questions, which rooftops had the best views, which walls were easiest to climb. She'd known all of that and a hundred thousand more she'd never be able to name.

But here, now, she didn't even know how to buy *food*. Panic replaced the pride she'd had when she lost the guards. With no clear idea of where to go, she just kept moving deeper into the city.

A riot of green opened off to one side. She'd watched someone enter a similar green space earlier, so they weren't off-limits. A dozen other invisible rules might govern them, but it was worth the risk. She stepped from the stone road onto a sandy path. The sound of splashing water pulled her across soft grass and between waist-high hedges to a shallow pool, its water so clear she could see silvery creatures swirling and flitting just beneath its surface.

Thana savored the first handful of water, but the second and the third and the fourth she didn't even taste. Soon, her stomach sloshed and she felt satisfied in a way she hadn't since before joining the caravan. She was still exhausted and sore and hungry and lost, but it was a start, and this small comfort brightened her mood.

She splashed water across her face—what a delicious luxury—then settled on her heels and watched the sleek, scaly animals dart through the water like lizards across hot stones. She could stay in the garden until nightfall, maybe even curl up and sleep beneath one of the hedges. But without glass overhead, she was exposed. Anyone could walk by and find her. No, she'd be safer off the ground. Higher up.

She peered through the foliage, scanning for an appropriate roof. If she climbed high enough, she'd be able to see how the city was laid out. She could figure out where Heru might have gone. He worked for the Empress, which meant he either lived in the palace itself or nearby. He certainly wouldn't live in the poorer parts of the city. And even if she was wrong, surely he'd have headed to the palace first to alert his Empress.

A building just south of the garden appeared to fit her needs. It was several stories high with a flat roof, and its brick walls looked easy enough to climb even exhausted as she was. As she stared up at the building, gathering the will and strength to start the climb, Thana found herself longing for Amastan's help. He'd know what to do.

How was he? It'd been several weeks. He should be up and walking around, reading old scrolls and laughing at her father's bad jokes. He hadn't been happy with her decision to go it alone. Maybe he'd come after her, join the next caravan and try to find her.

Thana closed her eyes. No. Amastan would never be that reckless. The family might take care of each other, but even they had limits. Amastan wouldn't come, and neither would any of her other cousins. Neither would her mother. She couldn't expect help. All she had was herself. She'd have to be enough.

But she had more than herself. She had her years of working closely with her mother, then years more with Amastan. What would he do?

His voice rang clear in her head, as if he were sitting right next to her. *What's the first step, Thana?*

The first step, always the *first* step, was finding where the mark was most likely to let his guard down—where he was most comfortable. All of Na Tay Khet was Heru's home, but where would he least suspect an attack? Where would he feel safest?

The palace. Even if he didn't live there, no one would dare attack him so near his Empress. There'd be too many guards and servants, too much protection and caution. If someone went through all the trouble to enter the palace, they'd be after the Empress, not one of her marab.

What then? How do you get in?

Thana closed and opened her fist. She had to get into the palace without drawing attention. Who lived and worked inside? She couldn't know for certain without careful observation, but she could guess. The Empress's guard. Her servants. Her healers and marab and close family. Slaves.

Who can you be?

Thana recalled the market, vivid and dense, and tried to place herself in that crowd. All those pale bodies, shoulders and chests bared to the sun. Then the slaves, skin brown as dates and heads shaved. Thana touched her head, her poof of hair almost a full inch long now. She was loath to cut it, but that'd be the easiest part of her disguise.

What about a distraction?

Thana shook her head. No, Heru wouldn't be easily drawn out. He kept his nose so close to his studies that he wouldn't notice if she set half the city on fire. The city wasn't his responsibility. She had to go to him.

Thana left the garden, Amastan's voice sharpening her plan. She methodically analyzed and discarded other angles of attack, from pretending to be a baker to hiding among the guards. It all came back to her skin, which was so much darker than most of the city's populace. She could disguise or alter many things, but her skin wasn't one of them.

No, her first idea was her best one. She'd infiltrate the palace as one of the Empress's slaves. She could learn the palace's layout and listen in on the gossip to find Heru. She reached the building and circled around, ducking her head and avoiding eye contact when someone passed. She turned into a narrow alley as if she lived there. No one stopped her.

Finally she lifted her gaze, picking out the handholds and obstacles on her way to the roof. It didn't look like a difficult climb, but up five stories without the safety of a rope still risked a long fall and a broken neck.

You can do this, said Amastan.

Thana took a deep breath. She just wouldn't fall. She rubbed her palms with dirt, then reached for her first handhold. She took the first ten feet at speed; she just had to get above eye level. No one would notice her after that. People didn't tend to look up.

She paused at the bottom of the second floor for a breath. She didn't look down. Her arms burned and her shoulder throbbed by the time she swung her body up and over the lip of the roof. Sweat dripped from her elbows and stung her eyes and her heart hammered in her chest, but she'd made it. She breathed deep, hunching over the pain, then straightened and turned and faced the city.

As she'd expected—and hoped—the height lent her perspective. She could see how the roads wound and twisted below, all converging on a ribbon of blue along the city's edge. The buildings flowed like dunes, rising and falling in rippling waves. And at their center, one building loomed over the rest, its walls angling inward and upward, a skirt of green at its waist: the palace.

A laugh bubbled within her, sudden and bright, and threatened to wrench itself free. As she looked across the city toward the palace, she realized that everything she'd planned—posing as a slave, sneaking into the palace, learning its layout and rhythm—looked exactly like what Heru had accused her of just hours before. Her schemes would bring her within striking distance of the Empress herself.

It was almost a shame that the contract was for Heru instead.

16

With her head held high, Thana walked through the outer ring of the gardens that circled the palace. No one stopped her. A night of rest—and a morning of preparation—had brightened her mood considerably. The task ahead no longer seemed so daunting. She even dared to hope that she could be on her way out of the city by day's end. The mark would never see her coming.

She'd climbed down from her rooftop sanctuary before sunrise and found the market already bustling and chaotic. Without the threat of guards immediately at her back, she was able to take her time and find the things she needed. For some, like the shaving blade and the extra knives, she'd traded the gold rings on her fingers, leaving her with just her poison rings. Others, like the kohl and the clay bowl, she'd simply taken. They were small and cheap and no one would be harmed by their absence.

Locating and acquiring the right clothes turned out to be more difficult. If she'd wanted to look like any other slave in and around Na Tay Khet, she could've been ready within an hour. Unfortunately, the Empress's slaves were held to a higher standard than a plain skirt and belt.

That's why she was here, in the garden. Thick kohl lined her eyes and she wore a beige skirt that she'd snagged off a clothesline. Her bare chest and arms made her feel naked in more ways than one—she had fewer places to hide weapons. But she'd made do. The new knives were strapped to each thigh, her garrote dangled from her charm belt beneath her skirt, and her darts filled an inside pouch.

She'd used the clay bowl to shave her head, worrying a hole through her lower lip the entire time. She couldn't risk any nicks. Then she'd washed every inch of herself before applying the dye just above her ear.

The marks she'd drawn wouldn't hold against close scrutiny, but she didn't plan on letting anyone get that close. She wasn't about to have herself branded for real, contract or not, and there were a dozen other ways someone could see through her disguise before it came to that. The success of her plan lay in a quick entry and exit, the exact opposite of every other time she'd infiltrated a mark's home. There were so many things that could go wrong that if she stopped to think about them, she'd back out. So she kept moving.

Now she just needed a slave's clothing, and she needed it before anyone noticed she didn't belong here. She passed towering palms and thick bushes, vibrant flowers and twisting vines. Even though it was midafternoon, a steady breeze and the cool breath of flora made the heat bearable, almost pleasant.

Thana had circled the gardens this morning before heading out for her supplies. A group of slaves had already been on the grounds, picking fruit and tending to the plants. A master watched over them, but his reign was lax. Clearly, slaves didn't try to run here. Their distinctive branding made it difficult for any slave to hide in this city.

Low voices accompanied rustling ahead. Thana bent over a bush to hide her face just as two slaves appeared with baskets on their arms. Their voices dropped to whispers when they noticed her, but they didn't alert the master or leave. Good. Thana watched them out of the corner of her eye as they pulled scrawny tufts of green and tossed these into their baskets, already half-full with more of the same. Thana copied their movements, pretending that her basket was just around the bush, out of sight. Then she circled away from them.

Two was too risky. She needed one alone.

Thana found her prey lost in her own world and drifting further away from the others with each step. She was a head taller than Thana and but still had to stretch up on her toes to pick bright yellow fruit. She didn't turn when Thana approached but continued humming a cheerful tune. Slipping the garrote around her neck felt like cheating, but Thana didn't have time for guilt.

A few moments later the unconscious slave, wearing Thana's wrap, was safely tucked between two large bushes. Thana walked with a basket loosely hanging from her fingers and a hum in her throat, a shimmery gold wrap around her waist and wide silver bangles on each wrist. A long necklace dripping with gold and turquoise came to rest between her breasts. It felt strange to wear this much jewelry. If this was what her *slaves* had, then what did the Empress herself wear?

Traversing the gardens was almost too easy. Thana paused and busied herself with whatever plant was nearest every time another slave passed. She spotted the slave master only once, but he didn't even glance her way. He was too busy watching the clouds whisping by and scratching his thigh with a long leather whip.

The palace sulked at the center of the gardens, an immense golden building topped by an impressive dome. Gems and polished stones spilled across its surface like stars. Turquoise and broad stretches of pale glass dominated the sides, but there were also sapphires, moonstones, and emeralds, all of them circling each other in glittering whorls.

Gold-covered pillars stood out front, inscribed with images dense and prolific and bleeding colorful paint. The whole of it hurt Thana's eyes. She passed broad, shallow pools that had been coated with gold and shone as painful as the sun. She passed carefully sculpted trees and towering cages full of vibrant, flitting and screaming birds. She passed more birds stalking the gardens uncaged, their long tails dragging uselessly across the grass, their puffed chests turquoise blue.

Despite the many temptations, Thana took care not to stare. Between the riot of color and the overwhelming displays of wealth was an unobtrusive, dark wooden door. A slave had just stepped out from that door and now closed it behind him. His gaze briefly met hers, then Thana was brushing past him and opening the door and stepping inside before he could try to stop her or say anything.

Just like that, she was in the palace.

She paused long enough for her eyes to adjust to the sudden gloom, then traded the green things in her basket for a handful of towels from the nearby shelf and continued down a narrow corridor. Her heart hammered and her nerves were on fire as she waited for someone to catch her out, to stop her, to challenge her. She was distinctly aware of each and every sound, every cough, every footstep, every brush of cloth from a passing slave, of the glass charms around her waist, the metal blades against her thighs, and the garrote's wooden handles tap-tapping her hip.

But she made it a step, and then another, and then another, without challenge. Torches lit the way, but blue light also drifted languorously from above, through squares high in the ceiling. The stone under her bare feet was cool, worn smooth by the passing of many others over many years. The walls were plain but for the occasional symbol that marked another hallway or door.

She pressed on, past washing and sleeping rooms, rooms where slaves pounded grain into flour, and rooms where slaves worked at towering looms, their shuttles clack-clacking in a familiar rhythm. Still, no one tried to stop her, or even talk to her. No one even looked at her twice. She was little more than a wild jaani, drifting unseen through the palace.

Eventually, the corridor spat her out into a courtyard. Now other people, some clearly important with their rich cloth and glittering gold, others more ambiguously dressed, joined the slaves. Their movements were at first chaotic, but Thana soon determined an order. While some drifted aimlessly, most moved toward the northern end of the courtyard and through a towering, ornate doorway. She'd bet her garrote that the Empress was somewhere on the other side.

But she wasn't here to find the Empress. Directly across from her was another entrance, less grandiose but equally impressive. Above the doorway arched paintings of people holding writing instruments and scrolls, some sitting at desks while others stood before long shelves. Altogether, the paintings gave her a pretty good idea of what was through that archway.

Despite her father's efforts, Thana had little but disdain for libraries. Nothing important and pertinent to life was ever found in one, just dusty scrolls about such-and-such drum chief and so-and-so's dispute. Thana had never found any information she could use in an old scroll. Everything she'd learned was either from her mother or through personal experience. Information needed to be able to change to fit its time and circumstances, something a scroll could never do. Libraries were unwieldy and static things, prone to hoarding only the stale ideas of the wealthy and stupid.

In essence, the perfect place for someone like Heru.

"Slave."

Thana twisted toward the voice. It belonged to an older man in flashy jewelry and a fine white skirt. Her heart sped back up; she'd been standing and staring for too long, she'd made a scene, it was obvious she didn't belong, he was going to order her to the other side of the palace, he was going to call the guards, he—

Thana swallowed and shut down her racing thoughts. She was fine. She belonged here. This was all perfectly normal. She lifted her gaze to his face, but didn't make eye contact.

"Senousert requested an assistant for the afternoon." The man looked her up and down, kohl making his already long eyebrows look like wings. "You look like you'd do for whatever the head librarian has in mind." He made a shooing motion toward the library. "Go."

Still processing the man's words, Thana headed for the library. The head librarian. Of all people—Thana brushed a hand across her hidden glass charms, muttering a silent prayer. Finally, a little luck.

The library was just as dark and stuffy as she'd expected. Ghadid had a handful of smaller libraries, most of which were hidden away in the private homes of wealthy merchants and drum chiefs. Her own father kept histories and records in their home, but that was different. She knew some of what to expect—the muffled silence, the musty air, the stench of old skins, the rasp of dry paper—but was unprepared for the sheer volume of it all.

The ceiling soared away and above. Cases stuffed with scrolls stretched in every direction. She stopped for a whole heartbeat just to take it in. Her chest tightened. Amastan should have been here. He'd helped her father with his histories and appreciated knowledge for knowledge's sake, no matter how old or outdated it was. In another life, Amastan would have worked here.

Thana scanned the shelves for any indication of where she should go. The floor rose up by a step a dozen shelves back, and again a dozen more. She headed for that step, passing solemn-faced people sitting on stools or the floor. Amusement and curiosity flickered freely across their faces as she passed, as open to the world as the scrolls they were reading. If she stayed in Na Tay Khet much longer, she might get used to seeing so many men uncovered. But for now, she had to fight the urge to avert her eyes.

Raised voices came from her right. No one had claimed her yet, so she turned to investigate. Tables were scattered liberally between the rows, most either completely empty or with a single individual perched at one end, a scroll or two at their elbow. One table, though, was overflowing with scrolls. On one side was a messy pile of half-open scrolls. On the other, a waiting tower of scrolls still tightly bound with string. Between sat a man in a white skirt, leaning back as he tilted an unrolled scroll toward the light.

The glass charms thrummed and warmed a warning Thana didn't need. She'd already recognized Heru, even with his back to her. Opposite him sat a woman, her elbows on the table and her forehead cupped in one palm as she pored over a scroll. Mo had found a red cloth to tie the braids back out of her face, a single splash of vibrance in an otherwise dull place. The sight of the healer, safe and whole and sane, made Thana's breath catch in her throat, then release with a silent, relieved laugh. Mo was alive. Mo was *fine*.

The tension that had tightened Thana's body from brow to toes for the past twenty-some hours finally released. She'd infiltrated the palace and found her mark, all in less than a day. She wasn't sure if even the Serpent of Ghadid could have done *this*. Now it was only a matter of waiting for an opportunity—or creating one herself.

Her gaze lingered on Mo a moment longer, taking in her furrowed brows, her smooth, water-drunk skin, the rise and fall of her chest, and her crisp, clean blue wrap, still worn high across her shoulders and throat. At least she'd been taken care of. Then her gaze snapped to the back of Heru's head and anger welled like blood in a fresh wound. How dare he—

"*There* you are."

A hand touched Thana's shoulder. Her own hand rose to slap it away, but she remembered herself in time and let her hand drop. The man was as old as dust itself and bent with time, his hair a half-forgotten wisp atop his head and his skin, almost as dark as hers, dotted with spots. Yet his eyes were still bright. He focused on her with an intensity that threatened to discover all of her secrets. Thana met that gaze with no small amount of effort.

"Are you all they could find for me? A *slave*?" said the man. This must be Senousert, Thana realized. "I asked for a competent and trained servant. I know they all assume I'm just a walking corpse, but you'd think they'd at least have some respect for her Imperial Highness's foremost madman." Senousert made a dry spitting noise.

Thana glanced at Heru to see if he'd overheard, but the mark was too engrossed in his research. Senousert followed her gaze and rolled his eyes upward as if appealing to the ceiling—or G-d.

"Oh, he won't hear me," said Senousert. "And even if he did, he wouldn't know an insult if it bit him between the nostrils. That man is as dense as spring mud. I simply don't understand how her Imperial Highness puts up with him. Clearly she possesses a great deal more patience than us lowly beings."

Senousert dropped his hands and some of the indignant spark went out of him. "But what am I going on about? There's so much to *do* and this pompous man is taking up all my time. I need you to clean up the stacks—you do know how to follow the basic organizing standards and read, don't you?"

Thana could read, but she didn't know the second thing about library organization. Her father had never bothered. She nodded anyway.

"Good. Go see Aohti over in the third tier. She'll get you caught up."

"Hey—librarian!"

Senousert pivoted, his hands clasped in front of him and his expression instantly subservient. "Yes, my master?"

As Heru barked out his request, Thana headed deeper into the library before he could notice her. She knew where both Mo and Heru were now, and they wouldn't be going anywhere soon. Hopefully whatever Senousert wanted her to do would let her keep an eye on them both. From the look of that stack of scrolls, she had some time to figure out phase two of her plan.

Unfortunately, her mark had picked the worst possible place to be killed. It was a little too quiet, a little too public, with no opportunity for distractions or chaos. Plus, Mo was at his side. Many of Thana's usual methods wouldn't work here.

Normally she'd pick poison, but although she had her darts, Heru had the box that contained her poison. She still had her knives and garrote, but those were for a quieter, more intimate scenario. At least she'd made it into the palace. It couldn't hurt to wait and watch for a better opportunity.

Heru had to sleep sometime. She'd just make sure he didn't wake up.

17

By the time the sun had set and slaves walked the aisles with glass lamps swinging from their arms, Thana was drowsy with boredom from stacking and sorting scrolls. Aohti had proven to be a tiresome young woman with an unfortunate attention to details—like where Thana was and what she was doing at all times. She'd only been able to sneak away once to check on Heru.

Thankfully, the mark didn't appear to be going anywhere. If anything, his stack of unread scrolls had only grown taller.

Thana was placing scrolls on a nearby shelf when a slave approached Heru with a wax-sealed letter. Heru took the letter and tossed it aside, unopened. Mo reached across, plucked it off the table, and popped the wax seal with her nail. She read the letter, her lips moving silently, and then she shoved the paper at Heru.

"It's from the Empress."

Heru looked up from his scribbling long enough to scan the letter. "We're not done here yet."

Mo frowned. "This is the *second* letter she's sent us. Shouldn't we respond?"

Thana reached for the top of the shelf just behind them, her fingers brushing and brushing again across the top stack of scrolls. She prayed for Aohti to stay away a little longer. She needed to hear this.

A second slave arrived a few minutes later, bearing another letter. Thana peered around the side of the shelf. This time Mo took the square of vellum from the slave and slapped it open on the wooden table. She traced the words with one finger. Then she stood.

"She knows you very well, your Empress," said Mo. "We should go."

Heru pulled the glass lamp closer and held the letter in its light. "I think she's threatening me."

"I'm fairly certain she is."

"Doesn't she understand the importance of the work I'm doing?" He cast the letter aside with no small amount of disdain. "We don't have time for this."

"I—but she's the Empress."

Thana pushed one of the scrolls out of reach. She let out a soft curse for anyone watching and grabbed a nearby stool. Standing on it, she could see over the top of the shelf.

"Fine." Mo's voice was tight with annoyance. Her fingers shook as she snatched and rolled up the scrolls she'd been reading. "I'll go and report for you."

"And have you misrepresent my research to the Empress? I think not."

Heru gathered half a dozen scrolls and stood. He cast around and his gaze snagged on Thana's over the top of the shelf before she could duck. He pointed a finger at her and suddenly she was back in Ghadid, standing in a dark room with an unconscious woman at her feet and a groggy Heru before her, the glass beads at her neck searing her skin.

But the charms at her waist remained the same tepid warmth they'd been since she'd entered the library.

"You," said Heru. "Get down here and help us carry these scrolls."

Thana obeyed, dropping out of sight before Heru could get a better look. Her heart raced from the moment of relived memory, the acrid terror of that night fresh on her tongue. She checked her skirt and ran a light hand across her shaved head, hoping that Mo wouldn't recognize her. She didn't worry that Heru would. Like with the Azal, he didn't look twice at slaves, and she'd disappeared from his world the moment the guards dragged her out of sight.

She didn't need to worry about Mo. The healer kept her gaze averted, her dark cheeks somehow even darker. It took a moment for Thana to realize that Mo was embarrassed by Thana's naked-ness. A smile tugged on the corners of Thana's lips. While she'd been forced to accept Na Tay Khet's strange fashion, Mo had been safely ensconced in the library, far from the markets and streets where such display was commonplace.

Heru began dumping scrolls into Thana's basket. He loaded her down with more scrolls than could possibly be necessary, then added the scrolls of his own notes. By the time Heru strode from the library, Thana's basket was precariously full and she carried even more scrolls tucked under her arms.

"Hey!"

Aohti bounded up to them, her youthful face full of self-conscious concern. She skidded to a stop in front of Heru and immediately wilted, losing half a head in height. She swallowed and forced her chin up.

"That's my slave—and those're the library's scrolls—and you can't just walk out of here with them—there are *procedures*—"

"I can do whatever I like with these scrolls and these slaves," said Heru, voice tight with impatience. "Now, get out of my way. I have to attend to the Empress. Or did you forget that I'm her second advisory marabi? I could have you drafted as one of my assistants if you continue to impede me."

"Aohti!"

Senousert shuffled toward them, the few remaining hairs on top of his head wild with the effort. "Let him go," he said, out of breath. He stopped and put a hand on a nearby stack to steady himself. "Sametket-sai may of course do whatever he wishes while he's our guest."

"But those are very old, very fragile scrolls that need to remain here and be handled with great care—" began Aohti.

The head librarian lifted his foot and set it on Aohti's big toe. She cut off with a yelp. Senousert turned his smile on Heru, but the en-marabi was already shoving past them both.

For a moment, Senousert's gaze fell on Thana and his smile cracked and worry leaked through. He looked from her to Heru and back again, eyebrows going up, then together, as if asking a question she should know the answer to. Thana could only shrug, almost losing a scroll in the gesture.

"Such a pity," said Senousert as Thana passed him. "That was a very helpful slave. She will be missed."

"Better her than me," grumbled Aohti.

The words floated after Thana and out the door into the still bright evening. She shifted her grip on the basket and risked losing a scroll to slip a hand into her pocket and feel the reassuring metal wire of her garrote. She couldn't kill the mark before or during his meeting with the Empress, but after . . .

Now that Heru had decided to make his appearance, he trotted across the courtyard with energy and purpose. Thana barely had time to register the towering gates and the gold coating every surface before they marched inside a long, broad corridor. At its end, Heru pushed through a pair of towering wooden doors.

They burst into a chamber so large, they might as well have stepped outside. The ceiling stretched up and away. Leftover daylight trickled through layers of drifting dust to mingle with the torchlight below. A haze fuzzed the highest reaches of the ceiling. Thana thought she saw stars, but surely that was a trick of distance.

Every inch of the room was painted or filigreed or stained gold. And etched into the gold were scenes painted black. Figures speared other figures and left them in pools of black paint. One whole section of wall was devoted to a sprawling battlefield littered with spear-struck, armless, or beheaded figures. Between the bodies crawled crocodiles, their body-crunching teeth fitted with diamonds and their eyes alive with rubies. They were demons come to drag away the defeated while the winning army advanced. Similar scenes marched around the room: the whole history of these people, or what they wanted their history to be.

Mercifully, Thana didn't have the time to examine the art—if it could be called that—for the mark's pace was swift and the room's far end demanded her immediate attention. A whole host of people waited there, hushed and still as statues. A dozen torches and a dozen tall mirrors spotlighted the crowd. Gemstones glittered and metal sparked under the light, but despite the opulence, the air was stale and still.

A fleet of guards stood before the host, their breastplates polished to a painful shine and the white of their wraps as fine as salt. They stood as straight and rigid as the spears clutched at their sides. Behind the guards stood people in skirts stained the color of fresh blood, the fabric dragging across the floor despite dozens of knots. Some held staffs, some incense burners, and others carried rolls of parchment. While their faces were uncovered by fabric, they were hidden beneath thick whorls and loops of kohl—either writing or pretty nonsense. These must be the Empress's marab.

More people were scattered between the marab and a high dais, their clothing varied but equally fine and abundant, their

features lined with kohl and their arms jangling with gold.
Slaves ghosted between them, filling a glass here, handing a note
there, their gold skirts helping them blend in with the riches on
display. But all of the glitter and gilding paled before the golden
chair on the dais and the woman who sat there.

The Empress Zara ha Khatet of the Mehewret Empire watched
over her court, back straight, eyes set deep in a wash of kohl. She
wore a dazzling white-gold headdress that covered her hair and
spilled over her shoulders. A gold diadem spattered with turquoise, emeralds, and sapphires sat on her brow. In the diadem's
center reared a stylized crocodile, its long snout bursting with
diamond teeth.

A wrap that could've been spun from pure gold covered the
Empress's shoulders and chest. Fine white needlework decorated
its edges and a belt cinched her waist. Gold jewelry so covered
her arms from her biceps down to her fingers that it was difficult
to pinpoint the shade of her skin. But beneath the thick kohl
around her eyes and the vermillion painted across her lips, the
Empress's natural beauty still shone. Standing in the Empress's
presence, Thana felt an urge to do or say anything that Zara ha
Khatet might ask. She swallowed the impulse; Amastan liked to
tease her for her weakness before beauty, but this felt different.
Like a compulsion.

Was this what it was like to be in the presence of such complete and absolute power? This *was* the Empress, and while
Thana might not like or accept her authority, that didn't negate
the fact that this woman was the most powerful person in the
known world. Anything Zara ha Khatet did or said became law.
The Empress could have any or all of them raised to drum chiefs
or beheaded on a whim.

As they approached the dais, the soldiers parted, then the
marab, leaving no one to stop Heru from walking all the way

up to the Empress's throne. Thana lagged behind as far as she dared, hoping to remain unnoticed. Heru finally stopped when the Empress raised a hand, the bracelets on her arm jangling a melody.

The mark bowed. Mo and Thana followed his lead. When the Empress waved her hand, he straightened. After the jangle of her bracelets had faded, the Empress spoke.

"Heru Sametket. You returned over a night ago and yet this is the first time you've deigned to answer our summons. What terrifically dire task have you deemed important enough to keep you from our presence?"

"Research, your Imperial Highness."

The Empress and her court waited for two whole heartbeats, but Heru didn't elaborate. The Empress's eye twitched.

"What . . . kind of research?" prompted a marabi, his voice nervous and high.

"The important kind." Heru sniffed. "Look, your Imperial Highness—"

"Silence," snapped the Empress. "Too often we have tolerated your indolence and your particularly childish need to hoard unimportant secrets like a miserable sand flea hoards water. Clearly this has led you to forget your place. Nearly a moon ago we sent you to that dust-covered hovel to begin negotiations—a mission that should've taken you at least a further moon to complete—and yet, here you are. Not only did you return early, you didn't report to us first and, further, you had the audacity to refuse our summons.

"We would not have suffered even the first insult from any lesser fool, but seeing as how we've granted similar liberties in the past, we were willing to let it be washed downriver. But a second—and *third*—insult is both unspeakable and unforgivable, even for our preeminent fool. You are walking a very fine line here, Sametket. If the next words out of your mouth do not fully and thoroughly explain your actions, we will personally introduce you and your foreign assistants to our imperial executioner."

Fear bit into Thana's confidence. The Empress had said *assistants*, plural. She couldn't have meant Thana. But who else—?

The Empress sagged back in her throne, as if all of that rage had burned too hot and left her hollowed out. Heru, for once, appeared uncertain. He shifted from foot to foot as he weighed his words. When he finally spoke, it was with none of the aloof impertinence he'd exuded earlier.

"I'm honored that your Imperial Highness has shown such restraint and benevolence," said Heru, carefully picking across his words as if they were hot rocks in a fire. "She knows that my work is of the utmost importance and also the utmost secrecy. I am loath to say that my mission in Ghadid was waylaid by a more pressing and dangerous issue that has come to my attention, but that's the truth. I am also hesitant to speak any more on such a delicate matter in the presence of so many ears."

The Empress raised one kohl-lined eyebrow. "If it's private council that you desire, then simply ask." She made a shooing motion toward the crowd. "Leave us. We'll summon you again when we have need of you. Atrex—tell him to stay."

One of the marab made a noise deep in her throat, but the others ducked their heads and started filing out. Within a few moments, it was just the three of them, the Empress, and a single guard whose white skirt was lined with black. A man all in silver had taken the guard aside before leaving and made several small hand gestures.

"What about him?" asked Heru, indicating the guard.

The Empress shook her head. "Atrex is deaf and never learned how to read lips. He can also cleave a man's head from his shoulders with a single swing of his sword. He stays. But what about your assistants?"

"She's a healer," said Heru. "She was with me when these terrible things first transpired. She can corroborate my story and fill in any details I might neglect. She is essential." He gestured to Thana without turning. "This other is Senousert's slave. She is carrying my research."

The Empress tilted her head, her earrings swinging with the motion. "That's not one of Senousert's slaves."

Thana's breath caught in her throat. She forced herself to breathe as she put on a mask of confusion and glanced from the Empress to Heru. It would be normal for a slave to be alarmed. But she didn't try to defend herself; a drum chief wouldn't let a slave speak without permission, so surely the Empress wouldn't either.

"Aohti's slave, then. She was in the library," said Heru, as if that explained everything.

Although Heru was no longer looking her way, Mo had turned toward her. Thana made the mistake of meeting Mo's gaze. Mo took a sharp breath, then quickly turned away, her fingers tightening around the wooden stake she was still carrying. As if the bound might attack them even here.

The Empress made a circular motion with two fingers, then pointed at Thana. Before she could react, the guard Atrex had shoved between Heru and Mo and grabbed Thana by her arm. He brought the blade of his sword to rest against her neck and pressed hard enough to cut through the first layer of skin. Thana hardly dared breathe.

"Your brand is incorrect and your skirt isn't knotted in the right places. You're not one of our slaves." The Empress waved her hand as if swatting a fly. "Behead her. We'll have the slaves clean up the mess later."

18

"No!"

Mo moved first, raising her makeshift staff as terror flashed across her face. The Empress lifted her palm. The deaf Atrex and his sword didn't move.

"What's this? You allow your slave to make such outbursts, Sametket?"

"She's not his slave!" said Thana, despite the blade pressing against her neck.

Heru half nodded, half shrugged. "She accompanied me from Ghadid, that is true."

"And this other?"

Thana's stomach dropped as she met Heru's gaze. He'd sold her out before, when he'd had little to lose. Now that he was in Na Tay Khet in the presence of his precious Empress, what would he do? Thana could see the words that spelled her death forming on his lips: *spy, liar, assassin.* In another moment, Atrex's sword would separate her head from her body and it'd all be over. Everything she'd done, everything she'd endured, just to become a headless corpse far from home.

"The same, in a fashion," sasid Heru. "If you must, I would prefer if you didn't behead her here. There will be quite a lot of blood and I've already had my sandals cleaned once since arriving."

Thana watched the Empress, waiting for the signal that would end her life. Then her mind wrapped around Heru's words and she turned her stare on him.

The Empress frowned. "You know this slave?"

Heru measured Thana again with his gaze and she could all but see the calculations behind his eyes. He was summing up every ounce that she could give him and deciding whether or not she was worth keeping around, alive. He'd already made clear that to him she was a resource, a pawn—not a person. But then Mo began to speak and his gaze slid to the healer and sharpened.

"She came with us, mai," said Mo. "Please don't kill her. She was there when the—the thing happened. Tell her, Heru."

Heru nodded to himself, as if he'd just decided something, then he straightened and met his Empress's gaze. "She might have additional insight into the problem. Perhaps you should put off executing her until we've extracted that knowledge."

The Empress touched a finger to her forehead. "If she came with you, then why does she wear the clothes of an Imperial slave, if poorly?"

"The three of us traveled to Na Tay Khet together from Ghadid, your Imperial Highness," said Thana. "We were separated at the city gates."

"And why was that?"

"A misunderstanding, mai."

The Empress's finger slid up until her whole palm rested against her forehead. "That still doesn't explain your presence in our library, pretending to be a slave."

"I was trying to catch up, mai."

The Empress stared at her for long enough to become uncomfortable, but Thana didn't flinch. She didn't dare; the guard's blade still hadn't moved. "A normal person might have sent word through our stewards at the front of our palace."

"Yes, well," said Thana. "A normal person would've had to

wait days for an answer, and even then been refused admittance. As a foreigner with neither name nor station, I wouldn't have been granted even that. By the time I'd received an answer, Heru and Mo would've been long gone. Which, considering the circumstances and the danger we're all in, would've been less than ideal, mai."

The Empress stared at Thana, not a single muscle moving. If it weren't for the steady rise and fall of her chest, Thana might've suspected Heru of something. As it was, Thana fought to hide her unease.

After almost a full minute had passed—Thana had counted her own heartbeats, loud and demanding in her ears—a twitch of the lips broke the Empress's blank expression. Then she leaned forward, her hands clutching the arms of the chair, and laughed. The sound was deep, almost guttural, and completely unexpected from such a slight figure. The Empress's laughter echoed throughout the throne room, redoubling on itself and twisting into something sinister.

Thana turned her head just enough to avoid cutting herself on Atrex's blade to exchange a confused glance with Mo, then tried to catch Heru's reaction. The thunderstruck en-marabi couldn't look away from his Empress. Her laughter thinned until it was only a wet hiccupping that she smothered with the back of one hand.

The Empress took a few deep breaths before straightening, her face once again an impassive mask. "We should have you executed for such impertinence. But it looks like this will make twice in a single day that we've exercised clemency against our own better judgment. Such willful disregard for authority is dangerous, but you are clearly ignorant of our customs. We hope you won't be among us long enough to create a real problem."

She pointed to Thana, then opened her palm and dropped her

hand. Atrex removed his blade and stepped back. Thana sagged to the floor. She took a moment to gather herself, then forced her shaking legs to hold her and faced the Empress with her head high.

"We have danced enough around the subject of our conversation," said the Empress, addressing Heru. "Tell us—what was so important that you came running back here without bothering to shake the fleas off first?"

"Someone is trying to kill me," said Heru.

Thana stiffened, but the Empress only waved a hand. "Correct us if we're wrong, but isn't someone *always* trying to kill you?"

"Yes, but this time the method troubles me," said Heru. "This was no unimaginative assassination attempt by some snot-nosed kid. This was something far more disturbing—a marabi of my own training, only significantly advanced." The fingers on Heru's hand curled into a fist and pressed hard against his thigh. "He has accomplished things of which I've only dreamed."

"Maybe we should bring him on," said the Empress. At Heru's full-body twitch, she raised an appeasing hand. "Only a joke, Sametket. Now, start from the beginning, when you first realized something was amiss."

Heru lowered his head, gathering his thoughts. When he spoke, his words were clear and precise. He outlined the first and subsequent attacks with methodical and impersonal language, never once attaching even a hint of emotion to the events, as if they'd happened to someone else entirely. He left out Thana's own involvement in his room at the inn, weaving her appearance in later when he attended the healers a second time. He described the writing on the backs of the dead in great detail, then explained his own realization of what—or who— that meant.

His account of their time with the caravan was clipped and

short, focusing heavily on their brief encounter with Djet himself. Then he skipped ahead to his research in the library. As he did, he grabbed a scroll from the middle of the pile Thana was holding and flicked it open.

"So far, I've only found a handful of secondary resources and one primary in my research, but even the small amount I've uncovered is enough to warrant the Empire's attention. The creature we met in the desert called itself Djet. I knew I'd read that name in my studies before. And I was right." Heru gestured at the scroll he held. "Djet Khentawpet was head marabi to King To of the first united dynasty, over three centuries ago. During his decade-long career, he became known for his obsession with immortality, and he was the first marabi to make use of the palace's lower wing for his research. He conducted experiments to determine the exact properties and constraints of a jaani in relation to its body and natural forces, like death.

"His groundbreaking research significantly expanded our knowledge of the jaan and advanced our ability to heal and quiet the possessed. It was also profoundly unpopular and eventually became the root of his undoing. Unfortunately, this occurred around the same time as the Great Division, when the First Priest to G-d declared any form of jaan coercion—at least, beyond the quieting of the possessed—anathema to G-d's will. The Priest coined the term en-marab for those who dared question him. His singular and narrow-minded understanding of the world led to the persecution of many great men.

"Djet's research placed him firmly among these en-marab. When the First Priest became aware of his impressive discoveries, King To was forced to charge Djet with high treason for crimes against G-d. Djet was convicted, beheaded, and his body divided into many pieces, each of which was burnt, the ashes buried throughout the kingdom."

"Did his research warrant such a reaction?" asked the Empress, eyes bright.

"Considering he worked to discover a way to rebind the jaani after the death of its body without risking insanity, thereby achieving a kind of immortality—I think not. His purpose was noble. King To was under a great deal of pressure from the First Priest, whose power at that time nearly rivaled his own. But then again, Djet might have been imprisoned like other designated en-marab of his time instead of so thoroughly executed if it weren't for the number of peasants that perished during his research. While Djet understood the theory of binding jaan, he had difficulties translating it into practice."

"What, exactly, was he doing?"

"The accounts vary, of course, and some of them are clearly sensationalized—"

The Empress waved her hand. "We don't need a discussion on historical accuracy right now. We trust your conclusions are sufficient."

Heru rolled up the scroll, shoved it back into Thana's pile, and grabbed another. He held it up for the Empress. "According to the historian Shedou, who was only a few decades removed from the occurrences, and therefore most likely to have written an accurate representation of what happened, Djet first tried to bind the jaan of peasants. When that failed, he realized that he couldn't bind a man's own jaani to his body—doing so would upset the fine balance between the two. He bound a wild jaani instead, which proved more successful. Unfortunately, since he first had to separate the peasants' jaan, their bodies failed, leaving him with an animated husk.

"Through much trial and error, he discovered that the bound jaan responded to written, physical commands. This led him to develop his particular script, the one we found on the backs of his men. Unfortunately, the creatures that resulted from these written bindings, the bound, were still devoid of independent thought, of real *life*, and their bodies, if left alone, withered away to dust."

"How did Djet solve that problem?" asked the Empress.

Heru snapped open a new scroll and pointed at a section entirely composed of symbols and numbers. "Jaan are dumb, wild things with little lingering energy for the purpose of sustaining life—that energy comes from the body. Djet needed to find a way to fill the role that the body served before it was severed from its jaani. But as far as he could calculate, there was no way to reanimate the body itself. He'd stumbled upon a seemingly unsolvable paradox: to achieve immortality, he had to bind his jaani. But to bind his own jaani, he had to first sever it, and doing so would kill him. An outside, self-sustaining source of energy was required to avert disaster." He looked up, locking gazes with the Empress. "Djet concluded that only a sajaami has anywhere near the kind of energy needed."

The Empress was leaning forward now, her hands curled around the arms of her throne, her knuckles gone pale. "But the sajaam are a myth," she said and her words were smooth, as if she'd said them a hundred times before.

"Djet didn't think so," said Heru. "He was absorbed with finding them at the time of his unfortunate demise. His work was left unfinished, but there were rumors that he hid his notes somewhere in the palace."

"Perhaps he was not so unsuccessful," said the Empress. "He appears to have returned to haunt us."

Heru nodded. "It's possible that he discovered the whereabouts of the sajaam before his execution, yes. But he wouldn't still be seeking to refine his methods if that were the case. I hypothesize that he found another way to cling to life and now he is searching for the sajaam to assure his immortality. Our only way of stopping him is to find the sajaam first."

The Empress propped her chin on a fist. "What does he want with *you*, though?"

"Obviously he is afraid of my superior intellect."

Thana snorted, but the Empress only shook her head. "That doesn't explain why he made you aware of his presence by attacking you first."

"He wants Heru dead because marab can unbind jaan, mai," said Mo. Heru and the Empress both stared at Mo. The healer shrugged uncomfortably. "If binding a jaani to himself is a necessary step toward immortality, then it follows that unbinding the jaani would be one way to stop him." She puffed out her cheeks, then added in a mutter, "It seemed obvious to me."

"But any marabi can unbind jaan," pointed out the Empress.

"Not every marabi is as well acquainted with Djet's particular research as I am," said Heru. "I am a unique threat and the only one who can stop Djet from achieving his goal. Nevertheless, I sent requests out to my colleagues as soon as I arrived in the city, asking those who might be qualified to lend their assistance. I've yet to hear back from any of them."

The Empress's eyes narrowed. "You sent word to your *colleagues* before you deigned to answer *us*?"

"It was important." Heru waved away the question like a persistent fly. "And it leads me to ask: where is Tamit? He wasn't amongst your court and he didn't answer my query."

"The first advisory marabi is away on business."

Heru's lips pressed into a thin, pale line. "Well. It does not matter." He gestured at Mo. "The girl is correct. Unbinding Djet's jaani will disrupt his plan for immortality. But I cannot be certain this tactic would work after he's bound a sajaami. Therefore it is of the utmost importance we find the sajaam before he does."

"We are confident that you will find them, Sametket," said the Empress. "But let us make certain we understand all of this. The creatures of a man who died centuries ago are menacing you. This man, once a skilled marabi like yourself, sought immortality during his lifetime—and apparently, beyond. He's discovered a way to bind his own jaani to his body, but without another ritual or source of power, his body will degrade and fail him. It's this source of power he seeks now, which you believe to be the sajaam of old stories. And you have found those sajaam."

"Correct," said Heru. "Except I've yet to find the sajaam. I have my suspicions, but it'll take further research before I can confirm anything actionable. Moreover, there's a separate danger inherent in not only discovering the location of the sajaam, but in their subsequent release. If the histories are accurate, then the sajaam were sealed for a very good reason—they are monstrous and destructive. At the time of their sealing, they were intent on wiping humans from the face of the world. Djet may believe he's all powerful, but it took many marab to restrain the sajaam once. We can't risk him releasing them again."

"But if you find the sajaam first, you can stop him," said the Empress. "Do that and you don't need to worry about sealing them again. We'd rather you focus your efforts on searching for and securing these sajaam."

"For that, I'll require full library privileges and absolutely no interruptions, your Imperial Highness."

"Of course. What a boon we have in you, Sametket. It was quite fortuitous that you didn't meet with a bad end on your journey. That would have been a shame." Her lips quirked in the briefest of smiles, there and gone in a heartbeat. "For the safety and security of the Empire, you must find the sajaam as soon as possible. Anything else you can discover about Djet's research, any further rituals he must perform before he can achieve his goals, even the location of his notes—find these things and report back."

"If I may ask permission to bring in all of my assistants to work on this—"

The Empress flicked one of her bracelets, interrupting Heru with a metallic *ping*. "You underestimate your strengths, Samet-ket. You are an incredibly powerful and resourceful marabi, other-wise you wouldn't have risen to such standing in our court. You were prudent to ask for a private conversation with us regarding this delicate matter. For now, we'd prefer to keep word of these unfortunate events out of the public discourse to avoid unduly worrying the common people. The less who know, the better. We trust you can handle the rest of the research on your own."

"Of course." Heru stood a little taller, talking over Mo's noise of protest. "I am more than capable. Do not fear, your Imperial Highness. This task is in the most competent hands."

"Be sure that it is," said the Empress. "And please, for the love of ourself and G-d, do not return with another, more press-ing problem after this. We don't have infinite patience. You are dismissed."

19

Mo waited until they'd left the throne room, passed the mob of marab and guards and sycophants outside, walked the long corridor, stepped into the thick night air, been intercepted by Senousert, been escorted to their own private suite in the library, and firmly closed the door before breaking her tight-lipped silence.

"*What*," said Mo, rounding on Thana, "in G-d's name, was *that*?"

"That was an audience before her Imperial Highness," said Heru. His back was to them as he shuffled and organized the scrolls on a long table.

"I wasn't asking you—wait, no, yes I *am*." Mo pointed at Heru, then Thana. "*You* were carted off by guards and accused of treason. And *you*"—she turned her finger back to Heru— "accused her. Now she's here, dressed as a *slave* of all things and the person *you* accused her of wanting to kill just laughed it off! I just—I don't—*what's going on?*"

Mo's face was flushed, her breathing uneven. A braid had come loose from that red ribbon, one of the few with a salas. Thana shoved down the urge to reach out and carefully tuck the braid back into place.

"Obviously, I didn't try to kill the Empress," said Thana.

"You were found out."

"Only because I wanted to be."

"She wasn't there to kill the Empress," said Heru, his back still turned.

"Then why did you *say* she was!"

Heru finally glanced back, annoyance creasing his brow. "I have my reasons. I don't have to explain everything to you. The girl needed an opportunity to explore Na Tay Khet on her own, free of my . . . influence. So I gave her one. And now she owes me." He loudly rustled the scrolls to indicate he was done with their conversation.

Mo let out a long, constricted groan. "I just don't understand what's going on between you two."

Thana smothered a smile. "I don't think I do, either," she said. "But I can assure you, I didn't come to Na Tay Khet to kill anyone." That much was true—she'd joined the *caravan* to kill Heru, but he was supposed to have been dead long before she reached the city. Now? She needed time to think. Heru's little history lesson for the Empress had shattered the remainder of her plans—that, and having her cover exposed.

Heru grunted, but didn't contribute. For some unfathomable reason, he'd decided to keep her secret. She'd expected Heru to rat her out a hundred times over as they'd left the Empress and returned to the library. He'd had every chance. And yet—he hadn't. Was this research, this problem more important to Heru than revenge? It didn't add up.

Then she remembered the way Heru had looked at Mo back in the Empress's chamber. He'd been perfectly fine having Thana dragged away by guards, but he must have decided that letting the Empress behead her in front of the healer would cost him any of her misplaced loyalty. It wasn't the research at all. He wanted something from Mo.

"So—what have you two been doing?" she asked, not wanting

to think about the implications of Heru's change of heart just yet. "Just hanging out with all these scrolls?"

Mo's expression softened. She turned to the table. "Heru brought us straight here. *He* hasn't slept, but I pestered Aohti until she found a bed for me." She yawned at the thought, one hand fluttering in front of her mouth as if she could contain her exhaustion. She set her makeshift staff on the table and waved her other hand at Thana. "And could you *please* cover yourself up already. You can stop pretending you're a slave."

"Ah. Right."

Thana reached down before remembering she'd traded her old wrap for a real slave skirt. There was no way the small scrap of fabric would cover her whole body. She looked at her feet, unable to meet Mo's gaze, her own cheeks warming with embarrassment.

"I—uh—don't have anything else to wear."

"By all that's holy and not," fumed Heru. "Would you two shut up and help me with this research? In case you don't remember, Djet's somewhere out there right now and every second we waste is another second he gains. I cannot—I *will* not—let him find the sajaam first."

Thana didn't look up, but she heard the rustle of fabric as Mo took a seat. Mo's words had left her feeling exposed and foolish. The dyed tattoo on her forehead, the shaved head, the ridiculous bangles, and the kohl-painted eyes no longer felt like a second skin, but a costume she itched to tear off.

"What are we looking for?" she asked, trying to ignore her self-conscious unease. "What are sajaam?"

Heru gave her a look thickened with disdain, but Mo pursed her lips. "You don't know?"

Thana waved a hand. "I know a little, but I don't understand why Djet wants them. They're just powerful jaan, aren't they?"

Heru held up a finger. "Not 'just.' Wild jaan are the untethered souls of those people who haven't yet crossed over, mere fragments of the potential they possessed while alive. Sajaam were the jaan of people with a great deal more potential—often powerful marab, but occasionally healers and lesser. Much like the guul, these jaan grew stronger in the wilds of the desert instead of wearing away to nothing. They developed their own sentience, of a sort, and some historians will claim they even named themselves the Sajaam. All agree that they became their own race, separate from both humans and jaan. They could reason, they could think, they could even plan.

"The Sajaam built their own society. They believed they were superior to those still bound to flesh. Some sajaam even believed they were more powerful than G-d. When the sajaam tried to rid the world of men and usurp G-d, the people of that time united to banish the sajaam to the third hell, where they have remained. Djet will be looking for a way to call them back from that hell, or a gate to go there himself."

Mo shook her head. "The sajaam weren't banished, though. At least, not all of them."

Heru fixed Mo with a thin-lipped stare. "Oh? You think you know more about the sajaam than one who has spent their life researching and understanding jaan?"

"There's another story." Mo crossed her arms but didn't meet Heru's gaze. "The healers know it, because it's about the first of us."

Heru took a seat at the table opposite Mo and extracted a roll of parchment from the pile of scrolls. He removed a pen from his wrap with a small flourish, dipped the tip in an inkwell, and then looked expectantly at Mo. After a moment, he tapped the end of his pen against the table and said, *"Well?"*

Mo started and lifted her gaze to his. She took in his pen and parchment and then wet her lips. "This is the way Enass told the story to me and this is the way her mother told the story to her." She took a breath and when she spoke again, it was with the rhythm of recitation.

"A long time ago, deep within the Wastes, the Sajaam kings called a meeting of their kind. Young and old came, powerful and weak. All agreed that the size of their kingdom, limited as it was to the Wastes, was no longer enough. They were power-ful beings who built sandstorms and reshaped dunes, who lived forever and ruled the sands and the skies.

"They deserved to rule more than the Wastes. They had watched as G-d-fearing man expanded his territory to the east and to the north and to the south. They had observed his wars and cruelty and crimes. Collectively, they judged him corrupt. The sajaam decided they would no longer share their world with man. They decided to rid it of him entirely. They decided they would rather be G-d.

"First, the sajaam stirred up a massive sandstorm and dried the land from the Wastes to the sea. Wells filled with sand and oases vanished, and what was once verdant land filled with dust and death. Villages and towns perished. Then the sajaam sent swarms of locusts to eat up any remaining crops, and to pes-ter and poison livestock. Last, the sajaam granted some of their brethren jaan will but not wisdom and hunger but not satiation. These jaan became guul, which decimated the Azal, whose life adrift had thus far shielded them from the worst of the drought and plague."

Mo paused for breath and touched the charm at her throat, as if for reassurance. "One of the Azal, a woman by the name Essif, recognized that these threats came from the sajaam and not G-d. She warned her tribe, then rode to the other tribes to give them warning. At each stop she convinced her people of the danger and took what marab they could spare. Essif crossed dunes and sand, mountains and gravel, to find every Azal marabi and bring them all together.

"Essif led the marab deep into the Wastes to find the source of the plagues. Upon their journey they fasted—for there was famine and their tribes could spare them no food—and they prayed. The further they went into the Wastes, the worse the winds' scouring became. So they wrapped themselves in camel hides to protect their bodies and they covered their faces with leather to protect their mouths and eyes. But they left one eye uncovered, so that they could see the way and watch for a sign from G-d.

"The first sign from G-d was a running wash. But instead of water, it was filled with blood. The marab discussed this sign but could not decide what G-d wanted of them. But Essif knew. She cut her arm and let her life's water flow onto the sand. The marab saw what she'd done and cut their skin, too, joining their water to hers. Their blood formed a circle which contained the sajaam within and kept the deadly guul out.

"The second sign from G-d was a burning tree. As they passed a stunted acacia, the only one of its kind for miles, the tree caught fire. But the flames didn't harm it and instead it grew taller and straighter and its withered brown leaves became green. Again, the marab couldn't decide what G-d wanted of them. But Essif knew. She broke off a branch from the burning tree, which did not diminish in the least, and walked the perimeter of the circle of blood. The marab saw what she did and each broke off a branch of their own. As they walked, the locusts were drawn to the light, only to burn up in the fire.

"The third and final sign from G-d was a salt-white camel, its hair as fine as dust, eating the branches and leaves of a thorny bush. Even this final time, the marab couldn't agree on what G-d wanted them to do. But Essif knew. She tore off the branches and leaves from the thorny bush and ate them. She was filled with the spirit of G-d. The sajaam, enraged that they couldn't leave the circle or engulf the marab with their swarms, lashed out at her with their wind and their fire, but they could not harm her.

"The marab saw what Essif did and each tore off the branches and leaves from the thorny bush and ate them. The spirit of G-d filled them. Thus empowered, they stood up to the sajaam as the demons railed against them. The sajaam scoured and bloodied their skin with sand and blinded their exposed eye, but the marab and Essif stayed firm.

"When the sajaam had exhausted themselves, Essif reopened her wound and spilled blood beneath their forms. This fixed the sajaam to the spot. With the power of the marab and the spirit of G-d, Essif bound the sajaam and transformed them to towering black stone. The sajaam were imprisoned within these rocks for all eternity for their folly. Now the rocks stand as a warning to any who might try to usurp G-d. And as a reward for her faith and devotion, G-d bestowed upon Essif and her heirs the gift of healing."

Mo's voice fell silent, but her story took longer to fade from the room. Heru looked up from his notes, the base of his palm black with ink from his hurried writing.

"That's a pretty story, but I have doubts as to its accuracy. Still, I wonder if perhaps Djet heard a similar story. If he has, then he'll try to find the location of these rocks instead of an opening to hell." Heru pressed a thumb against his nose, smearing it with black ink. "The woman's name was Essif. Now—where have I heard that name before?"

Heru rifled through the scrolls, pulled out one, and smoothed it flat. It was a map of the Mehewret Empire, which included not only Ghadid and the other crescent cities, but also the Wastes. While most of the map showed mountains, washes, dune fields, caravan routes, wells, and the names of towns and villages, the Wastes were only a stain of empty white parchment. *Almost* empty—a few mountain ranges had been sketched in its center, but they had no names.

"Essif, Essif, Essif," muttered Heru, stroking his thumb across the vellum. The thumb stopped over one mountain range straight west and innumerable miles distant from Ghadid. Heru snapped his fingers. "Fetch Senousert. I require everything he has on the Aer Essifs."

20

Thana would forever remember the subsequent week as a haze, those warm moments before a dream was fractured by reality. If only it could have lasted longer.

On the one hand, the days she spent with Heru and Mo in the Imperial Library were tedious and dull, testing and stretching Thana's patience further than ever before. Heru insisted on transcribing and combing through even the most insignificant details, to the point where Thana wished on more than one occasion that methodical planning and calm execution hadn't been drilled into her since birth, because oh how she wanted to simply *stab* Heru.

But the evenings were something altogether different. When the slaves came around with their lamps that first day, it had been Mo's idea to take a break. They'd left Heru with his stack of scrolls and scribbled notes and ink-stained hands and wandered out of the palace. No one had tried to stop them. No one had cared.

The river was just on the other side of the gardens. Thana heard the rush of water before she spotted the river beyond the trees, impossibly wide and blue. Then the path spit them out onto a wider street which ran right beside the river's edge. Dusk was settling heavy as a cloth, but the city showed no signs of slowing down. Even as they left the safety of the palace gardens

and crossed the road, people pushed past, merchants called their
wares, and children laughed and yelled and screamed.

Once they'd crossed the road, the only thing between them
and the rushing river just a few feet below was a metal railing.
Thana leaned against it, letting it hold her weight as she watched
the river run past, mesmerized by its constant motion. This close,
she could even taste the water in the air. Mo stayed back, her
gaze locked on the greater expanse of the river.

"It's so much more than I imagined," said Mo.

"It just keeps going," said Thana and then immediately felt
dumb. It was obvious to anyone with an eye, let alone two, that
this river held more water than Ghadid saw in a decade. She
tried again. "No one here must deal with pain or sickness."

Mo tilted her head and looked at Thana sidelong. "Na Tay
Khet doesn't have healers."

"What?" Thana frowned at the water. "Does the Empress
have something against them?"

"No, we just . . ." Mo pursed her lips together, trying to find
the words. "Healers are only born near the Wastes, in the crescent
cities. And we don't leave." She smiled self-consciously. "Well,
we're not supposed to."

"You mentioned that before. But why?"

Mo walked up to the railing and curled her fingers around
it. She leaned forward, a few of her braids falling free and tracing the lines of her round face. "There are so few of us to begin
with. The drum chiefs feared that if word got out, other cities
and people might be jealous. They might take . . . extreme mea-
sures to have a healer for themselves."

"Do you think that's what the Empress wants from Ghadid?"

Mo pursed her lips, then shook her head. "The Empress wants
power. If she really wanted her own healers, she could steal them
from the Azal when they come here to trade. She probably has."

"I would, if I were her," said Thana. "To never be sick again, or have to suffer through an injury. You wouldn't have to fear death with so much water nearby."

Mo laughed. "That's not really how it works."

"What do you mean? If you can heal everything—"

"We can only heal what the body itself could, given time," said Mo. "We can speed some processes up, but we can't stop time all together. Even with all the healers and all the water in the world, no one would be immortal. We just do what we can to prevent the preventable." She turned her head so that she caught Thana in a sideways glance. "Which is why we get a little irate about the particularly preventable."

Thana grimaced. "I promise to stay far and away from any dogs."

Mo rolled her eyes. "Why don't I believe you?" She straightened abruptly, then stretched her arm out over the railing. "But . . . you're right about one thing. . . ."

Mo reached further just as the water crested, which seemed to rise to brush her fingers like a cat. Water splashed across her hand and arm, darkening the edges of her sleeve. Then the wave was gone but a streak of blue remained, rolling up Mo's arm and across her shoulders and spilling down her body. Mo actually giggled, her dark eyes lighting on Thana's. She held out one glowing hand.

Thana took it. The blue spread to her, and with it a gentle, almost warm sensation. The little aches and pains of travel were smoothed away. Even the stress that had been building up in her shoulders and across her forehead was eased, if not entirely forgotten.

She smiled back at Mo. The blue faded and Thana became acutely aware that she was still holding Mo's hand. They stayed tethered that way for another heartbeat, hands entwined and gazes fixed. Thana realized Mo was actually, truly looking at her for the first time since they'd met. She dropped her gaze and hand, her stomach flooding with nerves, her throat dry.

What was she *doing*? She could all but hear Amastan chastising her for getting distracted, remarking on her tendency to fall for pretty faces. But Mo had become so much more than a pretty face and now was not the time to indulge in this incipient crush. A *healer* of all people, too. Shards and dust, she had the most inconvenient of tastes.

And yet . . . her own mother had met her father while on contract. He'd been the mark, for G-d's sake. What was a little indulgence among all this drudgery?

The silence seemed to pulse between them, given a life of its own. Thana didn't know how to break it, was afraid to. Thankfully, Mo broke it for her.

"Who are you, Thana?"

Thana laughed, but when Mo didn't, her nerves flared, hot as embers, and she turned back to the river. "I've already told you—"

Mo waved away her explanation. "Pieces and parts. Hardly enough to explain half the things you've done. You said you're here to keep an eye on Heru for the Circle, but I've never seen anyone fight like you did on the sands. You're fearless. The Azal abandoned us and fled, but you stood up to those bound like it was your job."

Thana held up a finger. "I *had* run into them before."

Mo puffed her cheeks and threw a stray braid over her shoulder. "Did you practice your knife throwing on them, too? And what about the guards at the gate? How did you escape them? And that disguise, that wasn't just playing around. That took real skill. My uncle puts on plays for the Telem neighborhood, so I've seen what goes into designing costumes. You've done that before."

Mo's gaze flicked across Thana's face, searching for an answer and afraid of finding it. Thana's stomach tightened into a knot as she watched Mo make the connections. She felt breathless in a way that had nothing at all to do with breath. When Mo's lips parted slightly in sudden understanding, Thana was almost relieved. At least she didn't have to tell Mo herself.

"Are you a performer? Do you play in the fights?"

Thana swallowed her laugh of surprise, but it still came out as a choked snort. She and her cousins liked to watch the performers put on their shows, especially the fights, which were laughable, contorted parodies of real fights. To be associated with their flamboyant and inefficient displays was an insult, yet Thana didn't correct Mo.

"The dogs," said Mo suddenly, realization lighting up her features. "Oh. *Oh*. It wasn't really dogs, was it?" She shook her head. "What a *waste* of water. You and your friends, hurting each other for fun. And you had the audacity to come to me afterwards."

The truth welled up in Thana's throat, pushing against the back of her tongue. She wanted to tell Mo everything, that she wasn't some bawdy entertainer, that she had a real calling, just as noble as healing—and just as necessary. She wanted to tell Mo about her great grandmothers and cousins whose bloodied hands had kept Ghadid safe. She wanted to tell Mo about Amastan and Illi and Dihya and Ziri and all her other cousins, ones who weren't assassins as well as those who were.

She wanted to tell Mo what had actually brought her across the sands and driven her to fight the guards and infiltrate the palace. That she had a contract to kill Heru, yes, but something else had complicated that simple task. A foolish need to see that the girl she'd just met over the back of a corpse was safe.

But the confession died in her mouth. She couldn't do it. If Mo thought that poorly about performers, who only hurt each other by accident, what would she think about an assassin? At least killing wasn't a waste of water, but somehow she doubted she could make Mo see it that way.

Thana remembered all too clearly Mo's righteous anger when they'd first met and she couldn't bear to see that return after all they'd been through together. If she confessed now, they wouldn't be able to continue working together. And they needed to, to stop Djet.

Yes, it was for the best if Mo didn't know. Not yet. Maybe not ever.

"We try not to get hurt," said Thana. And it wasn't a lie, not really. Mo's assumptions were her own and Thana couldn't exactly change those, could she?

Mo rolled her eyes. "You *fight* for fun." Then that gaze stole across Thana, lingering on her arms, her neck, before returning to her face. "I can see why the Circle chose you to keep an eye on Heru, though. The endurance and strength you must have from all that training. . . ." She trailed off, coughed, and looked away. "Is it awful that I'm actually a little glad this all happened? I feel guilty because people have died and there's a madman on the loose, but if Djet hadn't shown up, I'd never have seen *this*"—she gestured at the river, at the city around them—"and I'd never have met you."

The flutters Thana thought she'd banished came back with a vengeance. She didn't know what to say, so she opted for silence. It'd come off as enigmatic, if she was lucky.

"Can you teach me how to fight?"

Thana blinked, surprised by the question. She looked at the small healer, braids already cleaned of dust and hands as smooth as silk. She couldn't imagine her holding a weapon, but then she remembered Mo with the tent pole, swinging at the bound as if her life depended on it. Because it had. This was the first time she'd seen Mo without that makeshift weapon since that fight.

Mo swallowed, earnest face upturned. "Not with a sword. I don't want to kill anyone. But if the bound attack again, I need to be able to defend myself. And others." Her gaze clouded with pain. "Last time, I couldn't save anyone. I don't want that to happen again."

"I'm sure the Empress has a real staff somewhere that she can give you," said Thana. "I can teach you how to use one to keep the bound away. You'll still need to use a knife to break their bindings—"

Mo waved a hand. "Oh, I can do that just fine."

Thana thought about the hours they'd spend on the sands, trading blows and getting sweaty. "Great," she said, perhaps a little too brightly. "We can start as soon as we're done in the library. Somehow I doubt Senousert would take kindly to us sparring among his scrolls."

Mo laughed. She leaned close. Thana stiffened, very aware of the warmth and proximity of Mo's smaller body. Her gaze kept slipping to those wide lips and she'd become very aware of her own. She wondered if Mo was thinking the same. Did Mo even like women? It baffled Thana that anyone could say no to those curves and those lips and those eyes, so dark and warm and—

"It's getting late," said Mo. "We should probably head back."

Thana swallowed her disappointment. "Right."

But then Mo slid her hand in Thana's and that disappointment vanished.

After that first night, their evenings spent walking alongside the river or twisting through the city's streets stretched longer and longer, until dusk turned to night and Thana's feet ached come morning. She took care not to talk too much about herself, and instead turned the questions and conversations again and again back to Mo and her life. Thana learned about the test that had revealed Mo's innate healing ability when she was only a few years old, the seasons since then she'd spent at Enass's side, rarely allowed to leave, the elevation of her status and the sheer crushing responsibility of it all. Thana realized she'd never really understood what the healers went through. Maybe next time, she *would* be a little bit more careful during a fight.

All in all, it was a slow time, calm and quiet. And it was over too soon.

In the cramped library room, Thana stretched her legs beneath the table, a different mess of scrolls and maps covering its surface. A stale stench wove through the air. Heru pressed his finger against the corner of the map, triumph oozing from every pore. He could have lit up the room with his smug, burning pride.

"I can say, with almost ninety-four percent certainty, that our old and previously dead friend will be—or is already—headed here," pronounced Heru, leaning on his finger. "This mountain range in the middle of the Wastes known as the Aer Essifs."

"But we knew that a week ago," said Thana.

"We did not *know*," corrected Heru. He gestured at the papers. "We still do not *know*. But we can correlate from our sources and arrive at an appropriate conclusion. And that conclusion will take us deep into the Wastes."

Thana bit her tongue. Heru was right; they knew far more than they had at the beginning of the week. Most importantly, they knew now what Djet had discovered shortly before his temporary demise. As it turned out, Mo's story had been more than just pretty.

Djet's own research and notes had been burned along with him, but there were hints and rumors that a copy had been hidden somewhere within the palace, waiting for Djet's inevitable return. Absent that, Senousert had brought them any histories that even mentioned Djet.

Unfortunately, many of these were so extreme as to be completely useless. After Djet's death, his legacy had grown and spread, until he'd become more demon than man. He'd been blamed for the disappearances of marab, the murders of more than a dozen slaves, and even a plague that had desolated an entire town. It was doubtful that he could have been responsible for all of that. After his very public trial and execution, historians had taken to blaming him for anything outside the ordinary. But between the gaps and inconsistencies, they were able to piece together a semi-coherent story.

In his last year of life, Djet had become singularly obsessed with something beyond his experiments. He'd all but stopped eating, dismissed all of his assistants, and locked himself away in his study. Then he'd approached King To with a strange request: he wanted storytellers from every region of the kingdom.

The people who went before Djet returned physically unscathed, but refused to talk about what had happened. A pattern emerged: the storytellers came from the region nearest the Wastes and they were spiritual leaders of their tribes—close to, but not quite—marab.

One day, an old woman arrived claiming to have come from within the Wastes. When Djet asked her his questions, she flew into a rage. The accounts differed as to whether the old woman then disappeared in a cloud of smoke or cursed him, but she vanished and a few weeks later, Djet was caught trying to flee the capital with a dozen of the King's camels and men, the beasts burdened for a long journey. He was tried and executed shortly thereafter.

No source had linked his interest in the sajaam to his request for storytellers, but it was clear that Djet had been searching for evidence that the sajaam still existed in the world. He'd been searching for Mo's story.

Heru began rolling up scrolls. "As much as I'd enjoy spending another week in here with the both of you," he said dryly, "it's clearly time for action. If even a quarter of this is remotely true, then Djet is undeniably dangerous and already far along on his path to achieving immortality. He knows about the Aer Essifs and he was on his way to claim the sajaam for himself when he was finally caught. Our only consolation is that the exact location of the mountains remains unknown. Still, it may already be too late."

Thana didn't move. She could no longer ignore the reality of their situation. If it had just been her and Heru against Djet, she would've already slipped Heru poison and been on her way home. But Mo's presence complicated things. Mo was determined to see this through no matter what, and Thana couldn't—wouldn't—leave Mo to face such a monster on her own. Because if even half the accounts were correct, then Djet was a hundred times worse than Heru.

Djet had been power hungry, ruthless, and cruel. Alive, he'd practiced forbidden magic, bound people against their will, and killed numerous slaves and assistants in his pursuit of knowledge. Recently returned from the dead, he'd already endangered Ghadid with his creatures, decimated a caravan, and proven again and again that he had little regard for any life in his way. She doubted he'd be satisfied with immortality. Worse, there was every likelihood that when he released the sajaam, he wouldn't be able to control them.

Djet needed to be stopped. But doing so meant forfeiting her contract. There was no way around it. Heru might be the only one who could unbind Djet's jaani—he was certainly the only one who knew nearly as much about Djet's research as Djet himself. And if Heru helped avert a catastrophe and stopped Djet . . .

She couldn't kill Heru. She might even have to protect him. Either way, it meant the end of her career as an assassin. Her mother might understand. She'd once broken a contract to save Thana's father, although she'd later discovered that her employer had been conspiring to start a civil war, a fact that meant her contract had been invalid all along.

Unlike her father, though, Heru hadn't been wrongly accused. From what she'd seen, he was guilty of crimes against G-d and probably more. Still, she might be able to convince Kaseem that the circumstances were worth breaking the contract. But she'd never be able to escape the shame of failure and she'd have to live with that failure for the rest of her life.

So much for becoming a legend.

Or . . .

Or, if they somehow succeeded, if they found the sajaam and stopped this madman, then perhaps she'd become a different legend. Not an assassin, but a protector. A warrior. The falcon to her mother's serpent.

She could face Mo with honesty and a clean slate. She'd never have to mention her past because it'd never again intrude upon her present or future. Even if Mo found out about her previous contracts, surely her decision to quit, help Heru, and stop the inevitable destruction of their world would account for *something*.

In a way, this decision was a relief. She wouldn't have to find a way to navigate between her duty and her burgeoning affection for Mo. She wouldn't have to keep searching for ways to kill Heru—who seemed increasingly unkillable. She wouldn't have to keep playing a role, but could work honestly toward only one goal.

It was time to break her contract.

21

"You haven't tried to kill me in over a week. I'd appreciate at least another halfhearted attempt. The anticipation is starting to wear on me."

Thana glanced around, but no one was close enough to have overheard Heru's remark. She'd allowed him to walk his camel closer, assuming he'd want to drone on about his continued research, as he'd already done on several occasions. He spent every free moment, even while riding, scratching illegibly in his notes. But this was new and dangerous.

"Technically, it's been three weeks," she said. "And you haven't tried killing and binding anyone in a while. But you don't hear me complaining about it."

"That's hardly the same thing at all."

Heru stared ahead at the never-ending expanse of pale sand, his eyebrows knit together over his white tagel. His camel trod untiring at his side, its head down and swaying but, unlike the living camels, never jerking away to chew on errant tufts of grass. Why hadn't he taken one of the Empress's living camels? It was absurd that he'd display such an inconvenient loyalty to the abomination, but here they were, crossing the desert once more with the dust-cursed thing. The others in the caravan, merchants and Azal alike, gave the bound camel a wide berth. Maybe *that* had been his intent.

Although Heru had wanted to brave the desert alone to make better time, the Empress had insisted they join the next caravan to avoid undue attention and potential panic. Yet Thana had overheard the caravan's leaders talking about the payment they'd received to leave early and head straight for Ghadid, instead of circling to the north as they'd intended. The Empress must have decided some attention was acceptable.

"For one thing, it was *my* life at stake," continued Heru. "For another, that was necessary each and every time. But I'd appreciate if you refrained from mentioning it again."

Thana raised an eyebrow. "Is *that* what this is about? You want me to keep my mouth shut?"

"My abilities aren't pertinent to our current situation and might only serve to confuse and upset certain, potentially helpful, members of our party."

"Look, I haven't said anything and I'm not going to say anything." Thana pointed a finger at Heru. "Assuming you don't, either."

"I only wanted to confirm our ongoing arrangement in light of your changing relationship with the healer. You two have been spending a lot more time talking to each other and I'd rather certain elements remain unmentioned. I suspect the healer will continue being instrumental in understanding our shared adversary along with elucidating other particulars about the connection between jaani and body." Heru tilted his head to her in a nod, then turned his attention to the front of the caravan. This time when he spoke, his voice dripped with pained annoyance. "Ah. It looks like it might be time for the afternoon nap. What an efficient waste of time."

Still grumbling, he pulled his camel away from Thana. Off to her other side, bright blue cloth flashed between the darker, full-sky blue of the Azal as Mo returned from her rounds. Heru was right about one thing: since they'd left Na Tay Khet, she and Mo had been inseparable. Their evenings around the city had sparked a friendship, fanned that much brighter by the fact that they were the only two from Ghadid in the entire caravan and, aside from Heru, the only ones who'd faced undying bandits, stood in the presence of the Empress, and knew about Djet's danger. That kind of thing tended to bring people together.

But even without all those commonalities, Thana suspected she and Mo would have been drawn together. There was something about Mo's quiet yet firm demeanor, Mo's compassion for others, and Mo's delightful laugh that had wrapped around Thana and ensnared her. Like her cousin Amastan, Mo was serious enough for the both of them. But unlike him, there was a yearning for *more*.

Mo loosened the knot keeping her camel's lead fixed to Thana's pack and retrieved her staff. Before leaving the city, Mo had requested a sparring staff from the Empress to replace the wooden stake she'd been using. Thana hadn't made any requests, but she'd found a length of rope, a few extra knives, and the small bag of poisons Heru had taken when he'd betrayed her.

"Salaz says we'll reach the well by nightfall tomorrow and Ghadid within a week."

Thana glanced over the line of camels. "I guess we're making better time without so much salt."

A shout rang out from the front and was echoed along the caravan's length. Those still on camelback slipped off while the others began unrolling and staking out their tents. The sun was as hot as ever, but a cool undercurrent of wind now ran across their bare feet and through their hair and, at night, brought aching chills to their bones. The difference between being under the tent and out in the sun was much starker than it had been just a few weeks before.

Instead of setting up their tent, Mo tightened the knots of her wrap, spread her feet, double-checked her stance, then nodded once at Thana. She barely blocked Thana's first strike with her staff, and she stumbled under Thana's second, but she found her footing—and her flow—by the third.

They sparred for only a few minutes, but both were out of breath and scented with sweat by the time Thana signaled a halt.

"You're getting better," said Thana, unable to suppress her grin. "You almost got my knees with that last one."

"It's a lot more fun than I expected." The smile that had crept onto Mo's face while they sparred faded. Mo looked down at her hands, her staff clutched tight between them. "But it's not good enough. The bound won't be stopped by a tap to the knees."

"We've got all the way between here and Ghadid to practice." Thana picked uo the roll of tent cloth from their pile of belongings. "And then however long it takes us to find the Aer Essifs. You'll be a master of the staff by then."

Mo grabbed the other end of the tent's fabric from Thana and helped spread it out across the sand. "Have you thought at all about after?"

"What do you mean?" Thana freed a pole from the pack and pounded it into the ground.

"I mean—after we defeat Djet. After we return from the Wastes. After this is all taken care of." Mo brushed a braid from her face and pounded a third pole into the ground with her staff. "I don't know if I could spend the rest of my life in Ghadid. I thought seeing Na Tay Khet would be enough, but now I want to see more. Maybe that's the danger Enass tried to warn me about."

Thana placed the last pole and slid beneath the tent's welcome shade. Mo laid her staff on the sand and joined her. This close, Thana could smell Mo's sweat, warm and just a little salty. She thought about licking that salt off, but took a deep breath instead. She didn't know if that'd be welcome. Mo had been friendly enough, but friendly was one thing—Thana wanted another.

"You left once," said Thana. "What's stopping you from leaving again?"

Mo twisted her hands in her lap, staring out of the tent and across the sand they still had to cross. "That's what I'm afraid of. That and—what will Enass say when I get back?"

"Just explain that you were off saving the world," said Thana. "Surely all the lives you'll save by stopping Djet should earn you some time off."

But Mo continued to twist her hands. "I don't know. What if we fail?"

"We won't fail," said Thana immediately.

She took Mo's hands and held them in her own. Mo stopped twisting them and began chewing her lip. Thana wanted to take those lips between her own. She dug her fingernails into her palms instead.

"We can't fail," continued Thana. "We've got Heru, a very capable marabi, and you, an incredible healer, and me . . ."

She trailed off before she could say *the Serpent's daughter*. She opened her mouth to try again, but this time cut herself off when the only words that came were *an assassin*. Before she could try a third time, Mo answered for her.

"A selfless performer."

Performer. Thana's stomach plummeted at the lie. Sands cover it. What *would* she do when they returned to Ghadid? Would Mo expect to see her perform fights in the streets, all ridiculous movements and choreographed displays? Thana could already hear her cousins' laughter. No. Never. She had to tell Mo, and soon, before this infatuation became something more.

Just, maybe, later.

Mo's hand was on her leg. Thana wasn't sure how it had gotten there. She hardly dared to breathe, lest Mo notice and remove it. But Mo didn't and her gaze met Thana's.

"I wish I had your confidence," said Mo. "You almost make me believe that whatever comes next, we'll survive. At least I know you'll be there. So maybe we will."

"You give me too much credit," said Thana.

Mo's hand left Thana's leg and lifted to cup her face. Thana's breath stuck in her throat, heart pounding harder than a blacksmith's hammer. The desert fell away and all Thana knew was Mo's soft palm against her cheek, Mo's warm dark eyes, Mo's curving pink lips.

"Maybe," said Mo softly. "But I feel safer by your side. Whatever comes next, I want to spend it with you."

"I'm not going anywhere," said Thana.

"Good."

Then Mo leaned forward and kissed Thana.

All thought left Thana's head. She leaned into Mo, returning the kiss with all the pent-up hunger and need of too many chaste years. Mo tasted of water and almonds and salt, smelled of sweat and honey and something uniquely sharp. Her hand found the small of Thana's back, warm even through the layers of fabric, then the base of her neck, drawing Thana closer until there was no space left between them. Then her leg pressed up between Thana's and all thoughts about the lies or her contract or the bound or Djet vanished like smoke on the wind.

In the following days, they spent every moment they could together, sparring at each break, huddling close over tea through the hot afternoons, and entwining limbs under their shared tent at night. It had been one thing to lie to Mo before, when Thana could pretend they were only friends, but after Mo made her intentions clear, the lie weighed heavy on her chest. Thana told herself that she'd confess as soon as an opportunity presented itself, but each time a gap in their conversation left an opening, Thana's tongue grew as heavy as stone.

Guilt plagued Thana like a bad cold, rising up in her throat and waking her to stare at the tent's fluttering cloth while Mo snored next to her, warm limbs entangled with her own. Guilt muddled her thoughts, flushed her cheeks, and sickened her. It distracted her from keeping an eye on Heru, who daily withdrew further into himself and his scrolls.

But as each day passed, the desert endless and unchanging, her guilt shrank bit by bit until it became manageable. Her secret had not crashed through her in a moment of weakness and it hadn't bubbled up unwelcome in their conversations. Thana began to consider just letting Mo believe what she wanted. Why destroy the good thing they had for something as vague and fleeting as "the truth"? What did that even mean compared to what they were building between their bodies and their hands, with each caress and breath and kiss?

Thana had more pressing things to worry about, starting with what she'd do when they returned. Ghadid was only a few days away and, although she'd made the decision to abandon her contract almost a week ago, her tryst with Mo had shoved the looming consequences from her mind. She didn't know how to break the news to Amastan, let alone Kaseem. And her mother . . .

She just had to lay out what they'd learned in the right way and explain the unexplainable. She should have been planning and practicing her plea and deciding how to frame it, but every chance she'd had so far, she'd been distracted by Mo instead. Mo's long braids. Mo's warm hands. Mo's dark skin. Mo's soft touch.

Soon, too soon, she was going to be in trouble if she didn't do something, and now, but it was difficult to clear her mind long enough to make plans. The contract and Kaseem were so far away, as insubstantial as the shimmering mirages of water and mountains on the horizon. There was still time. It was easy—too easy—to push those worries away for another day, day after day.

Until one day, it was too late.

The news ran the length of the caravan that they'd be safely among Ghadid's platforms by nightfall while they were breaking camp that morning.

The fear started as a crack, hardly wider than a hair, but soon widened and spread and fractured within Thana as she helped Mo pack their tent and burden their camels. A blissfully heavy silence had fallen across the caravan in lieu of an excited murmur, everyone too overcome with the anticipation of real food, fresh water, and the luxury of an enclosed, windless space to break their daydreams with words. Camels grunted, sand fizzed across fabric, and leather creaked as the caravan readied itself.

Thana fought with her frozen fingers to secure her straps. Winter was closing in and the camels' snorts puffed out as miniature clouds. Thana's tagel caught and trapped her breath, warming her face, but she felt the cold in her hands and feet and creeping around the edges of her wrap. The stiffness reminded her how lucky she was to sleep curled beside another warm body each night.

The caravan began to move as soon as the morning tea was passed around. Thana held the hot glass close to her chest to protect it from the wind, which blew harder than usual this morning, throwing sand and grit into her eyes. Mo walked alone a dozen feet away, her head bowed in her morning prayers.

Ahead, Heru broke from the caravan and put some distance between himself and the rest of them before mounting his camel.

Once in the saddle, he pulled out a scroll and a pen and began scratching at the vellum. What did he plan on doing when they reached Ghadid? He'd probably hole himself up in an inn once again. But he might also plan to leave right away. She couldn't make assumptions.

Thana walked away from her camel, leaving it to follow the others. She needed to know what Heru expected when they arrived and she needed to be certain he wouldn't betray her as he had in Na Tay Khet. She'd wasted all her time worrying about what she'd tell her family and avoided thinking about what came after.

Ahead, Heru's bound white camel stood out in the darkness, his own white-clothed form hunched over his work. Thana's approach was as silent as a snake. Regret flashed through her; Heru was away from the caravan and thoroughly engrossed in his work. This would have been a perfect opportunity to finish her contract. But she'd made her decision.

She was only a few feet away when Heru shifted, looked up. She froze. He couldn't have possibly heard her. Was she out of practice? Then his camel stepped to the side and she saw the horizon.

A band of clouds glowed, curling and rising into the sky. For a moment, Thana was confused. Hadn't she been facing west? The sunrise should be behind her. Then the clouds thickened and darkened and began to spread like torch oil across the horizon, the glow inside a hazy red. She *was* facing west. The world lurched. That wasn't the sun.

"I suppose you already know what that is," said Heru.

Thana sucked in a breath, but he was still watching the cloud expand, become many. She closed the distance between them, her throat thick with fear.

"A fire."

This near Heru, she could smell peppermint and leather. But now the wind also carried the stench of smoke and flames. A paralyzing numbness started in her chest and spread outward.

"Looks like Djet arrived ahead of us," said Heru. "I was afraid of this. He'll be able to amass a great army of bound now. Although to what end, I still don't know."

"What is it? What's burning?" asked Thana. She was wrong, she was mistaken, it couldn't possibly be—

Heru turned to her, his face lit on one side by the orange glow of the rising sun and on the other by the red flames of a burning city.

"Ghadid."

22

Heru's tone held neither satisfaction nor amusement. He had stated a fact, one that cut through Thana as easily as a blade. Her city, her home, her family—

"No." She took a step back. Then another. "No. It's just a building that's caught. Poorly stored grain. Or—or a really large bonfire."

But the words sounded hollow, even to her. There was too much smoke, too much fire, spreading too quickly.

Heru said nothing. He only watched her and that was worse than any insult he could have thrown. An abyss unfurled in her chest and spread its cold, numbing tendrils through her veins. If she stood here much longer, she'd never move again.

"We have to go, we have to help them."

Thana started to run back to the caravan—nothing but flickers of light from swinging tea braziers now—but not before Heru said, simply, "It's too late."

No. *No.* It wasn't too late. The fire was big, but not *that* big. She could still reach them, still help put out the fire. It was a quarter of the city, maybe a third. A small disaster. Not a catastrophe. Ghadid needed her.

The caravan was boiling over with voices and movement. A group had formed in the front and at its center stood Salaz, the caravan's leader. Although the rising sun and brightening sky had diminished the brilliance of the fire's far-off glow, the dark smoke had become a night that sprouted and spread from the wrong direction.

Heru passed her on his camel and pulled up just short of Salaz. Mo cut through the crowd and intercepted Thana. Her face was ashen and her lips pressed tight as she took Thana's elbow and dragged her to a stop.

"They don't want to go any closer," said Mo.

"You mean they don't want to help."

"What can they do? It looks like the whole city's on fire. There's a well a day north where they can replenish their supplies, but they'd have to go now or risk running dry."

"Are you going with them?"

"Of course not," said Mo. "That's my home."

Thana pulled away from Mo and continued toward the group. Heru stood impassively by while the Azal gestured widely in a rare show of emotion, their voices tinged with fear.

Thana shouldered her way into the cluster and asked loudly, "What about the other crescent cities? Won't you go to one of them?"

Salaz shook his head. "There's no guarantee that what happened in this city didn't also happen to them."

"And what do you think happened?"

The Azal exchanged a look. A woman responded, "Clearly, the city has been attacked."

"There's no evidence of that," pushed Thana. "A few platforms are on fire, that's all."

"That's not just a few platforms," said Salaz. "No, come nightfall, there'll be little left of that city. I won't risk my people." His gaze flicked across Thana and the pity in his eyes made her even angrier. "I'm sorry."

"They need our help!"

Salaz stared at the ever-spreading smoke. "There's nothing we can do."

Thana clenched her fists. This was her *home* and all they could do was discuss it as if it were already a corpse. Her city wasn't lost. Even now, she knew her father would be directing sand and water efforts and her mother would be gathering their cousins. And Amastan—

A terrifying, heedless energy pulsed through her, wiping away the fear and cold. She stalked away from the group. She was going to help and she didn't care who joined her. She swung up onto her camel with practiced ease. She touched its neck—although whether to reassure the beast or herself, she wasn't sure—then yanked it away from the grasses and forced it instead to face the distant flames. The camel shuddered beneath her and took two steps back.

Mo appeared beside her, staff in hand. "What're you doing?"

"We don't know what happened, but we can still help. My family—" Thana swallowed, shook her head. "Look, while they decide where to flee, people are dying. If you want to dawdle here—"

"Who said I was staying?" Mo snatched the lead of a passing camel, drawing the beast to her. "I was just worried you'd insist on going off alone." Mo hoisted herself onto its back in one smooth motion. She laid her staff across her lap. "Let's go."

Thana spurred her camel forward, then leaned back and took the whip out of its holster. She gave the camel's rump a solid thwack. The camel grunted, but eased into a loping stride. Another thwack urged it into a full gallop. Thana held tight, digging her knees in to keep from being thrown off by the camel's rolling gait. She heard the beat of another camel's stride but didn't glance back. Mo would be close behind.

The dismal glow bulged and the smoke soon covered half the

sky. A westerly wind drove the clouds their direction. Something more substantial than wind or cloud drifted down like freshly plucked feathers. Ahead, the smoke now obscured so much sky that even the sand looked gray. No—that wasn't right. Thana leaned over and watched her camel's feet break through the gray to sand beneath.

The gray clung to her mount and clothes now. It neither dissolved nor melted, but accumulated in gradually thickening layers. Thana caught a falling clump on her tongue and tasted bitterness and smoke. Ash. Thana gagged. This was her home floating through the air.

The ash thickened, in the air and on the ground. Her camel's hesitation shuddered up through its stride and she whipped it on before it could balk. Ghadid reared up and out of the sands, its burning platforms so many warning beacons. Thana didn't heed them.

The level of destruction became more obvious as they neared, as did the ominous silence. There were no cries or shouts or other sounds of life. Only the fire's roar suffused the air. But that didn't mean her city was beyond help. Surely the distance was eating up any other noises.

Ahead, through the falling ash, a gray camel stood near the end of a metal cable. A figure hunched atop the camel, waiting. Thana drew her beast up a dozen yards distant, but the hope that flashed through her was quickly burned away when the glass charms at her waist flushed with warmth.

Then the figure straightened and some of the gray fell away, revealing white beneath. A white tagel, a white wrap, and a once-white camel, now smeared with ash.

"You took your time," called Heru.

Thana goaded her mount to join his, annoyed. She should've noticed when he slipped ahead of them, even with the air so thick with ash. Her camel shied, flared its nostrils, and pinned its ears back, refusing to near the dead camel. Thana pulled the beast away until it had calmed, then leaned back and followed the cable up with her gaze.

Smoke churned the air where the cable met the platform's edge, but Thana could just make out a carriage still locked in place, intact. Not that it could help them all the way up there; if she signaled for an operator, she doubted one would appear.

Mo pulled her equally skittish mount next to Thana's and followed her gaze. "How are we going to get up there?"

Thana dismounted and handed her lead to Mo. She rifled through her pack for a moment before finding a rope. Mo looked at her skeptically.

"I'm not very good at climbing."

"I'm not asking you to," said Thana. "I'll climb up and send the carriage down for you. But we'll have to leave the camels down here. The fire will spook them if we bring them up. They should be all right by themselves for a little while. It's not like anyone's around to steal them," she added bitterly.

"I don't think it's safe to go up there," said Heru. "Nor is there any reason. We have supplies enough to see us to the next well. There's more than fire and ash in your city—I can feel blood, too."

Thana looped the rope around her waist, ignoring him. She knotted it around the cable, then yanked on the knot to test it; it held.

"All right." Thana rubbed sand between her hands for a better grip. "If you don't hear from me a few minutes after I reach the top, you should probably run. Or come up and save me."

"The first option is more prudent," said Heru.

Mo put a hand on Thana's shoulder, then leaned in and kissed her cheek. "Be careful."

Heru made a strange, choking noise as Thana reached above her head to grab the cable. Then she jumped and swung her leg up, hooking it around the cable in one motion. Her shoulder protested, the weeks'-old wound not yet a memory, and she dimly realized she'd never gone back to the healer to get it repacked, and likely never would. She gritted her teeth and started climbing. Hand over hand, she pulled herself up and up. Within too few minutes, her arms were burning, her shoulder pounding, she was out of breath—and she was only a quarter of the way. She'd been too slack with her training while gone.

The mind is everything. Her mother's favorite saying. Thana pushed on despite the pain. Her arms obeyed. She inched ever upward, focusing on the cable just ahead.

Then she was over the lip of the platform, the metal carriage just out of reach. She unhooked her legs and swung down, the ground blissfully solid, her arms little more than jelly. Keeping the rope around her waist, she peered over the platform's edge. She tried to wave at the small figures below, but all she managed was a limp wiggle.

She untied the rope and examined the cable, which connected to the top of a tall metal pole. The carriage hung next to it. It was a simple construction: a flat square wide enough to hold several people and their bags, surrounded by a waist-high railing with a section that could be removed entirely to let people on and off. Blunt hooks curled at even intervals from both the railing and the floor. These secured the baskets and sacks and people and helped stop them from sliding off.

Thana had never operated a carriage herself, but she'd watched them carry goods and people up and down enough times to know how they worked. The operator would unlatch the carriage from the pole—like *this*—then take off the block that kept it from rolling down the cable—like *this*. Once the carriage was unlocked, the operator would undo the large knot at the end of a rope that kept the whole thing from careening, at great speed, to a sandy demise.

Although the operators were almost always large, bulky men, Thana had no trouble keeping the carriage under control as she let out the rope and guided it over the edge of the platform. With the help of multiple pulleys, the carriage was as light as dust.

The carriage settled with a poof of ash on the sand. Mo and Heru clambered on, leaving the camels and their belongings below. Thanks to the pulleys, the carriage ascended with slippery ease, but Thana still had to lean back and dig her heels in to keep it moving. By the time the carriage crossed over the platform's edge, her arms were about ready to give.

She heaved one last time on the rope, then looped it around the hook and tied a knot. Before she'd finished securing the carriage, Heru and Mo had stepped onto firm ground. Mo looked relieved. Heru looked around.

"The fire has barely touched this place," he announced.

Thana had avoided looking too close earlier, afraid of what she'd see, but a glance told her that Heru was right. Although the nearby buildings were gray with ash, they were otherwise untouched. While the roar of fire was louder up here, so was the silence where there should've been the clatter and hum of a living city. Instead of thrumming with life, the area around them echoed with abandonment.

The only thing out of place was the debris at the mouth of the road, shoved up against the walls of the buildings on either side. Chairs and metal tables and broken doors were all heaped on top of each other, as if someone had hastily cleared out their home of all its furniture and then some. Perhaps they'd thought they could save their things from the fire. Foolish.

Thana started down the road that would lead them to the platform's center. There might be no one at the carriage station, but that didn't mean they wouldn't find someone further on, someone who could tell them what had happened. A watchman, perhaps, or even a drum chief, walking their neighborhood to show support and maintain calm.

The smoke thickened as they headed away from the edge of the city, obscuring the rising sun and covering them with an edgeless twilight. Thana tied her tagel tight around her mouth to keep out the choking smoke. Her eyes smarted, teared up, blurred her vision. She stopped to rub them clear and that was when she noticed the blood.

It was everywhere. Smeared across the walls, the ground, even the sconces. Most of the blood had dried to a flaking brown crust, but some thicker pools had only just congealed. Thana had stepped in one of these pools. Now she jerked back, but the blood clung thick to the bottom of her sandal. A violent shudder tore through her and she tried desperately to scrape the blood off on the stones.

Mo stared wide-eyed at the mess, her nose and mouth obscured by her tagel. Heru glanced around with a curiosity that verged on appreciation, as if admiring a work of art instead of the scene of a slaughter.

"There must have been a large fight here," he said.

"But, if so—where are the bodies?" asked Mo.

A shiver touched Thana's spine despite the oppressive heat. An answer tickled at the back of her thoughts, but she shoved it away, refusing to acknowledge it. There was no evidence. Because that would mean—

No.

"If people died here, they would've taken them down to the crypts," said Thana, sounding more reasonable than she felt. "Everyone's just . . . on a different platform."

Heru raised his eyebrows as if to say, *really?* But for once he kept his mouth shut. Mo's expression darkened beneath her tagel.

They continued through emptied streets. Everywhere Thana looked, she saw the same scene: drying blood spattered across stones, bricks, and glass, but no bodies. As they crossed from one platform to the next, the blood gave way to burnt walls, broken glass, and smoldering ruins. The heat and smoke thickened and soon they passed the first fire, still burning through shattered windows. It was not the last.

Thana stopped to search a handful of buildings, pushing through broken or burnt doors to find only empty, echoing rooms. No people, no bodies—nothing. She searched only a half dozen before she gave up, the dread of finding another vacant room heavier than any lingering hope. It was as if the city had been emptied.

But that wasn't possible. *Couldn't* be possible. Ghadid wasn't a small village, easily overrun by bandits or sand. The city should have been—*was*—unconquerable. Even if an invading force had managed to cross the sands, even if an army had found a way to climb the cables, even if they hadn't been rebuffed by the citizens above, even if they'd somehow made it onto Ghadid's streets, there were still the watchmen, there were still the drum chiefs, there were still her cousins, nimble and able and deadly.

No one could conquer Ghadid. Yet clearly, someone had.

Despite the overwhelming evidence, Thana still expected to find someone, *anyone*, around the next corner. So she pressed on, leading Mo and Heru deeper into the city, trusting they'd follow her, knowing they had no choice. Heru's role had finally been reversed with hers. If he wanted to keep Mo with him, he couldn't let Thana go.

What does Heru want with Mo? asked Amastan, and not for the first time.

Thana pushed the question away as she came to a bridge between platforms. Or at least, what had been a bridge. Nothing remained now but the metal wires that had once supported wooden boards. One of two metal poles had been knocked down on their side of the gap, its wires dangling over the edge of the platform. But the other wires were still taut, one spanning the gap at ground level, the other at chest.

"Oh *dust*," moaned Mo.

"It's all right." Thana shifted her pack so its weight rested evenly across her back, then tested the bottom wire. "As long as you hold on, you won't fall. Just don't look down." The wire stayed firm under her foot. "I'll go first."

Heru waved a hand. "By all means."

Thana gauged the distance, then took a breath and stepped onto the wire. It gave a little under her weight, but held. She gripped the top wire, then began sidestepping across the gap. Thana made the mistake of glancing down only once. In the overcast gloom from the clouds and smoke, the sands far below were an indistinct blur. The distance made her stomach lurch. She kept her gaze fixed on the far side after that.

A thrum in the wire made her glance back. Heru had one hand on the top wire and was staring at her with an unnerving intensity. She misstepped, but caught herself. She met Heru's gaze. Despite his tagel, she could read his thoughts almost as he had them.

All it'd take was an "accidental" shake to loosen Thana's grip and send her tumbling to the sands far, far below. Or he could loosen the wire from its mooring just beneath his palm. He could also simply bind her jaani from a distance; Salid's charms should protect her, but the attempt might be enough to unsteady her. Either way, Mo wouldn't blame Heru. Thana swallowed and tightened her grip on the top wire, but didn't dare look away.

Heru made his decision and stepped onto the wire. Thana let

out a small breath of relief—of course he wouldn't *really* try to kill her—before finishing the crossing. Once Heru was halfway, Mo shoved her staff through the straps of her pack, then fixed her gaze on a rooftop opposite and put her foot on the wire. After that, she didn't look down once until she'd grabbed Thana's hand on the other side and had both feet on solid ground.

She gave a small, hollow laugh. "That wasn't so bad."

"I suspect your people burned this bridge themselves," said Heru. "From here on out, we should expect every bridge to be destroyed like this one."

Mo shot him a sharp look, her eyes wide. She leaned against Thana for support and held tight to her hand. This close, Thana could feel Mo's body shaking like a caught rabbit. Thana did her best to project confidence, even though she didn't feel it. She surveyed the new platform, but it was more of the same. Flames licked across rooftops and blood decorated every surface. There were more piles of furniture here, half-blocking the street. Broken glass littered the stones, glittering in the firelight and crunching underfoot.

"Over here," said Heru.

He'd hurried ahead and now stood next to a caved-in ruin of a building, what had once belonged to her neighborhood's glass-worker. Thana joined Heru. He pointed at something indistinct just beyond the shattered door. She peered through the shifting smoke and ashes at a charred and bloody hunk of wood or maybe it was—

Flesh.

Thana turned and breathed deep, trying to suppress the sudden urge to be sick. She closed her eyes and concentrated on the acrid taste of smoke until the nausea faded.

"It's an arm," said Heru helpfully.

Her mind's eye replayed the details for her. Now Thana could discern the hand and its fingers, the torn skin and bloody muscle, the dull white of bone protruding where an elbow had once been. Her stomach roiled again and this time Thana couldn't stop it. She bent over and was sick.

An arm wrapped around her waist and a cool, slightly damp cloth pressed into her hand. "You okay?" asked Mo, her voice low and close.

Thana wiped her mouth with the cloth. "I've been better."

Mo nodded, patted her back, then let go and approached the building. Still bent double, Thana closed her eyes and waited for the nausea to recede.

"The arm was torn off," said Mo from a distance. "See how the skin is ragged around the—"

"Please," said Thana. "Is this necessary?"

Silence. Then Mo said, "I'm sorry."

Thana straightened, wiped her forehead with the clean side of the cloth, and turned to the other two. What could have done this? No man, no bandit, no warrior. But then, she'd fought something like this once—twice—before. Yet it was too much to wrap her mind around. When she tried anyway, something twisted deep inside of her, numbing her. None of this felt real.

Thana forced herself to focus on the feel of the cloth in her hand, the hard stones under her feet, the air thick with heat and smoke. She couldn't let herself shut down, not now. She blinked away tears and tried to think. What would Amastan do?

But this wasn't one of their contracts. This wasn't a mark to find and kill. This was her whole city—her whole world—hollowed out and burned to ashes. This was a man who should have been dead.

"We know who did this."

"You think it was Djet?" asked Mo.

Thana met Heru's gaze. "Who else?"

Heru nodded. "That would explain the lack of corpses."

Mo gestured. "But the arm—"

"Yes," cut in Heru. "An arm. *Just* an arm. I'm fairly certain that is the exception that verifies my hypothesis."

"The towns that disappeared," said Thana through numb lips. "You remember—right before his death. We thought it was just more rumor and hyperbole. But what if it wasn't?" She pointed at Heru. "You said something about an army of bound before we came up here. What did you mean?"

"The question should be: why not?" said Heru. "An army of bound would be unstoppable. They could cross the desert in a quarter the time it'd take a living army, and they wouldn't need food nor water. The only thing that troubles me is why *now*?" Heru paused for a moment, gaze unfocused. "Unless he plans to use them for the sajaami. . . ."

"What're you saying?" asked Mo. "That Djet bound everyone in Ghadid?"

It was one thing for Thana to feel that suspicion creeping into her consciousness, but another entirely for Mo to voice it aloud. She couldn't breathe.

"No."

"Actually, I'm fairly certain she is correct," said Heru. "It'd explain the lack of corpses. But this category of large-scale binding takes time and forethought. There's no way he could have done this overnight, for instance. Djet must have been planning this since I first came to Ghadid—where are you going?"

Heru's voice drifted through Thana's awareness as if from a distance. Her chest ached, broken and cracked as wide as the gap they'd crossed moments before. If Djet had been here . . . if there were no corpses . . . if *everyone*—

Thana ran. Through the dull roar filling her ears she just

barely heard shouting—surprise, a question, then a command to stop. She ignored it.

She was only two platforms away from her neighborhood. She marked wrecked storefronts and charred signs and changed direction as needed. She dodged around more debris and climbed a heap that cut off a street entirely. Then she was on the other side of a gap she must have crossed, but couldn't remember. If not for the red, stinging lines on her hands from the hot metal wires, she could've flown.

No. Her heart and legs and arms pumped together, efficient as gears and just as merciless, throwing her forward, ever forward, toward a truth she didn't want—but had—to see.

Ahead, the street opened onto a platform's center, one just like the dozen plus they'd already passed through. Except here, one door was a dusty red, its once vibrant paint long since faded under the harsh sun. Thana knew the shape of that door even before she could see its details, could feel the weight of its wood, the turn of its handle.

But half of it was gone, burned away to ash and dust. Scorch marks charred the wall to one side and the long window that ran next to it was little more than a gaping, dark hole, its glass melted and dripping beneath it.

No.

Thana pushed through the door, its edges crumbling beneath her hand. She froze just inside, her heart stopped. The room where she'd mended sandals by the hearth, sharpened knives under her mother's exacting gaze, and sorted and filed her father's scrolls was barely recognizable. The floor and ceiling and walls were black with soot and scorch marks. The hearth stood out in the darkness, its stonework strangely pale. But the rest—

Thana's eyes smarted. Her father's scrolls. The shelves that had filled half the room. His life's work. All of it: gone. The shelves were broken piles of rubble and there was nothing left of the scrolls themselves save for ash.

She wanted to sift through the ash to find something, *anything*, to save. Then, after, when she found her father, she could hand him one undamaged scroll and starting again wouldn't be so impossible. Because if there was nothing to save, then that meant—then that meant—

Thana kicked through the debris to get to the stairs. Made of stone, they'd withstood the fire that had rushed through and claimed everything else. She flew up them, two at a time, her mind buzzing with emptiness, her cheeks wet.

No.

The second floor was a quiet, private space. One where her parents had talked late into the night with each other, with family, with cousins. One where her mother had brought younger cousins and showed them poisons, knots, and knives. Off this space were several doors, leading to bedrooms. Normally, these were closed. Now they were wide open, half-burnt.

Scorch marks curled up the walls. The pillows and cushions and rugs were gone, reduced to ash. But the purple cloth that her mother had hung on the wall was only half gone, its color a vibrant rebuke. Something dark had been splattered across it.

"No."

Thana slumped against the wall, dizzy and weak. She could no longer deny what had happened. Blood streaked across the floor, in spatters and pools and long, dragging marks. Her parents weren't here. They were dead and bound and it was her fault. The world crumpled, shrinking and shattering into too many uncountable pieces.

If she hadn't left—

If she'd only stayed—

If she'd *warned* someone—

This was her fault. She stared at the mess, searing it into her vision and memory as if her own pain could undue some of the horror. She'd killed her parents as surely as if she'd wielded the knife herself. Her ineptitude, her inability to kill Heru the first time, her idiotic decision to chase him on her own, her inexcusable irresponsibility in not involving the marab, her sheer *arrogance* thinking she could handle this alone. She, a mere child in the eyes of her family. She, with only a handful of contracts to her name. She, of all people, thinking she could become a legend. She might have laughed if she could feel anything but numb.

A wet cough snapped her out of those dark thoughts. Thana was moving before she'd even recognized the sound. It had come from inside one of the rooms: her mother's. Another, louder cough made her sudden flicker of hope flare and burn, hot and fierce and painful. It couldn't be—but *maybe*—

Thana stopped in the doorway. The window was shattered, but the room was otherwise as her mother would have left it: bed made, clothes folded, spare sandals beside the door. Thana looked at none of those. Instead, she stared at the huddled mess of flesh and cloth and blood just feet away. It stared back at her with equal surprise, then reached for her.

"Thana?"

23

"Salid!"

The charm maker was a mess. Blood oozed from ragged gashes on his arms, chest, and legs, and a chunk of flesh was missing from his neck. His chest rose and fell with shallow, shuddering gasps, but his eyes were open and bright. Thana crouched beside him and took his hand between hers.

"Thana . . ." His voice was hardly more than a whisper and even that much took a lot out of him. "What are you . . . doing here?"

"I could ask you the same thing," said Thana, matching his volume.

Salid's eyelids fluttered and Thana tightened her grip, but he didn't lose consciousness. "I knew this house . . . would be empty," he said. "I set some of the fires. I was supposed to set more, but . . . there were too many. I came here to . . . because . . ." He trailed off and lifted his arm, as if she could have missed the wounds.

"You'll be okay," said Thana. "We have a healer below. Save your breath."

She tried to let go of his hand to help him up, but Salid's grip tightened. "No. It's too late . . . for healers. You need to know . . . what happened."

"Below, you can tell me below," repeated Thana. "You're going to be okay."

But Salid ignored her. "Monsters. So many . . . started with just a few. Nobody knew . . . what they were. Not at first." He paused for a long moment, eyes closing, long enough that Thana started to worry, then his eyes snapped back open, found hers, focused. "They were our own. People died . . . but didn't stay dead. They came back . . . like a plague. Amastan guessed . . . I knew . . . we tried to stop . . . but too little. Too late. Your cousins fought . . . but too many. More climbed the cables. Came from the sands. And someone . . . led them. In red." He closed his eyes, his breathing shallower now, rasping. "There were so many. Too many. G-d."

"Shh."

Thana touched Salid's forehead and jerked back: he was as cold as a corpse. He was slipping away fast. She had to get him downstairs. If he died, she'd lose any remaining connection to her parents, her cousins, to Amastan. Salid would know where they were and what had happened to them. He must.

When he opened his eyes again, they were unfocused. "When we couldn't . . . stop them, we burned . . . the city. Amastan evacuated . . . the others. Your ma fought, but . . . too many. No one could have . . ." He shook his head, unable to catch his breath and continue.

"She—?" started Thana, but the question stuck in her throat. She wasn't sure she wanted to know the answer.

"The man was . . . too strong," said Salid. "Even for her. I'm so sorry."

Thana noted dimly that she felt nothing at all at the news. "You can tell me what happened later." She was finally able to slide her hand out from his. "You're going to live." She put every ounce of certainty she had left into that sentence and for a moment, she almost believed it.

Salid attempted a laugh, but it came out a harsh cough. "It's too late . . . for healers."

"No," snapped Thana. Her anger flooded back. "It's not. She's right downstairs. We have water. If you can't go down, I'll bring her up."

But as Thana stood, Salid reached up and grabbed her wrist, his grip weak but urgent.

"Don't—it's too dangerous—"

"There's no danger anymore," she said. "The city's empty. Just hold on—I can make it right. I promise."

Salid let out a dry chuckle. "Promise? Did you bring . . . my pages?"

Thana flinched. "I'm so sorry—"

"Shh." Salid squeezed her hand. "All's . . . forgiven. It doesn't matter. Thana . . . you can't stay. Leave me. Before I die. *Go.*"

He released her wrist and gave her a feeble push, but Thana didn't budge. His wounds, his breathing—he was right. There was no point in bringing Mo up; it would only upset her when she was unable to help.

"I won't leave," she said. "You deserve more than that. You helped our family for so long. And look—" Thana pulled aside her wrap, revealing the top of Salid's glass belt. "It's kept me safe. You should make more of these. I think you could make a small fortune, especially once the drum chiefs heard of them. And the Azal will love them, too—think of how useful they'd be in the Wastes."

She knew she was babbling. Her words sounded inane even to her own ears. But she couldn't stop herself. If she stopped, Salid would slip away.

"Thana . . ."

Her name was barely a sigh. Salid closed his eyes and slumped back. His eyelids fluttered and twitched, but he didn't open them again. Thana sat with him and held his hand, watched as his breathing grew more labored, then shallow, then intermittent. It wasn't long before the pauses between each breath were so deep that she had to check his pulse to see if he was still alive.

In the end, the next breath never arrived. His lips parted to let out a sigh and then his chest didn't rise again. Thana let go of his hand and it dropped, thudding against the floor with a finality that took all the air out of the room.

Her cheeks were damp, her eyes burning and blurring with tears. She didn't know when she'd started crying. She touched Salid's closed eyelids and muttered a prayer. Maybe Heru could perform the final rites and quiet his jaani, if only for a little while. But a little while might be enough for someone else to return and find him. After enduring all this, Salid deserved more than for his jaani to go wild.

Thana took her time standing. She dug her fingernails into her palms to feel something, but the pain that burst like stars in her hands was just as distant. She wanted to scream, to cry, to throw something, but she lacked the energy. All she could do was stare at Salid's body.

Your ma stayed to fight, but . . . too many. I'm so sorry.

Her mother, Tamella, the Serpent of Ghadid, the woman who'd stopped a civil war, killed a drum chief, and become a legend—dead. It didn't seem possible, couldn't be possible, and yet Thana couldn't deny it, not when her home lay in ruins around her.

And if even her mother had succumbed, then what about the others? Dihya, Illi, all her cousins, her father—? At least she could cling to the small hope that Amastan was still alive. But everyone else? Wounded, dead—or worse.

Thana's hands tightened into fists. A man had led the monsters.

Djet.

The horrifying understanding that had driven her across burning platforms for evidence that could prove her wrong now hardened into certainty. Djet had been here. He'd swept through her city with his monsters and enslaved her people. Her mother and her cousins had fought back, but it hadn't been enough. Now they were gone, bound to Djet's will and headed for—for where? For what purpose?

And Thana thought she could stop him?

A noise bubbled out of her throat, somewhere between a laugh and a sob. How could she stop Djet when even her cousins had failed? She was a fool. If she hadn't been so arrogant, so certain that she could live up to, even surpass, her mother's name, then she wouldn't be here, now, kneeling in blood and ash.

No, said Amastan softly. *You'd be dead, like your mother.*

Always logical, even when he was in her head. But it was all she could do to keep standing, let alone avenge a city.

Salid groaned, a rattling sound that came from deep within his chest. His foot kicked out, then his arm. Thana stepped back, not frightened, only wary. She'd watched enough people become bodies to know that this was normal, that this was a release of any lingering energy and eventually a release of their jaani. She started to turn—

Salid sat up. Thana jumped, a knife already in her hand. Salid's eyelids snapped open, revealing glazed, unseeing eyes. Thana shook her head, her heart lodged in her throat. This couldn't be happening. It wasn't possible. It wasn't *fair.*

Salid lunged. Thana stepped out of the way, tears already drying on her cheeks. As she clubbed Salid on the head with the hilt of her dagger, then swept a kick at his knees that sent him sprawling, she felt very, very old.

"It's not fair," she whispered as she pinned him to the floor with her knee.

"Not fair." Thana sliced open the back of Salid's wrap.

"Not. Fair."

The tip of Thana's knife was poised to cut through the marks across Salid's back, but his skin was unmarred. Thana stared, uncertain. Salid growled and twisted around, grabbing her by the ankle.

She slashed at his hand and jerked her foot free. She backed out of the room, watching with fresh horror as Salid stood, his gaze unwavering and vacant, his face slack. Part of her wanted to stay and fight. She wouldn't win, but that didn't matter, not anymore. There was nothing left for her here.

But part of her clung on tight, reminding her that Mo still waited somewhere outside. That someone had done this, that he was still out there, and he needed to be stopped. And if she died here—

She might become one of *them*.

That alone banished any lingering hesitation. Thana turned and ran. She took the stairs two at a time, using the wall to keep her balance. Salid's footsteps thudded behind, but too slowly. She'd easily outrun him. But she didn't slow down.

She hurtled across the bottom floor and through the door and slid to a stop. Glass crunched underfoot as she spun to face the doorway. Salid's shuffling approach was muted beneath the hiss of fire and the moan of the walls, weakened by heat and pressure. It was only midmorning, but the thick smoke and warm orange light darkened the day to evening.

Footsteps thudded from behind, at first a hollow echo, then louder as Mo solidified out of the smoke, braids loose and flying.

"Thana!"

Mo all but tumbled into Thana and threw her arms around her, hugging her tight. The hug only lasted for a heartbeat, then Mo shoved Thana away. She narrowed her eyes and clenched her hands into fists.

"What in all that's holy and whole is *wrong* with you? Why would you leave like that? If something happened to you . . . *why did you leave?*"

"I'm sorry," said Thana hollowly. "I'm all right. I . . ." She swallowed and glanced back at her home and its dark, empty doorway.

"Where's Heru?"

The en-marabi strolled out of the smoke. "Did I hear my name?"

"*G-d,*" muttered Thana. Then, louder, "There's someone in that building."

Mo made a startled noise. "Are they all right?" She moved toward the doorway, shifting her pack around so her waterskin was within reach. "I should check—"

Thana grabbed Mo's arm, stopping her from going any further. "No, Mo. They're—*he's*—not all right. He's not alive. Not anymore."

"Oh." Mo dropped her hand from her skin, but didn't re-shoulder her pack. Her other hand strayed to her staff.

Heru joined them and pushed up his sleeves. "Is he bound?"

Thana nodded. "But there aren't any marks. I tried that—I watched him die and he just . . . woke up again."

"I feared as much. Those comments by the historian Set regarding the empty towns prior to Djet's execution were concerning. I came up with a handful of hypotheses that might satisfy a historian, but still did not satisfy me." Heru sifted through his wrap as he spoke, removing a vial here, a satchel there, and a small blade. "I believe it was part of Djet's larger plan. He wanted to create many more like him—or at least bind them to his will. Something that could empty an entire town without undue hysterics from its neighbors would've needed to work fast and locally. Ideally, it'd use a single, ubiquitous vector. Like, for instance, water."

"Are you saying what I think you're saying?" asked Thana.

Heru paused what he was doing long enough to glance at her. "I'm certain that whatever you think I'm saying is most likely incorrect, considering your lack of expertise on the matter and overall lack of intellect." He turned back to the doorway and popped the cork from one vial. "The water of Ghadid is contaminated, likely with a contagion that turns all those who ingest it into bound when they die. I assume the binding mechanisms must not affect a person while they yet live, but once their body expires and their jaani is unable to leave, they awaken confused and belligerent, just like the bound we've already encountered. Djet is granting these people immortality, of a sort. All it would require to turn the entire city was a critical mass of dead, which could have occurred naturally as more and more people died and were bound—a cascading event."

So many. Too many. Salid had already told Thana all of this, if she'd only listened.

"Djet used *water*?" said Mo, horrified. "That's—that's just—"

"Ingenious," said Heru.

"—blasphemy," finished Mo.

Inside the building, something fell with a clatter. Then bare feet shuffled across stone. Heru removed a vial from his pack and poured a liquid thick as egg whites in a semicircle on the ground before him, then stepped back. Thana and Mo edged back with him, gazes fixed on the doorway. A moment later, Salid shot out as if he'd been thrown by some unseen force. His arms were outstretched, his mouth a froth of blood and foam. Thana winced at the sight. Mo gasped.

"That's—that's the charm maker," said Mo.

"Salid," supplied Thana.

"Oh G-d."

Salid rushed Heru, who was waiting impassively. Salid's hand scraped the air before Heru's face, but when his foot touched the edge of the damp semicircle, light flared and Salid was thrown backward. As the semicircle's glow faded, Salid shook his head like a rabid dog, spraying bloody foam across the stones. He growled and rushed Heru again, but was again rebuffed.

Unconcerned by the mad creature scrabbling at him only a foot away, Heru drew his blade across the underside of his arm. He bit the cork out of a second vial, then held it beneath his fresh wound. He caught several drops of blood, then covered the vial with his thumb and gave it a vigorous shake. Its contents glowed a fierce red, as if he'd caught the light of the dying sun.

Meanwhile, Salid rammed his body against the barrier over and over, his growl unbroken and growing louder. He clawed at the air and spat red froth at the ground. It was painful to watch, but Thana couldn't look away. For over a decade, she'd walked into Salid's shop and always been greeted by a jangle of bells and a wall of glass charms, at first with her uncle Usem, then later Amastan, and finally, this last time, on her own. Salid's charm belt thrummed with a bright hot heat, painful and searing. She welcomed the pain.

With a flick of his wrist, Heru sent the vial skidding across the stones. It came to a rest at Salid's sandals. The bound's whole body had turned to follow the vial's path and now he stared down at his feet. Then he pounced. He grabbed the vial with clumsy fingers and shoved it into his mouth, working the glass with his teeth. Some of the brilliant red liquid spilled from his lips like strands of bloody drool, but the rest went down his throat.

All at once, Salid's body spasmed. Heru stepped over the semicircle, now dark, and put a hand on Salid's shoulder. He turned the bound toward him while holding his other hand against Salid's chest. A light burst from between Heru's fingers and Salid writhed, trying to push Heru away. But the en-marabi held strong and a heartbeat later, Salid's mouth dropped open and darkness swarmed out.

The darkness arced toward the sky, then abruptly turned back sands-ward, as if yanked. It swarmed to Heru's hand held against Salid's chest, now a clenched fist. Then the darkness and the light both vanished. Heru stepped back. Salid crumpled to the ground, this time truly lifeless.

Thana detached herself from Mo and approached the body, passing Heru as he pocketed something still glowing. She turned Salid faceup and closed his eyes. She remained tense, ready for another attack. But this time, the body stayed still. It felt empty, too, in a way it hadn't before—before—

A hand touched Thana's shoulder. She started and went for a knife before realizing it was only Mo. She hadn't even heard the healer approach. Her whole body was trembling violently, uncontrollably, and the loud roar in her ears came from more than just the fire.

"When you're done having your moment, I need a healer," said Heru.

Mo jerked, but didn't move from Thana's side. She put a hand on Thana's other shoulder and gave her a reassuring squeeze. Thana swallowed, turned, and threw her arms around Mo. They pressed close; Mo was shaking, too.

"Or I can just slowly bleed to death over here," said Heru.

"While I respect your need for emotional and physical support, Djet won't wait for our permission to continue wreaking more such destruction. If you want to avenge your city, then we must act."

Thana pressed her forehead against Mo's, then took a deep breath and untangled herself. As much as she hated him, Heru was right. They couldn't waste time grieving. That could come later, if there was a later. Heru watched them impassively as he bandaged his hand with a length of cloth.

"All right," said Thana. "Do you have a plan?"

Heru's eyes almost crinkled in a smile. "I never thought you'd ask."

24

"First," said Heru. "You need to let go of my healer."

Mo wiped at her eyes, smudging ash across her cheeks. "We're going to need more water."

"I know where to—" started Thana, then stopped herself. "But we can't use it."

Heru sighed. "There are methods to circumvent the binding. Just—go before I bleed to death."

"Fine. I'll be right back."

"I'll come, too," said Mo quickly. "In . . . case."

"Yes," said Heru absently as he pulled out more vials from his pockets. "Do keep her from running away again."

With Mo at her side, Thana headed for a small, squat building just off the platform's center. Inside, there was barely enough room for both of them; Mo had to press close. A sconce on the wall held a cold torch, but enough light filtered through the doorway to still see. Thana pulled back the hatch set into the center of the floor, revealing a well-worn stairwell. Stairs spiraled tight and steep down past the platform's thick metal crust and into a hidden interior.

The lanterns lining the stairwell were still lit, their oil only half gone. That meant no more than sixteen or so hours had passed since they'd last been filled. Thana couldn't decide if that fact was encouraging or not. Would they find the poor slave who'd filled them down below?

Thana led the way, Mo's presence close at her back and reassuring. After a full, tight turn, the stairs opened onto a wide and well-lit room. Always before when Thana had come to get water, there'd been someone else here, either taking their share, hawking containers, or begging for a spare baat. Now the room was empty and the occasional clank from its center was as startling as a shout.

Thana paused at the foot of the stairs, but Mo pushed around her, heading for a small pile of abandoned waterskins. The curved face of the pylon itself stood at the center of the round room, its dull gray surface pitted and marred by splashes of brilliant orange decay. The font had been carved directly into the metal, forming a shallow basin at waist height. A pipe hung above the basin, its mouth orange with the same decay.

Thana eyed the familiar sight with fresh distrust. How had Djet poisoned the water? It didn't seem possible. Every pylon had a pump and every neighborhood had a gearworker who kept it safe and functioning. Only a gearworker had access to the inner mechanisms of the pumps and even they didn't fully understand how they worked. No one had access to the aquifer far beneath the sand that supplied the pumps and the city.

A disgruntled gearworker could have poisoned their own pump, but poisoning all of them would have required stealing the pumphouse keys from the drum chiefs. Yet, if Heru was correct, Djet had found a way.

Mo approached with half a dozen waterskins in her arms. She eyed the basin with equal wariness.

"The aquifer," said Mo. "That's the only way. Someone poisoned the aquifer."

"But how?"

Mo shrugged. "Does it matter? We'll have to take care when we leave. All the wells between here and the Wastes will be affected, too."

When we leave. Even though that had been their plan all along, Thana could no longer imagine it. What was the point? Djet had won.

Mo handed Thana the first skin. "How many more like Salid are out there?"

"From what he said, I don't think anyone's left."

Thana dug out a baat from the pouch she'd filched off Heru only a few days ago. The flash of smugness she felt as she fed the baat into the slot above the basin was gone as soon as it arrived. He wouldn't have been able to use those baats again anyway. And neither would she. What use was the currency of a dead city? What use was a contract without Kaseem? What use was a cousin without her family?

What use was *she*?

"But what if there's someone out there that I can still help? What if there's one person I can still save?"

"They left, Mo," snapped Thana. "They've all been turned into bound or they've fled—there's no one left. It's just us. And we can't stay here, either."

"I know," said Mo softly.

Thana flushed with guilt. She shouldn't have lost her temper. She bit her lip and pulled the lever next to the basin. Instead of looking at Mo, she stared at the water filling the skin. It didn't look contaminated. But what had she expected? A strange glow? A dark sludge?

"I know," repeated Mo as the water *glugg*ed. "I just . . . I can't stop thinking about what must have happened. I can't stop thinking about all the terror and pain they must have felt. What about my father, my sister? What happened to Enass? Everyone I've ever healed? What was the *point* if they were all just going to end up like the charm maker?"

Mo's voice broke. Thana glanced away from the basin as the first tear streaked down her cheek, closely followed by another and another. Thana swallowed, then took one of Mo's limp hands and held it tight.

"I don't know if I can do this," whispered Mo, voice thick. "I'm not like you, or—or Heru. I should never have left. What did I even accomplish by going to Na Tay Khet? Heru could have found all that out on his own. I was just being selfish. They needed me here. I'm not a fighter, Thana. I'm not strong. I'm falling apart just being in an empty city. I don't know if I can face what's out there, in the Wastes."

"You're stronger than you think," said Thana. The flow of water had finally stopped and she tied off the skin and set it down. "I've watched you fight and I've watched you heal. You're remarkable. And we'll need you if we have any hope of stopping Djet."

"Do we?" Mo swallowed. "Have any hope?"

It was a valid question. Thana looked around the small room, at the pump and basin, the leather skins and empty chairs, the metal walls and stone stairs. She'd thought she didn't have any hope left, and yet here she was, filling enough waterskins for a journey into the Wastes. What was that, if not hope?

Should they still go? Heru had a general idea of where the Aer Essifs were, but the Wastes were vast and they were only three. And on top of that, Djet had an army of bound at his command, an army made from the people she loved and hated and trusted and knew. Could she fight them, when it came to that? Could she stop them? Could she do what her family couldn't? What her mother couldn't?

What would Amastan do?

But he'd already done it: he'd fled, saving as many people as he could. She could try to find him and the survivors. Displaced and poisoned by Djet, they were still her people, still her city, and they'd need all the help they could get. They needed to know what they were up against, they needed Heru's expertise.

And then Djet would still be free, capable of doing this again on an even larger scale.

What would her mother do?

But her mother had already done it: she'd fought, and she'd died. If she were still alive, she would want to protect her own. She'd find Amastan and the rest and make absolutely certain no one else died.

But Thana wasn't Amastan and she wasn't her mother. She wasn't even an assassin, not anymore. What would she do?

Thana looked at Mo, at her tear-streaked cheeks and red-lined eyes, and she felt hope. It wasn't a grand feeling, a great unfurling or anything like that, but a simple bead of angry heat that burned hot and painful in her chest. But that was enough.

"We have to," said Thana. "It's our only choice. Because if we don't have hope, we stay here and die. But we can't let Djet win. We can't let him do this to another city or unleash the sajaam or whatever other horrible thing he has planned. But more than that—we owe it to those he's bound. Maybe this is our fault. Maybe we failed them. Either way, we can't stay here. They deserve peace."

"I know, I know. I just . . . I *can't*."

Thana folded Mo into her arms, feeling her body shake. She ran a hand across the top of Mo's head, her braids rough. So many salas were intertwined in them. Some red, some orange, some blue, but most were gray and brown strings. Thana quickly lost count. There were too many, and all of them had been people Mo had saved. A fierce pride filled Thana.

"You can," said Thana. "I know you can. You can't help but help people. You're kind when you don't have to be. There's a ferocity within you that keeps you healing even those who don't deserve it. And you'll do this, too, even though you believe you can't. And that's what I love about you."

Mo looked up, eyes watery and red. "Love . . . ?"

Thana swallowed, hesitated. The word had just come out, but in the midst of all this wrong, it felt *right*. The one thing she was absolutely sure of. Thana tilted her head down, brushed her lips across Mo's, and breathed, "Yes."

As Thana started to move away, Mo reached up and drew her back. This time their lips met and they didn't part again for some moments.

When they finally emerged from the pumphouse carrying the waterskins, Heru had settled onto the ground inside a circle of ash. He glanced up from writing and tapped his pen against the paper, gaze unfocused. Then he saw the skins and stood, attempting to brush off his white wrap but only ended up smearing it with black ash.

"Are you two finally finished? I knew your mechanisms were slow and tedious, but I vastly underestimated how much time they would waste. Let me see one of those skins."

Mo held out a skin to Heru. Thana set her burden down, warm all over in a way that had nothing to do with the pervasive fires and everything to do with Mo's lips and she couldn't help but feel a little guilty that she was thinking of Mo instead of the dead. She reached blindly for Mo's hand and found it. She squeezed. Mo squeezed back. Thana let go of some of her guilt; if this was how she'd survive the coming days, then so be it.

Heru opened the skin. He pulled his tagel down until it hung loose around his neck, then poured some of the water into his cupped palm and sniffed it. He tasted it. He gagged, spat it out, dropping the rest of the water as he clutched at his throat. His body shook as he coughed. He closed his eyes and curled his hands into fists.

Mo started for him. "Heru!"

But the coughing stopped before she reached him. Heru was doubled over, panting, but alive. He spat again, this time a wad of frothy red phlegm. Then he straightened.

"My hypothesis has just been confirmed," he proclaimed, voice rough. He pulled the tagel back over his nose and rustled through his bag. "The water was indeed the vector through which Djet seized control of the city and its people."

Thana drew a sharp breath, as if she'd been punched. It was one thing to suspect, but another to know. There'd been no way her people could have defended themselves against such an attack.

"Thankfully, I'm here," continued Heru. "This is a strong, but simple, binding that can be nullified if the correct steps are taken. I will need your blood."

Thana stepped back. "What? No. Absolutely not."

"Why?" asked Mo.

Heru spread his hands. "I can use my own blood if using yours is so repulsive, but doing so runs the very real risk of transferring Djet's control to me when you drink the water. I cannot be absolutely certain of the exact methods Djet utilized to create the original binding, seeing as how I have only had the opportunity to study his methods through secondhand sources and am hardly a scholar on the subject."

"How do we know you're not telling us the one so you can do the other?" pressed Thana.

He harrumphed. "If I had wanted to bind you, Thana, I could have done so upon our first meeting or upon the multiple times you've annoyed me since that eventful night. It is not skill or

opportunity I lack, but desire. If you want to continue question-
ing my motives, by all means avoid drinking any water until you
find another well, and then pray to your G-d that it isn't likewise
tainted."

"Fine," muttered Thana. "But if you're lying, I'll rip out your
throat when I turn into one of those dust-cursed bound."

"Considering your previous attempts at trying to kill me," said
Heru, "I'm not especially worried."

Mo drew a thin blade from a pocket and held it out to Heru.
"Here—use this. It's very sharp and won't cause scarring."

Thana's heart stuttered and her mouth had gone dry. She
forced herself to relax. Mo hadn't noticed. Mo hadn't heard. It
was fine—

As Heru took the knife from Mo, a frown creased her eyebrows. She looked from Thana to Heru, the question unasked on
the air between them.

"Yes," said Heru helpfully. "Thana's been trying to kill me."

Mo's hand dropped. "What?"

"*Hah.* He's only joking," said Thana. Her voice sharpened as
she glared at Heru. "Just like *I'm* only joking when I say he's an
en-marabi and he binds jaan just like Djet does."

"We all have our skeletons," said Heru. He took Mo's knife
and squatted next to the skins. "Mine is inside me. Hah—see?"
He looked up at them. "It's a joke. It was funny. Oh, fine."

Mo stared at Thana, sliding her fingers between each other
over and over again. "You never really answered me when I asked
if you were a performer."

Heru snorted. "She's no actor. Or if she is, she should find
another profession." He pulled out several small pouches from
inside his wrap and set them in a neat line before him.

Thana glared at him. "We had a *deal*," she hissed.

"What deal?" asked Mo.

"I don't see the point in lying to her anymore." Heru gestured at the destruction surrounding them. "Considering. I was only afraid that she'd take her healing services elsewhere, but now—where is there for her to go? We're all in this together." He placed a hand against his chest and cleared his throat. "It's true. I'm an en-marabi, and I am proud of it. I have devoted my life to the science of jaani binding."

Mo had stepped back and now crossed her arms protectively over her chest. "Please tell me you're both joking."

But Heru wasn't finished. "And Thana's an assassin."

25

"Mo—"

"Someone contracted her to kill me," continued Heru. "Thankfully, she's not very good at her job. I kept her close to keep an eye on her and also because it seemed you had some concern for her well-being. But I no longer see a reason to keep up our pretenses. We'll work together better if we know just what we're working with. Can one of you bring me a bowl?"

"But I'm not—I mean, not anymore—I wasn't—"

Mo brushed her hands up and down her arms. "I should have known. Your skills, your choices—G-d, I'm such a fool. I'd thought the Serpent was just a story. But everything you said, everything you did—was that all just to get closer to Heru? Was that the only reason you came with us? You never actually cared about anyone else." Her eyes widened. "You—you didn't dress up like one of the Empress's slaves just to find us, did you? You were there to kill Heru. If the Empress hadn't recognized you . . ." Mo put a hand to her lips. "And his waterskin on the way to Na Tay Khet—"

"I didn't go just because of Heru," interrupted Thana. "He'd left Ghadid, I could have broken my contract." The lie held some truth—it's what she would have argued to Kaseem, but her career would have been over just the same. "I went because of you. I didn't want you alone with him. He's just as dangerous as Djet."

Mo shook her head. "We'd only met that once, that time you were attacked by dogs. But those bite marks—that wasn't a dog."

Heru coughed. "She obtained those during her first attempt to murder me. We were unfortunately interrupted by some of Djet's bound. She's up to—what, is it three attempts now?"

Mo squeezed her eyes shut. "Please. Stop talking."

Heru counted on his fingers. "Yes. Three."

Thana balled her hands into fists, digging her nails into her palms. "That's not fair. He *earned* the contract. He's an en-marabi, just like Djet. You haven't seen what he can do. He deserves to die."

"No one deserves to die," said Mo.

"He binds jaan! When I first met him, he'd bound a woman to his will and used her as a shield against me. Are you really going to believe him over me?"

When Mo opened her eyes, they shone with unshed tears. "But is it true? Are you an assassin?"

Thana met her gaze. Some of her anger died; now she just wanted to throw up. "But that's all in the past—"

"Are you an assassin?"

"I had a contract on Heru when this all started, but I broke it." Thana gestured around them. "It doesn't even matter anymore."

Mo drew in a shuddering breath. "You lied to me."

"But Heru has been lying all along about what he is—"

"I didn't sleep with *him!*" snapped Mo. Her words echoed accusingly off the nearby walls. Mo took several deep, steadying breaths, then continued, "I know Heru isn't a good person. I've always known that. But you repeatedly and purposefully lied about your intentions every step of our journey. It's different because I cared about you—or at least the you that you were pretending to be. Now I can't even be sure you weren't just using me to get to him."

Heru cleared his throat. "You two . . . ?"

Mo glared at him. Heru held his hands up and made a show of turning back to his work.

"If either of you want clean water to drink, I'll need a bowl," said Heru to his tools and pouches. "I only wanted to clear the air," he added softly. "We have a long journey ahead that we likely won't survive. Since it's just the three of us, I thought we should all be more honest. I didn't know you two . . . ah . . ."

The fact that he sounded the tiniest bit remorseful filled Thana with anger. She stomped toward the nearest building and shoved her way inside. She found a bowl immediately, but lingered for another heartbeat to let her blood cool. She didn't need a contract to kill Heru, right? Her whole city was gone, she didn't need any excuse. But she knew she wasn't just angry at him; she was angry at herself.

When she returned nothing had changed. Mo was still avoiding her gaze and Heru was still staring intently at the ground. Thana dropped the metal bowl next to him and pivoted away. Heru plucked it out of the air before it could clatter on the stones.

Now that he had something concrete to do, Heru perked up. He poured water into the bowl, then measured out colorful powders from his pouches and dumped them one by one into the water, turning the liquid first a brilliant green, then a milky purple, and finally a colorless gray. Heru lifted his tagel to sniff at the water occasionally as he coached it through colors, but he never once glanced their way.

"I can't tell you to leave," said Mo suddenly. "There's nowhere for you to go. Alone, you'd die out here, and that would be a dereliction of the duty G-d gave me. At least *one* of us believes in the sanctity of life. I can't even say I won't heal you, because that would be a lie. But please—don't speak to me. Don't come near me. I can't handle it right now."

"Mo—" started Thana, but then thought better of it.

"Does that include me?" asked Heru, trading the bowl of water for Mo's blade.

"You're a G-d-cursed jackal, Heru," said Mo. "But you never pretended to be anything else."

"*I* never pretended to be anything else!" snapped Thana. "I am who I've always been! I've never tried to hide that from you, just the contract on Heru. That's it. That's the only thing."

"How many people have you killed?" asked Mo.

Thana's breath left her. "What? That's not—that's in the past."

Mo gave a bitter laugh. "So you *have* taken a life. And you still don't understand. What you do—" When Thana opened her mouth, Mo corrected, "—what you *did*—is directly opposed to all my training and all my years of work. I've done everything I can to save a life and still been forced to watch someone die. And now I find out that you've taken those lives."

"But that's not true—" began Thana.

"That's enough." Mo took a step back. "Please, Thana."

Heru coughed. "Well, now that's out of the way, can we get back to what's important?"

Without waiting for an answer, Heru sliced open his palm and, wincing, dropped Mo's knife. He squeezed his hand into a fist over the bowl until seven fat drops of blood fell, clouding the bowl's already murky surface. The red swirled and diffused in invisible currents, then the water cleared to a murk. Thana stared at the bowl to avoid looking at Mo.

"We haven't got all day," said Heru.

Thana looked up to find him holding the knife out to her. She took it and let the urge to slice open his neck fill her, picturing it, savoring it—and then she let it go. The blade's bite across her palm broke some of her anger, but the relief was temporary. The knife was too sharp to really hurt and for a moment, she couldn't even see the cut.

Then the blood welled up across her palm. Pain shot bright and sharp up her arm when she turned her hand over and formed a fist. She counted out seven drops, watching them splash, heavier than water, into the bowl. The murk thinned and dispersed until the water was merely chalky—clean enough to drink. But Thana wasn't even tempted. She set the knife down and stepped away, her throbbing hand pressed to her chest. The wound was already clotting.

While Mo cut and counted, Thana stared at the smoke-choked sky. It had to be midday, but only a yellow haze marked the sun. The flames crackled and hissed, the buildings groaned, and the wind whispered. It was almost peaceful.

Thana turned back at the splash of water. Heru was dividing the bowl's contents among the skins, shaking each in turn before tying off the neck and throwing the skin to the side. When he finished, he tossed the empty bowl aside, which bounced off the stones with a startling clatter. The metallic ringing still echoed as Heru turned his gaze upward, eyes inscrutable and expression obscured by his tagel.

He stayed that way for a heartbeat, two. Then his shoulders rolled forward and he dropped his head. "It is done. I'm tired and require rest. I would advise against beginning our journey into the Wastes until we've all had some time to recover."

"We can't stay here," said Mo with a hint of desperation. "What if there are more bound? Salid can't have been the only one left behind."

"I know a place," said Thana. "But I'm not sure you'll like it."

"If one of your leaders had a shelter, you should have mentioned it sooner," said Heru.

"No. Not a shelter." Thana pointed down. "Beneath the city."

Mo's expression brightened. "The crypts?"

When Thana nodded, Heru snorted. "Because nothing says safe from the bound dead like a crypt."

"No, she's right," said Mo, carefully not looking at Thana. "If Djet enslaved all the dead in Ghadid, then the crypts will be empty."

"Only those whose jaan haven't made the crossing. The other bodies are still ripe potential for creating more bound."

"We don't keep bodies without their jaan in the crypts," said Mo. "A jaani stays tethered to its body for seven years. In the last year, the marab remove the body and bring it to the sands for the seven year rite. Until the rite, the marab quiet the jaan in the crypts. There's no chance of a jaani going wild—it's never without escort. If Djet could bind those jaan, then they're already gone. Unless they were trapped within the crypt, there shouldn't be anyone, even bodies, down there. We don't keep the dead after their jaan is gone. For one, we don't have room. For another, that's just unsanitary."

Heru tilted his head. "You don't . . . keep your dead? Or at least entomb them?"

"There'd be nowhere to put them."

"Not even in the ground?"

"And lose them forever in the sands?" said Mo. "No, the marab burn the bodies. There's no reason to keep the dead around when their jaani is gone."

"Then perhaps your crypts are a prudent choice."

Thana started down the street. "Follow me."

The entrance to the crypt was a squat building at the rear of a small courtyard. Geometric designs adorned its roof and pillars, their bright colors dampened by the haze. Charms and string-work dripped from the open doors. A pot of gifts, mostly baats, remained undisturbed near the entrance. But the plain gray mats for prayer had been sullied and torn, their remnants tossed around the courtyard.

Thana had visited the crypt before, but she'd only been inside once—outside of funerals, only marab were allowed to enter. Normally, the crypt was awash with light and the scent of burning incense. Now, the crypt was quiet and dark. Like the pumphouse, its doors stood open and unlocked. Unlike the pumphouse, this wasn't normal.

Instead of incense, Thana smelled fire and burnt meat and oil, an uncomfortably pleasant combination. Streaks of blood shone brackish black across the wooden doors. Thana shuddered, then set her shoulders and stepped into the darkness.

Light bloomed behind her, sudden and sharp. Heru pushed past, holding a fistful of white light. Inside, more blood was smeared across the ground, but aside from a broken desk and a few scrolls trampled on the floor, the room was unscathed. Thana took a striker from its hook next to the door before heading for the bannister and stairs at the room's center.

The light turned and jumped as Heru moved around the room, inspecting what was left. Mo slammed the doors shut and slid the thick metal bolts in place with a reassuring thud. Thana started down the dark stairwell, but soon it was filled with that same, too-white light as Heru joined her. The stairs led to another, open door, which led into the crypt itself.

Like the pumphouse, the crypt wrapped around the pylon beneath the platform, forming a circle with a solid center. Thana walked the perimeter, lighting the torches with the striker. Mo had been right—the crypt was empty. The tombs were all bare, nothing but dark holes stacked four high and set deep into the walls. Torn cloth clung to the corners of a few, the only indication that something—some*one*—had lain within.

Thana paused in front of one empty tomb. Dust and sand

had accumulated at the edges, but the middle was clean. Heavy steps behind warned her of Heru's approach, but she didn't turn.

"Did your marab use the water to quiet their jaan?"

Thana thought back to her uncle Usem's funeral, the only one she'd ever attended. At the time, the marab had prayed over water, covered a piece of vellum with inscriptions, then cleaned the ink off with the water. They'd dripped the inky blend into her uncle's open mouth. "Yes, at first, but . . ."

"They do," said Mo. "Did. Weekly, anyway."

"That would have been enough." Heru surveyed the empty tombs. "It appears you were correct that the jaan would still be tethered to these bodies. Not a single one remains. The better for us—I'll go back up and seal the front doors. Once that's done, we'll be safer here than anywhere else. Of course, that's not a high threshold to pass."

Heru swept away and up the stairs, removing objects from his wrap as he walked. He took the light with him, but by now the torches were burning brightly. Thana glanced at Mo, hoping she was ready to talk, to repair what had been broken, but the healer was already walking away.

Thana sighed and eyed the tombs, briefly considering sleeping in one. Then she noticed the smear of blood beneath one tomb and, stepping back, across the floor. Now that she was looking, the blood was everywhere. Smears on the walls. Handprints across the floor.

Of course, the dead hadn't been the only ones in the crypt. What must the marab have thought when those corpses started moving, started climbing out of their tombs? The marab would have tried to stop them. They'd failed.

Thana shuddered. The stomp of footsteps on the stairs heralded Heru's return. He'd pulled his tagel down again. He still held the brilliant orb in one fist, but his other was streaked with blood and ash.

"That should hold for the night," he announced. "Now, I think it's time to plan our next steps. Djet is still out there—"

"Why do you want to stop him?" asked Mo sharply.

She'd moved in front of Heru while he walked and now blocked him with her staff, her body tense. Heru stopped and looked her over as if he'd been confronted by a growling kitten. He tried to go around, but she stepped with him.

"I know why *I* want to stop him," said Mo. "He destroyed my home. He killed my people. He's an en-marabi, a blasphemer of the worst kind." She paused for a beat, then added, "But so are you."

Heru tried going the other way around Mo and her staff, but again, she moved with him. "I thought my reasons were obvious," he said.

"I hope you'll forgive me if I don't take anything for granted right now."

"You're forgiven," said Heru. "But only if you get out of my way."

He darted suddenly to one side, but Mo moved just as quickly. Thana was smugly satisfied to recognize her training in Mo's movements. Heru huffed his annoyance.

"Not until you tell me why," pressed Mo.

"The Empress ordered me to."

"I don't think you care that much about your Empress's orders."

"Perhaps I don't want someone else to obtain immortality before *I* do. Now move."

But Mo continued to block him with her staff. Heru huffed again, shook his head, then opened his bloody palm: a warning. Mo's grip tightened on her staff as she stared him down.

"I could kill you right now and bind your jaani under my will," said Heru.

"You could. But you haven't and you won't. You need me."

Heru hissed, but it sounded more pained than angry. "I shouldn't need *either* of you."

"But you do."

"I *need* to get to my bags—" Heru tried darting around Mo again.

Mo's staff connected with his stomach and Heru let out an *oof* of breath. "*Tell me.*"

"Fine. You want to know?" Heru straightened and narrowed his eyes. "Djet has taken too much. Yes, I'm an en-marabi. I wear that label with pride. The en-marab aren't the demons and G-d blasphemers you want us to be. Djet gave the rest of us—*is giving us*—a bad name and I don't appreciate that. If Djet isn't stopped before he becomes immortal, he won't ever stop. They'll come for us again like they did in his time, and they'll be just as indiscriminate in their ignorance. All my years of research, every single one of them, will be for naught. I cannot—*will* not—let that happen. I've put too much time and effort and literal blood into my work to have some has-been dust-for-a-brain snotty up-start come in and take it all away from me." He slammed his bloody fist into his thigh. "Will you get out of my way *now*?"

Mo stood still for a moment, taking in Heru's words. Then she lowered her staff and stepped aside. "I don't think you have to worry about Djet giving the en-marab a bad name."

"I don't care what you think," snipped Heru, pushing past. "The en-marab are doing and have done more for the good of man-kind than any self-proclaimed, righteous, G-d-fearing marabi. It's because of our work that marab can even *quiet* jaan, and it's because of our work that there're fewer mad jaan roaming the desert."

"Because you *enslave* them!"

Heru stooped over the pile of bags and rifled inside of one. He freed a large leather box and turned it over in his hands.

Distracted, he said, "Yes, well, someone has to."

He slid the lid off, revealing several closely crammed scrolls. He spread one of these across the floor, weighing down the corners with pieces of broken stone. A familiar map scrawled across the scroll: the same one Heru had found back in the Empress's library. But it had been changed, marked up with scribbles in blue ink.

Heru smoothed out the scroll and surveyed his work. "We need to plan our next move and pinpoint exactly where we're going. We won't have the time—or supplies—to err or wander."

Thana picked out the new additions. They ran from simple circles, clustered at the western edge of the map, to full paragraphs in a language she didn't recognize. One line of blue ink traced their path, starting from Na Tay Khet in the upper east before plunging south, then turning west. The line passed through a sparse area before coming to a crescent of cities bordering a region that had been left completely void.

Between the crescent and the capital, the map had the occasional symbol for wells and various terrains, from the plains of sahar to the rugged, glossy rocks of regs. But the space beyond the crescent held nothing at all.

Or, it *had* held nothing when Thana had first seen the map. Now, blue ink filled the void.

Thana pointed to one of the new marks. "What's all this?"

"Hmm? Oh, that." Heru tapped a blue symbol that looked like a mountain. "I've been updating the map during the journey."

Mo hovered between Heru and Thana, curiosity getting the better of her. *"How?"*

But Thana remembered how Heru had perched atop his bound camel, working furiously on *something*. Now she pictured him trying to balance the map on one knee and a full writing set on the other. Too bad he hadn't lost his balance and fallen off.

"With the aid of the scrolls I borrowed from the library," said Heru. "My research wasn't complete when we left. I couldn't risk wasting any more time sitting idly in the city, but that didn't mean I couldn't broaden my knowledge during the predictably slow journey."

"You filled in the Wastes?" Thana tried not to sound impressed.

She must have failed, because Heru's smug pride deepened. "I did. At least, as far as the sources would allow. There's still a vast portion that can't be known, but what I have here is a start." He pointed at several of the mountain symbols. "By triangulating the locations in the stories with known landmarks, I have managed to place—with some small degree of error—the major mountain ranges that have been reported in the Wastes. The likelihood that one of these ranges in particular"—he tapped three symbols in quick succession—"is the Aer Essifs is so close to one hundred percent as to be actionable.

"Now, narrowing it down further has been integral because, as you can clearly see, these mountains are far enough from one another that to choose one means *not* choosing the others. We wouldn't have time to investigate a second potential site if we chose incorrectly. Therefore, it's of the *utmost* importance that we choose correctly." Heru pressed his finger on a symbol furthest into the Wastes. "*This* is where I hypothesize the Aer Essifs lie and where Djet will go—or has gone, if we are so unlucky."

Mo knelt and peered closely at the map. "You found them."

"It was no easy task, of course," said Heru. "No geographer or historian has traveled into the Wastes in living memory and the recollections of the Azal caravans that frequent its salt flats are deeply flawed, hindered as they are by their oral tradition. But I am confident in my conclusion. Djet will head here. And so shall we."

Mo traced an invisible line from the Aer Essifs to the crescent cities, her nail stopping at Ghadid. Their projected journey was longer than the one they'd just made, over more treacherous terrain, with no marked wells. And this time, it'd just be the three of them and all their camels could carry.

"How are we going to do this?" asked Thana. "We don't even trust each other, yet we expect to cross *this*"—Thana gestured at the Wastes—"and still be strong enough to take on the most powerful en-marabi that has ever lived? And *win*?"

"We don't have to like each other—" began Heru.

"But we *do* have to trust each other." Mo looked between them. "Thana's right—we've lost that trust."

When Mo's gaze flicked her way, Thana caught it. "I still trust you."

Heru grunted. "Trust is overrated. We have the same goal and I can sleep without worrying either of you will manage to kill me. With a plan, that will be sufficient. This isn't a marriage."

"We have no choice," said Mo.

"Can we at least pretend not to hate each other?" asked Thana.

They shared an uncomfortable silence, staring at the map as they reached a collective, silent accord. Or so Thana hoped.

Heru placed the orb in the map's center, its light now a soft glow. "I am sorry about the loss of your home and people, but we shouldn't dwell on what we cannot change. We should count our assets. We have a powerful en-marabi who knows more about Djet than anyone else—that would be me, of course." He touched his chest as if he were being modest. "Then we have a healer who can not only heal, but also find water." He gestured at Mo. "We also have three healthy camels, one of which can run several hundred miles without tiring. The other two . . . I can fix that."

"I don't think Mo's going to let you kill and bind the camels," pointed out Thana.

"She's right," said Mo.

"And we have a useless assassin who can provide a convenient fleshy meat shield in the event of an attack," finished Heru.

"I'm not useless." But even as she spoke, she worried that he wasn't as far off as she'd like. "I can fight."

Heru waved a hand at her. "As I said. I'm sure your antics will distract Djet's bound for a few minutes before they kill you. That aside, it's obvious that our first order of business when the sun rises is to bind the remaining camels."

"No." Mo crossed her arms. "I won't let you kill the camels."

Heru glared at Thana and grit his teeth. "It's for their own good, and ours. We cannot cross such a distance in time if we have to stop and rest our animals."

"I'm not going to argue with you about whether or not it's okay to *murder* our camels."

"It isn't murder. If anything, it's the exact opposite. I'm giving them immortality."

Mo shook her head, incredulous. "The same mindless immortality that Djet has given corpses?"

Heru shrugged. "They're camels."

"They're *alive*."

"We can talk about this later," broke in Thana. "What about Djet? How're we supposed to stop him?"

"That should be simple."

Heru retrieved a second scroll from his case. This he unrolled slowly, scanning the paper with a finger as he read. Leaning closer, Thana recognized that it was one of the primary sources, easily several centuries old. Like the map, though, the scroll was covered in fresh blue ink. Heru had scribbled notes, circled passages, and underlined words.

"We have to stop Djet before he frees the sajaam," said Heru. "If we're too late for that, we must interrupt the binding ritual.

If we're too late for *that*—I suggest we genuflect and beg for his mercy." Heru tapped the scroll. "Thankfully, the ritual will be easy to disrupt. According to this, Djet developed his binding method from typical marabi techniques. A circle of protection, a few choice herbs, and a seal, the last of which would utilize his own invented script. The seal will be the most difficult to break, as there will be built-in redundancies, so we should not let him reach that point.

"I also hypothesize that he'll use the myth of the sajaam's binding as his guide. In it, the marab used blood, smoke, and thorns—these three things will be instrumental in freeing them. The blood came from the marab and—" Heru stopped suddenly, his finger tracing and retracing the same note. He snapped his fingers. "The first advisory marabi and my colleagues. They never *did* answer me. Perhaps Djet has use for them after all. If we can remove them from the equation—ah, but I'm getting ahead of myself."

"If you mean anything other than evacuating the marab, I refuse to be a part of it," said Mo. "We can't stoop to Djet's level."

Annoyance flashed across Heru's uncovered face. "We will be forced to do many unseemly things before this is done. I won't rule out any in particular. I'm merely apprising you both of the situation as I understand it. Need I remind you that this man had no compunction sending his creatures into my room and destroying an entire city? To fight monsters, sometimes it helps to become one."

Mo tightened her lips, staring down Heru, but he didn't waver. After a long moment, she said, "G-d will provide."

"Maybe," said Heru. "But sometimes you have to help G-d along."

26

They discussed provisions and distances, then settled in for the night. Heru palmed the glowing orb, making it disappear somewhere within his wrap, but the torches remained lit. Thana pulled her wrap tighter and ignored the chill that came up from the stone floor. For the first hour, her mind jumped back and forth from her torn city to Mo's hurt as one might poke again and again at a bruise. And Thana was all bruise.

She thought she'd never sleep, but exhaustion eventually claimed her. When she opened her eyes again, her limbs were cramped and sore from lying on the hard ground. A dense quiet had spread through the crypt. She could hear her own heartbeat and the steady breathing of her companions. No—she frowned. Not so steady.

A faint blue glow suffused the area, covering everything. Thana slowly turned her head until she saw Mo. The healer sat cross-legged and straight-backed next to the pile of waterskins, her figure awash in blue. She held a bowl of glowing water in her lap. Although her lips were moving, her expression remained impassive.

Despite the thin wrap and cold stones, Thana felt comfortable and warm. For the first time in weeks, her shoulder didn't throb and the ache of travel that had settled in her legs and lower back had subsided. The scrapes on her palms and shins from climbing the cable were gone, her skin smooth and unbroken. Slowly, even her headache vanished.

Thana watched Mo through half-open eyes. With the blue suffusing her skin, Mo looked like an angel. The glow smoothed out her skin and her hair and her wrap, banishing darkness and shadow. In that moment, Mo was as delicate as a doll, as solid as a statue, and as inhuman as both.

The urge to go to Mo, to wrap her arms around the healer as she had on so many other nights, to feel her warmth and breathe in her citrus sweetness, hurt Thana as much as a physical wound, but one Mo couldn't heal. Heru had ruined that for her. Instead, cradled by the blue light, Thana closed her eyes and drifted back into a restless sleep.

Ghadid's smoking pylons were just fading into the east when the sky began to lighten and the stars winked out one by one. With a heaviness in her chest, Thana walked backward beside her camel and watched the horizon swallow her home. When she turned back around, she faced a seemingly endless stretch of flat sand, scattered with rocks. According to Heru's map, by day's end they'd be threading through a treacherous maze of dunes.

They'd spent another day in Ghadid before leaving. Mo had needed the rest and Thana had used the extra time to scavenge for supplies. Their camels had been grumpy but alive when they finally stepped from a carriage to the sands. Now the camels plodded along, their splayed toes sinking deeper and deeper as the hours slunk by. Each of them, even Heru, moved as if their jaan had fled, leaving only their mindless and dispirited bodies behind.

They stopped at midday for tea and huddled beneath a piece of stretched cloth, exchanging only a few words. Heru turned his back on them and hunched over a glass bottle he'd picked up in Ghadid. He was drawing something on it, over and over again, but Thana wasn't close enough to see what. She couldn't drum up the energy to care.

Instead, she closed her eyes against the blinding sand and carefully tended to the hot bead of anger and hope. Try as she might, she couldn't even be angry with Heru. His attempt to clear the air had been sincere, if severely misguided. No, all of her anger was directed at Djet. She tallied all the things Djet had taken from her and went over them as if they were the crimes of a mark. Her city, her people, her home, her family, her cousins, her love, her mother, her *future*. That anger was the only thing keeping the heaviness from choking her, the only thing keeping her going, step after step after step. Because without it, what did she have left?

They traveled into the night, keeping to a caravan's schedule although they hadn't discussed it. When the moon rose, they made camp. When the moon was overhead, they set out again. The heat quickly dissipated and even Heru walked to stay warm.

When dawn oozed across the sands, the world had subtly changed. Instead of an expanse of flat sand, one horizon was now choppy. The wind had picked up, become a steady breeze that spit sand and sucked the heat from their bones. As they approached, the horizon grew and spread, towering higher and higher: a dune field.

They entered the dunes around midday. Their afternoon rest was short, a shared sense of urgency forcing them onward. Heru checked his map to estimate the size of the dune field, but the effort was wasted. They were in the Wastes now and Heru's additions could be off by miles.

The dunes grew around them from rolling hills to sleeping giants. As they walked through the valleys, the only sounds were the *shh-shh-shh*ing of the camels' feet and the occasional creak of leather. They turned and wound between the dunes and soon Thana lost all track of time and direction.

The sun sank on their second full day in the Wastes and the dunes' shadows stretched with it, until everything was blanketed in shadowy twilight. This time, the heat lingered, thick and dense as an oven's. As the stars came out and the wind picked up, Thana thought she saw a flash of light. She'd dismissed it as a trick of her tired eyes, but then it flashed again. Thana peered more closely ahead, the afterimage still burning her vision. She found herself staring at the tail of Mo's camel.

The tail swished. The light flashed. Thana's mouth went dry.

Then her heart picked up with a panicked beat. She held up a hand to test the wind. Its direction had changed; now it blew hard from the east, whistling past her ears. The sky was clear, if occasionally hidden from sight by the black hulk of a dune. But between one dune and the next was something darker.

Then the darkness flashed, lightning arcing from one cloud to the next, illuminating the towering storm wall from within. The clouds glowed a bloody red, and then were swallowed up by the dunes again.

Thana urged her camel into a trot. She'd fallen back, ostensibly to keep watch, but really to remove the temptation to talk to Mo. The healer had asked for space and by G-d, Thana had given it to her, even as it broke her own heart. But now was not the time for space.

"Mo!" she shouted. "Heru!"

Leads were pulled, camels turned. They both glanced around—Mo with a wild, startled motion, Heru with distanced curiosity. He spotted the stormwall first, his gaze locking on to it over Thana's shoulder.

"What is it?" asked Mo.

"Sandstorm," said Thana. She rustled her wrap, sending a shiver of sparks down its length. "Bad one."

Mo's eyes widened, flicked from the sparks to behind Thana. The moonlight gave her skin a liquid metallic sheen that would've been breathtaking at any other time. Now, Thana had no breath left to take.

By the way Thana's mouth was dry as cotton and her head pounded and her nose trickled blood, this storm was going to be bad. Even in the middle of a relatively sand-free, flat expanse, a traveler could be inundated. Here, surrounded by dunes—

It was a death trap.

A white light blazed in Heru's hand. Thana turned away, but the damage was done. Spots danced in her vision, obscuring everything. The light faded to a pale pulse, only as bright as the moon, and just as round: it was coming from the small glass orb. Heru held the light aloft as he studied their surroundings. Thana eyed the orb, knowing and not knowing what it was, what it contained. But she pushed her fresh disgust away; now was not the time.

Sand surrounded them. Overhead, it flew in intermittent sheets, obscuring the stars. They had two options: climb the dunes and risk the full fury of the storm, or shelter between them and be buried. Heru glanced from Thana to her camel and raised his eyebrows meaningfully.

"We can't outrun the storm," she said.

Heru raised his eyebrows still higher.

"We have to take cover while we can." Mo slipped from her camel, couched it, and began untying her bags. "We'll pray to G-d the dunes give us enough protection."

"Or I could bind your camels and we might stand a reasonable chance of surviving," said Heru.

Mo didn't even look at him. "No."

"Entire armies have been buried by lesser storms," wheedled Heru.

"Then you go on yourself," said Thana.

Heru muttered under his breath, but didn't spur his beast into motion. After another moment, he even dismounted.

"We're going to die," he said.

Within minutes, they'd heaped their supplies and skins at the base of a dune. A blanket covered the heap and a tent stake stuck out of its middle. After the storm, the stake would help them locate their supplies. If they didn't drown in sand themselves.

The living camels had settled on their own, tucking their legs beneath them and closing their long-lashed eyelids. Heru's camel remained standing, staring unblinkingly at its master and the light oozing from his hand. He had to firmly guide it down.

They sat with their backs against the camels, tagels dampened to trap dust, a cloth ready to be pulled down across their eyes, and a stake in hand. They waited for the storm.

The moon blurred red and, as a whistling roar swept between the dunes, went out. The stormwall broke around them, hissing like a thousand snakes. Thana pulled the cloth over her eyes and ducked her head. She struggled to breathe through the damp cloth, but she didn't dare take it off. When the storm hit, she could still see the light in Heru's hand, even through closed eyes. Within minutes, that light was gone and they were plunged into darkness.

Then the whispering began, as intimate as it was indecipherable. Drums beat in her ears—or was that her own heart? The charms at her waist grew warm, then hot. They burned her skin, but she didn't dare remove them. They were the only thing protecting her from the wild jaan riding the storm.

She focused on the sensation of the wind and the sand. A glow suffused her surroundings, at first white, then red. She began reciting pieces of prayers, any phrase that crossed her mind. *G-d be merciful, G-d be good, may G-d bless and watch over this house—*

The whispering grew louder, but not clearer. Then, all at once, it was gone. The wind began to slacken. Thana opened her eyes and watched the world grow a little less dark. Soon the storm had passed entirely, leaving behind an empty silence.

Thana stood, or at least tried to. She'd been half submerged in sand. She dragged her arms free and tugged at the cloth around her mouth and eyes. When it came off, she gasped and drank in the night air.

The stars had returned and the moon was well past its zenith. After the storm's darkness, the moonlight was as bright as day. Thana struggled to her feet just as the camels shifted and rose, sand cascading off their backs. Two poles still stuck out of the sand, but a third was cast to the ground near a set of footprints.

"Mo?" said Thana.

Light flashed and blazed white, blinding her. Too late, she raised a hand. The light dimmed and lowered and after another moment, Thana could discern the outline of a person.

"I hope the storm didn't addle your senses so much that you would confuse me with that thin waif of a girl," said Heru. "Speaking of which—you might want to help her out."

One of the poles was shifting, sinking into its mound of sand.

"Mo!"

Thana was at the healer's side, shoveling sand away with cupped hands. She uncovered bright blue cloth and dug faster. She found a shoulder and heaved Mo sideways, out of the small sand hill. Mo flailed as they fell, catching Thana in the nose, then they were both coughing and spitting up sand. Mo tore the cloth from her face and sucked in air like a gift from G-d.

"How long was I under there?" Mo stuck a finger in one ear

and began wiggling it around. "I could feel the sand creeping up, then I couldn't breathe and the next thing, you were here."

"I don't know." Thana held out a hand to Mo, who took it and stood on shaky legs. "But it looks like we survived the storm."

Heru had moved behind them to examine their supplies, so Thana's back was to the light and her vision clear when the first shadow tumbled down the dune. Thana didn't stop to think. She pushed Mo aside with a barked *get back!* and freed two knives.

She'd spotted a second and a third shadow right behind it, loping across the sand on all fours like jackals in full stride, but something was wrong. They were too big for jackals, their front legs too long, their snouts truncated, their eyes—

The first launched itself at her. Thana sidestepped as she thrust her knife into its chest. She was already turning to take the next creature, but it passed her, aiming for Heru. He stumbled back, raising the orb as if that could stop the creature, but it ignored the orb and slammed into him. Heru let out a high-pitched squeal.

Then Thana was there, one hand around the creature's throat. She yanked it back and slammed her hilt down hard on the base of its skull. She was rewarded with a satisfying *crack*. The creature crumpled, but wasn't dead yet, only dazed. Heru met her gaze and nodded appreciatively. Then he knelt and shoved his palm against the creature's chest before it could rise.

Thana freed another knife. The third creature had paused a few feet away, watching with open curiosity. Since her charms were burning, she'd assumed these were Djet's creatures, but those had never stopped and watched and *thought*. And the creature's eyes—they glinted in the blaze of Heru's light, but they weren't flat and dead like the eyes of the bound. These flared with life barely contained.

Now as the creature tentatively approached the circle of pale light, Thana could see it better. Its head was shaped like a cat's, tiny snub of a nose flat beneath two wide, oval eyes. Its body was a mad mixture of jackal and man, all odd angles and tufts of wild fur. Long, wickedly curved claws sliced through the sand like so many knives.

A name bubbled up from the stories her father had once told her when she was young: *guul*. According to those stories, the guul were either the jealous creation of the sajaam or they were jaan that had learned how to survive and even thrive by scavenging corpses. Normal jaan lusted for a shell of flesh to call their own again, convinced that to return to life all they needed was a living body. Guul were an inversion, the jaan who'd realized they could create their own bodies out of the dead.

Guul were as mad as wild jaan, but in their madness, they retained a sense of self. They could plan. They could work together. And they understood that a living body could quickly become a dead one.

The third guuli locked gazes with her. Thana snapped her garrote free. The guuli barked and rushed her. Thana held her ground. The guuli closed in, but before she could strike, it veered sharply away. Toward Mo.

Thana lunged for the guuli, too slow. Mo shrieked. The monster's claws tore through her wrap and her upraised arm. Thana slammed her shoulder into the guuli. It released Mo and tumbled with Thana across the sand, snapping its claws at her eyes.

Thana jerked her head to one side. The claw's tip narrowly missed her eye, grazing her cheek instead. The guuli pinned her to the ground, sitting on her chest and baring a mess of collected teeth that jutted and crowded its mouth. Its breath reeked of sweet rot and hot sand. It tore at her wrap, wincing back even as it tried to hook a claw under her charms.

Light blazed behind her and Heru barked in triumph. Mo hissed through the sand at her other side, the first guuli right behind her. But Thana couldn't help her, couldn't get out from under the guuli sitting on her. The more she fought it, the further the guuli pushed her into the sand, until the sand was cascading into her eyes and nose and mouth.

"Thana!"

Thwack.

The guuli fell to the side. Mo appeared above, a hand outstretched. Thana took her hand, warnings tumbling from her mouth, but as soon as Thana was up, Mo was already turning, her staff raised. She struck the first guuli and it stumbled back, dark smoke leaking around the knife Thana had left in its chest. Mo swung again, but this time the guuli grabbed her staff and refused to let go. Thana loosed another knife, but was jerked backward before she could help. The third guuli had hold of her wrap and it was dragging her toward it.

Thana slashed through her wrap, cutting herself free. The guuli stumbled back, surprised. Thana unlatched her belt. The glass charms glowed white hot, spilling light as bright as Heru's orb across the sand. The guuli cowered in the light, covering its head with its long claws. Not entirely sure what she was doing, Thana stepped forward and, keeping hold of the belt's ends, dropped it around the guuli's shoulders.

The guuli howled. It shook and trembled and then it fell apart, arms and teeth and claws and skin and broken torso all tumbling to the sand. A dark haze burst free, sweeping toward the sky. It broke apart in the wind, but before it was completely gone, another light flared behind Thana. The haze thickened and swirled and streamed back.

Heru stretched one hand up to meet the haze, the orb burning between his fingers. The haze whirled and pulsed—once, twice—before being sucked into the orb. The light dimmed and the skin around Heru's eyes crinkled with a frown as his gaze flicked to Thana. Then past her. He shouted—

The last guuli slammed Thana to the ground. It wrenched the belt from her grip, its fingers falling off even as it flung the belt away. The glass sang as it arced through the air, then hit the sand with a soft *thump*. The guuli pressed its collapsing body against Thana, its catlike eyes flaring with burning light.

Thana tried to push the guuli away, but its body gave and her hands crunched through dry flesh and loose bone. It fell apart even as a thick haze obscured her vision. Her nose and mouth and eyes were burning, dry, *scorched*, and it didn't matter that she couldn't see, because everything was light and darkness and flame.

Distantly, she heard her name. Something slammed into her chest, cool and slick, but she couldn't open her eyes. Then the pain began and Thana tumbled into the darkness.

27

Cool water splashed across her cracked lips, both a pain and a balm. Voices stirred around her like gusts of wind, indecipherable and opaque. Her skin and lungs and blood and organs burned with a fire that sloshed and churned within her. She couldn't tell if she was lying down or standing up, if she was surrounded by fire or sand or air.

Another voice chittered in her head and images of dunes and mountains and camels flashed before her eyes. Bloodied and torn corpses. Jagged stretches of flesh. Ripping, tearing winds and flashes of lightning. With these images came rage and hunger and joy. At times, she thought she knew what it was like to soar above the Wastes, to ride the winds of a sandstorm and surf in its wake of destruction. She knew centuries of wandering and hunger and, before that—before that—

She knew the touch of a man, skin smooth and hands delicate. She knew the scent of flowered soap, colorful hair, the weight of seeing glass across her nose. She knew creations of metal and smoke that rumbled across the Wastes, needing neither water nor grass. She knew glinting birds that drew clouds across the sky. She knew the bustle of people close and rank with sweat and spices, and the feel of metal attached to skin—and mind.

But sand and rocks and endless pale blue sky outweighed and overwhelmed the rest by years and decades—centuries. She'd been trapped in this desert for so long, had inhabited only a handful of bodies, only to be exorcised again and again. This time would be different. This time, she would *live*.

SLAP

Thana jolted. For a heartbeat, she was two—the one who remembered whole centuries of dust and sand, and the one who only remembered a city in the sky, once whole, now destroyed. Then the centuries faded and her eyes opened and she was on her back, sand in her mouth and nose and ears, dizzy and sick and burning. *Burning.*

"She's awake!"

Mo's face filled her vision. Thana squinted. The sky was brighter. But the last thing she remembered—it had been night. Her memories flooded back: the fight with the guul, the sandstorm, the journey into the Wastes. Thana started coughing, choking on sand and dried spit, and couldn't stop. She sat up and the world tilted with her, dizzyingly fragile.

Her waist burned. Her fingers found the edges of the glass belt even as she shied away from touching it. The belt's heat pulsed in time with her heart, an ebb and flow that left her flush and frail at intervals. The guuli was still inside her. She could feel it, as surely as if it were breathing down her neck. But its grip had loosened.

Mo pressed a waterskin into Thana's hands. Heru stepped into her line of sight, peering at her with his peculiar intensity.

As Thana took a sip of water, Mo asked, "How're you feeling?"

The water was like nothing Thana had ever tasted. She couldn't stop herself from gulping it down. Only once the skin was empty could she answer Mo.

"Alive."

Mo's faint smile faded to a frown. She took the skin from Thana and replaced it with one half-empty. "Take it slower with that one. You'll make yourself sick."

But Thana couldn't stop herself from drinking just as fast. The second skin disappeared even quicker, but her thirst remained. A finger of worry twisted inside her, but she couldn't voice it for want of more water.

Heru pressed a cool finger against Thana's neck. "Fascinating." He pulled back. "She's burning up and her pulse is elevated. She's drinking too much water, yet her eyes are clear. I wonder— are you sane?"

Thana squinted at him, her thoughts slowed by the guuli. It took her a moment to process the question. "I am. Praise be to G-d."

"Praise be to G-d," whispered Mo.

Heru nodded. "Those charms you're wearing are muddling the guuli's influence. Typically, charms would *repel* an attack, but since the healer put the belt back on *after* you idiotically took it off and got yourself possessed, the charms are instead keeping the guuli in check. If I were you, I wouldn't remove it again. You would burn up, and I don't mean that figuratively."

"Can't you do something to remove the guuli?" asked Mo.

"Potentially." Heru peered at Thana, fingering the tagel over where his beard would be, if he had one. "But I have neither the resources nor the time. Plus, as much as I loath to admit it, extracting a jaani of this particular type is a delicate process that would benefit from the assistance of another, equally skilled marabi. I *could* attempt it, but if I were to fail—which is a highly probable eventuality—the ramifications would be dire for all of us. We would be less that much in water and burdened with a homicidal, fully corporeal guuli. Also, she would be dead."

"Isn't there something we can do?"

"Water," said Thana, her tongue already thick and dry. "Give me water."

"You're a healer," said Heru. "You know what you can do."

Mo looked away. "We don't have enough water to heal her."

"You have other resources besides water at hand."

"I don't know what you mean." But Mo didn't meet Heru's gaze.

Heru gave Thana a pitying glance before straightening and heading for the camels. "Then the only solution is to travel as fast as we can. Of course, we could leave her behind. She *probably* wouldn't die. Those charms will last some time and the thirst should only drive her mad, not kill her. No, the guuli breaking through and burning her up from the inside is what will kill her."

Mo ignored him and offered her hand to Thana. "Can you stand?"

Thana took Mo's hand and heaved herself up. She leaned on Mo as her head swam and the sands briefly darkened, threatening to slip out from beneath her feet. Then the world stabilized and the dizziness passed. It took all of her focus just to follow Mo to the camels. All she could think about was water—how'd she ever taken it for granted? She could see the pumps, feel the cool, moist air inside the pumphouses, and hear the gurgle of liquid. If only she could just hold her head under the fount—

"Thana?"

Thana had stopped. Mo was a few paces ahead, worry creasing her brows. Beyond Mo, Heru bent over one of the camels and pressed his hand against its neck. The beast's head drooped and its body jerked, then its eyes flicked open and it stared, unblinking. It lurched to its feet to stand next to the other two, which were just as still, just as lifeless. Thana had enough sense not to say anything.

Mo took Thana's elbow and guided her the rest of the way to the camels. Heru had already mounted his. He flicked the lead impatiently.

"Get on. The sooner we leave, the sooner we can get her help."

Mo hesitated, her hand hanging outstretched toward Thana's camel. The beast stared back at them with blank, glassy eyes. Mo placed her palm on its neck. "This camel has no pulse."

"They died in the storm," said Heru, busying himself with something on his saddle. "I bound them for expediency."

Mo met the camel's glazed gaze. "They were alive when the guul attacked." She closed her eyes and let out a *whoosh* of breath, then turned to Thana with feigned brightness. "Right. Let's get you on this camel."

"Water?"

"Not yet. You've already had most of a skin, Thana. We don't have much left."

Thana swallowed a whimper. Her insides were burning and parched, her throat sore, her tongue heavy and rough. But the water they had still needed to last for untold days yet, split between the three of them. So she concentrated on this moment and ignored the next. Right now, she needed to mount her camel. She twisted the camel's lead around her shaking fist and let Mo help her up.

Heru led the way, threading his camel through the dunes. Their camels followed, unbidden. He goaded his beast into a trot, then a gallop, and soon it was all Thana could do to stay on.

Thana settled into the camel's rhythm, the sand flying past at a sickening speed. Meanwhile, the guuli exulted; this was familiar, soaring through and above the dunes along the edge of a storm, everything fire and heat and lightning—

Thana shook her head, fighting back to reality. She wasn't a guuli. She was a woman riding a very unhealthy camel and she needed to stay that way. The guuli wanted her to lose her concentration and fall. She couldn't let that happen.

The minutes then hours crawled past and Thana's thirst deepened. She tried to think of anything but water, but when her focus slipped for even a moment, she was swept away by the memory of its cool taste, its soft splash, its slickness dripping between her fingers.

The ground thumped her hard on the back and she stared at the gray-blue sky. She didn't even remember falling. A shout rang through the air—her name—and camel hooves slid through the sand beside her head. Mo slid an arm beneath her shoulders and helped her sit up. Thana leaned into Mo, hoping she wouldn't draw away.

"Are you all right? What happened?"

"Water," said Thana.

Mo squeezed her eyes shut. When she opened them again, they glistened. Heru thundered close before pulling his camel up sharp. He peered at Thana, full shadow cloaking his expression. He shook his head.

"We'll have to tie her down. We can't afford to waste any more time."

"She needs more water."

"She'll drink everything we have," snapped Heru. "And she'll still burn up from within and die."

Mo crossed her arms. "We can find more. I'm not letting her die."

"I'm not either," said Heru. "She saved my life when the guul attacked and I will see that debt repaid. But I refuse to let baseless hope cloud my reasoning. So no, I won't sit and wait for you to find water. Every moment we linger is a moment closer to the guuli inside her winning. I doubt you'll be able to do what's necessary when that happens."

Mo fixed Heru with a cold stare. "Don't underestimate me."

Heru matched her stare. "You haven't given me a reason not to. You're capable of so much more than I've seen you do. Water is just a proxy for blood, after all."

"I'm a healer, not an en-marabi."

"There is less of a difference than you might wish. We each do what we believe is necessary."

"Then at least give me time to do the ritual," said Mo.

She helped Thana stand. When Thana didn't collapse, she let go and retrieved her bowl. She filled the bowl with water and placed it on the ground just out of Thana's reach. Thana stared hungrily at the water, all other discomforts forgotten. Her focus cut through the haze in her mind like a thrown dagger. The guuli was rising up, filling the spaces within her, but she didn't have the strength to fight it.

Mo traced a circle in the sand around her and the bowl. She didn't see Thana lunge. The bowl was already halfway to Thana's lips when Mo turned. She smacked it away, spraying water across the sand where it instantly vanished. Horror flashed across Mo's face, followed by anger, then shame. She grabbed Thana's hands and pressed them between her own.

"I'm so sorry. I shouldn't have done that. But you have to understand. You can't interrupt me, you can't cross the circle, and you *can't* drink the water. Trust me—if you can follow those directions, soon you'll have more water than you can dream of."

Thana forced her trembling hands down to her sides, nodded. But Heru dismounted with a grunt of disgust.

"You can't reason with a guuli," he said before he grabbed Thana's arms and, twisting them behind her, forced her to her knees.

The guuli struggled against Heru, but her sudden strength soon waned, the charms burning a reminder against her skin. Thana sagged in relief. Mo had watched, biting her lip. Now she filled the bowl again.

Mo retraced the circle in the sand. She stood tall in its center, then let her head and arms go loose. Only her fingers moved, twisting and twitching as they traced shapes in the air. Blue suffused her skin, darkening it even further, reaching down her arms and legs to her exposed fingers and toes before diffusing into the air as a blue haze.

The air thickened, stinking of water and electricity, but no storm filled the horizon. Mo shuddered and the haze twisted into a swarm, which tasted the air like a snake, darting one way, then the other. It rose away, higher and higher until it crested the dunes, then it turned north, west, still tasting, still searching. Thana struggled to stand and follow, but Heru's grip tightened.

"Patience," he growled. "If you want to survive this, you will let the healer do her work."

The wind had a pulse to it now, a cadence like the rhythm of speech. The blue haze settled on the west, then coiled in on itself like a rope. Mo straightened, tilting her sweat-drenched face to the sky as she drew the blue back in. The haze pulsed around her with its own heartbeat, settling against her skin and wrap. Then it vanished.

The water in the bowl was gone. Thana's thirst, however, was not.

Mo smudged the circle in the sand with her toe, then turned, the whites of her eyes now a faint, pulsing blue. "We head west."

Heru tied Thana to her camel. Rope kept her arms down, so she couldn't reach the knots to free herself, and more rope anchored her between the camel's neck and hump. Thana didn't have the strength to struggle. It turned out that being tied up was more comfortable; it took her less effort to stay mounted, even as the camel galloped.

Mo led the charge with Thana's camel close behind, its lead tied to Mo's bags. The dunes flashed by at a dizzying pace. Thana's wrap caught and snapped in the wind and sand sprayed her face, kicked up by Mo's camel. Her own camel's rolling gait soon made her sore, then outright pained. But overriding the discomfort was her growing thirst, a desiccation within that demanded all of her attention.

Mo leaned over her camel's neck, a blue haze occasionally flashing around her. When it did, the ghost of a snake would snap across the sky, pointing them toward water. They covered more distance in an hour than should have been possible.

The dunes ended abruptly, towering beside them one moment and receding into the distance the next. Ahead stretched flat sand, which melted into a sea of bright salt, cracking underfoot. Mirages of endless lakes and ponds and rivers shone with promise just before their camels' feet crumbled them into salt and dust.

Thana slipped in and out of consciousness. All around her blazed white and hot. She closed her eyes against the glare and when she opened them, nothing had changed but the sun's position. No, that wasn't quite right—tiny pinpricks spotted the horizon ahead. Thana stared. Were they real, or another mirage?

She blinked and the sun slid and the dark spots spread and stretched upward, thrusting into the sky. For a few delirious moments, Thana was confused enough to know they'd come full circle, that Ghadid stood just ahead, whole and safe.

But these were no pylons. As they approached, the spots separated from five to seven, then to eleven, thirteen. Darkness covered the space between them, spilled in front.

Mountains. Ragged and black, they were impossibly tall and narrow, like figures frozen in time. Even in her muddled state, Thana remembered Mo's story about the sajaam, how they'd challenged G-d and been transformed into pillars of rock. It felt as if Mo had told that story months, even years ago. But it had only been a few weeks.

The sun was setting and its dying light threw the mountains into sharp relief. Their shadows stretched toward the three of them, never meeting. Even at this unrelenting speed, they were still hours away.

Then the sun was gone. Night leached away the colors and light and details along with the sun's warmth, yet Thana could see the mountains rising ever taller and closer, a darkness that blocked out the stars. Her gaps in consciousness widened and the pillars of rock blinked closer and closer.

When she next came to, the moon had risen. The mountains were so close Thana wanted to reach out and touch them, but what caught her attention were the flickers of orange light at the base of one. Mo spotted them, too. She slowed her camel and waited for Heru to catch up.

"Fires," said Heru.

"There's a camp ahead." Mo flushed blue and pointed. "That's where we're headed. They have water."

Heru peered into the distance as if he might uncover more from the darkness through sheer force of will. "A well?"

"No." Mo twisted around to look at Thana. "But they have water and they should have a marabi, too."

Heru scanned the flickers of orange as if they contained a message. "They might even have two."

"But who could be out here?" Worry gnawed at Mo's voice. "From the look of it, that's a big camp. If they're not bothering to hide their fires, then they're not worried about being attacked."

"There's only three of us," said Thana. Her throat was raw and her words came out scratched, but they were audible. "They won't see us as a threat."

"The possessed girl is correct," said Heru. "Besides, they wouldn't dare hurt a marabi of the Empress."

"Don't assume that the people in the Wastes know anything about your Empress," said Mo.

"Do you want to help your friend or not?" asked Heru.

"Because we can sit here and waste time wondering about something that doesn't matter or we can go to that camp and demand to see their resident marabi before the girl dies."

"We're going," said Mo. "I just . . . wanted to make certain we all agreed, considering the risks."

"Risks!" Heru barked a laugh. "We have *riskier* things to worry about than a camp in the Wastes. Come on, girl—if you're afraid of these sand fleas, then I'll lead."

Without waiting for an answer, Heru smacked his camel, which jerked into a full gallop. Mo swallowed a complaint and Thana grabbed tight to her ropes as their camels followed.

The flickering flashes of orange settled into stable pinpricks, which separated into individual campfires. Smoke hazed into the sky and swept across the stars, which blinked in and out like beacons. The salt sea receded and soon their camels' feet scattered stone and gravel.

When they were close enough to see the flames of each campfire and the dark silhouettes of pitched tents, a shape detached itself from the camp and approached them at speed. Heru lit the tea brazier and held it aloft. Thana squinted, trying to see who was nearing and read their intent. Her hands fought the rope, her fingers itching for the familiar smooth feel of a knife hilt.

A man on horseback solidified out of the darkness, his face obscured by a tagel. Both the tagel and his wrap were a deep and vibrant red, delicate gold embroidering their edges. The man reined in his beast just beyond the circle of Heru's light, allowing the night to obscure him. His eyes glinted as he studied them.

The horse pranced in place, full of its own nervous energy. Thana thought of all the water the camp must have to sustain such a beast and grew agitated. She needed to be *there*, not out here. But she resisted the urge to kick her camel into a gallop and leave these fools behind. Her charms flared even hotter as the guuli fought back, then finally cooled to their previous heat.

The man raised an empty hand in greeting. "Heru Samet-ket," he said, voice gravelly and raw, but somehow familiar. He stepped his horse into the circle of light. "You were expected over a day ago."

Heru tilted his head to one side. "Bo Tamit? What are you doing out here?"

Thana recognized that name from somewhere, but her thoughts were growing increasingly ponderous and difficult to parse. All she could think of was water. It was so *close*—

"Tamit?" Mo looked between Heru and the man. "You mean, the first advisory marabi?"

"Yes," said Tamit. "And her Imperial Highness is expecting your audience. You would do well not to make her wait."

28

Empress Zara ha Khatet's tent shone like a torch in the dark, its gold fabric glowing with the light of the many campfires around it. Thana had enough presence of mind to note the ten or so guards stationed just outside, but the scent of water was too close, too distracting. She strained against the ropes holding her.

Tamit handed his reins to a waiting slave and asked, "What's wrong with your friend?"

Heru cut the ropes around Thana. "The heat has made her unwell. She requires rest and water."

Mo started to say something, but instead pressed her lips tight and frowned, eyes flicking between Heru and the other marabi. As soon as the ropes lost tension, Thana sagged and slipped to one side. Heru caught her as she fell and helped her stand with uncharacteristic gentleness. Her legs, however, refused to cooperate. They buckled and then she was flat on her back, staring at the sky. Voices stirred around her, loud and brash but already distant and receding even further until they were little more than a pulsing echo.

Thana woke inside a tent. Her skin prickled with chills and her head beat insistently as the voices shifted and grew louder. When she noticed the bowl of water in front of her, she grabbed and drank it all in one gulp.

"—heat sickness," Mo was saying. "In the aftermath of the sandstorm."

Metal bracelets clinked. "We had no trouble with sandstorms," said a familiar voice. "Ah. Your friend is awake."

Heads turned toward her, but Thana ignored them to look for more water. The bowl had held so very little and that brief taste had only stoked her thirst. A slave dropped a skin heavy with water in front of her. She unknotted the neck with trembling fingers and drank deep, not bothering to keep the water from dribbling out of her mouth, over her chin, and down her neck. For a brief moment, it was enough: the guuli was satisfied and Thana could think again.

With the skin clutched tight between her hands, she took in the room. At its center sat the Empress, flanked on either side by red-robed marab and bare-headed slaves. Tamit stood at her right shoulder, his wrap the color of blood and his eyes as dark as midnight. Atrex, the deaf guard, stood at the Empress's left shoulder, one hand on the hilt of his sword, his gaze clamped on Heru.

"Thana." Mo started toward Thana, but Heru stuck out an arm, holding her back. Worry warred with relief across her face, which out of everything, comforted Thana the most. If it took being possessed by a guuli for Mo to speak to her again, she'd take it.

The Empress leaned forward. "How are you feeling?"

"I'm fine." And Thana *was* fine. If it weren't for the flaring heat inside her chest and the still present, if distant, thirst, she could have even felt normal. As it was, this was the most coherent she'd felt since the storm. As Thana looked around again, this time more carefully, her worries flaked away one by one like rust off an old knife.

They were safe. They were no longer alone.

"Good," said the Empress. "We're glad we could offer aid."

"I don't mean to sound ungrateful, mai," said Thana, her tongue still thick from lack of water, "but what is your Imperial Highness doing in the Wastes?"

The Empress folded her hands in her lap. "We were just discussing that with your friends. But first—is there anything else we can do for you? We've been told all about your trying journey. Please, relax. You're safe here."

Thana opened her mouth to say *more water*, but then swallowed the request. She still had half a skin. Instead, she shook her head. "Thank you, mai."

"You'll all enjoy the respite you've earned, of course," said the Empress, indicating the rest of the room with a sweep of her arm. "Breathe deep, for your troubles are over. We were able to locate this distant place thanks to all of your diligent work. The notes you left behind were quite meticulous. We were correct in assigning such a capable group to the task. We only regret not perusing those notes sooner—if we'd known then what we know now, we might have saved you such a troublesome journey."

"By distant place, you don't mean the Aer Essifs?" asked Heru.

"Patience." The Empress held up a hand. "But yes—you're in our tent, which is situated at the base of one of the pillars in the mountain range commonly referred to as the Aer Essifs. After reading your notes, we directed all of our librarians to search the palace high and low for this notebook you described. We believed it might be useful in your endeavor, if it even existed."

The Empress had Heru's complete attention. "You found it."

"Yes." Her smile brimmed with self-satisfaction. "It was a simple matter of leaving no stone unturned. Quite literally."

Heru stepped forward. "I must see it."

"Patience," repeated the Empress. "You will see it in due time.

The notebook's contents helped us comprehend the enormity of the situation. As clever and resourceful as you are, we realized we'd made a terrible error in sending you on this mission alone. It will indeed take an army to defeat Djet."

"So you know how to stop him, mai?" asked Mo.

"We do." The Empress smiled. "And it's a simple thing, now that you've arrived. But don't worry about the threat. Before the night is out, Djet will be a man of history once more."

"Where is he?" asked Thana. "He had a lead of days on us—he should be here by now."

"He is near."

"If that's true, I must see his notes immediately, your Imperial Highness," said Heru. "Therein lies the key to stopping him."

The Empress waved a hand. "Tamit has already secured that key. That's why we are here tonight, camped at the base of the Aer Essifs. Your research gave us the name of these mountains, but Djet's notebook helped us locate them. We suspect the Wastes keep many secrets. But don't worry—in another hour, the time will be ripe to begin and we can put all of this behind us. Your part in this story is at an end. Relax. Rest. Our slaves will attend you."

Thana's fingers twisted around the waterskin as she fought the urge to drink, a fight which she soon lost. The skin was emptying quickly and she didn't want to find out what would happen when the water was all gone. Her mind was clouding again and although she realized the significance of what the Empress was saying, she couldn't yet find relief. Why hadn't Heru asked for help with removing the guuli yet? What was he waiting for?

"The notebook?" pressed Heru.

"Of course, Sametket. Perhaps a second glance will elucidate our situation further." The Empress snapped her fingers. "Tamit, if you would be so kind."

"I cannot believe you found it," said Heru, breathless. "It should have been destroyed when he was. And now—all that knowledge—I have to see it. I must understand. I have so many questions." He ran a hand through his uncovered hair; his tagel hung around his neck, smeared with dust and ash and blood. "Where is it?"

"Another tent," said Tamit. He beckoned to Heru, who all but trotted across the room to join him.

Heru followed Tamit out without a backward glance. Thana pushed down the thrum of concern that rose in her throat; he'd be fine. They were safe. To reassure herself, she gave the room another glance, her gaze snagging on Mo. She and Heru were both a mess, their wraps stained with dust and blood and ash and soot. Mo's braids were in disarray and several hung loose from their tight weave. But while Heru was still bright-eyed and engaged, Mo was haggard and worn, her expression blank with exhaustion.

Thana ached to go to her, to hold and comfort her, but she wasn't sure she could stand. Besides, Mo didn't want anything to do with her. The memory struck sudden and fierce, like a trodden snake hidden between stones. Mo had begun to care about her again out there in the Wastes, but that had been Mo the healer, concerned about the guuli. Now that they were safe, Mo would go back to ignoring her.

Before Thana's thoughts could spiral any further, Tamit returned, alone. He crossed the room to stand again at his Empress's side. As Thana studied the first advisory marabi, she couldn't shake the feeling that she'd seen him before: a tall figure in a blood-red wrap, eyes as dark as midnight. With what felt like a world-tilting lurch, Thana finally placed him: Tamit had been at Drum Chief Eken's party. And then later, at Idir's inn.

Why?

"If I may be so bold as to remind your Imperial Highness,"

said Tamit, gaze fixed ahead, "we have preparations to complete before we can begin the ceremony. Some of the marab are still incapacitated from the march—"

"Ah, yes," interrupted the Empress. Her gaze fell on Mo. "We've heard wondrous things about the ability of healers near the Wastes. If you'd grant us an hour of your time, we would benefit from your assistance in our healing tents. Our journey was quick, but not painless. Semma will show you where you're needed most."

Mo glanced at Thana, her expression tight with uncertainty. "But Thana needs—"

"Your friend will be given a room and all the rest she requires," said the Empress gently. "When he has a chance, Semma will see to her personally. Of course, we do understand if you'd rather not help . . ."

Mo bit her lip, then turned away from Thana and nodded. "I'll go."

An older man in a faded blue wrap stepped forward, bowed to Mo, and then gestured for her to follow. Mo cast one last glance at Thana before leaving the Empress's tent. Thana resisted the urge to open her mouth and tell her *no, please stay*. Apprehension squeezed her chest tight. Too many terrible things had happened to them. Despite all the evidence, she still couldn't believe they were truly safe.

But they were in the Empress's camp, surrounded by soldiers and marab. They couldn't be safer. Djet wouldn't be able to touch them here.

Thana fumbled with the waterskin, spilling some across her wrap before it touched her lips. Then she drank deep, too deep. When she forced the skin back down, it was almost empty. She needed to ask the Empress for help.

Thana cleared her throat, but before she could form the words, the Empress spoke. "It appears that we are finally alone, assassin."

Thana's focus, previously disjointed and fuzzy, sharpened to a fine point.

"You're misinformed, mai," she said. "That was only a ruse Heru played. It wasn't true."

The Empress stood and stepped down from her chair, her bracelets jangling. "Your contract was not on us, that part is true. But don't lie to me, Thana."

She silently counted her weapons in a fruitless attempt to calm her suddenly galloping heart: three knives across her chest, a longer blade on one thigh, a set of rings, and her garrote. Everything else, including her poison darts, were still with the camel. With aching slowness, Thana unfolded from the floor and stood. "How—?"

"Why didn't you complete your contract?"

Thana's mouth was drier than dust. She moistened her lips, took a swig from the skin, and croaked, "What?"

"Were you not paid enough?" The Empress took a step forward; Thana matched her with a step back. "We'd only heard praise for your family and their professionalism. Yet, here we are, two months on and the contract is still open. At this point, we're not certain you still intend to complete it. If you've had a change of heart, simply say so. We can come to a new . . . arrangement."

"I—you—" Thana fought for words, drinking more water to settle her thoughts. But she was dangerously low. "You can't mean—?" She gestured in the direction Heru had disappeared.

"You aren't stupid, girl. What other contract is there? Yes, we sent Tamit ahead of Sametket to secure a contract and ensure its completion."

"But—why? He's your second advisory marabi."

"We needed him dead," said the Empress. "Now that he's here—and still alive—we might have a use for him yet." Her gaze hardened into something dangerous. "You, on the other hand—

we were assured that if you failed to complete the contract, your body would belong to us. And here you are. How convenient."

"There were intervening circumstances," said Thana quickly. "I was attacked by Djet. And anyway, Djet's threat is more dire than any contract. It's not an excuse, but surely you must agree. You sent Heru to *stop* Djet. You still had a use for Heru, otherwise you could have ordered him killed while he was in the palace."

"The situation had changed before he reached our palace. We wanted to know what he knew. But we are the Empress of Mehewret and we do not broker in forgiveness. The terms of the contract were clear. You broke the contract; your life and body are forfeit."

Pulse thudding in her ears, Thana counted the other people in the room. There was the Empress herself, small and lithe but weaponless. Tamit, who likewise carried no visible weapons, but whose fingers curled as he listened. The guard Atrex, whose gaze was focused on her, hand on the hilt of his sword. That left two red-clad marab and four slaves who hadn't moved since Thana woke.

The slaves would hide or run at the first sign of a fight. She could have killed Heru a hundred times if it weren't for her bad luck, so she wasn't too worried about Tamit, but the guard—

Why is there only one guard? asked Amastan for the first time in weeks. *Either she doesn't think you're a threat, even though she hired you, or—*

Or she knows something that I don't, finished Thana.

This wasn't what it seemed.

The Empress was watching her, a smile spreading across her face. A chill touched Thana's spine and set her nerves on fire.

"You're not here to stop Djet."

No one moved. Thana's gaze flicked from guard to slave to marabi and horror slithered and uncoiled within her along with understanding. All of the Empress's subjects, save Tamit and Atrex, were as still as stone. They weren't breathing. And their eyes—how had she not noticed their eyes? They were glassy and dead, like the bound in Ghadid and in the desert. Like Salid's eyes had been. His charm should have warned her, it should have blazed hot and painful . . .

. . . as it had been doing since the guul attacked.

"G-d." Thana slipped a knife into her palm, but her weakness was returning, her thoughts becoming slippery and thin. She should take another pull of water, but there was only a mouthful left and she didn't dare take her eyes off Tamit.

"No use calling on your G-d now," said the Empress. "There's only us."

"What did you *do*?"

The Empress laughed, delighted. "Do you think we're going to waste our time by explaining everything to you? We've got a schedule to keep."

"Yes, actually, I was hoping you would," said Thana, the words rushing out. She fought to stay centered and focused, but the thirst was creeping up her throat as the guuli roused. She could taste the hot acrid wind before a storm, could smell nothing but burnt metal and hot sand. *Not now, not now.*

Tamit's hand closed around something in his pocket. Salid's charms had protected Thana from jaan and guul and Heru, but she wasn't certain they'd protect her from Tamit. But he'd need to touch her before he could do anything to her jaani and she had her knife and the shreds of her wit and—

A warm hand fell on Thana's shoulder. She jerked around and stared into the Empress's dusky beauty. She'd been so focused on Tamit and containing the guuli that she hadn't registered the warning jangle of the Empress's bracelets. This close, Thana could see the flaws in her skin, the wrinkles and folds that betrayed her age, the raw redness around her eyes from days and days of riding through the Wastes, the dark cracks in her lips where blood had dried, the dust in the edges of her clothes and across her scalp. Her breath reeked of roses and rot.

"No," said the Empress. "We don't think an explanation is necessary."

The Empress's grip tightened until Thana's whole arm went numb. Salid's charm burned, searing her skin. Tamit closed the gap between them and produced a stoppered vial, its contents smoky and opaque, from his pocket. He yanked the stopper out as the Empress's fingers wormed their way between Thana's teeth, forcing them apart.

It all happened too fast for Thana's dulled senses. She tasted metal and dust and a cloying sweetness, like date juice, as the vial's liquid poured into her mouth. She gagged and tried to spit it out, but the Empress closed her hand over Thana's nose and lips. Desperate for water, the guuli swallowed.

The Empress released her. Tamit shoved the stopper back in and palmed the vial. Then he simply watched. The room was silent. Salid's charms were so hot, they must be burning through her skin, her muscle, down to her bone, but charms couldn't stop whatever Tamit had done.

The liquid washed through her, chasing away the guuli's desiccating touch. The smell of hot wind and sand flared, so sudden and powerful that she might've stepped into a storm—and then it was gone, leaving nothing behind but a burnt taste. The thirst vanished, along with the haze that had wrapped tight around her head. Thana felt whole again, if exhausted. Then all of her aches and pains rushed into the gap the guuli had left behind, the worst of which was around her waist: the charms were on fire.

"I came to ask, on line ninety-two—wait, what are you doing?"

The Empress and Tamit ignored Heru standing in the tent's

entrance, a thick, poorly bound manuscript in his arms. Heru's gaze flicked across the three of them, expression giving away nothing. Then he tucked the manuscript under his arm and pulled his tagel over his nose.

"I said—" began Heru, approaching.

But Thana didn't hear what he said. She'd begun to shake and a humming filled her ears and drowned out everything else. The Empress held Thana's arms down as they tried to fly up, no longer her own, even as her consciousness sharpened. It was as if someone had cut all tethers between her mind and her body. She could only wait and watch as the guuli twisted into itself and ripped away from her.

The Empress pressed her palm against Thana's chest, something sharp and solid between her fingers. She leaned in, digging the object into Thana's breastbone. The room spun and burned white and then something was screeching up her throat like scorching bile and forcing her mouth open and pouring out of her.

The room went dark. A moment later, the hum turned to a buzz and stars burst in the blackness. A coarse rug scraped across her cheek and upper arm. She was cold all over but for the charm, which now pulsed with a soothing warmth. Beneath its glass, she could feel the scrape of new blisters.

Stay still, said Amastan. *Don't move. Think.*

Thana stopped trying to open her eyes. She breathed in through her nose and out through her mouth, staying as quiet as possible. She searched herself, but found no lingering scrap of the guuli. The Empress had removed it. Why?

"What did you do?" asked Heru, his voice closer now. Calm. Curious.

"You should recognize the procedure," answered the Empress. "After all, you refined it."

"Yes, yes," said Heru. "But I see no reason to remove her jaani."

A second chill pulsed through Thana. Only the Empress *hadn't* taken her jaani—she'd removed the guuli. The Empress hadn't known Thana was possessed and had failed to differentiate between the two. The urge to get up and run was strong, but she held still instead. She was in a camp, surrounded by hundreds of the Empress's soldiers. The Empress had her camel and supplies and they were days and weeks away from any city or town.

And then there was Mo.

Mo.

Fear sliced through the chill and in its wake came fury. The Empress had sent Mo away, had purposefully isolated them. She'd been planning this. She'd offered them safety and Thana had been so tired, so desperate to believe her. And now Mo was in danger. Her fury tightened into resolution: the Empress would pay for this. In the meantime, Thana needed a plan, and to make a plan she needed to know what was going on, which meant she needed to act like a body recently relieved of its jaani: dead.

"Justice has been done," said the Empress. "This girl was a danger and a fool. Her carelessness might have ruined everything we've been working toward."

"I was not aware you'd been taught how to remove jaan," said Heru.

A toe prodded the small of Thana's back. Thana's heart jumped. Heru would realize she wasn't dead. He'd notice she was still breathing, he'd understand what had happened, and he'd betray her. He had no reason to help her, not now that he had everything he'd wanted. Thana inched the hand trapped under her side closer to her thigh and the knife strapped there.

"There are many things of which you aren't aware, Sametket.

For one, you kept close company with this girl, but she'd been contracted to kill you."

"I knew that," said Heru dismissively. "And I'm glad she's dead. I only wish you'd allowed me the privilege."

Thana's hand froze halfway down her side—was he that dense?

"What are you doing?" asked the Empress sharply.

Fingers brushed Thana's neck, so sudden that her swallowed cry still came out as a muffled squeak. She squeezed her eyes shut and tried not to breathe while Heru took her pulse.

The fingers lifted and Heru said, "I only wished to confirm that the severance was clean and complete. After many years of performing similar jaani nullifications, I've learned through experience to check. There's little fun involved when a piece of jaani remains to cause trouble. Trust me."

Thana's lungs burned with held breath. Her hand continued toward the knife. She'd take Heru first.

"You dare question our—"

"You'll be pleased to know your work was meticulous," interrupted Heru. He paused, then added with dripping reverence, *"Your Imperial Highness."*

Thana let out the breath she was holding as quietly as possible. Relief blew through her—he hadn't given her away, thank G-d—followed by confusion. Heru was *protecting* her— why? He must have realized something was off about the Empress and her actions, but that didn't seem like enough of a reason to stop him from betraying Thana. She could only think of the night they'd spent in Ghadid's crypt, when Mo had pressed Heru hard enough to get an emotion aside from disdain out of him. Heru had shown real anger then, more than he'd shown even when Thana had failed to kill him. But was that anger enough to go against the wishes—and outright orders—of his Empress?

"May I ask what she would have interfered with?"

The Empress gave a tinkling laugh. "Oh, we are so glad we kept you around. You never fail to amuse us. We're here to open the Aer Essifs and release the sajaami trapped within, of course."

". . . of course," echoed Heru. "And Djet?"

"Djet has been dead for centuries. As powerful as he might have once been, no one survives being hacked into pieces and scattered around the kingdom. We've merely resumed where he left off with his research. We are the Empress of the Mehewret Empire, we are a god among our people, and soon we'll be immortal and a god among *all* people. It's only befitting us. If you join us, as Tamit has wisely done, then you may share in our glory and power. How do you answer, Sametket?"

Heru hesitated, but only for a heartbeat. "I see no point in declining glory and power. But, I will aid you under one condition. Allow me to handle the assassin."

29

That dust-cursed son of a—!

"That's an interesting request," said the Empress. "But as you've already observed, she's dead. What could you possibly want with her?"

Thana's fingers curled around the hilt of her knife. Not yet, but as soon as Heru touched her, she was going to make good on her contract. She was surprised at how much his betrayal hurt. She'd thought they'd come to an understanding in the corpse of her home. Obviously not.

"It's an interesting opportunity," said Heru. "I doubt you know all the troubles this girl has caused me. She hasn't stopped trying to kill me since we first met and, although those attempts were inevitably futile, the whole experience has left me less than favorably inclined toward her. Call it my due, if you will. I've been curious about how the anatomy of these sand fleas might differ from normal men for some time. But I can do the dissection later—just promise me you won't harm the body through some token ritual or binding. That would compromise the integrity of any data I might collect."

"We were going to add her to the seal, but one less bound won't affect its strength. Fine. You may have the body to use as you see fit. But not now—we must begin the ritual soon if we're to complete it before sunrise."

"Sunrise? Why—?" Heru paused, cleared his throat. "Oh. Of course. Jaan are weakest at sunrise and sunset, the liminal phases of the day. You suspect sajaam will be, too, and you plan to release a sajaami when it'll be easiest to control."

"Correct."

"And this seal—since the specific circumstances of what you're attempting negate the efficacy of traditional reagents and writing used to bind jaan, and since the sajaami is already bound within inorganic stone, then you are forced to utilize the more general and less efficient method of a physical seal. But what do bound have to do with a seal?"

"Everything," said the Empress.

"Have you instructed them to draw the seal?" asked Heru. Then he sucked in a sudden breath and snapped his fingers. When he spoke again, it was with barely contained excitement. "The bound *are* the seal! That's—dare I say, that's brilliant." He began pacing, his footsteps drumming out his eagerness. "A seal is only as powerful as its components, of course, and while a seal of blood is traditional, it's not alive. Because the bound contain jaan, this creates a sympathetic component to the seal which even a powerful sajaami shouldn't be able to break. But how will you compel the sajaami once it's trapped in the seal?"

The Empress sighed. "Your questions grow tiresome. We don't have the time to explain the details and intricacies of jaan binding, especially those you should have learned during your studies. Come, we must begin."

"After all this is done, though, if I may ask for an audience with you so we might discuss the writing system Djet invented and how you—"

"*Heru Sametket.* We appreciate your interest. Now is *not* the time."

A pause, then, stiffly, "Yes, your Imperial Highness. I apologize."

Another pause, then Heru cleared his throat. "But can I beg one final indulgence? I'm ablaze with curiosity as to the seal's construction. Did you find the schematics in Djet's notes or—?"

The Empress snapped her fingers. "Tamit. Locate the pertinent section for Sametket so that he can hold his tongue for more than a minute."

"Your Imperial Highness."

The rustle of papers filled the silence. The touch was sudden and unexpected: a hand settled on her shoulder, warm and alive. Before Thana could free her knife, Heru's words hissed in her ear, spiked with peppermint.

"I repay my debts. Play along."

The hand lifted and he stepped away just as the shuffle of paper ceased. What debt? She wouldn't trust Heru with a spool of thread, let alone her life.

Then she remembered: the guul. She'd stopped one from sinking its talons into him. She'd saved him without even thinking. Was that enough?

"Here," said Tamit. Vellum crinkled, exchanging hands.

Silence. Then, "Ah. I see. This is a most complex design. It would have to be enacted on a grand scale. But where would you find a sufficient number of bound this deep within the Wastes?"

When the Empress answered, a smile carved through her words. "Why don't we show you?"

A jangle as the Empress stood. Then footsteps, moving away from Thana. The jangling tracked the Empress across the tent.

"You will see for yourself on our way to the sajaami's prison," said the Empress. "Then, finally, you can be of some use."

Fabric rustled and the footsteps faded into the distance, soon smothered by sand. Thana didn't dare move until she'd counted to a hundred and more in her head. When she dared crack open an eye, no one was waiting for her. She opened the other, then slowly, carefully, pushed herself up.

Her head swam with the movement, but otherwise she felt fine. Then her breath caught: she wasn't alone. Three slaves remained in the tent. Thana was on her feet, the knife in her hand, before they could move.

But the slaves didn't attack. They didn't move at all. Even their gazes were fixed forward, unwavering. Thana shifted, but the slaves didn't even look at her. She relaxed out of her fighting stance and approached one, but the woman never blinked. Thana knew they were bound—*by the Empress,* a little voice reminded her—but this stillness was new.

Thana stepped around the slave, turning as she did so that she could keep an eye on all three and avoid exposing her back. She reached out a hand behind her and backed up until she felt the slippery smooth fabric of the tent. Only then did she turn. She pulled the fabric to one side, revealing the night beyond. Warm light spilled out from the tent, silhouetting her shape on the sand. Thana stepped out and let the tent flap fall behind her.

She noticed the smell first: fetid and foul and a touch sickly sweet. Not quite what she'd have imagined an army would smell like, but she'd never been around one before. She waited while her eyes adjusted, listening for any indication that someone had seen her. It wasn't as fully dark as she'd expected. A quarter moon gave some light. Campfires flickered all around, their light broken by the dark shapes of smaller tents and motionless figures.

Thana's heart jumped into her throat. She was surrounded by the Empress's soldiers. They couldn't have missed her when she left the tent, yet none of them moved to stop her. None of them moved at all. She started breathing normally again after another minute of silence, broken only by the spit and crackle of the fires.

Salid's charms thrummed hot and uncomfortable against her blistered skin as they responded to the presence of so many bound. Because that's what they were. Thana picked her way through the camp, cautiously at first and then with less care, because everyone she passed was just like the Empress's slaves: motionless and dead. Unlike the bound in Ghadid and with the caravan, these didn't bother to chase or attack or engage her in any way. They could've been asleep, if not for their staring eyes.

At the camp's center hulked one of the mountainous pillars. With nothing else to guide her, Thana threaded through the camp toward it. She didn't know what she'd find when she reached the pillar, but she knew what she'd do: stop the Empress.

The how eluded her, but she had her knives and her rings and her garrote. She was the Serpent's daughter. She'd find a way.

She was so focused on the pillar and what lay before her that she didn't at first notice what else was wrong with the Empress's army. Strong, healthy men stared at her, but so did old men as well as boys too young to wear the tagel. Women, too, were mixed in with the men, their ages just as varied. None wore a uniform. Some were missing limbs. They looked as if they'd been conscripted straight off the streets.

Thana didn't know when she'd stopped. She was breathing in shallow, staccato gasps, her chest too tight to draw enough air. Her vision had narrowed so that she could only see the man standing in front of her. He wore a dark green tagel, a light green wrap tied tight around a wiry torso. He stooped, back bent. His cane was missing.

"Kaseem."

Dried blood matted the side of his head, adhering the tagel against his ear. More stained his wrap from the shoulder down. Kaseem's gaze was as empty as the others'.

The world tilted and Thana stumbled back. She made the mistake of looking around. The man next to Kaseem wore a stained yellow tagel and a belt dangling herbs: he sold soaps and scents on the next platform. A few steps away stood a woman with pockmarked skin and wild hair: a beggar from the alley near the inn. Next to her was the baker's boy and beside him was the innkeeper himself, Idir.

There were more and more of them, people she knew and people she recognized and people she'd passed more than once in the street. Her city. Her people.

It was like losing Ghadid all over again. Thana swallowed bile and locked gazes with Kaseem. She stood there for some minutes, too afraid to look away, lest she see someone else she recognized. Kaseem had never been a cousin or a friend, but she'd known him, spoken with him. He hadn't been nice, not exactly, but he'd never been cruel. He certainly hadn't deserved this.

Amastan.

Salid had said Amastan had evacuated part of the city and fled, but that was no guarantee he'd survived, that he'd made it out. He could be here, standing with these corpses.

She forced her hands down to her sides and took a deep breath, then another. She focused on the sand beneath her bare feet, the wind sapping warmth from her skin. She couldn't fall to pieces now, not before she'd found and saved Mo from a similar fate. Not before she'd killed the woman responsible for this.

Anger flared, chasing away the shadows in her mind. It hadn't been some centuries-old en-marabi with no regard or understanding for what he'd done. It'd been the Empress, the woman who had sat on a golden throne and laughed with—*at*—Thana, who had smiled and sent them on their way, knowing what they would find when they reached Ghadid.

To the Empress, they'd been nothing but playthings, pawns

in a game between her and immortality. Thana had completed contracts on marks far better than her.

Thana tore her gaze away from Kaseem and fixed it on the ground. She started walking, marking feet instead of faces. It felt cowardly, but she knew that if she saw her mother or her father, if she saw Amastan—she wouldn't be able to continue. And she had to, for their sake.

She slipped between the bound like a mouse through shadows. When she finally looked up, the first pillar of the Aer Essifs towered ahead, its dark shape blotting out the stars. The moon had sunk behind the western horizon. How long had it been since she'd left the Empress's tent? And what day was it? Sunrise should have been many hours away, but from the faint sheen in the east, it was going to be much sooner.

Firelight glowed around the base of the pillar, turning the dark stone orange and red. The pillar was as tall as a pylon and twice as wide. As Thana neared, she could make out a group of people circling its base. Most wore red, their heads uncovered: the Empress's marab. They trembled, bound physically by heavy chains and ropes. Among them stood several healers, their blue wraps bright splashes of color in the dark. Where had the Empress found them? She must have plucked them from Ghadid when she'd plundered the city. Thana searched for Mo. She felt a pang of relief, then guilt, when she found her. After all, the Empress clearly had use for healers and Thana had delivered Mo to the Empress herself.

Around the marab and healers stood another circle of men, these menacing in their stillness. They wore the gold uniform of the guards of Na Tay Khet and each held a long, sharp spear. As Thana approached, the light caught their staring eyes; the guards were as dead as the rest of the camp.

Thana slowed, slipping her feet through the sand so the sound of each step was no more than a dry hiss. She didn't worry about being seen: campfires circled the area, lighting it well but also blinding anyone within to the dark of the rest of the camp. As long as she didn't get too close, she could watch the Empress's ritual without being caught.

The Empress and her small entourage had only just arrived. The guards turned and gave her a stiff salute. The Empress passed them and her chained prisoners without acknowledgment. She reached the base of the pillar and laid her palm on its rock. Then she leaned in and pressed her cheek against it. She gave the rock a gentle caress, fingers trailing across stone as they might a thigh. Then she pushed back, her features hardening with resolve.

Heru stayed with Tamit beyond the circle of guards and surveyed the scene. Mo didn't look around. Her head hung loose, braids obscuring her face. Thana longed to go to her, to strike off those chains and flee, but she wouldn't make it far with the Empress and her guards right there.

For now, Thana only had one advantage: the Empress thought she was dead. Heru had given her that much and she couldn't risk wasting it. She had to stay back and keep quiet until she had a chance to strike.

The Empress spread her arms and turned to her captive audience. "Sunrise comes. Our time draws close. We have awaited this moment since we first drew breath and the world knew us as Empress. Now we claim what is rightfully ours. We will be known as a god. Thus, we begin the ritual." She snapped her fingers. "Bo Tamit—the dagger."

Tamit held up a bundle of white fabric, which he unfolded to reveal a small, rust-stained dagger. He went down on one knee and presented the dagger to his Empress, hilt-first. She took the weapon and held it up, turning the dagger this way and that as she examined it.

"This was a great undertaking in and of itself," said the Empress. She glanced at Heru and beckoned to him with the dagger. "Don't be shy, Sametket. Attend your Empress."

Heru set his shoulders and—with a half second of hesitation that only Thana noticed—walked through the guards to join Tamit. He kept his gaze fixed forward, hands like stones at his sides. Thana had spent enough time with him to realize that he was, of all things, *nervous*.

"The ritual of release contains three distinct elements," continued the Empress. "These elements mirror those that the marab of old used to originally imprison the sajaam. This dagger represents part of the second element: fire. As an experienced researcher, you already know that rust is a simpler, slower fire. It eats up iron in the same way flame eats wood."

The Empress slid the dagger's blade across her palm, splitting the skin. Blood beaded in the wound, then dripped from her hand. The Empress held her fist over the sand, letting the blood fall into the shallow trench circling the base of the pillar.

The healer Semma stepped through the circle of marab, a bowl pressed to his chest with one gnarled and twisted hand. With the other, he took and held the Empress's bleeding hand. A blue haze coursed from the bowl down his arms and spread across the Empress, startling Thana. But of course the Empress would have found and kept her own personal healer; she'd probably plucked him from an Azal caravan. After a heartbeat, Semma let go and stepped back, head bowed. But the blue haze lingered, clinging to him like a late winter fog. The Empress examined her hand, the cut gone and her skin whole once more.

Vain—and a waste of water. The cut would have healed quickly on its own. Thana could all but hear Mo chastising the Empress. But when Thana looked, Mo wasn't even paying attention. In fact, Mo had hardly moved.

With her other hand, the Empress removed her belt and undid the knot of cloth at her shoulder. Her golden wrap fell away in a cascade of shimmering light to pool at her feet, revealing her sand-pale body. The Empress had perfectly carved curves, her stomach smooth and free of the marks of childbirth, her breasts no larger than teacups. She kicked away the wrap and stepped out of her gold sandals, fully naked but for her white headdress.

Tamit stepped forward, a sky blue wrap in his outstretched arms. He held it up for the Empress to put on. She turned, holding out her thin arms, and revealed the mess that was her back. Where the front of her body was smooth, almost flawless, the Empress's back was a knot of scar tissue from her shoulder blades down past her tailbone. The scars formed a script similar to what had been on the backs of the bound.

But Thana didn't have to ask Heru to know these were more than experiments, as those had been. These scars were the results. The Empress had already bound her own jaani.

Tamit covered the Empress with the blue wrap and helped her tie and knot the fabric in place. The fabric swirled like liquid as she turned and held the dagger out to Heru.

"Your turn, Sametket," she said. "If you truly desire to work with me and be rewarded for your faithfulness—cut out your eye."

30

Heru raised his hand, but didn't take the dagger. "I'm not sure I understood you correctly."

"You did." The Empress was smiling now. "The marab who imprisoned these sajaam lost their right eye to the cause. The sajaami in this rock must believe that the same marab have returned. You of all people should understand the value in adhering to the proper procedure. Take the knife, Heru." With her other hand, she gestured past him.

Heru stepped back just as Tamit and one of the guards closed in. But it wasn't one of the guards with glassy eyes. Atrex was still alive, his eyes clear and alert. He had one hand on the hilt of his sword.

"I'm certain this isn't necessary," said Heru. "If it's a sympathetic tie you're attempting to forge, then I can assure you that there're far less painful—and messy—options available. For example, we could cover one eye, assuring temporary in lieu of permanent blindness. Or, alternatively, we could dry the eye over a flame or scour it with sand. Again, less painful and far less untidy, and both within the skills of your healer to reverse. My notes indicate that the sajaam weren't known for their intelligence. The reference to the loss of an eye could also have been metaphorical, in which case I'd suggest—"

The Empress gestured and Atrex grabbed his throat, ending

Heru's rambling with a gurgle. He struggled for a moment, but Atrex was easily twice his size. Heru sagged.

The Empress cupped Heru's chin with her palm and lifted it, forcing him to look at her. "We know you're not squeamish when it comes to such matters. We've seen what you do with the prisoners we've granted you."

"Yes, well, mostly my assistants do all the hands-on work. I actually have a weak stomach. They're always telling me not to watch when they're performing the practical experiments because I might contaminate the equipment, so really, I'd understand if you'd prefer I observed from a distance instead."

The red-robed marab watched their exchange with disdain—and with only one eye. The healers remained unscathed, at least physically. Mo's gaze kept flicking toward the Empress, then settling, lost, on the sand. Thana's chest tightened. Time was falling, too fast, and she needed to do something, to stop this and free Mo before the Empress used the healers in her plan. But how? And what?

She closed her eyes. *Amastan*, she called silently, hopefully. *I need you.*

But her mind returned only echoes of her own fear. Amastan wasn't there.

A wet, squelching sound yanked her back to the present. Heru gurgled his pain deep in his throat, but didn't cry out. The Empress straightened, something red and wet and stringy pinched between two fingers. She made a face and tossed it over her shoulder.

"Healer," she snapped.

Semma grabbed Heru's arm, the blue haze already snaking up and around Heru's head. The steady drip of blood from Heru's chin slowed, then stopped. Thana couldn't see what remained of his face and didn't want to.

"Good." The Empress offered Tamit the knife. "Your turn."

Tamit took the dagger without hesitation. Thana looked away, but nothing could block out the wet squelch as Tamit removed his own eye. He grunted once, then his eye joined Heru's in the sand. Thana looked again when the air glowed blue, sealing up the ragged wound where Tamit's eye had been. When Semma was done, Tamit had a dry, crusting hole that could've been years old instead of moments.

The ritual was moving quicker now and Thana needed to stop the Empress before it was too late. But how? If she had her darts, she might have had a chance to strike the Empress before her guards or Tamit could react. With only her knives, rings, and garrote, she had to get close to the Empress—much closer. But a whole brigade of bound guards stood between her and her mark.

Absently, Thana unscrewed one of her rings, then stared in disbelief. She always emptied her rings unless she planned on using them, but she must have missed this one. White powder filled its shallow impression. She quickly secured it again. The last thing she needed was to accidentally poison herself. She checked her surroundings, thoughts whirling. If she had some water, she could coat one of her throwing knives with the poison. Then, maybe, she'd have a chance.

But there was no sign of water nearby, only the bound and their fires, and her mouth was as dry as sand. A shattered glass bowl lay half-buried at her feet, but its contents were long gone. Still, one shard curved to form a basin, in which she could mix the poison. She just needed something to mix it *with*.

The solution was so obvious Thana took another moment to accept it. Then, gritting her teeth, she drew the blade across her own palm. She squeezed blood onto the glass, drop by drop, until there was enough.

Shaking, she tore off a piece of her wrap and bandaged the wound. After taking a deep, steadying breath, she unscrewed the cap of her ring and gently tapped out the poison. The white dust dissolved in her blood and together, the two turned black.

Meanwhile, the Empress was still speaking. "We return to this place of treachery and pain to undo what was once done, to unmake what was once wrought, to reforge what was once broken. We prove our penance through our eyes and renounce the thorns that empowered us, the fire that weakened you, and the blood that bound. Through the same, we will release you. Through thorns, fire, and blood—you will be freed."

The wind stirred, no stronger than a breath. But it was enough to emphasize how very still the air had been only a heartbeat before. Thana dipped her knife into the poisoned blood, turning it until its blade was coated. She perched it on the rim of the broken bowl to dry.

The Empress raised her hands. "Thorns."

The bound guards moved as one, shifting their grip on the spears from underhand to over. The spears were unusually shaped. Instead of a uniform thickness throughout, these tapered to a point. In lieu of a sharp metal head, the wood had been whittled down to a needle-fine tip and blackened by fire.

Like thorns. With that realization, Thana knew what was about to happen. The circle of guards tightened around the imprisoned marab and healers. Thana steeled herself; she wouldn't look away.

The guards struck. The spears slid into the marab's backs and out their chests. The marab crumpled to the ground with muffled screams and dragged the healers chained to them down. A few healers cried out. One started to sob. Mo caught herself on her knees and refused to let the chains pull her to the sand. She struggled to stand again, but the bodies on either side weighed her down.

"Fire," said the Empress.

Flames flared skyward all around the camp until its edge was one unbroken wall of fire. Tents caught and burst and somewhere, someone cried out. The relative silence was gone, replaced by the fire's all-consuming roar. The wind whistled, high-pitched and frantic, catching and dragging at Thana's wrap. She checked her knife; it was dry.

"Blood."

The Empress stepped behind Tamit and slipped the rusted dagger from his hand. He tried to turn with her, but the Empress grabbed his tagel and yanked his head back, exposing his throat. She slid the blade through his neck from ear to ear. Blood poured down Tamit's front, darkening his red wrap to black.

The Empress dragged his quaking body to the foot of the pillar. She held his opened neck over the trench until the gush of blood slowed to a trickle, then finally stopped. The sand drank up most of the blood, but a red stain lingered and spread. The Empress dropped Tamit's body and turned to Heru. The wind was now a gale and the sand felt as if it were shaking.

"I'm quite grateful that you chose him and not me." Heru's voice was as fragile as a bird. "Now we only have to share all that glory and power between the two of us."

The wind tore at the Empress's headdress, ripping away feathers and tilting it to one side. Her blue wrap, now spattered with Tamit's blood, shook and snapped. Without a word, the Empress advanced on Heru, leaving bloody footprints in her wake. A haze suffused the air around her like that of a healer. But instead of blue, this haze was white. The color of bones and maggots and salt seas. Of death.

The pillar shuddered. Pieces of rock broke free and fell. Sand splashed into the air at their impact. Thana weighed the poisoned knife in her palm. She had one chance.

Heru turned and ran. He only made it a few stumbling steps before Atrex had him, first by the arm, then by the shoulder and throat. Heru shoved a hand against the guard's face and gritted his teeth. Atrex slapped Heru on the side of the head. Heru's hand fell. Blood dribbled from his lips as Atrex carried him back to the Empress.

Thana pulled her tagel over her mouth and stood. She scanned the scene, confirming her plan one last time—inasmuch as it could be called a plan. The marab sprawled dead next to the trench, the guards once again frozen in place, their spears caked with drying gore. The Empress watched Atrex approach. Semma stood to one side, hands fluttering, useless.

And the pillar loomed behind them all, shedding stone and sending out tremors that stirred and shifted the sand.

Atrex dropped Heru before the Empress and stepped back, one hand on his sword. The Empress knelt, grabbed Heru by his hair, and hauled him to his feet.

Thana approached, no longer bothering to hide. She stepped into the circle of firelight and set her stance. The Empress yanked Heru's head back. Thana aimed. The Empress touched the dagger to Heru's throat.

Thana threw.

The rust-covered dagger bit into skin just as the poisoned knife struck the Empress's shoulder. Her fingers spasmed open and the dagger fell. For a heartbeat, the world stood frozen: the Empress's stunned expression, Heru's closed eyes and sagging body, the flickering flames, the bound guards, the chained healers, the stone prison, and Atrex.

Then the Empress dropped Heru to grab the knife in her shoulder and Atrex spun, sword already drawn, scanning for the offender. His gaze caught and narrowed on Thana. He didn't wait for an order from his Empress—Atrex charged.

Thana ran. She weaved between the bound, trying to confuse and lose him. She was faster than him, and soon she was doubling back toward the pillar, Atrex a safe distance behind. The Empress had pulled the knife from her shoulder and was studying it, lips pursed. She looked up as Thana came running through the bound guards. She tossed the knife aside.

Two guards grabbed for Thana, but they were slow and clumsy and Thana was thrumming with energy. She was finally in her element. No more waiting and hiding. Only action and reaction. Thana dodged and pivoted, heading for the chained healers.

Heru had put a few feet between himself and the Empress. He stooped and picked up the rusted dagger. He held it in front of him as if it might hold the Empress off as he kept backing up, step by step. He didn't seem to be in immediate danger, so Thana focused on rescuing Mo.

The Empress's voice boomed too close behind her. "We took your jaani. You should be dead."

The ground shuddered again, hard enough to throw off Thana's balance. She stumbled and fell just a foot from the first healer. The girl—for she was hardly older than sixteen—tried to shy away but her chains stopped her. A few bright-colored salas stood out among her short braids. From the style of her wrap, she had to be from one of the other crescent cities.

"You're too late," said the Empress.

The charms around Thana's waist had been burning hotter and hotter as she neared the pillar and now they let out a piercing whistle. With a loud *ping*, the first charm exploded, its hot glass slicing through her skin and wrap. The second shattered as a hand grabbed her shoulder and spun her around. Thana stared up into the Empress's face, paler now and glistening with sweat.

In her other hand, the Empress held Thana's knife, fresh blood still drying on its blade. "You cannot poison *us*."

Thana responded with a knee to her stomach. The Empress let out a *whoosh* of breath, but instead of letting go, her grip tightened. Behind her, the bound guards were closing in, spears pointing at Thana. She didn't need to turn to know that the guards were also behind her. She was trapped.

The Empress smiled wide and dug her fingers into Thana's shoulder, forcing her further to the ground. "You cannot stop the inevitable. You should have *stayed* dead."

The ground shuddered again, but the vibrations were different this time. Instead of rocks thumping to the ground, the guards had all collapsed. The Empress jerked, then hissed and shoved Thana away. Thana hit the ground and rolled back up into a crouch, fists up. But the Empress was no longer fixated on her.

Chest heaving, Heru stood in the center of a circle drawn in the sand. He'd dropped his arms, but blood dripped from his hands and the knife clutched in his fist. The guards were face-down and motionless. Quieted.

As the Empress stalked toward Heru, Thana seized the opportunity he'd given her. Her third charm shattered when she reached the bloodied trench. One of the healers covered her head and cowered away from Thana, her clanking chains barely audible above the roaring wind. Thana grabbed the nearest link and followed the chain to a lock. She stared blankly at it. She didn't have a pick and she'd used her last throwing knife to poison the Empress.

The roar of the wind intensified until it was all Thana could hear. A rock struck her shoulder as she tried to fit her remaining blade—a long, curved dagger—into the lock. She grabbed her shoulder, the pain blossoming a moment later along with blood. Despair and hopelessness ate at her, but she wasn't done, not yet. She wrapped her fingers around the rock that had hit her and bashed at the chain. When the metal refused to even dent, Thana growled her frustration.

Her fingers picked through the sand for something, anything, and slipped across a jagged piece of Salid's charm. The thick glass he'd used had shattered into chunks and this one could easily have been a small dagger. Her blood already stained it, turning the blue glass a bright red. She jabbed its point into the lock and felt the first tumbler click. Gritting her teeth and ducking her head against the flying sand, she wiggled the shard until a second and third tumbler clicked. She hardly dared to hope when she yanked hard on the lock, but it opened and released a portion of chain.

It was a small victory. Several locks remained, tethering the healers to each other and the ground. The shard had cut Thana's hand deep and now her blood made the glass too slick to grasp. The wind spat sand into her face and eyes, making it harder and harder to see. She tore off a piece of her wrap and twisted it around her bleeding hand. With this makeshift glove, she was able to free the shard from the lock.

Thana felt along the chain for the next lock. The Empress had been lazy in at least one respect: all the locks were the same make, so once Thana figured out how to spring one, the rest were easy. The first healer was freed and sent stumbling away from the disintegrating pillar. When Thana looked back, Heru was crouched on the sand, blood staining his arms. The Empress was only a few feet away, but she stood frozen in place, both hands clutching at her throat.

Thana kept moving. She didn't know how much more time Heru could give her. The next healer scurried away, whispering prayers under her breath. A third stayed kneeling no matter how much Thana pushed or yelled at her. The fourth and last was Mo, dark eyes wide with relief.

"Your hands," said Mo when the last lock opened. The wind snatched her words, but Thana could read her lips.

"We have to get away," said Thana.

She pulled Mo to her feet, the chains falling away like water. Mo glanced toward the healer still kneeling in the sand, but—

CRA

CK

Thana's ears sang. Pebbles rained down, catching on her arms and head in painful bursts. Thana glanced up just as the pillar of the Aer Essifs split in two.

Thana didn't think. She grabbed Mo's hand and ran. Rocks fell all around, some as small as sand, others as big as boulders. One large rock slammed into the ground only feet away, crushing a marabi's corpse. Thana swerved around the rock, one hand over her head, the other clutching Mo's.

They passed the collapsed guards, just starting to twitch and move again, then the Empress. She sputtered and clutched at her throat, eyes wide and skin even paler than before. Thana allowed herself a small amount of satisfaction—the poison *had* worked— and then the fourth charm sang and shattered.

A trail of blood guided them to Heru, just beyond the first bound. Thana grabbed the fabric of his wrap and yanked him along. Behind, the mountain crumbled. Stones tumbled and struck the ground, sending out more tremors. The wind sang through the air, kicking up dust and sand. Thana yanked her wrap up over her mouth and nose. Already her eyes and throat burned from the dry air. The last two charms whistled and shrieked, their heat searing.

Once beyond the radius of falling rubble, Thana slowed and turned. The pillar was completely gone, a haphazard heap of debris the only sign it had been there at all. A buzzing darkness filled the air in its place. The ground still trembled beneath their feet, but had otherwise stopped trying to throw them off balance.

The flames encircling the camp flared, black smoke billowing into the brightening sky. A deep rumbling suffused the air, as if a herd of spooked camels were bearing down on them. Thana backed up until she could feel Heru and Mo's reassuring presence, then she slipped her garrote free.

"I couldn't stop her before she set the ritual in motion," said Heru, his voice thin. "The sajaami is free."

"Won't the Empress's seal trap it?" asked Thana.

"Perhaps. But if she's dead, it won't hold for long."

"You killed her?" Mo's voice was almost as thin as Heru's.

"Thana poisoned her, I weakened her further, and the falling rocks we so narrowly avoided ourselves will have finished the job."

"We are not dead."

The words echoed all around them in a chorus of broken and gargled voices, high and low, scratchy and clear, and yet, unmistakably, the Empress's. Heru closed his good eye, resignation smoothing out the wrinkles in his face. Thana tightened the garrote between her fists, scanning the crowd of bound. The people with glazed eyes had turned as one to face them.

"That's reassuring," said Heru. "Now if you'll just let us go on our way, we'll stop interfering with your plan."

"Heru," hissed Mo.

"She's not going to let us go," said Thana.

"The assassin is correct," chorused the bound.

"No." Heru snapped his eye open, all traces of resignation gone. He pressed his lips together and took a grating breath. "You will let us go, because I refuse to die without first integrating all that I've learned here into my own research. Besides, you cannot attack us, your Imperial Highness, not without disrupting your seal. Any moment the sajaami will break free and if your seal is not intact, you'll be unable to capture it." Heru began rolling back one of his sleeves. "So you'd better let us go if you don't want to lose your sajaami."

"That's not an option," said the Empress. "We have more than enough bound to share. We built redundancies into this system. We have you to thank for that; you suggested it in your notes."

The bound nearest them unfroze and lunged for Heru. Thana

didn't think; she stepped in front of Heru and kicked the first out of the way, then whipped her garrote across the other's face. Mo sank between them, hiding from the onslaught. Thana didn't expect her to fight after what she'd already been through. Besides, the Empress had taken her staff. That was all right; the bound would have to kill her to get to Mo, and Thana wasn't about to make that easy.

"Go on, Heru!" Thana elbowed a third and ducked the swipe of a fourth. "I can distract them!"

Heru nodded. While Thana whirled around him, taking out one bound at the knees and sending another stumbling back with a kick to the chest, Heru drew a circle. Thana's next punch landed on a bound's temple and she was rewarded with a satisfying *crack*. She moved with a liquid smoothness, all her fear abandoned at the base of the pillar. After all, what did she have left to fear?

Then she turned, bringing her arm back for another punch, and hesitated. She recognized the bound charging at her. He was the blacksmith's apprentice. And the person dragging their foot just behind him was their neighborhood's gearworker. The woman coming at her from the side had always stood outside her front door with a pipe and a ready smile.

In her distraction, the blacksmith's apprentice slammed into her, ripping the garrote from her hand, his fingers like claws around her throat. Thana scratched at his eyes, but of course that did nothing. Her own neighbors were trying to kill her. No— not neighbors anymore. The Empress had seen to that.

Thana growled, grabbed the bound's wrists, and twisted until its grip broke. Her foot connected with his sternum and he went sprawling. Breathing heavily, Thana reset her stance as another barreled at her. But before it could reach her, the ground heaved. The bound stumbled and then collapsed as if their muscles had dissolved.

Heru held his arms up, blood rolling down to his elbows, his face even paler than usual. His whole body shuddered. He sank to his knees. Mo ran to him, reaching for a waterskin at her belt that wasn't there.

Behind her, toward the center of the camp, the darkness that had poured out of the pillar had coalesced. Now it seethed and pulsed and tossed sparks around the camp. The darkness broke and split and in the space between formed two eyes and the thin line of a mouth. Those eyes narrowed at the sand below, where a figure in blue stood with upraised arms.

"Who has freed Nejm?"

The voice was the roar of wind across the sands before a storm, the crash of thunder through a deluge, the rumble of a mountain moving. It reverberated through Thana's bones, and it was all she could do to keep from falling to her knees.

"The Empress Zara ha Khatet of the immortal Mehewret Empire," answered the Empress through the mouths of every one of her thousands of bound. "You are in our debt—and bound within our seal, sajaami Nejm. Don't waste your energy trying to—"

"You dare seal Nejm?" boomed the voice, the darkness flaring first red, then bone white. *"Nejm, who is so powerful G-d themself had to seal us away? Nejm, who even a hundred marab could not defeat? Nejm, who has ruled the Wastes for thousands of years and will rule for thousands more? Insignificant mortal, you cannot comprehend the power of the sajaam. We have watched your empires be born and die. This seal will not hold us."*

As the sajaami spoke, its form swelled and spread until the turquoise sky was engulfed in its darkness. The burgeoning sunrise was night once more and the only available light bled from the fire around the camp's periphery.

Thana touched her waist, counted: two glass charms remained. By the way one was vibrating, she was about to be down to one.

Soon, she'd have no protection at all. But then, Salid had never intended his charms to go up against the strength of a sajaami.

"No," said the Empress. "You underestimate the strength of this seal. Or have you seen one of this make before?"

Mo reached Heru and grabbed his still bleeding arm. He didn't resist, only slumped further toward the ground. Mo searched her immediate area, lips pursed, and caught Thana's gaze. "I need water. He's badly hurt."

"I . . . have not," admitted the sajaami. *"But no mortal seal is a match for my strength."*

"I am no mere mortal."

Thana cast around, but the only things nearby were the motionless bound. The wind kicked sand into the air and screeched past, its voice deep and raw. No, that wasn't just the wind. The sajaami was screaming.

The Empress was still speaking, but her words were a mere murmur beneath the sajaami's storm. The few guttural, clipped words Thana picked out from the noise slipped across her mind, unattainably foreign. They sounded exactly how Thana imagined the marks across the backs of the bound would if they were ever uttered.

With a single, abrupt movement, the bound took a step inward, then another. Step by step, they tightened the seal and closed in on the camp's center and on the Empress standing there, arms open and head thrown back. Fire split the sky in a sudden arc, but this was no lightning. Another arc struck the Empress, wiping her and her guards from sight in a blinding blast of light. But when Thana's vision cleared, the Empress still stood, arms outstretched. The guards around her were gone.

"How dare you!" seethed Nejm.

The darkness surged westward across the camp. But when it came to the camp's fiery edge, it spilled to either side, unable to go any further. Nejm gathered itself again and this time surged east, only to meet a similar fate. The sajaami flew from side to side like a bird trapped in a cage, but no matter how much it raged and roiled, it couldn't venture beyond the edge of the seal.

All at once, Nejm coiled tight in the seal's center, then dove straight down at the Empress like a hawk after its prey. It sliced through the air, trailing darkness and whorls of fire in its wake, claws and teeth and eyes forming and reforming at its head. The Empress didn't flinch, but opened her arms even wider.

The sajaami collided with her and both vanished in a blast of roiling darkness. The ground shook, sending a jolt through Thana's bones as severe as if she'd been thrown from a window two stories up. Heru stumbled, but Mo caught him before he could fall. The bound scattered and toppled like stones. Gouts of sand and dust exploded into the air, obscuring the sky with haze. The sun crested the horizon and its light suffused the haze, filling it with a bloody glow.

Silence fell like a heavy blanket across the camp and just as smothering. Thana's pulse beat louder than drums in her ears. A hand touched her arm. Mo stood nearby, Heru leaning heavily against her.

"Is she dead?"

A dry cough answered and a heartbeat later was echoed throughout the camp. Mo's hand squeezed Thana's arm as dread squeezed her throat. A deeper cough, then a long stretch of silence. Thana freed the dagger strapped to her thigh—her last blade—and fingered its hilt. Finally, when she couldn't stand the silence any longer, she started forward. If the Empress wasn't dead, then Thana could catch her while she was still weak.

But Mo refused to let go. "Thana, no!"

A dry rasping scraped across the sands from all sides, queerly hitched and all wrong. The hairs on Thana's arms stood up as goose bumps prickled her flesh. All at once, she realized the rasping was a soft laugh. The Empress was *laughing*.

A form condensed in the haze. It approached them, the laughter scratching from its throat. The haze peeled away, revealing the Empress, her blue wrap torn and smeared with blood, but she was otherwise whole. Alive.

"It worked." Her eyes were bright, her grin wild. "We did it. After all these years, all that planning, finally, *finally*. Look at us!" She gestured at herself with a childlike glee. "You should be proud of us, Sametket—we managed something you've only ever dreamed of. All those years you spent on your research and experiments and work, and for what? Nothing but dust and defeat. Does it pain you that we accomplished what you could not? We hope so—you were always such an insufferable little snot. But you were useful in your own way. Out of all our marab, your research proved most invaluable, you kept our people's ire off us with your antics, and you refused to see what was happening all around you."

Mo moved closer to Thana, her whole body trembling. Heru let go of Mo and straightened, but he was still shaking. Blood trickled down his arms, unwilling to clot.

"I congratulate you on your accomplishment, your Imperial Highness," said Heru through gritted teeth. "But now you have no need for us. If you'll just step aside so we can find our camels—"

"You may address us as 'your Holiness and Highest,' for there's now nothing between us and G-d," said the Empress. She stopped a couple dozen feet away from them. "And you're correct—as individuals, we have no need for you anymore."

The sand stirred as every single bound turned and began to shuffle toward them. Thana could feel the stares of a thousand pairs of dead eyes on her, each as heavy as a brick. Her dagger might as well have been a toothpick.

"Instead, you will join our army."

31

The bound charged. Before Thana could turn, run, or do anything, cold fingers wrapped around her chest and yanked. She stumbled forward with a cry. The second to last glass charm blazed hot and let out a thin whine. When the fingers tugged again, the charm shattered, raining hot shards of glass down her hip and thighs.

"Stay in the circle!" snapped Heru.

Mo grabbed Thana's shoulders and pulled her back just as Heru finished drawing a circle in the sand around them with his sandal. Then he stood in its center, rolling up his blood-stained sleeves, his breathing ragged and sharp.

"Come here, little sand flea," sang the Empress. "We took your jaani once before. We don't know how you restored it, but you belong to us now."

Mo's grip on Thana's arm tightened. "What's she mean?"

"After she sent both you and Heru away, she tried to remove my jaani," said Thana. "But she didn't know about the guuli. She removed that instead."

"An amateur mistake," scoffed Heru, although his breathlessness leached away some of his scorn. "Any who has studied jaan as long as I would have noticed that there were *two* jaan within Thana. My initial suspicion of the Empress's intent was well-founded."

"Is that why you didn't mention the guuli?" asked Thana.

"The Empress's appearance in the Wastes at the base of the very thing we sought was simply too fortuitous," said Heru. "Life is never that simple."

"So why didn't you say anything sooner?" pressed Thana.

"I wanted to see what she would do," said Heru. "If I had played my hand too soon, she would have slit both of our throats. Unfortunately, it appears that her thwarted attempt to take your jaani created a link between you two, which the former Empress will try to exploit. So would you *please* stay within the circle."

Thana nodded, mute. The tug came again, but Mo held her tight and kept her from leaving the circle. Just beyond the thin line, the bound swarmed dense as flies after season's end. They were completely surrounded.

Heru found the strength to draw his knife across his arms a third time. Blood fell, quick and profuse, staining his wrap and the sand. Heru swayed, his skin losing all color even as Thana watched, but his feet were planted wide and his lips pressed together with fierce determination and somehow he remained standing.

One of Mo's hands entwined with Thana's and she pressed both to Thana's chest. Mo's heartbeat pulsed against her back, reassuring and strong.

"I'm sorry." Mo's whisper tickled Thana's ear. "I shouldn't have gone with Semma. I should have seen what she was so much sooner. And I shouldn't have judged you for your past."

Thana squeezed Mo's hands. "She would have tried to kill you, too, if you'd stayed."

"She's going to kill us now."

"No," said Thana, realizing as the word passed her lips that she meant it. "We're going to stop her."

Heru barked out a single, incomprehensible word. Then his

will burst from him and rushed across the circle, tackling the bound. Men and women and children all with dead eyes collapsed midstride like so many empty skins. The ground shuddered as they fell and silence rushed into the void.

Heru dropped his arms, nodded to himself, then fell to his knees and crumpled forward, face-first into the sand.

"Impressive," said the Empress. "But that little trick won't work on us."

Mo squeezed Thana's hand before breaking away and going to Heru's crumpled body. She laid two fingers against his neck, then pried the knife from his fingers and began rolling up her own sleeves.

Thana tilted her head back to meet the Empress's gaze. Whatever she did, it had to buy Mo enough time to heal Heru. Only an en-marabi could undo those terrible marks and sever the Empress's jaani once and for all. Heru had been right; an assassin wasn't much use against the horrors of a sajaami and an immortal Empress. But if a distraction was what Mo needed, then she could be that distraction. Thana would be anything, as long as Mo lived.

Thana stepped out of Heru's circle. Immediately, the last charm burned hot, but it didn't shatter. Not yet. The Empress widened her arms as if welcoming Thana into an embrace.

"Ah, our little assassin," she said. "You thought a simple poison would stop us. We didn't appreciate the inconvenience." She made as if to pluck a string out of the air before her, and Thana felt something sharp deep inside her chest. "You shouldn't be alive. We pulled your jaani out ourselves and we haven't made an error with that procedure in years. However you survived, it's clear that our mutual friend lied to us when he checked you earlier. Perhaps he learned something after all."

Thana only half listened to the Empress's spill of words. She weighed her last knife in her hand, then sighted along the blade. The dagger was much bigger than her throwing knives, but not so big that the shot would be impossible.

The Empress's fingers played through the air as if tying stringwork. The tugs strengthened. Thana stumbled once before spreading her feet and bracing herself. The tugs had their own predictable pulse. Thana counted, breathed deep, and between one and the next—*threw*.

The dagger struck the Empress in the throat. She jerked back, hands going to her neck. The tugging stopped. Thana rushed her. She'd pull the knife out herself and sever the Empress's head while she was still weak. Even with her jaani bound, she couldn't survive *that*—

The Empress plucked the dagger from her neck. Blood sprayed in one short burst, then slowed to a trickle and stopped. The Empress traced the wound in her neck as it knit back together. Before Thana had run a dozen feet, only a streak of blood marked where her dagger had hit. Thana slid to a stop.

The Empress's lips quirked up. Before Thana could react, she'd thrown the dagger. It was a clumsy throw, but Thana felt the impact in her thigh. Her leg gave out and she fell with a cry to her knees. Pain followed, sweeping through her bright and furious like a flash flood.

The Empress stalked toward her. Thana's fingers slipped around the knife in her thigh, now her only weapon. But she hesitated. She didn't know the extent of the damage and if she pulled it free, she could bleed out. On the other hand, if she didn't, soon there'd be nothing between the Empress and Mo. She had to give Mo more time. Thana gritted her teeth and yanked the knife out.

Blood pulsed down her leg. When she first attempted to stand, her leg buckled and she hit the sand hard. Thana rode out the wave of dizziness, then removed her tagel and tied it around her leg, just above the wound. This time when she stood, her leg shook but held. The blood had slowed.

The Empress swept her fingers through the air as she drew close. Thana braced for another pull. But no pull came—instead, the Empress lunged and yanked the dagger out of Thana's blood-slicked grip. She followed up by sending her elbow into Thana's throat.

Surprised, Thana's hands flew up and she stumbled back. The Empress stepped in close and Thana felt pressure against her stomach, *in* her stomach. The Empress twisted the knife.

No. The thought echoed through Thana's head as she fell back onto the sand. The sun was over the horizon now, its light transforming the Empress into a silhouette as the woman dug her knee into Thana's chest and wrapped cold fingers around her throat. *Not like this.*

"*Thana!*" Mo's cry came from far away, barely cutting through the ringing in her ears.

The Empress grabbed Thana by the hair and slammed her head against the ground. Dark spots burst in Thana's vision. She scrabbled at the Empress's sides, but her aim was off, her fingers weak. All she wanted to do was curl around the pain screaming in her gut.

"You should have stayed down, little assassin," said the Empress. "You should have finished your contract and never left your city. We tried to help you. We sent those bound to kill Heru for you. You should have let them. *This* could have been avoided." She slammed Thana's head down again for emphasis.

Pain spiked through Thana's skull, sharp as a razor. Her fingernails found skin, but she was only rewarded with another head slam. Her thoughts slipped away like sand, and a cold calm seeped through her body. Her mother's words flitted through her mind like a stray butterfly: *you will know you've lost when you can stare death in the face and only know calm.*

This was it. The Empress was going to bash her head in or Thana was going to bleed out from her wounds and then it'd be over. A not-so-small part of her accepted, even welcomed the end. She was so tired of fighting. She'd failed a hundred times. She'd lost everything: her friends, her home, her family. The Empress had won.

She could only hope she'd given Mo plenty of time to heal Heru or get away. That would be enough.

Thana closed her eyes. The calm helped her endure the pain that ran through her body in searing flashes. The world drifted away from her and she was floating. Cold. The heat was leaving her, pumped out of the gashes in her thigh and gut, sucked away by the air and the sand.

It was okay. She'd see her mother again, her father, her other cousins. Her city was gone, her duty was done. What was an assassin without her city anyway?

A cool sensation slid across her skin like silk. Thana opened her eyes. The Empress had paused mid-bash, but her fingers were still wrapped tight around Thana's throat. A blue haze suffused the air, clinging thickest around the Empress and herself. Feeling fled Thana's body, leaving her numb and rigid. The Empress, too, seized up. Only her eyes betrayed her panic.

This was healer magic. *Mo*—Thana tried to form her name, but her lips refused to move. Her stomach and thigh itched, then pulsed with pain, which spread out from her wounds and across her skin and down into her bones. She could feel the skin knitting together even as it felt as if she were being ripped in two. The dagger fell from her stomach to the sand with a soft *plop*.

The Empress gasped and shoved herself back, panting and wide-eyed. She clutched at her throat, then her chest. She tried to swat away the blue haze. But already the haze was dissipating on its own, the wind sweeping the rest away in small gusts and eddies.

"No," said the Empress. *"No."* She locked eyes with something just over Thana's shoulder. "What have you *done*?"

"I healed you."

Thana turned. Mo stood only a few feet away, remnants of blue clinging to her hands. Thana tried to find a bowl of water, but there was only sand at Mo's feet. Confusion filled the void of her emotions. Water was the very essence of healing, it was the life force that renewed and revitalized. Mo couldn't have healed even the smallest wound without water. So where had she found enough to heal Thana and the Empress both?

"You *bitch*." The Empress shook, clutching at her arms, at her face. She fell to her knees, catching herself on her palms. "Our jaani—"

"—is still there, just no longer bound. And the scars on your back have been healed." Mo took a step toward Thana and some of her calm fractured. "Are you all right?"

Thana's fingers had curled into the skin of her chest. She dropped her hand and took Mo's proffered palm. Mo's face was smeared with dust and dirt and blood that Thana hoped wasn't hers. Her braids were loose and wild and spilled around her face. Despite the disarray, her eyes and cheeks were vibrant, alive.

Then Mo's eyes widened. She gurgled a croak and staggered forward. Thana tightened her grip and twisted around. The Empress was still panting on her knees, but her eyebrows were furrowed, her lips were pressed into a thin line, and her hatred was knife-sharp and focused on Mo.

Thana didn't think. She threw her arms around Mo. The last charm let out a loud whine, burned hot. It shattered and broke just as Mo sucked in a deep breath and the Empress hissed.

Thana let Mo go and cast around for a weapon. Her dagger was nowhere to be seen. The sand must have claimed it, as it had claimed her garrote earlier. That left her own hands, the wrap in tatters across her body, and the metal wire at her waist that had once held Salid's charms.

Thana undid the clasp and snapped the wire between her hands. It felt achingly familiar, and why shouldn't it? Aside from missing the wooden dowels at the ends that would've made tightening it easier, the wire was a garrote.

The Empress had clambered back to her feet. Murder smeared her features, twisting her beauty into something unrecognizable. She locked gazes with Thana and gave a vicious smile.

"Even unbound, we're still an en-marabi with a sajaami, girl," said Zara ha Khatet. "You can't stop us."

"And I'm still an assassin," said Thana.

Zara ha Khatet laughed. "A failed assassin. You couldn't even kill *Sametket*. You have no contract and no city. You're nothing."

Thana gritted her teeth. "I'm so much more than nothing. I am Thana Basbowen."

The bodies of the fallen bound began to stir. Some jerked, but others climbed to their knees, then their feet. Zara extended a hand toward Thana, lips moving soundlessly. Thana rushed the Empress, expecting pain. She'd already crossed the distance between them, wire taut between her fists, before she realized that no pain was coming, none *would* come. The pain had been part of the charms' resistance to Zara, and now the charms were gone. If she let Zara touch her, she'd rip Thana's jaani right out of her.

A familiar calm filled Thana. She might not have any protections left, but neither did Zara. Mo had erased the marks that bound Zara's jaani. She was no longer immortal. Thana had one chance, and only one, to stop Zara. She could end this contract, once and for all.

Years of training guided her movements. Too late, Zara real-ized that Thana wasn't going to stop. She tried to step back, out of the way, but Thana's fist met her stomach. Zara doubled over and as her head came down, Thana looped the wire around her neck.

Zara's hands flew up, grabbing at the wire. Thana wrapped the wire around each hand, replacing the missing dowels with her fists. Zara fell to her knees, eyes bulging. Thana fell with her. She twisted her wrists. The wire cut into Thana's hands. Blood rolled down her arms to her elbows, dripped to the sand.

Zara stopped trying to free the wire and grabbed Thana's arm instead. Fresh pain tore through Thana, so sudden and hard that she jerked back and loosened her grip. She could taste blood in her mouth; she'd bit her tongue. She swallowed and steeled herself against the pain. The edges of her vision grew dark. She tightened her grip.

The pain passed. The hand slipped from her arm. Zara was falling, her lithe body suddenly heavy and dense. Thana fell with her. She wound another loop of wire around one fist, tightening the garrote, but the mark no longer resisted. She was quiet and still. Thana didn't let go.

A hand touched her shoulder. Thana jerked and the Empress jerked with her. Another hand covered her own, warm and gentle.

"Thana. Let go." Mo's voice was close to her ear. "It's done. She's dead."

32

Mo untangled Thana's hands from the wire. The metal had cut deep, scouring bone. Yet Thana could barely feel the pain. All of her senses were numbed by a dull roar, a thrumming that built inside her like an approaching storm. Mo wrapped cloth around Thana's hands, stemming the flow of blood.

When Thana finally took in her surroundings, she was startled by what she saw. The sun was fully in the sky, its light strong and pitiless. None of the bound moved. Thana wasn't sure they could. Something had happened to them, changed them. They no longer resembled fresh corpses, let alone people. They were withered husks, as if they'd been left exposed to the sun and sand for years. Some lay on the ground as if they'd been struck down, but some were frozen mid-motion, a hand outstretched here, legs bent to leap there. Others stood like statues and nothing remained of their skin but leathery tatters across brown bones.

The fire encircling the camp was little more than embers now. The pillar was gone, a mound of rocks the only remains of the mountain. Nearby, the rest of the Aer Essifs towered, untouched and intact. Tents had collapsed, blown apart by the sajaami's storm. The scene was one of great destruction. Only she and Mo moved in the stillness.

"—Heru?" asked Thana, the word barely more than a croak.

As if in answer, Heru straightened up from where he'd been

bending over one of the corpses. He glanced their way, shouldered something, and shuffled over.

"He's feeling much better now." Mo's hollow voice betrayed
her exhaustion. "He's gathering samples."

Thana waved weakly at the destruction. "What happened?"

Mo didn't meet Thana's eyes. "A great deal of water is needed
to heal an untethered jaani. Blood is more than nine-tenths
water. I . . . used what was available."

"You drained them." Thana stared at Mo. "Heru kept saying
he knew about healers who used blood, but I thought it was just
wishful thinking."

"They're not healers." Mo's reply was sharp. "Even done to
corpses, it's desecration. What I did—what I've done—is blasphemy."

Thana tried to laugh, but only succeeded in coughing. "And
I killed my employer. I'm pretty sure *that's* not allowed in my
family."

"You don't understand—" began Mo, but she cut herself off
with a shake of her head.

Thana held out her bandaged hands. "I don't. But maybe we
can fix that."

Mo glanced at her, then took Thana's hands gently between
hers. "I had to stop her. I had to save you. I couldn't lose you." Mo
sucked in a shaky breath. "I can't pretend you never lied to me, but
I also can't pretend that almost losing you didn't terrify me. The
past—you're right, it doesn't matter anymore. Can we try again?"

Thana pulled her close and wrapped her bandaged and bloody
hands around Mo. They stayed pressed together, sharing hitched
breaths, until the *hiss* of shifting sand betrayed Heru's approach.
They parted reluctantly, Mo furiously wiping at her eyes and
Thana uncertain if she would ever be capable of crying again.

"I'm fairly certain that with enough time and resources, I'll be able to accurately replicate her efforts here, although I doubt ever to such a grand scale." Heru stopped beside the Empress's corpse and gazed down at it with a mixture of disdain and respect. "She made some grievous miscalculations that unfortunately brought her much further, much faster than she could handle."

Heru knelt next to the corpse and pressed his thumb against her twisted neck. He frowned, then fished a glass flask from the folds of his wrap. When Thana had last seen the flask, it'd been only loosely covered in a looping, floral script. Now dark brown writing completely covered the glass. Heru pulled the cork out with his teeth, breathed into the bottle, then covered the opening with his thumb and shook it. He drew Thana's throwing knife from another fold and turned over his arm.

"Oh no you don't," said Mo, moving to stop him. "No more blood."

Heru shook his head. "This is necessary. The sajaami is still in her and we cannot leave it there. It will linger, but not as long as a jaani. It will tear away within a few more hours and then our chances of recapturing it will be close to zero. I, for one, refuse to let a perfectly good sajaami go to waste. I've been working on the seal on this bottle since we left Na Tay Khet. I'm confident it'll hold the sajaami. Besides, if it isn't sealed, the sajaami will terrorize the Wastes, creating sandstorms and floods the likes of which haven't been seen in epochs. I'd rather *not* see such."

"But the en-marab who originally sealed the sajaam needed many of their kind and a mountain. What makes you think a little glass bottle will hold one now?" asked Mo.

Heru met her gaze with his remaining eye. "The en-marab have had centuries to learn, girl. We know far more in this modern age than those ancient husks ever dreamed of."

Without waiting for Mo's permission, Heru flicked the blade across a recently healed cut, reopening the skin. He squeezed five drops of blood into the flask, then dragged a finger across the blood oozing from his wound and scribbled fresh letters on the outside of the glass. The blood faded from brilliant red to dull brown, matching the rest of the writing on the flask. Heru tightened the sleeve of his wrap around the fresh cut, knotting it with the expertise that came from frequent repetition, then pressed the open flask to the Empress's blue lips.

With his other hand, he closed her eyes and covered her nose. Then he began muttering words under his breath that sounded almost intelligible. The Empress jerked, eyelids flying open, but Heru had shut them again before either Thana or Mo could react. In another heartbeat, a dark, seething substance poured from her mouth and into the flask. As soon as the last trace of the darkness had left her lips and swirled within the glass, Heru shoved the stopper in place and gave it a firm shake.

The darkness inside spun violently, then dissolved until the flask appeared empty. Heru slid it into his wrap. He took a moment to gather his breath.

"That should suffice until I can commission a more permanent housing situation for our ancient and inimical guest." Heru wiped his forehead with the back of one hand then closed his eye as if shutting out pain. "Now, do either of you have a plan for getting away from this mess and back to proper civilization? I am in dire need of a bath."

The days after consisted of little more than sand and sun. The nights, however, were filled with terrors. Thana woke the others on more than one occasion with her screams. Mo insisted on using some of their dwindling water supply to help Thana sleep, but that only stopped Thana from waking up. She still saw the faces of the people she'd once known and loved withered and misshapen by death and desiccation. She still felt the Empress's cold body beneath hers, the tear of metal wire through flesh, the pain as the Empress ripped into her jaani.

Thana itched for a knife. Without one, she might as well be naked. In their rush to leave the camp, Thana had forgotten to look. They'd set out as soon as Heru had found their bound camels, still dead but intact—more or less. Nothing else had stirred in the camp. If anyone—or anything—had survived, they'd left before the sajaami was released. Thana hoped that included the healers she'd freed.

They hadn't found much water, either. Only a skin or two had survived the winds and the stones and the fires still intact and full. That was barely enough to see them out of the Wastes, and nowhere near enough to get them to Na Tay Khet. They'd have to stop in Ghadid.

After surviving a seal made from the bound corpses of her people, stepping into the hollowed-out city again should have been easy. But Thana's skin ran cold at the thought and her chest felt as if it'd been cast in metal. Only a few weeks ago, she would've given everything to return home. Now she wished for any way to avoid it.

But wishing was as useful as dust and one evening, still far to the east, metal blinked back the light of the setting sun. Thana was a hundred times grateful when Mo suggested they make camp so that they could reach Ghadid in daylight. She needed time to prepare.

That night, Thana had her worst nightmare yet. She woke with a start, panting for breath. Mo made a noise and turned over, fingers curling around Thana's knee beneath their shared blanket. Thana held her breath and studied Mo's face, the light from the small fire enough to watch the fragile flutter of eyes moving beneath closed lids. Mo still had both. It was just a dream, *just a dream.*

Thana brushed a braid from Mo's face. The braid was choked

with dust and unadorned; Mo had removed all of her salas early in their journey. Thana hadn't tried to stop her, but she hadn't been able to look away either as Mo jerked the colorful ribbons and strings from her hair and let them drift to the sand, one by one by one. Thana rubbed her hand, remembering the pile so small and insignificant. Then she winced; her palms were well-bandaged, but the gashes made by the makeshift garrote had been deep. She wished again for a knife, even though it would have been useless in her hands.

The nightmare's unease clung to her like thick webs. There was no point in trying to go back to sleep. Thana rubbed the grit from her eyes and left their tent. The sky was awash in liquid stars, no moon in sight. The Way of Silver Straw wound across the stars, a streak of brightness that was almost—*almost*—enough to see by.

At first Thana assumed the flickers were more stars, their light distorted by their proximity to the horizon. But the longer she watched them, the more her unease thickened. These spots of light had a warmth to them that the other stars lacked, and their flickering was random and chaotic. Almost like—

fire.

"You see it, too."

Thana spun, bandaged hand going for the knife she didn't have. She immediately regretted turning. The light from the fire, even though it was little more than embers, hurt her eyes. She shielded them, but the damage was done.

"I've been watching those lights for the better part of an hour," continued Heru. "I can state with a high degree of certainty that no, those aren't stars and yes, it appears that something is on fire. However, none of the fires have spread and a handful appear to have shrunk—at least, in regards to the amount of light they're giving off. This brings me to the conclusion that the fires are controlled and, by extension, someone is controlling them."

"You're saying someone is alive up there."

"Or close enough."

"We need to go."

Thana turned away, already going over what she needed to re-pack and how best to wake Mo. Energy buzzed through Thana for the first time in days. Energy—and something else, something hard and sharp that she thought she'd left behind in the Wastes: hope.

But Heru didn't budge. He scratched at the corner of cloth hiding his empty eye socket. Although Semma had fully healed the wound, Heru had taken to wearing a slash of white fabric across his forehead. "Let's not be hasty. We cannot know who has started those fires or for what purpose. For all we know, they could be bandits—"

"No. It's them. I know it. Salid said before he, before he—some survived."

"We can wait until morning."

"You can," said Thana. "I won't."

She knelt at the edge of their tent and placed a hand on Mo's warm calf. "Mo love, wake up—we need to go."

Mo sat up as quickly as Thana had. She blinked away sleep, fingers fumbling through the blanket for her staff, finding it, gripping it tight. "What is it? What's happening?"

"There are people in Ghadid."

"Yes," said Heru. "But we don't know who—"

Mo set the staff across her lap and began pulling her braids into a knot. She'd run out of ribbons. "What? How do you know?"

"Campfires," said Thana, already pulling the tent from its stakes and folding it in on itself.

Mo retied her wrap, then peered at the sky. "It's not even past midnight yet. Shouldn't we wait for dawn?"

"They don't know about the water. We can't let it happen again."

Mo dropped her gaze to Thana, her lips pressed tight. She nodded. "You're right. If there's any chance we can get to them before they drink the water, or before someone dies—"

Heru snorted his annoyance. "The chances of you intercepting either situation in a timely manner are slim. In all likelihood, it is much too late and they've already had their fill of the water. If anything, that's more of a reason to wait until light; at least we'll be able to see them when they attack us."

Mo bit her lower lip, but didn't look at Heru. She stooped, started folding the blanket. "I can't take that chance, as small as it may be." But there was little conviction in Mo's words; she was doing this for Thana.

Heru continued to protest, but when they broke camp a few minutes later and goaded their bound camels to a gallop, he was with them. The stars shifted, but the fires stayed along the horizon. As they neared, Thana realized the fires were clustered in just one neighborhood. Seraf. *Home.*

The pylons grew and stretched upward until they towered overhead like mountains. Thana cast around for a way to ascend, but she had no rope and there'd be no carriages waiting for them. She steered her camel toward one of the cables; she'd just have to climb. Easy enough, after everything else she'd done.

As soon as Thana dismounted, though, a light flared on the platform's rim. She looked up and could just make out flames thrust over the edge: a torch.

"Hello down there!" called someone, voice deep. "Are you sane?"

The elation that burst in Thana was almost as cold as her fear. Alive. They were *alive.* But what were Azal doing in her city? And the question—Thana honestly wasn't certain.

Thankfully, Mo found the words before she did. "We are sane. Praise be to G-d."

The torch jerked. "Praise be to G-d. May he do well for you."

"And you," chorused Thana and Mo.

"Are you in need of rest and shelter?"

"Yes," said Mo. "We have traveled long and far."

"So if you would kindly let us up, that'd be great," added Thana.

The torch hovered over the edge of the platform for a moment, as if considering, then abruptly disappeared. Pained creaking filled the air and a carriage dropped over the platform's side. Thana stared in disbelief as it descended, swaying back and forth on the cable. She hadn't expected the guard to be so trusting. Shouldn't they be afraid of another attack?

As they hobbled and unburdened their camels, Heru led his on, then stopped and blocked Thana's way. She tried to move around him, but he held out his hand. Her throwing knife lay in his palm.

Thana's breath caught. She snatched the blade from his hand without thinking. Her fingers curled around its short hilt with the ease of familiarity and she brought her arm back as if she were going to throw. But she dropped her hand instead and met Heru's gaze with no small amount of confusion.

"I kept it with me in the very likely event we were attacked by the angry guul and unbound jaan that populate the Wastes," said Heru. "But since we've left the Wastes behind and will once more join the living, it will benefit us all if you have the knife."

"You're not worried I'll try to kill you?"

"Your employer is dead," said Heru. "And I have proven my use to you, as you have proven yours to me."

The corner of Thana's lips twitched up in a smile. "Coming from you, that's high praise."

Heru abruptly turned away. "Yes. Well. Don't let it go to your head."

Thana watched him help Mo with her camel. Then, shaking her head, she slid the throwing knife into its sheath and heaved a bag onto the carriage. As soon as they'd secured their packs to the hooks, the carriage jerked and began moving upward.

A young man with a low-tied, dark blue tagel waited for them at the top. Behind him, another man and a woman worked the crank. The woman secured the lever, her hair in two long braids, her wrap a dusty rose. The second man was broad-shouldered and muscular, his blue tagel obscuring everything but beetle-black eyes. Thana wondered what she and Heru and Mo must look like, with their fading bruises, blood-mottled clothes, and dust-choked skin. They'd be indistinguishable from iluk. But with all the sand they'd crossed, they *were* iluk.

"Welcome to Ghadid," said the young man, his words much richer when they weren't being yelled. He pressed a hand to his chest. "I'm Bilel, son of the bright Namara. This is Azhar and Sofin"—he indicated the woman and the older man—"both of the same tribe."

"You're Azal," said Thana. She didn't mean to sound so disappointed, but the breath had been sucked from her. She'd hoped—no, *known*—she'd find her people here, returned from whatever hiding place they'd found to weather the storm. But of course, that had been a baseless, even ludicrous hope.

Bilel inclined his head in agreement, but Sofin spoke, his voice silky smooth. "Who is it you seek, ma?"

"The people who lived here."

Sofin grunted, but whether in recognition or pity, Thana couldn't decide. Azhar let out a long, soft breath.

"I'm so sorry, ma." Azhar put her hand on Thana's arm. "I regret to inform you that a great and terrible thing happened here—"

"We *know*," snapped Heru. "The water was poisoned and the dead woke and slaughtered everyone. The Empress of the Mehewret Empire took the dead and brought them into the Wastes to release an old evil and gain ridiculously incomprehensible powers. Only she was an *imbecile* and lost those powers—and now here we are. Sans a large, bound army of the dead, of course. We left that behind. I wouldn't advise going too deep into the Wastes."

Azhar had raised her hand when Heru mentioned the water, but Heru hadn't bothered to stop. Now she coughed and said, "What do you mean about the water?"

"It was contaminated with a magic that would bind the jaani of the drinker so that upon their death they'd become mindlessly chained to the Empress's will, but half of that equation has been taken care of and it will be a simple thing to cleanse the entire aquifer, given time. Just, try not to die for a few days."

Sofin looked alarmed, but Azhar only laughed. "The Wastes must have addled your minds, friends." She motioned to Thana. "But not everyone who lived here died in the tragedy. Some escaped. I'm hesitant to offer false hope, but if you're looking for someone—"

Thana's heart sped up. "Where? Where are they?" She stepped forward, but Mo's hand tightened around hers, stopping her from going any further.

"Many died in the siege, yes, and many more succumbed to the curse, but a handful managed to flee the city. They hid in the Wastes with other refugees and Azal—Ghadid wasn't the only city hit by this curse. When the danger passed, they returned. I can take you to their leader, if you want."

"Please."

Azhar bowed her head. "This way."

The Azali woman led them across the platform and past forms huddled next to small, contained fires. Some work had been done on the buildings here and there. A door replaced, glass cleaned away from broken windows, a roof retiled. And, but for the occasional pile shoved to one side, the streets were clear of debris.

They crossed a bridge with new wooden planks and then they were only one platform away from home. Thana could have found that red door with her eyes closed, but she resisted the urge to start running. She wasn't sure what she'd do if it was still broken, her platform untouched. Her chest tightened and her palms grew slick as they crossed another bridge. Beyond flickered more fires, contained and under control. Beyond, the streets were clear.

Then her feet left the bridge and felt the firm, familiar stones of home. There were no piles of debris here and some of the buildings even had a fresh coat of paint. Doors had been rehung, if not replaced completely, and torches burned in the sconces along the road.

Yet, instead of hope, Thana only felt dread. Too much had happened. Too much had gone wrong. Once before she'd thought she'd come home, only to find destruction. Now her city was being reconstructed, but it was still different. The should-be-familiar surroundings were like shouts on the wind, distorted and off. Even the light was wrong: the orange-hued glass around the torches was all broken, gone.

As Azhar led them mercilessly toward the center of the platform, Thana's feet dragged. She should stop. Turn around. She didn't want to see this. Couldn't. And yet, some force drew her onward, step by step.

A fire burned at the platform's center, fueled by shattered wood and balls of dung and hemmed in by the crumbled stone from destroyed buildings. Gaps like missing teeth loomed between the houses circling the center where the buildings had been completely torn down.

People clustered around the fire, conversing in low voices and passing a brazier of tea. Azhar held up a hand, stopping Thana, Heru, and Mo. She went on ahead. Thana couldn't help but look around the circle; one door was bright with fresh red paint. Her door.

Azhar had only begun to speak when the tone of the conversation around the fire abruptly changed. One man set his teacup down with a clatter and started toward them. He wore a dusty green tagel and was as tall as Thana and just as lean. What started as a fast walk soon became a limping run. Hope caught in Thana's chest like a spark from a striker, but she couldn't let it flare, not yet.

He skidded to a stop still a dozen feet away. "Thana?" His face above the tagel was flushed, eyes searching hers. "Please G-d, let it be you and not a jaani come to torment me."

Thana's heart stopped. And then she was throwing her arms around her cousin and holding him tight, because she'd know that face and that voice and those eyes and that tagel anywhere.

"Amastan."

"I got you. I'm here," said Amastan. His voice sounded so different when it wasn't in her head.

"I thought you were dead," said Thana.

"It's all right, I'm not. I'm here, I'm alive. *You're* alive."

The numbness that had sat heavy on her chest since Thana had first seen her city in ruins finally broke. It wasn't fine. It would never be fine. Nothing could be the same again and she knew that now, knew that better than she'd known anything else. Killing the Empress couldn't undo the damage she'd caused.

"We'll rebuild," said Amastan. "You'll see. You're here and I'm here and that's what matters. It's the only thing we can do."

Thana pulled back. Mo stood only a few feet away, her smile tense with pain. Heru was being lead to the pumphouse by a lanky girl with long braids—*Illi*. Beyond, more and more people filtered out of buildings and streets, some yawning, some rubbing their eyes, but all drawn by the outburst and spectacle. They weren't all Azal, but they weren't all from Ghadid, either.

Amastan followed her gaze. "More survived than I thought possible. The other cities were completely decimated, but we took on their survivors. We were all out there on the sands together, until it was safe enough to return. Our cousins were amazing, you should have seen them. Illi must've taken down a dozen herself. And your father, well . . . he has always been levelheaded when it was needed most. He's gone to the other neighborhoods to help with the recovery efforts, of course. I'll send someone to find him, let him know you returned." He swallowed. "But Salid stayed behind and . . . your mother—"

Thana didn't want to hear him say it. "I know."

Amastan took a deep breath. "We burned her body on the sands. I can take you there later, if you want."

Thana's sob startled her. It was brief, but sudden and sharp. Her mother hadn't been in that seal, she hadn't been one of the bound. It was a small thing, but the relief burst inside her and burned away some of her grief.

"I do," said Thana.

Amastan took her by the shoulders and peered into her eyes. "What happened?"

But Thana shook her head. For the first time since Ghadid had been destroyed, she could see a future. One where Ghadid was rebuilt, one where she found a new home, a new purpose, a new life. The construction and people around her were here, now, a reminder of what they'd all survived but also a promise of what was to come.

"Not now." Thana took Amastan's hand. "Can you show me around first?"

ACKNOWLEDGMENTS

This book was decades in the making, and I could easily thank decades-worth of people for all the help, love, encouragement, and support they've given me. A writer is grown daily by their own words and by others', and no encouragement is ever wasted.

Thank you to the Tor team for all your ongoing work. Thank you to Larry Rostant for such an amazing cover. Thank you most particularly to Diana M. Pho, my editor, who first believed in this not-so-little queer book and made sure everybody else did, too.

Thank you to my agent, Kurestin Armada, who saw the potential in Thana and co and who has unwaveringly stood up for this book for all the many, many years in between.

Thank you to Elesha Teskey, who answered my panicked online call for help when I desperately needed to cut 10k words out of a manuscript and gave me a crash course in brevity.

Thank you to my beta readers—Eldridge Wisely, Penny Morris, and Sarah Doore—who have put up with multiple drafts over the years and are just as confused as I am as to what's real anymore.

Thank you to my agent-siblings in the Armada, who have cheered me on and been just such a fantastic hype squad. You guys mean so much to me.

Thank you to the 2019 Debut Authors group for being such

an understanding and safe place to exist and emote through all this.

Thank you to the Pima County Public Library, in whose well air-conditioned building I wrote 90 percent of this book.

Thank you to my parents, without whose support and love I'd never have made it half this far, and who have always accepted who I am. Not everyone's that lucky.

And of course—most of all, always, forever—thank you to my wife, Sarah, my rock and my dragon. Without you, there would be no Ghadid. Simple as that.